SCHO

The Phoenix was gone,
Xavier.

Yet, Magneto was still there.

Floating above us, sporting his original uniform and helmet, he hovered like a purple and scarlet titan over the cracked concrete. Magneto gestured and half the army vehicles left the ground, levitating on imperceptible magnetic waves to join him high above the installation. He frowned at the scrambling human soldiers, not with disappointment, as he would during my later interrogation, but with anger and mistrust, hate and arrogance. Magneto radiated an air of earned superiority. This version was no friend to humanity – this was the O.G. Master of Magnetism, proud advocate for Homo superior rights and leader of the Brotherhood of Evil Mutants.

ALSO AVAILABLE

MARVEL XAVIER'S INSTITUTE

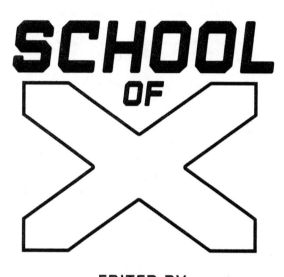

SCHOOL OF X

EDITED BY
GWENDOLYN NIX

ACONYTE

FOR MARVEL PUBLISHING

VP Production & Special Projects: Jeff Youngquist
Associate Editor, Special Projects: Caitlin O'Connell
Manager, Licensed Publishing: Jeremy West
VP, Licensed Publishing: Sven Larsen
SVP Print, Sales & Marketing: David Gabriel
Editor in Chief: C B Cebulski

Special Thanks to Jordan D. White

First published by Aconyte Books in 2021

ISBN 978 1 83908 106 4

Ebook ISBN 978 1 83908 107 1

Cover art by Heri Irawan

Distributed in North America by Simon & Schuster Inc, New York, USA
Printed in the United States of America
9 8 7 6 5 4 3 2 1

ACONYTE BOOKS

An imprint of Asmodee Entertainment Ltd

Mercury House, Shipstones Business Centre

North Gate, Nottingham NG7 7FN, UK

aconytebooks.com // twitter.com/aconytebooks

CONTENTS

YOUR FIFTEEN MINUTES

Jaleigh Johnson

"I thought we were going to watch a Christmas movie," Benjamin Deeds complained as the television lit up the dark common room with the fiery explosion at the top of the Nakatomi building, framing a panicked John McClane leaping to safety.

"This *is* a Christmas movie," Fabio Medina argued as he settled into an ancient, weary beanbag chair that was more bag than beans, cradling a plate of pepperoni and mushroom pizza slices. "It transcends."

That profound observation made him the target of multiple groans and several popcorn missiles from Eva Bell, who was draped on the sagging couch next to Celeste of the Stepford Cuckoos. Her sisters, Irma and Phoebe, were sitting on the floor next to Benjamin in a puddle of blankets and pillows. Christopher Muse and Avery Torres had grabbed the faded paisley armchairs that everyone jokingly referred to as "mezzanine seating" near the back of the room, and David Bond lounged on the floor next to Fabio, eating pizza with one hand and plugging a finger-sized hole in the beanbag chair to keep it from shedding its contents all over the food.

OK, so they weren't exactly living the dream, but the room was still theirs for the night.

Fabio lived for movie night. He no longer remembered whose idea it was, but over the past several months, it had become a ritual for the students to huddle around the television on Sunday evenings to watch a selection of movies from a cobbled together donation box assembled by the students and faculty. The only rules were: everyone took turns picking the movies, and no network television or real-world news allowed. They all had enough to deal with during the week with classes, training sessions, and all the worries and fears that came alongside being one of the few groups of mutants left in the world. Sunday nights were a night to escape and cut loose.

"Fabio's got a point, though," Benjamin said as the credits rolled a few minutes later. "This film redefined what makes a movie hero."

David chuckled skeptically. "It's popular, but it's not like it reinvented the wheel or anything."

"What's your ideal movie hero then?" Fabio challenged. Movie debates were almost as much fun as the movies themselves.

"They have to be relatable," Avery said, balancing her sketchbook on her updrawn knees while she reached for another fistful of popcorn.

"Agreed, but there's something to be said for larger-than-life qualities," Christopher put in, leaning back in his chair. "Movie heroes drop the best one-liners at the perfect moment. They get to walk away from the fiery explosion looking all kinds of cool. The rest of us wish we could handle a crisis like they do."

And they're loved by everyone in the end, Fabio thought, as he wiped his fingers on a paper towel. Not that he needed to be a John McClane out there saving the world. He had a soft spot for other movie leads, too – the hard-boiled detectives and spies – the smooth characters who could talk everyone in circles with a twinkle in their eyes.

He wouldn't mind if the real world was a bit more like the movies. In the movie version of his life, he would have a codename that wasn't susceptible to the obvious jokes that came with being a mutant called *Goldballs*. In the movie version of his life, his powers would come with cool laser sounds – *pew! pew! pew!* – and not *poink!*

He sighed. Why was one of those sounds so cool, while the other one made people giggle uncontrollably?

It wasn't like he didn't know who he was in this great cinema of life. He was well aware he was the sidekick, the comic relief, the butt of the joke. If he was lucky, he wouldn't also end up being the one sacrificed to advance the plot in some way. That was probably the best he could hope for, and he'd accepted it.

Sort of.

But to be the hero just once, to have his fifteen minutes of fame and glory... now that would be awesome.

The others were arguing over the next movie. Celeste said, "It's my turn to pick."

"Then pick," Benjamin said. "It has to be a movie."

"I know that." Celeste rolled her eyes. "I'm just saying, what if we mixed it up one of these nights? Did karaoke? It could be fun."

Next to her, Eva nodded enthusiastically, but Irma and Phoebe raised their hands in a simultaneous thumbs-down gesture. Seeing this, Celeste flushed and glared at the pair of them.

That was weird. Fabio couldn't remember the last time he'd seen them at odds. Or sitting so far apart. Something else was different, too. It took him a minute, but then he realized Irma had dyed her hair black, in sharp contrast to the others' blonde look. He started to say something about it, but abruptly the word "karaoke" penetrated his pizza-fogged brain.

"Hold on." He sat up in the beanbag chair with a loud crinkling of vinyl. "Benjamin's right, this is *movie* night. Karaoke is against the rules." And the laws of nature.

Celeste opened her mouth to argue, but seeing that Eva was her only ally, she deflated and burrowed into the couch cushions. "It was just a suggestion," she mumbled. "I don't really care what we watch." There was a glint of moisture on her cheek that might have been a tear, but she quickly turned her face away from the rest of them before Fabio could be sure.

He hoped he hadn't upset her by shooting her down. Maybe he'd been a little harsh, but it was *karaoke*. The thought of getting up in front of everyone and singing made the pizza churn in his stomach.

Movie heroes never had those kinds of problems, either.

"Hate to break it to everyone, but we probably shouldn't start another movie tonight," Christopher said, pointing to the clock on the wall. It was almost midnight. "Early training session tomorrow in the Danger Room, remember?"

There was a chorus of groans as one by one the students peeled themselves out of their chairs and nests of blankets to start cleaning up the food. It looked like a minor storm had blown through the room, but they eventually sorted it out.

As Fabio carried a stack of greasy plates to the garbage cans in the kitchen, he couldn't help but feel a pang of longing. Despite their grumbling, he had no doubt that tomorrow everyone would get a chance to shine somehow in their training session. He was scheduled to go first thing with the Stepford triplets, whose psychic powers were so strong, he knew he'd barely have to try in order to receive a passing grade. He supposed he should have been happy about that, but it just reinforced the role he'd been assigned in his own life.

Always the sidekick, never the hero.

He'd fallen asleep at his desk again.

Any minute now, Magneto was going to yell at him and everyone in the classroom would laugh. Not cruelly, just... you know, there goes Fabio, sleeping in class again, ha ha, of course.

Maybe if he lifted his head slowly and wiped the drool on his sleeve, no one would notice.

A hand grabbed his shoulder and gave him a teeth-rattling shake.

"Medina!"

"Present!" He jerked his head up, looking blearily around the classroom. Had the lights dimmed while he slept? Everything looked gray and dull – more so than usual – almost as if the entire room had been painted in black and white.

Wait a minute.

He squeezed his eyes shut and opened them again. Shut. Open. Everything *was* in black and white. And he wasn't sitting in a classroom. He was slumped behind an old wooden desk in a cluttered office that looked like it belonged in a different century. Big metal filing cabinets lined one wall, and a small couch was pushed up against another wall near the door. The desk's surface was littered with papers and dirty coffee cups. An old rotary telephone sat near his right elbow.

He wasn't alone in the room.

Three women stood in front of the desk. They were identical, from their shoulder-length hair to the style of their skirts, and all three of them wore soaring high heels that looked terribly uncomfortable. The one nearest him had her hand on his shoulder. She'd been the voice he'd heard, the one who'd woken him. That voice was familiar somehow, but he couldn't place it.

"What's going on?" he asked around a huge yawn. Was he still dreaming? He dug his fingernails into his palm until it hurt. Nope, not a dream.

"Detective Medina," the woman who'd woken him said impatiently. "We had an appointment. Surely you haven't forgotten?"

He had absolutely no idea what she was talking about. He looked at the other two women for a hint, but they only stared at him expectantly.

"I… yes, our… appointment. Of course." Nope, he had nothing. His underarms were damp with sweat. What was he doing here? Where was here? *Who* was he again?

He felt like he should have the answer to at least one of those questions. The fact that he was hazy on all three threatened to send him into panic mode. His gaze swung wildly around the room, looking for something to help him out. The office door had a pane of glass set into its top half, and on the outside, there was a sign. It was backwards from his point of view, but he managed to read it anyway.

Medina Investigations.

"Detective Medina?" the woman said again, a hint of desperation in her voice.

Suddenly, a sense of wellbeing washed over him, like a cool breeze on a hot day. Medina turned his head. There was a small window in the wall to his right. He took in his faint reflection in the glass. He was dressed in a weathered trench coat and an old but stylish fedora.

That's right. He was Detective Medina of Medina Investigations. This was his office.

When he looked back at the women, he gave them an easy smile. "Don't worry, I never forget an appointment."

The woman who'd woken him straightened up, looking more confident now. "My name is Celeste, and these are my sisters, Irma and Phoebe."

Again, that sense of familiarity washed over Medina, those names bouncing around inside his head like balls going *poink poink poink*. Celeste, Irma, Phoebe. But they'd never met before. Had they?

"What can I do for you?" he asked, getting back on track.

"Detective Medina, I won't waste your time. I just need fifteen minutes to tell our story." Celeste paced the small office in agitation, her hands clasped in front of her. "My sisters and I were on expedition in the Amazon, where we discovered an ancient treasure." She nodded to Irma, who reached inside a large bag she had propped against her hip. She pulled out an object roughly the size of an ostrich egg.

"I assume you've heard the legend of the Golden Sphere," Irma said as she put the object on his desk.

He laid his hands on the smooth, cool surface, fighting back another rush of familiarity. "Of course," he said. "Everyone knows the legend of the Golden Sphere."

Right?

"Word got around that we found it," Phoebe said, coming over to the desk and taking the sphere out of his hands. She gave it back to Irma, who slipped it carefully into the bag. "Now there are some very bad people chasing us."

"What sort of 'bad people' are we talking about?" Crossing his arms, he leaned back in his chair.

"The usual," Celeste said. She stopped pacing and perched on the edge of his desk, as if to take the weight off her high heels. Really, those shoes looked awfully uncomfortable. "Thieves, criminals – they all want the sphere for themselves. We need protection until we can decide what to do with it."

"All right, I'll take your case," he found himself saying without stopping to think about it, "but my protection fees are steep." He leaned forward, elbows propped on the desktop. "Now, first things first. Do you know if you were followed here?"

Celeste shook her head firmly. "We kept a close eye out," she said. "No one saw–"

She was interrupted by the loud *rat tat tat* of gunshots shattering the window.

"Get down!" Medina shoved his chair back, and all four of them hit the floor as more gunshots rang out in the small office.

"They found us!" Celeste shouted, panic rising in her voice as she crouched next to her sisters. She threw her arms protectively over the pair of them, shielding them with her body.

Medina fumbled in his bottommost desk drawer for the revolver stashed there. He army-crawled across the floor to the door. "Follow me and stay low!"

They ran down a narrow hallway to the back door of the building, which spilled onto a dimly lit alley. He herded the sisters behind him, leading the way with gun drawn, watching the inky shadows for any signs of movement. There was no sound except the huffs of their breathing. The air was crisp with late autumn cold.

Rounding the corner of the building, he halted and cursed.

The street dead-ended in a brick wall.

Wait, that didn't make any sense. He'd gone this way a hundred times to get to his car. It should be right there.

Gravel crunched behind them. Medina whirled to see a trio of figures emerging from the shadows at the other end of the alley. Their faces were obscured, but he could clearly see the guns they held.

Irma and Phoebe stepped forward, shielding their sister. Medina raised his own weapon, but he wasn't fast enough. Three sharp pistol cracks rang out, and a dull pain punched Medina in the shoulder. Next to him, Irma and Phoebe dropped to their knees, spots of blood darkening the fronts of their blouses.

"No!" Celeste screamed, but Medina couldn't get to her. His world had gone hazy and soft, and he was sinking into darkness.

He was staring up at the stars. Ursa Major winked at him as if it knew something he didn't. A cold wind pushed through the thin fabric of his bodysuit.

Wait, what?

He sat up, his ears ringing faintly as he stared down at

himself. He was dressed all in black, a mask covering his face. Glancing around, he realized he sat on the roof of an extremely tall building. A voice called out from behind him.

"Medina, get over here! The countdown clock is at fifteen minutes!"

Right, the bomb.

He stood on legs that were a little wobbly. He touched his shoulder, rubbing away a faint ache. What had he just been doing?

"Medina!"

He turned. Celeste, Irma, and Phoebe, wearing identical black bodysuits, were crouched around a bulky metal cylinder with a countdown clock in its center. Its red digital numbers tracked how much time was left before they were all blown to bits. Less than fifteen minutes now. A panel hung open in the cylinder's bottom, wires spilling out like entrails. Celeste was frantically separating them, trying to find the ones they could splice to disarm the bomb.

He sprinted over to the group, joining Celeste in the mess of wires. The city's biggest crime boss had discovered Medina's elite team of assassins' headquarters in the building below. They'd planted the bomb, and now if he didn't disarm the device, the explosives would level the building and five city blocks.

They were running out of time.

Medina glanced up at the countdown clock. He blinked, and the timer was at two minutes. Wait, how had that happened? It had just been fifteen! Hadn't it? His palms were sweating beneath his gloves as he frantically worked the wires.

"We've got company!" Celeste cried as the whirring of helicopter blades filled the air. Four black cables fell from the craft, which hovered thirty feet above the rooftop. Four assassins wearing the crime boss's signature crimson suits rappelled down and landed on the roof, brandishing knives and swords.

"Phoebe and I will hold them off," Irma told him. "You two keep working!"

The sisters darted across the roof like vicious shadows, engaging the other assassins. Medina finally found the elusive red wire and began splicing it with the two green wires Celeste held in her trembling fingers.

"It's going to be OK," he told her. "They've got this. We just need to focus on disarming the bomb."

He twisted the wires together, and the countdown clock stuttered, but kept going. A vague sense of unease tickled the back of his mind as he worked. Was this really how bombs got disarmed? It almost felt like he was picking wires at random, and he wasn't even sure he knew how the mechanism worked.

No, this was right. This was what he had to do. He was part of an elite team of assassins, and he would protect them at all costs.

Celeste screamed.

Medina jerked his head up in time to see one of their attackers pulling his sword out of Phoebe's stomach. She clutched the wound and fell limply to the ground. Irma was now surrounded.

"Take over!" Medina shoved the wires at Celeste and ran to help Irma, but as he moved, he noticed a shadow shift in one corner of an adjacent rooftop. "Sniper!" he yelled, diving and rolling as a hail of gunfire peppered the air. He jumped to his feet, but one of the assassins was bearing down on him, blade ready.

Desperate, Medina spun and tried to dodge, but the blade sliced smoothly into his shoulder. Distantly, he heard Celeste scream again as the beep of the countdown clock echoed in the air, ticking down to zero.

The last thing he heard was the sound of a terrific explosion, a ball of fire filling the air. Then he saw nothing at all.

He woke to the sound of gunfire and a revving engine, the reek of oil and gasoline searing his nostrils. It was suffocatingly hot. His white tank top stuck to him like a second skin.

They'd been pinned down in the chop shop. Celeste, dressed in shortalls and a bandana, crouched against the opposite wall beneath a shattered window, holding up a gun and firing blindly at their attackers outside.

"We have to get the sphere out of here," Phoebe said, sliding behind the wheel of the rocket red Mitsubishi parked near the garage door, handing the legendary Golden Sphere to Irma, who huddled in the passenger seat.

Yes, they had to get the sphere to safety. But instead, they'd gotten trapped after the gangsters hunting them had discovered their shop.

Wait, was that right?

There was a sharp ringing in his ears, and his mouth felt funny, like it was full of cotton. His shoulder ached like someone had punched him hard, but when he reached up to touch it, there was no wound.

"We're fifteen minutes from the border," Celeste said. Keeping low, she crossed the concrete floor and dove into the passenger seat of a second Mitsubishi, sky blue with a spoiler that went on for days. "Medina, we have to cover my sisters!"

He looked down at the gun and car keys he hadn't realized were in his hand. He felt so strange, like he'd done all of this before. Well, maybe not exactly this, but some version of this. What was happening to him?

"Medina, we need you!"

They always needed him. And he would come through.

Except... no, that wasn't right. He hadn't come through. He'd failed, and it kept happening, and...

"Medina!"

He sprinted to the blue car, throwing himself behind the wheel. Celeste slammed the button to raise the creaky old garage door. Tires screeched as they peeled out of the shop into the humid night, trailing close to Irma and Phoebe's Mitsubishi.

They were going to get away. No car in the city could match these deadly twins for speed...

"They've got a rocket launcher!" Celeste screamed as the rocket-propelled explosives streaked toward the cars. Medina spun the wheel, but he wasn't fast enough.

Explosions engulfed both cars, but the fire didn't burn. Medina felt a stabbing pain in his head, and the ringing in his ears grew more intense.

Then there was nothing.

"Detective Medina!"

"I'm here!" He'd fallen asleep at his desk again. Celeste stared down at him, worry and fear in her eyes. He must have been lying on his shoulder. It ached abominably, and there was a loud ringing in his ears.

He looked up at Celeste. Wait, how did he know her name? He'd never met her before, or the other two women standing near the door.

No, of course he knew them. Irma and Phoebe. They were psychics...

No, they were in trouble. They were going to ask him for help with... something.

"We need to protect the legendary Golden Sphere," Celeste said, as if she could read his thoughts. She placed the vaguely egg-shaped sphere in front of him on the desk. It made a soft *poink* sound as it came to rest.

And with that sound, Fabio remembered.

Fabio Medina.

Not the detective in a trench coat in this black and white world. Not the leader of an elite team of assassins. Fabio Medina – Goldballs – like the one sitting on the desk in front of him. And the sisters who'd come to seek his help were the Stepford Cuckoos.

None of this was real. Or at least, it shouldn't be.

"Detective–"

"Let me think a minute!" He hadn't meant to shout, but he was scared. How long had he been living inside these weird movie moments? What was going on?

He tried to remember the last time things were normal. He'd been among friends. There'd been food. Movie night, that was it. They'd been discussing movie heroes. Did that mean this was some elaborate dream brought on by too much late-night pizza and action flicks?

He shifted in his chair, and a jagged bolt of pain went through his shoulder, making him grit his teeth. No, definitely not a dream. But why couldn't he remember anything past the movie night? There'd been something going on the next day. He vaguely recalled getting up early and heading to the Danger Room.

That was it.

Emma Frost had paired him with the Stepford triplets for a telepathic training exercise. Obviously, something had gone very wrong.

"Celeste," he said, looking up at the closest sister. "Do you know who I am? Who I *really* am?"

She looked at him in confused impatience, her forehead wrinkling. "Detective Medina, we don't have time for games. This is serious."

He couldn't agree more. "My name's Fabio. I'm not a detective. I'm one of the X-Men, and so are you. None of this is real."

She scowled, as if he wasn't making sense. "You're *Detective Medina*. You're supposed to be the best at what you do. That's why we came to you. You solve crimes, you right wrongs, and you help people who need help."

"And if he can't help us, we need to get out of here," Irma snapped, grabbing the sphere. "We have to get this to safety."

"OK, first of all, I *am* trying to help," he said. "Secondly, do you even know where we're supposed to take that thing?" When they just stared at him blankly, he plowed on. "Think about it. We're all in black and white. Doesn't that strike you as odd?"

The three of them stared down at themselves, but only Celeste seemed unsettled by what she saw. Irma and Phoebe looked at each other in confusion. "We look like we always have," Irma said slowly.

Gunshots shattered the window, sending them all diving for cover. Great, he'd forgotten about this part of the scene.

"Out the back!" he yelled to the others, herding them toward the door. He had to find a way to get the triplets to remember who they really were. They were psychics. If anyone could get them out of this, it was them.

They ran down the long hallway, but this time, when they exited the building, Fabio turned everyone right instead of left, avoiding the dead end.

He rubbed his shoulder as they ran. Celeste noticed and said, "Were you hit?"

"No," he said, trying to sound reassuring, but it felt like he had been hit. His head hurt. The ringing in his ears was constant now. It seemed to be steadily getting worse with each deadly vignette they went through. Was it possible they could die here, caught in some kind of psychic trap?

"We should split up," Irma said as they came to an intersection. To the left, the road ran between two tall warehouses, and to the right was an all-night diner. "Our car's two blocks away. Phoebe and I will go get it and pick you up."

"No," Celeste said immediately, as Irma glared at her. "We're not separating. It's too dangerous."

Something tickled the back of Fabio's mind as he watched them argue. This had happened before, too. In all the movie scenes, there was a moment when Irma and Phoebe tried to act on their own, without Celeste. Then everything went wrong.

Did that mean something?

"Fine," Celeste was saying, "we don't have time to fight, just get the car."

Fabio had a sinking feeling as the two sisters started to walk away. His fears were confirmed when four men with guns stepped out, seemingly from nowhere, to block their path. "Hands up," the lead man barked. He had a thick, square jaw and the beginnings of a beard. "Give us the Golden Sphere."

Fabio's thoughts whirled, his mind replaying the plot of every heist movie he'd ever seen, trying to come up with a way out. These scenes always ended in tragedy, but why? Was it possible they could rewrite the script by doing things differently?

"We'll give you the sphere," he blurted out before the triplets could say anything.

Celeste looked at him as if he'd lost his mind. "We can't!"

Why not? he wanted to shout in frustration, but he kept his cool. He glanced over at Irma, who held the sphere tightly in her hands and glared at him. OK, no help there. He took a deep breath and let it out, turning to face their enemies. Time to see if he could change the ending of this scene himself.

"You want a gold ball?" Hands up, he spread them wide and tried to make his lip curl in amused disdain, just the way the movie heroes did right before they laid waste to the bad guys. "Have a bunch."

Poink!

Poink!

Poink!

Poink!

Poink!

Poink!

Gold balls flew from his body, catching the gunmen completely unawares and knocking them off their feet. They opened fire as they fell. A stray bullet struck Fabio in the shoulder – always got him in the same spot – and this time, the pain that ripped through him was so intense it drove him to his knees. The gold balls vanished as if they'd never been there.

"Run!" he cried feebly, but Irma wasn't listening. Over Celeste's scream of protest, she ran to his side and hauled him to his feet. With her help, he tried to run, but the pain made his head swim.

One of the gunmen rolled onto his side and fired again. Irma was suddenly a dead weight at his side. They slumped to the ground together, and all Fabio could hear were Celeste's screams.

He looked over at her as his vision began to darken. She was unhurt. But how? She was standing right in front of the gunmen. There was no way they could have missed her.

He fought the darkness reaching up to claim him again. This was important. He needed to figure this out. Celeste was never hurt in any of the movie scenes. It was always him, Irma, and Phoebe.

Celeste. She was at the heart of this somehow. He had to get through to her.

He woke with a gasp and sat up. He was on the roof of a building again.

Oh no, not another bomb.

Gray predawn light filled the sky, but the wind carried a strange, foul scent, like something had been rotting in the sun. He didn't remember this movie set. Was it new?

Celeste laid her hand on his shoulder. She was dressed in ripped jeans and a sweat-stained t-shirt. He wasn't looking any better in a faded camo jacket and cargo pants, and he smelled like he hadn't showered in a week.

"Sorry to wake you," Celeste said, her voice grim, "but they're coming."

"Who's coming?" he asked, but then he shook his head. It didn't matter. Whatever it was, it would kill him again, and he wasn't sure how many more of these scenes he had in him. His shoulder was on fire, and his thoughts were sluggish. It hurt to concentrate.

"Celeste," he said, grabbing her wrist when she started to turn away from him. "You have to snap out of it. None of this is real."

She wasn't listening. "We've only got a little ammo left, a few grenades," she said, "so when they start swarming, make them count. I have to go check on my sisters."

He tried to ignore the tightening in his gut when she said *swarming*. "We've done this before," he said, trying to be patient. "It always ends the same way. Why? Are you causing this?"

"Seriously?" Her fists clenched as she stared at him in disbelief. "You think *I* brought about the zombie apocalypse?" She stabbed a finger angrily at the surrounding rooftops. He followed the gesture and broke out into a cold sweat.

A horde of grotesque, bent-limbed zombies shuffled toward them, their flesh gray and rotting, the reek of them filling his nostrils and making his stomach roil. He glanced over the nearby ledge where dozens more zombies scrambled slowly, creepily up the side of the building. Faintly, he heard the sound of shuffling and moaning coming from the floors below them. They were trapped up here.

OK. OK. Breathe, Fabio, breathe. Panicking would just hasten their demise, and he had no desire to be eaten alive by zombies, psychic trap or not.

He squeezed Celeste's wrist, ignoring her angry protest. "I need you to remember," he pleaded. "We were having movie night. At the Institute. Remember the Institute?" He stared into her eyes, willing her to listen. Was that a flicker in her expression? He plunged on. "The next day we were supposed to do a telepathic training exercise. You and your sisters connected to me psychically. Something went wrong, and now we're stuck in these movie scenes that end in me and your sisters dying, but never you. It's *hurting* me, Celeste, so I bet it's hurting them, too. We need to find a way to break this cycle before someone gets killed for real."

When he mentioned her sisters, Celeste's eyes widened. He'd been right. That was the key.

"You were upset with them last night," he said, piecing it together on the fly. The sounds of zombie groans were getting closer. He could hear their blunt nails scrabbling for purchase on the window ledges and grooves as they climbed the building. It made his skin crawl.

"I... that's not..." But Celeste was thinking now. He could see it. Some of the fear in her face was being replaced by confusion and doubt.

"You wanted to do karaoke. We told you no, and you were hurt. I noticed, and I should have said something to make you feel better. I'm sorry. I was wrapped up in my own stuff." He was babbling now. "I was thinking about how much I wanted to be a movie hero, and you–"

"I was afraid my sisters were leaving me behind."

Fabio's breath caught. He stared at her hard. "Does that mean you remember?" He barely dared to hope.

She squeezed her eyes shut and let out a long breath. When she opened them again, she nodded. "We let our thoughts intrude on the training exercise and lost concentration. Now our worries and fears are all tangled up and manifesting in bizarre ways."

So that was it. Fabio's obsession with movie heroes had

gotten them stuck in a loop of movie scenes, and Celeste's fear of losing her sisters wasn't allowing any of the scenarios to end happily.

Emma Frost had warned them about the dangers of being distracted during telepathic exercises. Now they were seeing the consequences firsthand.

"Can you wake us up?" Fabio demanded. "I don't know how much more of this we can take before it breaks our minds."

On the opposite side of the roof, Phoebe screamed.

Fabio turned in horror to see a line of zombies cresting the rooftop. Irma and Phoebe opened fire, but there were far too many of them. The horde descended, and they disappeared under a pile of gray bodies.

"No!" Celeste tried to run to them, but Fabio held onto her. She was strong and desperate. It took everything he had to keep her in place.

"This isn't real!" he insisted. "Your sisters are OK, and they're still with you, even if you're fighting, because you're family. If you really want to help them right now, you need to get us out of here!"

"I can't!" Tears rolled down Celeste's face, but her cheeks were red with fury. "I'm trying, but nothing's happening! I hate this! I don't even like these dumb movies!"

Under normal circumstances, Fabio would have been outraged by that comment, but since they were about to be murdered by a zombie horde, he let it pass.

And he suddenly had an idea.

"In the last scene, I was able to use my powers and take control of the story for a few seconds," he said. As he spoke, he lobbed one of the grenades as hard as he could to the other side of the roof. He and Celeste ducked as the explosion sent a ball of fire mushrooming into the sky. Zombie parts flew everywhere.

"I remember," Celeste said, grabbing her rifle to pick off zombies as they came onto the roof. "But it didn't work. You and my sisters still got shot."

"I think it's because you originated the psychic connection," Fabio said, tossing another grenade. "So, you're the only one who can fully control it. You should be able to do whatever you want here. Think about it. Do you know how to shoot that rifle in real life?"

She looked down at the gun in her hands, brow furrowed. "So, you're saying I should try to think bigger? Change the whole connection?"

"Exactly! I think fear is what's holding you back." The horde was getting closer. There were hundreds of zombies clustered on the surrounding rooftops now. "You have to move past it. But whatever you do, please do it fast!"

"Change the story," Celeste murmured. "That makes sense. Change it to something I love." She turned sharply to look at him. "We need this to be a musical!"

"A what now?" It was the only thing she could have said to distract him from the ravenous zombies.

"A musical! We change the movie scene into something that won't kill us. What better than a big musical number?"

It was actually a great idea, and it just might work, except for one thing. "I can't sing," he said in a choked voice. "I'm terrible. There's no way."

Mouth flattening, she grabbed him by his shirtfront and gave him a shake. "I ran from gunmen in two-inch heels and fought assassins in an itchy unitard in your version of this nightmare," she hissed. "Use the mic, songbird."

He gulped. "O- OK. What mic?"

"The one in your hand."

He looked down, and sure enough, his last grenade had turned into a shiny silver cordless microphone. Celeste's rifle had become another one in sparkling gold. She raised it to her lips and without hesitation belted out the opening verse of a familiar song, a tide of orchestral accompaniment rising from nowhere to support her.

Oh, for the love of... She'd picked "We Go Together", the ending number to Grease.

What happened next was one of the strangest, most impressive things Fabio had ever seen.

As Celeste launched into the song, the psychic vision picked up on her energy, almost as if it had been waiting all this time for her to take control. The sun rose past a bank of gunmetal clouds, saturating the rooftop scene with orange, red, and purple light. Their filthy clothes morphed into tight pants and stylish leather jackets. The zombies froze in place as the clear, ringing notes of Celeste's chosen song filled the air. Slowly, they began to sway in time to the music, crooked limbs flapping weirdly with the beat. It was horrifying. It was unnatural.

Fabio couldn't look away.

Celeste elbowed him in the ribs, and he realized he hadn't joined in the number. He hadn't been lying about his lack of talent, but at that moment he decided he didn't care. Celeste's plan was working.

He sang, moving awkwardly in time to the music, but the microphone took his words, mixed them into the psychic stew and churned out a performance that even Travolta might have been proud of.

This was nothing like the movie musical he barely remembered. It felt more like they were a cover band performing their own version of the song, and the crowd of zombies responded. They clapped and swayed and gyrated and suddenly, transformed. No longer were they a ravenous horde bent on consuming everything. They were a supporting cast, adults and children dancing and singing and smiling while Celeste led them in the closing number and its nonsense lyrics that everyone could just bop along to.

That's why she'd picked that particular musical and ending song, he realized. It was light and fun, a celebration of love and freedom and the possibilities of the future. Fabio threw back his head and closed his eyes as the scent of fresh flowers and the feeling of endless hot summer days filled the air, replacing the stench of rot and death. He felt Celeste take his hand and give it an encouraging squeeze…

And then he was opening his eyes to find himself lying on the floor of the Danger Room, his weight pressing his shoulder painfully into the hard floor. Students and instructors clustered around him, their faces breaking into relieved smiles.

"How long was I out?" he croaked as they helped him sit up.

"Not long," Triage said. "About fifteen minutes."

Later, after an extended stint in the infirmary to make sure no permanent damage had been done during the psychic vision, Fabio found Celeste in the television room digging through the box of old movies.

"It's amazing how many of these I recognize now, even

though I've never seen them," she said as he sat down across from her. "You really know your movies."

"Well, you smashed that musical number," he said, rubbing the back of his neck self-consciously. "Listen, I wanted to say thanks, for getting us out of that vision."

She shook her head, her expression troubled. "It was my fault we were stuck in the first place. My sisters and I have always done everything together, but lately it feels like we couldn't be more different." She picked at a loose bit of cardboard on the box lid. "Obviously, I'm not handling that very well. I need to talk to them, but they don't remember anything from the vision, so I don't know how I'll explain everything." She sighed. "Anyway, I'm sorry you got pulled into my fears and worries."

"You weren't the only one responsible," he argued. "If I'd been less obsessed with the whole 'movie hero' bit, we might never have ended up in those gunfights and explosions." He felt his cheeks warm. "So, you know all my dark secrets now. It must seem pretty silly, me imagining myself as all these larger-than-life characters."

"I'm sure you're not the first person who wished they were the hero of an epic movie," she said dryly. "Your secret's safe with me."

He was relieved to hear it, but he realized he couldn't leave it like that. Not when it wasn't the whole truth. "I had another reason," he said quietly, "for wanting to be the hero."

"What was that?"

"Everyone loves movie heroes." He stared down at the covers of the DVDs in the box. "People aren't afraid of movie heroes. They accept them, cheer them on, all that stuff. Well, isn't that what mutants want, to be accepted by the world? If we could be heroes like in the movies, surely that acceptance would come easier?" That's what he'd hoped at least, deep down inside.

She gave him a sad smile. "Maybe, but it's easy to embrace something that isn't real. Life is a lot messier and more complicated." She reached across the box and laid a hand on his arm. "But you came through for *me* today when I needed it. You were a hero, even if the rest of the world doesn't know about it."

She was right. No one else would ever understand exactly what went down in that vision, but they'd been there for each other, and that kind of acceptance was better than any movie. It was real.

"Thanks," he said, and took a deep breath. "For what it's worth, I think you should try talking to your sisters, even if it's hard. And if it helps, I'll support your bid for karaoke night next week."

Her eyes brightened in surprised pleasure. "Really?"

"Yes," he said before he could rethink it. "I'm going to be terrible, and you'll regret you ever suggested the idea, but anything for a friend."

Should he have used the word 'friend'? He wasn't sure, but somehow it felt right. When a slow smile spread across Celeste's face, he knew that it was.

"You're on, Medina."

CALL OF THE DARK

Robbie MacNiven

Time was running out.

Graymalkin knew he'd probably been gone too long already. His next class was about to start. If he left now, he would only be five minutes late. If he delayed any longer, he'd be punished with rerunning combat drills for the rest of the day.

Yet, he stayed where he was, sitting in a chair in the corner of the room. It was the only upstanding piece of furniture in the space. Several tables lay collapsed in on themselves, and several more chairs broken, on their sides. The floor was littered with old books, broken glass, crusty food cartons, and even less identifiable detritus.

He had picked up one of the books earlier, trying to discern its purpose. It appeared to be some sort of manual or operating script, though its instructions were too opaque and its state of decay too advanced for comprehension. It had fallen apart in his hands, pages black with rot.

Time was running out, and Graymalkin didn't care. Combat class was about to start, specifically the night-fight drill, part of this semester's course and held once a week. The Danger Room would be configured to represent a city street after dark, or a sewer tunnel, or a subterranean cavern. Zero illumination. Total dark.

"They shouldn't let you run those drills," Victor Borkowski had told him before their first session, last week. "Maybe you can tell me if I'm about to run into a wall or something?"

Vic had been joking, of course. Graymalkin's mutant powers were derived wholly from the dark. As a youth he'd been buried alive by his father, a punishment for what the snarling zealot had called Graymalkin's unnatural attraction to his own gender. That had been over three hundred years ago. The experience had unlocked latent mutant powers, a plethora of abilities – in the dark he was stronger, faster, more resilient, more active, and aware. He should have been more than a match for the school's dark-scenario training. And yet, increasingly, he was finding that he was not.

He was afraid of the dark.

A flashlight sat propped up by one of the broken tables, its beam picking out the rough-hewn rock of the walls and ceiling. The room was buried, like the rest of the Xavier Institute, deep below ground, a further irony that was not lost on him. The inhabited parts of the school, such as the dorms, lecture theatres, recreation halls, and the Danger Room, were hardly welcoming. They were cramped spaces formed from old monotone concrete and iron girders, with bundles of exposed cabling snaking along the walls and ceilings and air circulation systems that rattled and coughed like an old rheumatic. The place was almost homey, especially when compared to what lay further down.

No one Graymalkin spoke to seemed to know the full extent of the complex. He doubted even Principal Summers was certain how deep it went. When it had first been built it had served as a Weapon X facility, a government facility dedicated to experiments designed to exploit the deadliest traits of mutantkind. It had been repurposed by the X-Men into its current role: a school – and safe haven – for gifted mutant children. In Graymalkin's experience, though, the switch was skin-deep only. It was akin to a cosmetic redecoration. Light and life had been brought back to echoing halls and dank corridors that had lain in silent darkness for years, but while the dorms now had beds, the canteen smelled of fresh cooking, and naked lightbulbs, humming generators, and clicking lecture theatre projection screens had driven back the shadows, the soul of the place remained the same. Behind the schedules and the art class sketches the walls were still cold and hard, the room and corridor layouts bleak and utilitarian. As far as Graymalkin was concerned, this was still the Weapon X facility.

That became even more apparent when he left the well-traveled, well-lit spaces and ventured down. He wasn't supposed to, but it wasn't difficult to slip away, not when he knew he had no choice if he wanted to confront his fear. From the outside, the school's defenses were solid, the few hatches that led to the world beyond blast-proofed and heavily alarmed. Inside, though, the place was porous. Ventilation shafts, maintenance tunnels, and access panels all led down into a place where no amount of renovation was going to banish the facility's origins.

Graymalkin leaned over, his chair creaking dangerously, and picked up the flashlight. He took in the dilapidated room one more time, then flicked the switch.

This was the worst part, right after he'd killed the illumination. He could see as well in the darkness as he could in the light, but it took him a few moments to adjust from one to the other. He was blind for seconds, and totally defenseless.

His heart began to race. Every sense ramped up until they were poised on a painful, delicate razor-edge. He could feel everything, the stale, clammy air, the firmness of the chair beneath him, the heavy weight of the bedrock surrounding him. Sounds that had gone unnoticed before, deleted by his mind as irrelevant, demanded his attention. He could hear the skitter and scrape of what he took to be small rodents nearby, and the dull, constant throb of the Institute's primary generator, somewhere above. His own breathing, his own heartbeat, his very thoughts, all seemed uncomfortably loud. And there, far away, was the telltale buzz, a noise he'd started to hear more and more during his visits to the facility's depths.

He tried to settle himself. It shouldn't be like this. He had made so much progress over the past year. With Vic's help, he'd conquered a multitude of fears. He no longer dreaded the fact that the entire school was entombed underground. He had left the worst of his night terrors behind. He now understood the power darkness gave him – power he could use for good. It was a part of him, not something to shy away from. He hadn't been so afraid of it for a while, not like this.

He stood up, holding the inactive flashlight. The darkness seemed to coil and shift around him, but there was nothing there. He knew that. He could see clearly enough now. Was lack of vision not the root of the fear caused by being in the dark? It stemmed from fear of the unknown. Yet he was not blind. He could see that there was nothing here to be afraid of.

He moved to the door and looked out. To his left lay a narrow emergency stairwell that led back to the Institute's inhabited levels, while directly ahead of him was a corridor, dilapidated and semi-collapsed, old cabling hanging like jungle creepers from the cracked and broken ceiling. It was worse the further down he ventured. He'd discovered much after deciding to explore the school's depths several weeks earlier, initially seeking the sort of calming solitude he didn't think he could find even in his locked dorm room. He had unearthed a forbidden, half-forgotten realm of dusty chambers and crumbling tunnels, many of them partly fused with the bedrock they'd been burrowed into. They were laden with age and stale with disuse. Their function remained uncertain – cabinets lay empty, and gaps marked where heavy machinery had been removed. Still, the cold soul of the place lingered, more tangible here in the echoing, lifeless spaces than further up, where it was masked.

It made him afraid, and that fear drove him to return. He knew he had to face those fears. There was nothing that need disturb him in doing so.

Nothing stirred in the corridor ahead of him. He tried to recall the poetry he'd learned recently.

Deep into that darkness peering, long I stood there wondering, fearing,
Doubting, dreaming dreams no mortal ever dared to dream before.

It was from Edgar Allen Poe's *The Raven*. A nineteenth-century author who still, it seemed, retained some renown. Vic had been amused when he had spotted him reading from a Poe anthology in the canteen. He'd asked if he had started going through his emo phase, a term he'd struggled to explain adequately to Graymalkin, beyond the fact it seemingly included a good deal of angst. Graymalkin had shrugged and suggested he might be, making a mental note to conduct further research on the matter.

Poe spoke of a darkness that was at once familiar and unknowable. Graymalkin could understand that. The problem was the darkness felt as though it kept growing increasingly unknowable. It had not held such fear for him for some time, yet now it did. During the night drill the week before, he'd frozen, unable to move. Summers had canceled the session and given him an absence of leave for the rest of the day. When Vic had come to him, asking what had happened, he'd been unable to explain. He had been afraid, but he didn't truly know why.

He understood fear itself – it had been a companion for slow, suffocating centuries after all, one of the only constants as he had drifted in and out of a paralyzed fugue. He also knew that fear sometimes wasn't reasonable, that it couldn't be bargained with. Still, as he looked down the corridor, feeling an unshakable sense of apprehension, he tried.

There's nothing there, he told himself. He forced the words out past his lips. "There's nothing there."

"There's nothing there."

The repetition made him jump. He immediately felt foolish, realizing his voice had echoed, nothing more.

What had become of him? Jumping at shadows, at his own voice? He had spent too long down here. It was time to get to class before an afternoon's combat drills became a whole day.

"I'm a fool," he said out loud, wanting to hear the words repeated back to himself.

Only this time, they weren't.

Graymalkin went still. Nothing in the corridor ahead of him moved. He hadn't so much as turned his head since first speaking.

So where had his echo gone?

The most immediate explanation, the one that set his heart racing once more, was that it hadn't been an echo in the first place.

He made for the stairwell, still feeling foolish, but acting by instinct now. He darted for the entrance, moving whiplash-fast in the total dark.

Just as quickly, something struck him. He dropped his flashlight and went down with a grunt, the wind driven from his lungs. He rolled, senses keen, ready to lash out in turn, to bring down whatever apparition stalked him.

He found himself looking into his own white eyes. A figure, tall and gaunt, its skin a pallid gray, ears pointed. It wore a black and yellow X-suit.

It was him. A doppelgänger, an exact replica. It looked down at him without expression from a few feet away, blocking the route to the stairs.

Graymalkin's breath came back with a gasp. He stared, not daring to move, hardly daring to speak.

"Who are you?" he managed.

A ridiculous question, he realized. The apparition said nothing. Instead, it struck him again.

This time, Graymalkin matched its speed. He threw himself back, the fist passing by his face, the follow-up falling just short as well.

"What are you?" Graymalkin demanded, his voice firmer than before as he put more space between himself and the creature.

It sneered, an ugly expression, one that he was unaccustomed to. "I am you, Jonas."

"That is impossible," Graymalkin replied, trying to fight through the fear and confusion seeking to paralyze him. "This is a dream. A night terror."

The double didn't answer. It attacked again.

This time it was too fast. Graymalkin managed to block the first blow with a forearm and take the sting from the second with a desperate twist of his upper body, but he couldn't stop the third before it slammed into his chest, or a lashing foot that thumped into his calf. He fell back once more, almost driven into the room he'd come from.

Shock made him defensive, but the pain touched off a spark of anger. He snarled and hit back. An uppercut, a jab to the stomach, the cycle repeated then reversed. None landed cleanly, the force taken from them with a flurry of counters.

The exchange had started and finished in the blink of an eye. In the dark, Graymalkin's power was absolute. But then, so, seemingly, was his double's.

"This cannot be happening," he said as he relented, panting. The double showed no sign of exertion or discomfort.

"This fear you have developed, it is pathetic," the double said. "How can you, of all people, be afraid of the dark? It is where you thrive. Where you are strongest."

"I'm not afraid," Graymalkin said.

"Liar," the double said. "Have you ever said those words truthfully?"

"What do you want from me?" Graymalkin asked, desperately trying to buy time while he figured out what was happening.

But the double didn't answer. It attacked again. Graymalkin dodged backwards, but he struck the side of his head on the doorway to the room he'd been sitting in before. Sharp pain lanced through his skull and birthed a constellation of stars across his vision. He stumbled and cringed from the series of blows that fell across his shoulders and back, bringing his arms up to shield his head.

In a last-ditch effort, he snatched the double's wrist and hauled him in with all his strength, managing to bring him down. They grappled, Graymalkin feeling the terrible strength he was competing with, the power of the darkness that surrounded them given form.

He wrenched himself free so that he was on the other side of his twin, with nothing now between him and the stairway. He lunged for it.

The double surged after him, snagging his heel. He went down, but as he stretched, he reached out to grasp his fallen flashlight. He twisted, pointing it at the double as he rose to strike, white eyes glaring at him.

"Darkness there and nothing more," Graymalkin snarled, and turned on the flashlight.

He'd expected the sudden light to rob them both of their power, to take both the incredible speed and terrifying strength out of the fight and leave his opponent blinded. But the effect of the beam of illumination was altogether more absolute.

In an instant, the double was gone.

Graymalkin let out an involuntary moan. He darted the flashlight's beam about, afraid the double had darted away before he'd been able to flick the switch. There was nothing, though, nothing in the rundown corridor, or in the room he'd left, or in the stairwell.

He regained his feet, shaking, the light still on. His powers recoiled at it, but it was better than the alternative. Better than being left in the dark.

He made for the stairs, not daring to look around any further. As he ran, his feet ringing from the rusting metal rungs, he could hear a voice – his own – rising up after him.

"I will see you again, Jonas."

There was a knock at Graymalkin's door.

Someone had already tried that earlier in the day, and his communicator had buzzed several times since. He hadn't answered any of them. He sat on his bed in his dorm room, with every light on.

A part of him was convinced he'd dreamt the entire episode in the Institute's underbelly. The only problem with that, besides the ongoing pain of where he had been struck, was the fact that if he'd been asleep, he still hadn't woken up yet. The thought was just as disturbing as the idea that he had a ruthless twin lurking somewhere beneath the school.

"Gray," said a voice from the other side of the door. "Gray, it's Vic. You going to open up?"

Graymalkin didn't move. Part of him wanted to kill the lights, so it seemed as though he wasn't in, but he didn't dare give the darkness free rein once more.

"Principal Summers wants to know where you are," Vic went on. "I told him you were sick. But truth is, I'd kinda like to know, too."

Graymalkin closed his eyes, wishing his best friend would go away. There was no hope that he would be able to explain this to him without sounding insane. In fact, what if he *was* insane? What if the soul that had remained trapped underground for so long had finally, abruptly snapped?

"Listen, Gray, I know sometimes you need space," Vic called out from beyond the door. "That's OK. We all do sometimes, even a cool kid like me. But I need to at least know you're going to be OK. That's my duty, as a friend. So open this door, or I'm going to use my big scaly green lizard arm to break it down."

Graymalkin knew that tone. When it came to his friends, Victor Borkowski had a stubborn streak. He knew he wasn't joking about the door.

He got off his bed and opened it. Victor – alias, Anole – looked up at him with an expression that was at once stern and concerned.

"Gray, your head," he exclaimed, immediately entering the room, his eyes fixed on the injury Graymalkin had sustained when he'd been driven back into the door frame. The blow had left behind a light scabbing and a swelling the size of a small bird's egg. It still throbbed dully.

"What happened?" Victor demanded, anger entering his voice. "Who did this to you?"

"Myself," Graymalkin said, almost blushing as he realized the unintended implications of what he'd just said. "I fell," he added.

"Next you'll be telling me you tripped in the dark," Vic said, unimpressed. "Give me names and I'll sort it out. Was it Kid

Gladiator? The Stepford Cuckoos? I swear, I'll break every single one of–"

"It wasn't a student," Graymalkin interrupted, trying to quell Victor's mounting anger. "At least, I don't think it was."

"What's that supposed to mean?"

"I wish I knew," Graymalkin said earnestly. "Trust me in this, Victor. It's nothing."

Vic looked at him with an expression that perfectly encapsulated his view of Graymalkin's "nothing". Graymalkin found he couldn't look his friend in the eye. Lying had never come naturally to him, but what else was he supposed to do? If he couldn't explain what had happened to Victor, who had shared the best and worst moments of his life since the day he'd been hauled from the earth, he knew there was no chance he'd be able to tell Cyclops, Frost, or anyone else running the school.

For the first time since that moment of rebirth, he felt truly alone again.

"I'm going to check in on you later," Victor said with a look of defiance. "I'll keep up the story about you being ill. But in exchange, I want you to have a long, hard think about what you want to tell me when I come back tonight. This isn't right, Gray. You've saved my life before; don't think I'm going to ignore you when you're in trouble. That's not how real friendship works."

"I know," Gray allowed, finally forcing himself to look his friend in the eye. "I'll message you later, Victor."

Graymalkin knew Vic would do his utmost to help him, and that in turn meant it probably wouldn't be long before he discovered what had happened beneath the school.

Graymalkin couldn't allow that – he was determined to resolve this alone – and he couldn't run the risk of whatever he'd discovered getting loose. What if it came up into the Institute? What if it replaced him?

The night passed with painful slowness. Vic called him in the evening, and he answered his questions long enough to allay his concerns until the morning. Graymalkin lay awake with the lights on for hours afterward, too afraid to sleep but too exhausted to do anything else. On several occasions he thought he heard movement outside his door but didn't dare draw back the blinds on the window that looked out into the corridor. He closed his eyes, desperately willing away whatever terrible spirit or mocking curse had attached itself to him.

At some point he must have fallen asleep because he realized his double was in the room with him. It stood by the bed, looking down at him in the dark. The lights were off, though he didn't remember turning them off. Its eyes were different now from his own – gone was the milky white gaze, replaced by a jet-black glare.

Graymalkin froze in horror. The thing spoke. In the background, there was a distant buzzing noise.

"Did you think you could simply leave me behind, Jonas? That you could forget about me, or I about you? Come, we have been together far too long for that."

The double snatched Graymalkin by the throat. He cried out, sat up, shielded his eyes.

The lights were on, dousing his room in harsh brilliance. He looked around wildly, heart beating against his ribs. The double was gone as if he'd never been there at all.

He looked at the clock on his nightstand, and realized it was just after six am. He wasn't sure when he'd fallen asleep, if he had.

His first instinct was to call Vic on his communicator. He checked himself. It had been a dream, nothing more. The story was no more credible now than before. There was no point in telling him.

He forced himself to get up, have a shower and sit aimlessly in it before getting dressed. His first class of the day was early, at half past eight. He resolved to attend. He needed company, a means to reinforce the desperate hope that he'd been imagining things. Maybe he'd even open up to Vic later on, once he'd wrapped his head around everything, try to explain it all. If anyone would believe him, it would be Victor.

The first lesson of the day was culture class. Ordinarily, it was Graymalkin's favorite. The topics were wide-ranging, but usually involved recent history, sociology, and investigation into the place of mutantkind in the wider world. They provided him with a window into the modern age and helped him understand how much things had changed over the three hundred years since his imprisonment.

Today, though, he was barely listening. The subject was official government responses to mutants throughout the twentieth century. They were passing over the Weapon X project, including the use of the Institute's current home as a testing facility for experimental weaponry. Graymalkin's mind was elsewhere, at least until Ms Pryde said his name. His heart racing, he swore he could detect a distant, faint buzzing sound.

"Jonas?"

His attention snapped back to the whiteboard. He realized, with a sudden surge of embarrassment, that the entire class was staring at him.

"My apologies, Ms Pryde," he said hastily. "Could you repeat the question?"

"I asked who initially founded the United States Weapon X project," she repeated sternly. "Given I told the class less than five minutes ago, I hoped you would remember."

Graymalkin's thoughts scrambled desperately for the answer. He swore the buzzing noise was getting louder.

"Professor Thornton," he managed after what felt like an age. Ms Pryde nodded.

"Partially correct, though that was only an alias. Megan, could you perhaps give us the full answer?"

Pixie, sitting beside Graymalkin, looked up from the page she'd been pretending to study.

"Truett Hudson," she said brightly, after only a moment's concentration.

"Thank you, Megan," Ms Pryde said, glancing again at Graymalkin but saying nothing more to him before continuing the lesson.

"Pro tip," Pixie murmured, leaning over to him as Ms Pryde told the class to turn to the next chapter. "If you spend five seconds reading the board behind her, the answer's probably already up there."

Graymalkin muttered his thanks. Ordinarily he'd have been deeply embarrassed at being caught short in front of the entire cohort. Right now, though, he barely cared. He felt as though the very walls of the classroom were closing in around him. He could still hear the buzzing.

"You OK?" Pixie asked him. Concern laced her voice, though she sounded casual. He tried to reassure her, tried to ward off the fear and panic that were steadily taking hold of him. His words faltered, though.

"What a miserable coward you have become."

The voice seemed to come from nowhere, and everywhere at once. It made him start and look about, terror gripping him. His neighbors on the nearest desks looked at him askance, though there was no sign that anybody else had heard the voice. His voice.

"*It's too late to turn back now,*" it carried on. The buzzing had increased in volume, as though whatever was causing it was steadily drawing nearer. "*You belong to the dark, Graymalkin.*"

"Jonas?" Pixie asked. He realized that he had stood up so fast that his chair had clattered over. The entire class had gone deadly silent. Everyone stared at him. He looked around wildly, convinced he would see his own face among them.

"Jonas, what's wrong?" Ms Pryde asked, seeming genuinely concerned now. He looked from her, to Pixie, to the classroom door.

"I'm sorry," he managed to say, heading for it. "I need to be excused."

He stumbled out into the corridor, closing the door hard behind him. The space was empty. The buzzing sound had gone, though he expected to hear the voice again at any moment.

What was happening to him? How had it followed him all this way into the light, into the life he'd built for himself at the Institute?

He began to walk down the hallway, breaking into a run. He heard the classroom door open behind him, Ms Pryde calling after him, but he didn't stop. The lights above him flickered, throwing the corridor into darkness for the briefest moment. It made his skin crawl.

He reached his dorm and locked the door behind him, panting, shaking. He'd left the lights on, though the bulb in his bedside lamp seemed to have failed. He tried turning it on repeatedly, then fumbled through his drawer looking for a spare. There weren't any.

The voice said nothing more. He sat down on his bed, pulse racing, too afraid to close his eyes for even a moment, certain that if he did so, his twin would be standing before him when he opened them again.

Gradually, the panic subsided. He found he could breathe normally again. He listened, afraid he would hear the strange buzzsaw noise again, or the voice, or even just a knock at the door. But there was nothing. He was alone.

He tried to tell himself that that was a good thing.

It took him the better part of an hour to get up from his bed. He fumbled around in one of his drawers for a minute until he found his flashlight, dropping it into the rucksack hanging off the side of his headboard.

He was out of options. Whatever was wrong with him, it was worsening, and rapidly so. Something had happened to him down there, something that had changed him, corrupted him, perhaps. He was afraid of it, afraid of the dark itself. He couldn't go on like that, not when it had been his companion for so long.

There were no other cures that he could conceive of. He had been taught, by Victor and by others, that running from his fears did no good. They always caught up eventually. It was far better to turn and face them. That was what he would do. Face the darkness. Reclaim it.

He pulled the rucksack on and heard a buzz. It was his communicator, he realized, lying by his bed. He'd forgotten to take it with him to class. After hesitating, he unlocked it.

Pixie had messaged him, asking if he was alright. The message bore into his very soul. No, he wasn't alright. No, there was nothing she could do about it. This wasn't a case of opening up about his emotions or sharing the burdens of his past. This was a real and present danger, to himself and perhaps to the Institute as a whole.

And only he could deal with it.

He waited until lack of movement in the dorm corridor caused the lighting to go on energy conservation mode. Then, leaving the communicator behind, he tightened the straps on his rucksack and opened the door.

Graymalkin descended into the depths.

He did so in darkness, though he feared it. That much he now fully admitted to himself. He was afraid of the shadows, of what they hid, of how they lied. He was no longer himself.

His heart thumped as he stepped out into the corridor where he had first encountered his double. It sat as it had before, empty and lifeless, utterly abandoned. He turned in the space, his senses painfully keen, expecting at any moment to be struck.

But there was nothing, not even the voice in his head.

He must have been imagining it all. That was the only rational explanation. Carefully, he reached up and touched his head, where it had been slammed into the doorframe by the phantom. Pain flared beneath his fingertips, real enough. He glanced at the door where it had happened. It stood there, unmarked, giving no indication of whether what he remembered had been real or not.

He felt a pulse of anger, brought on by his confusion and uncertainty. This thing, whatever it was, mocked him with its silence. It was down here, waiting, watching, doubtless amused by his vacillations. Well, he had come here for it, and he would not be leaving until he had put a stop to its taunting.

He followed the corridor to the next set of stairs and descended them as well, discovering another tunnel at the bottom. This was the deepest he'd gone, the furthest out of bounds from the Institute. Here the facility barely seemed manmade at all. The walls were uncut rock, patched in places with damp subterranean moss. Naked lightbulbs, long burned out, hung from loops of cabling that snaked along the tunnel's uneven ceiling. Doors had been carved into the stone on either side, seven in total, four to the left and three to the right.

He tried the first one, tentatively, his senses straining. The room within was as abandoned as everything else he had seen so far. It was bare except for a few old rusting tables and metal swivel-chairs. It seemed as though it had been some sort of viewing area or control space – the far wall was bare glass, and beyond it was a chamber that contained several large machines, cobwebbed and inactive. Graymalkin was still coming to terms with the dizzying array of technology that proliferated the twenty-first century, but from what he'd seen so far, the machines looked like giant, more complex versions of the tower units that powered personal computers. He found himself wondering what had required such computational power, and why the engines had been left to rot, rather than hauled out with the rest of the machinery that seemed to have once filled the facility's now-empty spaces.

He checked the next door, and then the next. More grim, silent rooms met his gaze, forlorn and forgotten. In the first there was a sunken pit that, judging by the empty sockets, had once held some sort of large electronic device that could be observed from the sides of the room. The second was filled with rows of empty cabinets. He thought he heard one shiver and rattle slightly when he entered but, after a minute of standing frozen, he could detect nothing more.

It was only when he reached the doors standing at the end of the tunnel that he heard the voice again.

"I wondered if you would come."

It came as a whisper, right in his ear.

He lashed out, wicked-fast in the darkness. His fist passed through air, and he found himself turned half around, hunting through the shadows, his flesh prickling with fright.

"I'm not afraid of you," he told that darkness, and the darkness answered.

"You are," it said, in his own voice, riven with scorn. "If you weren't, I wouldn't be here."

"Where?" Graymalkin demanded, turning in a circle, panic threatening to overwhelm him. "Where are you?"

"What am I, where am I?" the voice repeated. "I'm you, and I'm right here."

Something cannoned into Graymalkin's back, pitching him hard into the doors at the tunnel's end. They gave way with a crash. He hit the floor beyond, scrambling up instantly, braced for a second blow.

His double stood in the open doorway, framed by it. There

was no amusement on its face, no mockery, only hatred. It chilled Graymalkin, dousing his determination with dread.

"I've come to banish you," he said, trying to muster his courage once more.

He half-expected the double to laugh, but its spiteful expression remained unchanged.

"You can no more banish me than banish your very self," it told him. "What hope can you have against one such as I? I am you, with all the pathetic fears, all the quivering self-doubts, stripped away. I am the superior version. You are unworthy of me."

"That isn't true," Graymalkin responded. "I do not know from where you have come, shadow, but you aren't me, and you aren't superior. You are a cruel, bitter creature. Whatever made you, it failed to teach you empathy."

"Empathy is what makes you weak," the double snapped. "You are soft, malleable. You could be so much more. You have the potential to be the strongest, greatest mutant this Institute has ever produced."

"Only in the dark," Graymalkin pointed out.

"Which you fear," the thing retorted. "A further embarrassment."

"If you are so superior, then prove it," Graymalkin said, spreading his arms with a confidence he did not feel. "Let us see who is the stronger."

The double struck. Graymalkin was ready for it. A flurry of punches, a kick, all met with thumping parries. He went on the counter instantly, going low then high, aiming first for the thing's gut – a diversion – then nearly catching it on the jaw.

It gave ground, and they broke apart, both panting slightly.

Graymalkin nodded. "Not so superior, it seems," he said.

The thing snarled and attacked a second time. Now it mirrored his own moves, feinting low before switching to short jabs directed at Graymalkin's face and chest. He did his best to block and divert, grunting at the weight behind each blow. The double didn't relent, and in a surge of desperation Graymalkin went back on the offensive. He took a hit to the right side of his ribs and got in close, pounding a fist into the double's stomach and forcing it over. He grabbed it by the shoulders, intending to bring a knee up, but suddenly it wasn't there. The thing had simply vanished.

He barely had time to register the disappearance before he sensed a presence behind him. He threw himself to the side, the desperate motion enough to ensure the blow only caught him on the shoulder. He lashed out as he turned, trying to drive it back and regain his guard.

Somehow it had gotten behind him. In the darkness their motions were both lightning fast, as were their reflexes. Graymalkin should have been aware of its movement, capable of matching its speed. Yet he'd lost track of it as surely as someone without his abilities would have.

He gave ground. The double's face was a terrible rictus of hatred, every blow seemingly driven by pure loathing. Graymalkin managed to snatch its wrist and twist, momentarily ending the rain of blows and turning them about once more. The double delivered a chop to his forearm with its other hand, the spike of pain forcing him to let go.

He faltered. The double was about to attack again, its aggression relentless. It had no interest in talking, it seemed, or in explanations or negotiations. There was nothing more

Graymalkin could do, not right now. He still had a backup plan, but he didn't want to use it yet, not until all other options were exhausted.

So, he ran. He turned and threw himself down the corridor, on into the darkness deep beneath the earth.

Vic was poised, about to deliver his line, when the intercom system crackled.

"Victor Borkowski to the principal's office, repeat, Victor Borkowski to the principal's office."

He glanced at the rest of the cast, sighed theatrically, and tossed the script down onto the chair next to him. They'd been in rehearsals for the semester's performance of *Les Misérables* during lunch breaks for the past week. Of course, he'd known every line by heart since the age of ten, but there were only four days to go before opening night and he was still trying to coax Tempus along in her role as Eponine.

He'd have been annoyed, if he wasn't already so worried.

Scott Summers was waiting for him in his office. He must have been running one of the combat drill classes, because he was wearing his black and red X-suit, rather than a shirt and tie. The unblinking red glare of his visor followed Vic as he sat down across the desk from him.

"Good afternoon, Victor," Summers said. His expression was as serious as ever, a fact that Vic didn't find at all reassuring. He began to fear the worst.

"I wondered if you might have a look at something for me," Summers said, grasping the edge of the monitor that occupied one corner of his desk and partially swiveling it so Vic could see the screen. It was divided into a dozen sections, each one showing a different hallway or classroom. He realized he was looking at the Institute's security camera footage.

"These are from this morning," Summers said. "Look at the dormitory hall footage, please, and tell me what you see."

Vic did so, locating the section showing a recording of the dorm corridor. As he watched, something seemed to flicker down it. It was early enough for the lights to still be on low, but the sudden motion triggered their sensors and caused them to switch to full. By the time they had, though, whatever had darted down the corridor was gone.

"Did you see it?" Summers asked.

"I saw something," Vic allowed.

"I've been down to Graymalkin's room," Summers said. "He isn't there. You came to me yesterday and told me you were worried about him, that something seemed off."

"I did," Vic admitted. He'd spoken to Pixie and Cipher about Gray, had tried to work out how best to help him, but ultimately he'd come away with nothing. He had never known Gray to shut him out so thoroughly. It had left them all feeling helpless. It was Cipher who'd eventually convinced Vic that the best thing would be to confide in Summers.

"We think Graymalkin has been leaving the Institute," the principal went on.

"And going where?" Vic asked, surprised. "The nearest town's too far away to reach easily. We'd know if he was gone long."

"He hasn't been going out, as such," Summers said. "He's been heading down."

The words sent a chill through Victor. He'd been trying to work out just what Graymalkin had been struggling with, but he'd never considered the possibility that, whatever it was, it was related to the warren of tunnels that lay beneath them all. He'd never ventured down himself, had never felt the urge that some of the other students at the Institute seemed to share. It felt like there was nothing but bad news down there. The thought of Gray, alone in those undisturbed, silent depths added a new layer to his concerns.

"You did the right thing in coming to me, Victor," Summers said. "I'm glad that you trust me. I'm going to repay that trust. Graymalkin has ventured out of the Institute's bounds. He needs to be brought back. I very much doubt that myself, or any other member of the faculty, will be capable of doing that. You, however, have been his best friend since he enrolled at this school."

Victor stood up, hands planted on the edge of Summers' desk.

"Just tell me how he got down there," he said.

"Stairwell eleven," Summers replied, tapping the communicator on his desk. "You have yours?"

Vic felt the pocket where he kept the device. Summers nodded, his expression grave.

"I will be sending a member of staff to follow you and ensure you're both safe," he said. "You'll be ahead of them, because I believe you're best placed to resolve this issue, but if we discover there's any direct danger to either Jonas or yourself, you're to withdraw."

"I'll bring him back," Vic promised, voice riven with determination. "You have my word."

After the door to Summers' office closed behind Victor, the communicator on the desk clicked. Summers hesitated before accepting the transmission and opening the channel.

"You're sure about this?" asked a man's voice.

"Yes," Summers said, attempting to sound certain. "You were absent from the Institute last semester. You don't know what they did in New York, when the Purifiers tried to take them."

"I've read the report, twice," the voice replied. "You are fortunate they proved to be so competent, Summers. Or so lucky."

"If you doubt them, you can see for yourself," Summers said. "Follow them but keep your distance. We don't know exactly what we're dealing with yet, and we don't know how Jonas might react."

"What if it's the device you think it is? Should I destroy it?"

"Better to bring it back so we can verify it. There may be more, and we need to be sure."

"And at what point do I intervene?"

"You be the judge of that, Erik."

Graymalkin didn't get far.

The tunnel he'd taken opened out into a large, cavern-like chamber. The ceiling and walls were bare jagged rock, though the floor consisted of smooth tiles, scuffed with the tell-tale signs of equipment removal. Much of it still remained, though – there were chairs and work islands, littered with old, rusting detritus. The walls were ranked with more of the large computing devices Graymalkin had seen earlier, as well as what appeared to be subsidiary offices and work spaces.

He had barely taken in his new surroundings before he realized that his double was already waiting for him. Somehow, it had gotten ahead of him. He felt an upwelling of despair as he came to a halt inside the chamber.

The thing offered him the ghost of a smile.

"I told you," it said. "Faster and stronger. When will you admit to your weakness?"

Pain spiked inside Graymalkin's head. He cringed, touching his brow. The grating shriek of a buzzsaw filled his hearing for a moment before vanishing. "What... is happening to me?" he gasped.

"You're splitting apart, Graymalkin," the double said, its smile gone. "Finally."

It attacked once more. Distracted by the pain in his head, there was nothing Graymalkin could do to stop it this time. His sight blurred as a blow caught the side of his head, another pounding his jaw, then his ribs, pitching him over.

"Is that it?" the double demanded, standing over him and cracking its knuckles. "Is that all the resistance you intend to offer me?"

Graymalkin hissed with pain, trying to think through the incessant buzzing as it returned, making his skull ache. There was a light flashing on one of the workstations, he realized, some piece of equipment that was lying discarded amongst the facility's abandoned junk. He had only registered it when the double's boot lashed out, catching him in the side and defeating his attempt to get up.

"Won't you even fight to preserve yourself?" the thing demanded.

"I... told you," Graymalkin managed through gritted teeth. The rucksack he'd been carrying had slipped onto one shoulder. "I didn't come here to fight you. I came here to banish you."

"I am your darkness, Graymalkin," the double scoffed, its black eyes glittering. "I am the eternal night within your soul. You cannot banish me."

"Light can always banish darkness," Graymalkin said, and pulled the flashlight from the rucksack. He pointed it at the creature and flicked it on.

The sphere of illumination caught the double square in its center. It didn't so much as flinch. It stood above Graymalkin, its black eyes shining, unperturbed and whole.

"You fool," it said. "You cannot simply shine a light and banish away your fears. This darkness – this power – it is within you, always."

The thing hit him. It was with a speed and force he could not match, not now that the flashlight was on. His own powers were rendered impotent by its light, yet this creature that wore his body like a puppet seemed wholly unaffected by the illumination.

Graymalkin cried out in fear and pain as the blows fell, curling into a fetal position on the chamber's cold, hard floor. He couldn't escape it, he realized. It was going to kill him, down here amidst the abandoned detritus of a project spawned from terror and hate. It was going to take his soul the way it had already taken his body, consume him and eat him up. He was being buried as surely as his father had buried him with shovel and dirt. For a second, he even thought he could hear the scrape of the blade over the hideous, grating buzz that was now filling all of his senses.

In raw desperation, he cried out for help. There was no response, though, none but the pounding of fists.

He was alone, and that, Graymalkin realized, was how he was going to die.

Victor followed the sound of the saw.

It was intermittent and distant, but he was sure he wasn't

imagining it. It echoed up from the facility's depths, from the dark desolate rooms and tunnels he was descending into.

He had brought a flashlight, a lance of illumination he used to banish the shadows. It didn't feel like enough. The darkness crept in all around him, leering and full of threat. It sent fear crawling through his body, but he forced himself to carry on, ever deeper, down derelict stairwells and along jagged corridors chiseled from rough bedrock. Cyclops had put his trust in him, and Graymalkin was relying on him, whether he realized it yet or not. He wouldn't let either of them down.

As he passed down one corridor, he thought he caught the silhouette of a figure in the corner of his eye, framed by one of the adjoining doorways. He wheeled sharply, his powerful right arm raised to ward off an expected blow, but his light shone straight through into an empty, junk-littered room. He frowned.

For a split second, he thought he'd recognized the figure's outline as his own.

Get it together, Vic, he told himself. He carried on. The buzzing sound was almost painfully loud now. He was convinced he was on the same level as it was. He began to hurry, just before he heard a voice, crying out over the hideous sound.

It was Graymalkin.

"Gray!" Vic shouted, breaking into a run. His voice echoed back at him weirdly, rebounding with different intonations along the tunnel. The sound of his footsteps seemed to multiply, so much so that he felt as though someone was running, right behind him.

There was a set of doors at the tunnel's end. He banged through them, flashlight poised, riven with an aggression born out of fear.

He saw Graymalkin immediately. He was curled up about

halfway into the cavernous room, close to one of the numerous workstations that covered the floor. A discarded flashlight rolled on the ground next to him, its beam throwing crazed shadows through the echoing space. It was not the only source of illumination, though – something amidst the junk on the table above flashed intermittently, emitting bursts of harsh, white light. It matched the pitch of the saw noise that felt as though it was carving away at Victor's brain.

"Gray," he shouted over the discord, rushing to his friend's side. He placed a hand on him, rolling him over. Graymalkin cried out with the sort of primal fear Vic had only seen his friend display when he was in the clutches of one of his night terrors. His face was streaked with tears and his eyes were red-raw as he looked up, uncomprehendingly, at Vic.

"Y- You shouldn't be here," he stammered. "It'll take you, too!"

"What will?" Vic demanded, looking around, probing the darkness once more with his flashlight. "What's down here, Gray?"

"We are," he stammered, clutching at Victor's wrist, the force of his grip painful even against the thick knots of green-skinned muscle and spiny ridges that Vic had developed on that arm.

"I don't understand," Vic said, cringing again as whatever was on the table continued to emit its brutalizing noise.

"We're all down here," Graymalkin said, his eyes and voice taking on a feverish intensity now. "All of us. Our shadow-selves. It belongs to them. The dark. All of it."

"I don't know about that," Vic said, prising himself from his friend's grasp and standing up. "Doesn't seem so dark down here at the moment."

He went at the workstation, swiping aside the junk piled atop it to reveal the device bearing the flashing light. It was a metallic box, plugged via a nest of cables into a port in the table's surface. A control panel, its buttons inscrutable to Vic, occupied one flank. The light was situated on top. The sound, he realized, didn't seem to be emitting from any one part of it. It was in his head.

There was movement behind him. He glimpsed Gray back on his feet, swinging at an assailant Vic couldn't see, seemingly trying to protect Vic. Vic had no idea whether there was something invisible there, or if it was Gray's imagination.

"This machine is active," Vic shouted, reaching back to touch his friend's arm and pointing at the blinking device. Gray's eyes found a moment's focus.

Then, pain struck Vic.

Victor collapsed, crying out, clutching his skull. Graymalkin looked from him to the strange machine his friend had pointed out. He couldn't let the darkness take Victor.

His double was nowhere to be seen, but he had no doubt it would reappear just as quickly as it had first vanished when it seemed as if Graymalkin might momentarily overpower him.

Acting on impulse and desperation, Graymalkin reached out, snatched the cluster of cabling, and yanked on it, hard.

The effect was immediate. The light went out.

The pain in Vic's skull began to recede. Blinking, he found his feet, just in time to catch Graymalkin as he in turn collapsed. He realized Gray had disabled the device, ripping out its wiring. The hellish grating sound was gone.

The sudden silence in the cavern was painful in its intensity.

Just before Gray had cut the strange device's power, Vic had been sure he'd seen his own twin, grinning at him from the other side of the workstation, there and gone again as the white light strobed on and off.

With a shudder, he checked Graymalkin's pulse and breathing. He was unconscious, but alive.

"What did you get yourself into down here?" Vic murmured, casting one more look around the cavern and back at the now-inactive device, before stooping to heave Graymalkin's limp body up over his shoulder.

"Lucky you're such a skinny kid," he told his unresponsive friend, patting his back. "And that I've got the biggest right arm at the Institute. No need to say anything, though, you can thank me later."

Graymalkin sat up sharply. He was in bed, though it was not his own.

There was light though, that was the most important thing. Light and the presence of others. Victor was at his bedside, and so was Principal Summers.

"It's OK, buddy," Vic said, putting one large hand on his shoulder, face full of concern. "We've got you."

Graymalkin glanced around the room – the Institute's infirmary ward, he realized, its starched white beds unoccupied by any bar himself. He had no memory of getting there. The last thing he recalled was Vic standing over him, down in the facility's depths. He flinched as pain flared in his head.

"I would advise you to make no sudden movements, Jonas," Summers said, his crimson visor fixed squarely on Graymalkin. "It will take time for both body and mind to heal."

"Did you see it?" he asked them both, his fear rising once more. They didn't know. He had to tell them.

"Who?" Vic asked.

"My… my double. You have to believe me. There's something down there–"

"When I found you, there was no one else," Victor said. "But there was a machine in among the debris of the old facility. You broke it."

"That's right," Graymalkin whispered, askance. "I don't understand."

"There is a good reason the depths of this place are out of bounds for those at the Institute, Jonas," Summers said, his tone taking on the merest hint of a reprimand. "This is no ordinary school. It was once a primary place of research for the Weapon X project, and more besides. Governments sought to mold our kind into tools of destruction, and likewise developed the tools that would help them do so. I believe you unwittingly discovered one such piece of functioning equipment while you were down there."

"It creates… a twin?" Graymalkin asked, struggling to understand Summers' claim.

"Only in your mind," Cyclops went on. "It was an illusion, at least in part, but a truly powerful one."

"That was no illusion," Graymalkin said, holding up one arm, showing the bruising starting to discolor his gray skin. "It would have killed me had Victor not helped."

"Your injuries, from what we can ascertain, were accidental. Unintentionally self-inflicted," Summers said. Graymalkin looked at Victor, who offered his friend an unhappy shrug.

"Like I said, when I found you, you were alone," Victor

explained. "I saw no one else… except perhaps myself, briefly. It was pretty freaky, but hey, I'm handsome as ever."

The humor did little to mask Victor's concern.

Summers nodded. "We believe the device is called a psychosis splicer," he said. "It was designed to emit frequencies and other disorienting stimuli to help fracture a mutant's consciousness. Its creators believed they could change the mindset of their test subjects and thus influence the powers they displayed."

"When I found you, you were afraid of the dark," Victor said. "More than I've ever seen since at least New York. The dark is where you're strongest."

Gray tried to rationalize what he was being told, but that much did make sense. At some point in the past few weeks, he had started to develop fears and doubts he had never truly appreciated before. Concerns that didn't feel like they belonged to him.

"I would assume this wasn't your first trip beneath the school?" Summers asked.

"No," Graymalkin admitted. "I've been… going out of bounds for a while now."

"And slowly exploring deeper and deeper, I would imagine," Summers said. "The psy-splicer would not have an instant effect. It requires proximity and time. Every moment you spent drawing closer to it gave it longer to work on you, sawing slowly through the essence of your mind. Eventually, you began to hallucinate seeing your double."

"He was terrible." Graymalkin's words faltered at the memory. "Cruel and spiteful. A thing of the dark."

"The splicer would amplify parts of a mutant's power and

personality and suppress others. Your connection to the dark formed its own consciousness within you, collecting your insecurities. From what I understand, those who invented this device believed they could ultimately use it to bend mutants to their will."

"I hadn't been down before yesterday," Victor said. "So its effects were less severe. Still, if you'd been experiencing what I felt in those moments for weeks, I'm amazed that you lasted so long. That you went back to face it."

"I thought I was going mad," Graymalkin admitted quietly. "I suppose in a way I was, though it wasn't my own doing. I have never known fear like it."

"You should've told us," Vic said, squatting beside the bed so he was at the same level as Graymalkin, looking him in the eyes. "After all we've been through the past year, you should've trusted us to handle it."

"I was not myself," Graymalkin said, feeling suddenly ashamed. He had allowed himself to become prey to a devious artifice, his thoughts twisted and bent to dark purposes. He had feared everything and trusted no one. He struggled to put the memory of his double – or the imagining of his double – from his mind. Was that truly him? Was a corner of his mind, the dark that had festered for so long beneath the earth, really so full of hate and malice? Did he carry such potent emotions within, hidden like jagged rocks beneath the surface of a glassy, unreflective lake?

"This… splicer," he began, his thoughts turning to a flurry of possibilities, none of them pleasant. "How was it still active? Surely it has not been transmitting since the facility was abandoned?"

"That I do not know," Summers said, his voice becoming guarded.

"What if someone found it and turned it on?" Vic said, taking up the train of thought. "What if it's an attempt to compromise the Institute? To attack it?"

"The possibility has been considered," Summers said. "But it's not something for either of you to pursue. I'm told that your recovery will take time, Jonas, and you are not to exert yourself. Victor, you are to provide him with companionship and peace of mind, as you have done in the past, until he is well again."

"Did I completely destroy the splicer?" Graymalkin asked.

"We're not sure," Summers said, "but rest assured, Jonas, the faculty are dealing with it."

The tall figure passed through the darkness in silence, his white cape hanging heavy about him. A glossy metallic helm obscured his head. It gleamed in the illumination of his flashlight, which floated steadily beside him, just beyond physical grasp.

Magneto paused as he entered the cavern. He could feel the potency of the wreckage all around him, the forgotten wonders of a cruel age. They brought back painful memories, full of the wickedness of man and the bitterness of a past he had left far behind.

He stepped up to the workstation, the flashlight picking out what he'd come for. The psy-splicer remained incongruously amidst the junk abandoned in the old facility. He could see how Graymalkin had ripped out the wiring, but he could discern no other damage to its frame. He had unplugged it, not destroyed it.

Did it still function? Was it what they believed it to be? Summers had told him to bring it back to the school, where it could be examined. But if it was already broken, there would be no point. And if it wasn't… well, there was only one way to be certain. A moment's reactivation was all it would take for him to be sure.

He reached out, grasped the tangle of wires, and slotted them back home, one by one. For a while, nothing happened. Then, without warning, the white light on top of the device blinked on, reflecting back from Magneto's dark eyes.

Graymalkin was dozing off and alone in the infirmary ward, at his own insistence. Vic had been tired, he could tell, and Gray didn't want to be more of a burden. His only request was that he left the lights on.

He rolled over, seeking a cold patch of pillow, his mind growing sluggish. For the first time in weeks, he felt a degree of peace. Even the migraine lingering in the depths of his skull had eased.

Just as his eyes began to close, he realized he had seen something, something that, when he looked again, wasn't actually there.

A figure, standing in the darkness of the corridor outside, looking in at him through the ward window, its black eyes glittering.

UNCATCHABLE

Cath Lauria

Every machine had a voice, and each voice was unique. Learning to hear those voices was one of the coolest things about Hijack's mutation, in his opinion.

Except when you were torturing them, it turned out. Then it sucked.

The engine of the Volkswagen Golf GTI screamed in Hijack's head as they careened around the corner of the Roanoke Docks frontage road, three endless seconds behind the confident, hyper-competent lead car. Simultaneously, Cipher screamed in his ear, "*Slow down!*"

Hijack contemplated screaming, too, just to complete the circle of chaos, as the two other lead cars closed ranks in front of him, like a moving wall.

This was *not* the relaxing, two-hundred-mile-per-hour street race that David Bond had envisioned for himself a few hours ago.

It was supposed to be a chance to stretch his skills, a time for David to step away from his role as a fledgling X-Man at the New Charles Xavier School for Mutants and remember that, oh yeah, he *was* in fact an adult capable of making his own decisions. Not some green – literally, in one case – teenager with no life skills who might be able to dodge bullets, but had no idea how to pay their own bills. Not some kid who was still learning how life worked. David was in his *thirties*, for Pete's sake, it was embarrassing to be lumped in with them all the time.

It wasn't that the other students weren't good people… by and large. It wasn't that he didn't have a lot to learn himself – being a mutant, especially one whose powers emerged later in life, was a head trip. His roommate in particular was a good kid, as kind-hearted as you'd expect a healer to be, but David…

Well. He had a roommate. A *roommate*. Like this was a boarding school, or worse, summer camp. He was just *waiting* for Professor Pryde to start the bonding exercises. One verse of *Kumbaya* and David was out of there.

The Golf was his way of asserting his independence, something just for him. David hadn't been a car guy before his mutation emerged; he'd been a professional illustrator, and the most attention he'd ever paid to cars was making sure he got the paint color right. But ever since his ability to control vehicles had manifested, it had turned the way he saw anything with an engine on its head. What had been an impenetrable black box before was now innately understandable, like he'd not only learned a foreign language overnight, but he could create other languages with it.

David could do more than understand the voice of a vehicle; he could control how the vehicle moved, every aspect of its behavior. He could make a simple wind-up toy do a freaking tap dance if he wanted it to. And this car, Tiger? Tiger was his escape to a place of complete control, to something that was just for him. Nobody else in the school cared about an old beater like this, not when they had a Blackbird to go gaga over. And if he *happened* to sneak it off campus to take part in the monthly Roanoke Races, a local street racing event, then no one would care enough to stop him.

Except Cipher, apparently. He should have known he wouldn't get out clean, even though he kept his speed to a near-noiseless crawl as he exited the school's basement lair. Honestly, he'd expected a professor to be the one to intervene, not Cipher. He hadn't seen her coming... then again, no one saw her coming if she didn't want them to.

"Where are you going?"

"*Sonuva–*" David whirled from where he sat in the front seat to look at the passenger side of his vehicle, where Alisa Tager had suddenly become visible, sitting with her arms crossed, a disapproving expression on her face. Almost a foot shorter than him when they were standing up, they were the same height sitting down. She had her thick black locs held back with a bandana, and her brown eyes were full of suspicion.

"Get a bell, kid."

"Even if I had one, you wouldn't hear it unless I wanted you to," she said. "Now, where are you going?"

"What's it to you?" Even as he said it, David wanted to kick himself – acting pugnaciously wasn't the way to deflect attention, especially with someone like Alisa. She was a tough kid, someone who'd pulled off living with them like a ghost for who knew how long before she was discovered. They didn't know each other well, but they'd been ... friendly acquaintances before this, he'd say.

There was nothing friendly in her expression right now, though.

"It's the difference between you leaving here or not," Alisa replied stubbornly. "I'm leaning toward *not*, though. It doesn't take a genius to figure out that a student sneaking a private vehicle out of the basement lot at midnight is probably bad news. So how about you tell me what's going on?"

David rolled his eyes. "Oh please. If this were really a problem, you think one of the professors wouldn't have stopped me by now? Someone with more authority than you?"

He saw a hint of doubt enter her eyes ... not enough to keep her from pushing, though. "Still. Stop the car."

"Ask politely."

Now it was Alisa's turn to roll her eyes. "*Please* stop the car."

"No, thanks."

She scowled. "I could make you stop the car. Phase right through you and leave your nervous system twitching so bad you can't even find the gas pedal, much less drive a vehicle."

Ah, OK, they were jumping right to the threats, then. "And I could speed up to a hundred miles an hour in less than a second and a half and slam the passenger side of this car into the cement wall over there." It would totally burn out his engine, but he could do it. "Want to see if you can phase your way out of that?"

Alisa looked away, and David immediately felt like a jerk. "I just don't like people sneaking around," she said after a second. "It makes me nervous."

That was ... yeah, that was reasonable. "OK, look." He

stopped the car and turned to face her more fully. "I'm going out, yes. I'm going out late because that's when the event is, not to be extra sneaky or anything. You seriously think nobody knows I'm doing this, with two of the strongest psychics on the planet in the building? I'm not you, Alisa. I can't block telepathic detection." Although, man, would he like a power like that. "I need to get away for a little while, and the street race is a fun way to do that without everybody and their sister asking me what the heck I'm doing and bothering me nonstop."

Alisa paused for a second, then smiled. "Are you saying I'm bothering you?"

"Yes." And she knew she was, little smart aleck. "Will you get out now so I can get there before the freaking race starts without me?"

"I'd rather go with you."

She'd... rather... "What? *Why?*"

"So you have someone to watch your back, of course!"

David groaned and resisted the urge to bang his head against the steering wheel. "It's a street race, not an anti-mutant rally or a re-enactment of the O.K. Corral."

"You're totally missing the point, Hijack."

"What's the point?" he snapped. "What can possibly be the point you're making here except annoying me for the sake of being annoying?"

"It's about teamwork," Alisa said quietly. "That's a big part of why we're here, isn't it? To learn how to be a team. I get wanting space to do your own thing, I really do, but..." Her mouth tightened. "Even when we're trying to stay out of the way, bad situations have a way of finding us, it feels like." David thought about her recent mission with Anole and Graymalkin and wisely kept his mouth shut. "I don't want you to get into something without having some backup around."

"All I'm going to get tonight is a win in this race," David said. "Which will be harder with a passenger on board slowing me down."

"Look at it this way," Alisa said with a smirk. "If none of the professors have come down here to stop me from coming along, it's as good as permission that I should be here, isn't it? That's *your* standard, after all."

"You can be psychically invisible!"

Alisa shrugged. "Not to Jean. But I'm not shielding right now anyway, I promise. Come on," she wheedled. "Let me come along. I can't sleep and I've never been in a street race before and I'm…" She stopped talking and looked away from him, down toward the floor.

You're what, bored? Nervous?

Lonely?

God, David was such a sap. "Fine," he snapped, and sped up Tiger. The Golf's engine revved as they jetted forward out of the subterranean lair and up toward the moonlit school grounds. He had to slow down then – it wasn't graded for cars, and he'd almost broken Tiger's axle in a pothole more than once. The first bump threw Alisa back against the passenger seat, and she cast him a disgruntled look as she reached for her seatbelt.

"Freaking fine, come along. But you stay invisible the whole time you're there, got it? The people in charge didn't clear a guest, and I don't want to risk getting disqualified because they don't know you."

"How do they know *you*?" Alisa countered as they hit the

road leading to Roanoke, an hour's drive distant. More like two hours for a normal person.

"I heard about it and decided to check it out." Actually, he'd heard the cars first; three of them, roaring along the road closest to the Institute, machines that were massively overpowered for their size – nothing else came close to having an engine sounding like that, that wasn't a logging truck around here – meaning he had to check them out. Once he knew their voices, he could follow them, and what he found when he did was...

Well. It was something.

Noisy, mostly. With cars, and with people. People with oil under their fingernails, people who smelled like gasoline and engine grease, people who *knew cars*. Who knew them far better than David did, honestly. That first night he'd arrived as a tourist, but after some cajoling he managed to convince one of the guys to let him take a turn on the quarter mile. And that...

That had been a revelation. Sitting inside a powerful machine like that, a machine that David could *feel* the limits of better than any one of the gearheads out there could intuit even with all their expertise, had left him breathless. And pushing it to the max? That had left him grinning like the Cheshire Cat, especially when his quarter-mile clocked in at five and a half seconds.

There had been a lot of questions that night. A few accusations, a few offers to hire him, and one decent fight between another driver and the guy who owned his car that ended with David taking the other guy's ride out and doing the same race in even less time. Once he'd proven himself and shown an interest, *then* came Tiger. Technically she belonged to Liam, his sponsor, but after a couple of solid months' work on her, she *felt* like she belonged to David. God knows he wasn't about to hand the keys back over anytime soon. Not until he won the race.

He'd come so close last time, too.

"Uh huh." Alisa didn't sound convinced. "So, finding this place was just a crazy random happenstance, then?"

David glanced at her. "You like *Dr Horrible's Sing-Along Blog*?"

"Is that on TikTok?"

"Never mind." He sighed and focused on picking up the pace. There were different kinds of races throughout the night, but the one David definitely didn't want to miss was the Roundabout. It was the distance race, following a series of roads around the outskirts of Roanoke, and it was considered the main event. David could see why... especially given who won it last time.

How they'd won it, he still didn't know. The mysterious driver in the red leather was as much a mystery to David as their car was an open book – and their car was incredible, but it still shouldn't have been able to beat him. That was down to the driver, who had to be something really special. Maybe David would get a chance to strike up a conversation with them this time.

The racers gathered on one of the older concrete docks, made to accommodate passenger ferries back when Roanoke was more than just a bump in the local lake economy. There were around fifty people or so there – a pretty good turnout, considering they all had to be on the lookout for the cops. No bystanders had ever been hurt during one of the races, as far as David knew, but it was still pretty illegal, and even with moving locations and dates each month, it was only a matter of time before the cops got here to break up the party.

Hopefully not before they had a chance to race, though.

David parked Tiger on the edge of the group and glanced at Alisa. "Remember, invisible."

She wasn't looking at him. She was looking at a pair of dark vans parked on the other side of the dock. "What are those for?"

David shrugged. "I don't know. Mobile DJ? Crappy food trucks? A place to spend quality time with your significant other?"

She squinched her nose up. "Gross."

"Welcome to adulthood, it's pretty gross." He got out and shut the door, then saw Liam wave at him and went to join him next to his BMW. "Hey, Liam." Behind him, he could hear Tiger's shocks ease – Alisa had just phased out, then.

Have fun, kid.

"Davey! Hey, man, get over here and tell me what the heck you've done to your engine. I could hear it from a mile away."

David shrugged and smiled. "Just added a few special parts to give it a little more juice."

"Special parts?" Liam raised one of his bushy eyebrows. He worked on boat engines by day and car engines by night, and was the one who usually made the pick for where the meetup was going to be. He dressed like a lumberjack, but David had realized after a few months of living here that plaid was more of a way of life than a deliberate fashion choice. "Like from what, a freakin' F-16?"

David laughed. "Not quite." *From a Blackbird, actually, but nobody needs to know about that.* The mini-rockets weren't powerful enough for the Blackbird anymore, and they would have just gone to waste if David hadn't repurposed them. They were his one-shot-wonder trick, something that had the potential to completely do in his engine but would most certainly help him take the lead before that. "I won't blow anybody up, I promise." *Nobody except maybe myself.*

And Alisa. Crap.

He'd have to warn her to phase out if things got too hot.

"I've heard that before," Liam said glumly. "Poor Carlos, man. He was a legend, but he pushed his Mustang too hard. The battery explosion wouldn't have been so bad if he'd just done some basic maintenance on his fuel lines, but *nooo ...*"

David zoned out a bit while he listened to Liam grumble, looking around for the usual suspects. He recognized cars better than people these days, and saw the same mix of Hondas, Nissans, and Chevys that he'd seen last time, as well as the twin Corvettes that acted like chasers for Red Leather's Camaro, getting in the way of anyone who tried to pass them. Not that they'd managed it with David, but they'd sure as heck tried. But where was the Camaro?

"Hey. You got the route down, right?"

David refocused on what Liam was saying. "Yeah, I got the map you sent. Not too different from last time."

"Not too different, but make sure you steer clear of the road construction by the South Bay Bridge, you got it? They're doing some major work there, and if you get onto the bridge by accident, you better hope your car can fly, you know what I'm saying?"

David grinned. "What do you want to bet that I can get my car to fly?" *For, like, two seconds, but it still counts.*

Liam held up his hands. "Oh no, I'm not takin' that bet. No way. I don't want to encourage you maniacs to do something even wilder than you already do."

"Speaking of maniacs..." David glanced around again. "Where's last race's winner?"

"Last time?" Liam chuckled. "Try every time! Although you gave her a run for her money, huh?"

"Her?" David perked up. "The Camaro's driver is a woman?"

"Try 'lady', and way outside your comfort zone, son," Liam said.

David scoffed. "You don't even know my comfort zone."

"No, but I know an ass-kicking in waiting when I see one." Liam patted David's shoulder. "Stick with driving your car and leave the ladies alone, Davey."

"But–" Just then, he felt a tug on his elbow. He ignored it. "I just want to know if she–" Another tug, this time gripping his jacket and holding onto it. David couldn't shake Cipher off without looking like he was having muscle spasms in front of Liam. He forced a smile. "I'll be right back."

"Sure thing."

David walked back to his car and got in. A second later Alisa materialized beside him.

"What was that?" he demanded. "When I said be invisible, that includes not interrupting me when I'm trying to work!"

Alisa rolled her eyes. "Right, because standing around gossiping about people is super professional."

Oh my god. I brought my mother to the Roanoke Races with me. David took a deep breath to help hold onto his fraying composure. "You need to–"

"The vans are full of guns."

Wait. What?

"Guns," Alisa repeated, as though she'd given David a chance to respond. "Big ones. I saw a few crates of AK-47s, some other styles of assault weapons, and a lot of extended magazines. I think this whole thing is a front for gun-smuggling."

David struggled for a second to comprehend it. "No. Liam wouldn't do that."

Alisa arched her eyebrows. "Oh, really? The guy over there handing out cheap drinks while wearing a ten thousand-dollar watch wouldn't be part of that sort of thing?"

David blinked. "How do you know how much his watch costs?"

"Are you kidding me? It's on every second influencer's wrist these days." She stared at him for a second, then shook her head. "Never mind. Jeez, you're the most geriatric millennial I've ever met."

"Wait a second," David said, willing to let the geriatric thing go as his mind whirled in circles. "You're telling me that you think this race is, what, some sort of cover for a gunrunning operation? What would be the point of that?"

Alisa shrugged. "I mean, think about it. If you've got a regular shipment coming in, cops are bound to get wind of it eventually. Why not give them something else to focus on? Set up a dumb, flashy street race where you rope in whoever you can find and pit them against your own drivers, then set them loose so that the actual product can be moved in anonymity?

"It's still a bulky kind of plan," she said, frowning, "but it's the sort of thing an adrenaline junkie might do. It lets them toy with the cops *and* the locals with impunity, pretty much."

If David got any more out of his depth, he was going to be underwater. "Liam doesn't strike me as an adrenaline junkie."

"No." Alisa glanced behind David and grinned suddenly. "But she sure does, huh?"

"She?" David turned around and, sure enough, there was Red Leather stepping out of her Camaro. Now that he knew what to look for, he could see it; the natural sway in her hips, the way the leather was just a bit bulkier over her chest. Why had he ever assumed she was a man?

Probably your internalized misogyny. And look at you, absorbing something from Professor Frost's lectures after all.

David exhaled heavily. "Well, hell. OK." He ran a hand down his face, watching Red Leather strike up a conversation with her two backup dancers, so to speak. She left her helmet on the whole time, which now that Alisa mentioned it *did* seem pretty suspicious. "You might want to start walking back to the Institute, because this is probably going to take a while."

Alisa stared at him. "What is?"

"Taking down the gunrunners, of course." He watched her jaw drop and let himself enjoy startling her for once. "What, you expect me to just call the cops and fill them in on this?"

"Well... I mean..." Alisa bit her lower lip. "That would be safer, wouldn't it?"

"If everything went exactly the way it was supposed to, sure," David said. "But that would mean taking a lot of things for granted, like the cops listening to someone who didn't want to identify themselves because they didn't want to potentially expose the school. Even if they did listen, they'd have to actually find the vans. If they did *that*, they'd have to be able to stop the vans without being shot by the people inside, surrounded by guns and ammo, or the people in the cars who would be pulled from the race to swoop in and save their score. Any way you look at it, it goes badly for the cops, at least tonight."

"Oh."

David nodded. "Yeah, *oh*. So get a move on, and I'll–"

"I'm still coming with you."

He groaned. "Are you kidding me? You realize this is going to be dangerous, right? Not just because we're going to be moving fast."

"I can phase if things start looking bad," Alisa replied, her expression mutinous. "You're the one who's going to be in trouble if people start shooting, not me. So let me help you."

It wasn't worth arguing about it anymore, and they didn't have time anyway. Red Leather was heading back to her car, flanked by her Corvette lieutenants, and Liam was getting off his butt and grabbing the familiar neon-green flag he used to start the races.

"OK," David said, closing his eyes for a moment. "OK, OK..." Using his power, he reached out to the cars around them until he had the voices of the important ones locked in his head. The vans were Clunky and Clumsy, the two backup cars were Growly and Grunty, and Red Leather's brutal machine was just Red. Its engine purred in his mind like a lion, ready to go from contented to threatening in less than a second.

"Drivers, get ready!" Liam shouted, raising the flag. David scowled at him even as he tightened his hands on the steering wheel. That son of a... almost as an afterthought, he reached out to Liam's car and, with a mental wrench, broke every single piece of the steering column. *Save yourself with* that, *you–*

"And go!"

Tires squealed, engines roared, and the race was officially on. David felt threads of his power drift out ahead of him, each one tethered to one of the lead cars – Red, Growly, and Grunty. It was disorienting, feeling their movements while being surrounded by the leashed fury of his own car, eager for his attention. So disorienting that for a long moment he couldn't move at all, until Alisa smacked him on the arm and shouted, "Get going already!" David slammed his foot down on the gas, and they were off.

There weren't that many cars in the race, maybe nine or ten total, but right now they were all between David and his targets, and that just *wasn't acceptable*. He maneuvered around the first set of them like the nothing they were – the drivers were young and eager, but they didn't know how to handle their machines. The next one he managed to pass before they left the docks behind, screaming in from behind it on the water side of the frontage road and losing a layer of rubber to gravel before cutting them off. He could sense the driver's frustration in the way he pounded his foot against the gas pedal, trying desperately to get more out of a car that simply didn't have any more to give.

Jerk, thought David, and he decided to let the guy focus his anger on another pedal. He pulled up to the side of the next car in line and, just as they started around the curve that would lead them toward town, he disengaged the driver's clutch. Not the brakes – those still worked, and pretty well if the way the little Honda beside him practically shuddered to a stop on the side of the road was any indication.

The Honda's sudden movement was enough to spook Mr Angry Driver right behind them, though, and when he slammed on *his* brakes halfway through the turn–

Well, *those* tires didn't do so well in gravel. He spun out and did two and a half circles before impacting the heavy chain at the edge of the final pier. He didn't go through it – they weren't going fast enough to have that kind of power yet – but it did enough damage to end his race.

So long, sucker. David flipped him the bird as he sped away from the docks toward the eastern edge of Roanoke.

"He can't see you, you know," Alisa hollered over the sound of the engine, one hand tight on the handle above the door as they took the next turn too sharply.

"Not the point." It wasn't about what the other guy saw, it was about how what David did made him feel. And right now, he was feeling the need for speed. He could see the next car in the distance – too much distance. He urged Tiger faster, and she roared in agreement.

The next driver was better yet than the last two – nowhere close to Red and her tails, but better. The GT-R, with more hardware shoved into it than any single vehicle should have, flared with a sudden infusion of NOS as they began to close in, widening the gap between them considerably. It would have been a good play, if it wasn't for the way the car's front axle wavered under the force of its own weight, its instability compounded by the increased speed. All it took was the slightest nudge from David and–

The front of the car collapsed, its bumper impacting the road and sending up a spray of sparks as the metal undercarriage gouged out a scar in the asphalt. David had to jerk Tiger hard to the side to avoid hitting them, which sent Alisa's head into the passenger side window.

"Hijack!"

"Buckle up, Cipher." David flexed his fingers against the wheel and grinned sharply. He could see the taillights of Red and her followers ahead of him, entering the industrial part of Roanoke. "We're about to have some fun."

"Why do I doubt tha– *whoa! Slow doooooown!*"

It was easy to get lost in Tiger's rhythm, her engine singing a triumphant anthem as she gained on the lead drivers. Part of David couldn't believe he'd never cared much for driving before his mutation emerged; he'd been so blind. This, the pull and pulse of metal and gasoline, the shrill scream and squeal of the tires as he rounded turns so sharply that any other car, any other driver, would have burned out – it was pure glory, an exultation, sheer exhilaration. Part of David wanted to keep the race going, but...

The other two tethers in his mind, bright red lines leading back to the vans, were moving now. They were heading vaguely parallel to this route, but on the other side of town. They were moving fast, though. Fast enough that they'd be pulled over if they were caught. Which meant the cops had to be–

"Weee-ooo-weee-ooo-weee-ooo."

–distracted. Shoot, and here they came now, turning quick around the corner of a Tim Horton's and rattling into position behind him. They weren't all that close, maybe a hundred yards back, but David had to keep tabs on them with his mutation. Them, and the vans, and the lead car and her cronies, plus Tiger. That was... a lot all at once.

"You're losing speed," Alisa said, her voice tight with... concern? Maybe. Or maybe that was her way of expressing anger or frustration – David hadn't paid close enough attention to her to tell. Seemed like an oversight. "Why are you losing speed?"

"Too much to think about," David replied, gritting his teeth. "Too much to keep track of." He should be paying attention to his own car, pushing it to catch Red and the others, but if he didn't keep close enough tabs on the vans and their guns, then it didn't matter as much if he caught up to the lead cars. The gunrunners would still get the job done. "The vans are heading for the highway south of town. If they make it before we get there–"

Alisa nodded her head. "And the cars ahead are going to bypass the highway. I get it. OK." She firmed her jaw. "OK, I can help. I can do this."

"Do what?"

"Lead the cops to the vans."

David shook his aching head. His vision was starting to blur. "How? You can't feel them with your mind, you might miss them."

"Get me up next to one of those cars and find out. Where's your cell phone?"

"Center console."

She used her phone to call his, then opened up his center console so the phone was clearly audible. "Should have brought our communicators," she muttered. "This'll have to do, though. Are you going to speed up, or do I have to step on the gas for you?"

David gritted his teeth and sped Tiger up, closing the distance between them and the lead three cars fast. Growly was a little closer, darting over into the oncoming traffic lane now and then like David was going to do something dumb like try to pass him to get up to Red. Which – no, of course he wasn't going to do that. What a waste of time.

"You could stop their cars, right?" Alisa asked as they closed in. "Even if your brain's kind of busy right now?"

"Sure," David scoffed. "But we're trying not to get anyone killed tonight. You know how much force the driver would take if I just went and locked up his brakes? Whiplash would be the least of it." He urged Tiger closer. "How close do you need to be?"

She looked nervously at the car ahead of them, biting her lip. "A little closer? Side by side would be better. *I* want to survive the night, too, after all."

"You could just stay phased."

"And climb my way out of the ground?" she snapped. "Do you know how irritating it is to fall into the *freaking* ground?"

"As irritating as sitting here listening to you?" David asked. He glanced into the oncoming traffic lane – the nearest set of headlights were pretty distant. He had time. He pulled into the left lane and roared forward with a burst of speed.

"Almost as irritating as you!" Alisa shouted as she phased right through her seatbelt. A few seconds later, Tiger was level with Growly. Alisa crouched down on the front seat, readying herself, and then…

She was gone, visible for a second as a shadow leaping into space before she vanished. A second later, Growly began to slow down, then suddenly swerved. Alisa must have phased through the driver.

"No, nope," David said. It hurt – his whole head was pounding like a pneumatic hammer now – but he took full control of Growly's steering long enough for Alisa to finish taking out the driver.

When he felt control reengage, and heard her say over their open line, "OK, OK, I got it!" he let go, willingly releasing the car to her. "I'm going to lead the cops toward the highway," she said. "Tell me if I go off course."

"I will."

With that, she jerked the wheel around so hard that Growly's wheels spun out, and did a donut – a *donut*, jeez, who knew she had such a knack for visual puns – right in front of the incoming cop cars, which skidded to a stop to keep from hitting her. Then Alisa peeled out right in front of them, heading southwest as fast as she could go. The cops gathered themselves and raced after her.

Which left David to race after Grunty and Red.

It was easier, having Alisa driving the other car. He still paid attention to it – he wasn't about to let her get in trouble when he was the whole reason she was here at all – but he trusted her to handle herself. She could keep the cops engaged, she could close the distance with the vans, she could keep herself safe. And he could track down the leaders of this escapade.

Grunty was *not* pleased with the loss of his fellow chase car. He wavered back and forth between David and Red, the Corvette's big, wide tail an effective barrier to moving forward. When David reached out and tapped Grunty's brakes, just to see what happened, he got a barrage of bullets out the driver's side window for his troubles. "Whoa!"

"What, what?" Alisa yelled over the phone. "Are you OK?"

"The guy ahead of me is armed and not afraid to show it."

"So?"

So? What does she mean, so? "So, I don't want to get shot!"

"Guns are just simple machines, aren't they?" she demanded. "Make it jam when he tries again!"

Oh right, that was… yeah. "Stop knowing more about my mutation than I do," David muttered, surging forward until he barely touched Grunty's rear bumper. Distantly he smelled the scent of burning oil – Tiger's oil pan had sprung a leak. Not a bad one, not yet, but it wasn't going to get any better at a hundred and fifty-seven miles an hour. Had one of the bullets ricocheted off the ground? Was it just bad luck? That seemed to happen a lot, to David.

"Just jam the gun, Hijack."

He wanted to snark at her, but it also wasn't like she was wrong. David tapped Grunty again, reached out with his power and…

Click. He jammed the slide of the gun. No matter what the driver did, that thing wasn't going to unstick now. Of course, the guy might have another one in there, which meant this next move would have to be fast. David barely felt capable of being fast right now, with the way this headache had come on. *Time for some sympathetic magic.* After a fashion, at least.

He pulled up next to the car, aware that the oncoming truck headlights, which had been a comfortable distance away thirty seconds ago, were now dangerously close. Then he reached out to Grunty's steering column, synced it with his own, and jerked his car over into the proper lane just before the big rig, its horn blaring, missed him by less than a foot on the left-hand side.

Grunty went careening off the shoulder and toward the woods. The driver was frantic on the brakes, but it wasn't going to help. David took a second – just a second – to lock up Grunty's entire fuselage. The car groaned, and the driver rattled around like the last TicTac in the box, but he was OK after the car stopped.

"Did you get him?" Alisa called out over the phone. "Hijack, are you OK?"

"Fine," he said, forcibly disengaging his mind from the ruined car. "I got him, I'm fine. You?"

"This is a lot different than any car I've ever driven before." Cipher sounded a little disgruntled. "There are all these extra buttons..."

"Don't push those!" David could only imagine what some of those buttons did.

"I *won't*. Jeez, I can handle myself."

Wasn't that the truth. After tonight, David wasn't going to say a single word to her about who was the adult, because it was clear she'd been adulting better than him, and probably most of the other people in the academy, for years.

It was kind of sad that she'd had to, though.

Head in the game. Red was the only one left for him to take out. No matter who was behind this caper, without a stellar driver like her, at the very least they'd think twice about pulling this in Roanoke again. David got a bead on Alisa's car, then the vans. "You're about half a mile out from interception just north of the highway. Cops still following you?"

"Like glue. I'm going easy on them."

"Good. Go easier. You want the cops to come in behind the vans, after all. Feel free to cause an accident."

"I've got it," she affirmed. "Where are you?"

David looked around, then bit back a curse. "Heading for South Bay Bridge."

"Wait... didn't your evil friend say that it's under construction? David? *David!*"

He didn't answer Alisa – he couldn't. He had to focus now, had to get Tiger closer to Red.

You don't have to. You're not monitoring everyone now; your head feels better already. You could stop her from here. Stop her cold.

He could… but he didn't want to. It was risky and ridiculous, chasing down this bright red Camaro and its mysterious driver for no reason other than to prove that he could outdrive her after all, but David couldn't remember the last time he'd felt this alive. He wasn't going to stop, not now.

He pushed the Golf to the limit of its capacity and beyond. The engine block was getting dangerously hot, so he shunted that heat as much as he could to other parts of the car, which meant that the hood, the frame, even underneath his seat all got uncomfortably warm. There was no way Red should still be driving so smoothly, not at these speeds, and yet – every move was precise, every second controlled. Was she a mutant? How could she not be, and maintain that kind of control? Was she someone David knew, or knew of?

Maybe he'd find out once he ran her off the road. The bridge was coming up, suspension arches rearing out of the darkness like the legs of an enormous insect. It was clearly marked as under construction – beyond that, it was missing pieces in the middle. *Do not pass go, do not collect two hundred dollars.*

Oh, I'm gonna collect.

Red hesitated for a moment before committing to the bridge – why? Was she scared, or did she think David would be?

You could die. You control every part of this vehicle, but you don't control the ground and you can't stop gravity. You could die up here.

David knew he wouldn't, though – somehow, he knew it. Tiger sizzled with heat and stress, and ahead of him Red Leather was racing like hell for the gap in the bridge. Their side of it was slightly higher than the other side – would it be enough to propel her and her monstrous Camaro over safely?

He felt Red soar to nearly two hundred and fifteen miles per hour, and then...

She flew through the night sky, a trail of sparks behind her, moonlight glinting off her sleek red frame. She flew like a hawk... but she landed like an elephant. Red screamed in agony as she broke apart, and her driver fought a losing battle for control before the car spun out and skidded to a smoking halt. David could have cried, if he hadn't been so concerned for his own life.

Time to power up. It wasn't how he'd envisioned using his jets, but he wasn't going to say no. He fed fuel from special reservoirs to the Blackbird attachment at a hundred feet out, and–

Tiger didn't fly like a bird of prey. She flew like a meteor, like a shooting star, going so fast so quickly that David was pressed back into his seat from the power of the g-force. He shot over the gap in the bridge, shot over almost all the rest of the bridge, too, and landed on the other side with a spine-shattering crash that should have left him broken.

It didn't, of course. He knew Tiger, knew how to make her into a cradle, to get her to hold him steady even when everything around him was falling apart. David felt the bump, for sure, but he wasn't hurt.

The same couldn't be said for his baby, who he brought to a stop as quickly as he could without breaking her completely. Oh god, her engine was *toast*, he was going to have to replace the whole freaking thing after this.

But the rest of her was salvageable. That was the important part. "You did so good," David said, patting his car's dashboard. "So good, Tiger."

"–vid. David! Are you OK? Did you get her?"

For a second David wanted to ask "Who?" before he realized Alisa was talking about Red Leather. "I'm on her," he said, and got out of his car just in time to watch Red's windshield explode outward in a shower of glittering shards. A second later Red Leather crawled out, shaky but still able to stand on her own two feet. She stood in front of her ruined car and tore her helmet off. Now to find out the driver's identity…

Her hair was short and dark with sweat, her face sharp and thin with a kind of bladelike beauty to it. When she turned her eyes on David, they were full of venom… and something like respect. There was no recognition, though.

He didn't know her, either. Not Psylocke, not Reiko, not Madeline Pryor… holy crap. Maybe she was just human after all.

Human and *awesome*.

She raised her left hand and very clearly flipped him the bird, then began to run in the opposite direction. "Shoot," David muttered, getting out to follow her, but he could already tell he wasn't going to make it in time. He couldn't even overtake her in a vehicle, since both of theirs were non-operational now.

Well. At least she wasn't going to be able to call the vans for a pickup. Speaking of that…

"Oh, crap." He lunged back into Tiger and grabbed his phone. "Alisa? Everything OK?"

"Where have you *been*, you jerk?" she demanded, her voice too-loud from nerves. "I've been calling your name for two minutes! Did you get her?"

"Sorry." He glanced back toward the abandoned Camaro. "No. I didn't. Did the cops find the vans?"

"Yep. I only had to cause a small traffic accident to do it, but I managed to get one of the back doors open and shoved a crate of the guns out onto the pavement. The cops were very distracted. And speaking of distractions…" In the distance, David heard a familiar engine voice. Growly was getting close. "I'm surprised you haven't said anything about me coming to get you."

"Eh, I knew you wouldn't leave me here to hoof it," David joked.

"Of *course* not." There was a second of silence, then, "I really like driving this car."

"Good, 'cause you're gonna need to tow Tiger back to the Institute with it."

"No, I mean… I *really* like it. I think I'm going to keep it."

David laughed, feeling lighter than he had for weeks. What a night. What a *race*. He'd caught the uncatchable car at last. And he'd had someone to share it all with, too, someone to help him do what was right, someone to make it all work. "Let me know if you want some help tuning it, it's running a little rich right now."

"I'll do that." Headlights flared in the distance, Alisa getting closer and closer to South Bay Bridge. "I could, um, help you fix Tiger up, too. If you want. I mean, team effort, right?"

"Yeah." David's cheeks ached from how hard he was smiling. "Go team."

EYE OF THE STORM

Amanda Bridgeman

Santo raised the large boulder over his head as the lightning flashed like frenzied paparazzi and the rain ran off him like rivulets of sweat.

"And the crowd goes wild for Rockslide, the superhuman wrestling champion of the woooorld!"

Flexing his large granite arms, he tossed the boulder into the middle of the swollen river, sending water splashing high and waves smashing onto the already battered muddy banks. Raising his arms in victory, he mimicked the sounds of a cheering crowd.

"Would you like some time alone with your rocks there, big guy?" Iara said. She stood, hands on hips, appraising him with her intense brown eyes.

"Hey, I'm just trying to enjoy myself while we toil," he said. "I don't know what you did over at the Jean Grey School, but at the New Charles Xavier School we like to have some fun."

"We can have fun once the work is done," Sooraya said, standing further along the bank, her long black niqāb damp and flapping in the strong wind. "If we don't levee this river and it floods the town downstream, there'll be humans all over this mountain. That won't be good for your school."

"No, it won't," Santo said. "The best thing about *our* school is its secrecy. We gotta protect that at all costs." He cracked a wide granite smile, his snow-white eyes alight with mischief. "But that doesn't mean we can't have fun while we do it. Besides," he glanced around the skies, "I think the rain is easing."

"It's the eye of the storm," Sooraya said, glancing about, too. "The worst is yet to come."

"Relax," Santo said, heaving another boulder into the air, "we'll have this levee done before then."

"I'll start checking the foundation beneath the water," Iara said, as she lowered her head in concentration. She twitched and groaned as her skin turned rough and gray, and fins sprouted down her back and along her muscular legs. She looked up again, her brown eyes now black, her teeth enlarged and sharpened, then she turned and dove beneath the waves.

"Man, it must be cool to swim underwater like Shark Girl," Santo said.

"I'm sure it has its benefits," Sooraya said, eyeing the water. "But like all of us, I'm certain there are times she wishes she was just human, too."

Santo glanced at Sooraya, but before he could question her comment, she turned away.

"I'll go assess the stability of the banks downstream," she said, vanishing in a cloud of sand and flying away on the wind.

"Dust and Shark Girl," Santo grunted, shaking his head. "Why did I get lumped babysitting the moody transfer students?"

Swimming beneath the water, Iara pressed her hands against the foundation of the rocks to test their stability. The rock wall Santo was building seemed sturdy; the weight of the heavy boulders nestled deep into the sand to provide a solid structure upon which to build upon. They'd been out here for hours now and this was the third and final levee they'd been asked to build. The system rolling over them was being hailed as one of those "twenty year storms", and local weather bureaus had been issuing alerts that escalated as each hour passed.

Having checked the river earlier and witnessing the rising water line, Cyclops, the principal of the New Charles Xavier School, had requested measures be put in place to ensure the stability of the river and its banks, and to guarantee no unnecessary attention was drawn to the school's vicinity. Iara, given her ability to breathe underwater, was naturally selected, along with Sooraya because she knew how to work sand. She guessed Rockslide was there for his strength, although part of Iara wondered if he was there to keep an eye on them.

Was this some kind of test to see if Iara and Sooraya would fit in at the New Charles Xavier School? It was no secret that both had been struggling to belong at the Jean Grey School, and Wolverine himself had suggested the transfer, thinking a change of scenery might help them decide who they were, what they wanted, and where they wanted to be.

Iara was angry at Wolverine for suggesting the transfer for

the term. The X-Men were supposed to be helping her, not passing her off when things became too hard. Then again, maybe Wolverine wanted her to see the other side in the hope that she would return. Deep down she sensed that Wolverine understood her sometimes uncontrollable anger. Maybe he knew better than anyone that she needed to wander in order to find herself, to heal herself.

Iara had to admit, though, finding herself through hard labor wasn't what she'd been expecting. She wanted to learn to control her mutant abilities for a higher purpose, not plug up a river! All this work was making her hungry. There'd better be a good meal and a hot fire waiting for them when they returned to the school, she thought.

Iara saw a flash of silver in the corner of her eye and glanced around. Through the rushing water, she made out the familiar shape and shimmer of a fish of some kind. It was a little bigger than her hand, swimming steadily against the tide but not making any ground. It sure picked a hell of a time to try and swim upstream.

She focused back on the rushing water and the growing rock wall, feeling the impact vibrations every time Santo added another boulder to the stack, and sensing the pull of the river's current lessening with each rock that held back the flow. With every added boulder, Iara paused, watching the wall carefully, but it held steady. The levee would soon be complete.

The flash of silver caught her eye again and she turned to stare at the fish. It was still there. It was a little odd, she thought. She wondered what it was doing, why it didn't swim harder to get where it was going – especially while there were still gaps in the wall for it to pass through. Though she could identify most fish in the ocean off her homeland of Brazil, here in this Canadian river, she wasn't sure what kind of fish it was. She noticed its eyes looked lifeless and glassy. Maybe it was tiring. She watched it curiously as it swam in its suspended animation-like state, not moving anywhere, the continual flash of its silver body hooking Iara's attention.

And more importantly, her hunger.

It was starting to give her an idea...

Maybe a snack was in order? Maybe this fish was so weakened that it couldn't forge ahead. Maybe she should save this fish the hassle of fighting a current it could not win against. Maybe Iara should put it out of its misery.

Snack time it was!

With one swift kick of her powerful legs, she lunged, shooting through the water and slamming her jaws down on the fish before it knew what had happened.

She instantly recoiled in pain.

Her teeth did not sink into tasty flesh. In fact, they didn't sink into anything. The fish was as hard as metal.

Iara pushed herself backward, leaving a trail of blood, *her* blood, in the water and watched in disbelief as the fish swam awkwardly away, its metal torso dented from her powerful teeth. She rubbed her gums in pain and confusion.

What was that thing?

Santo and Sooraya's conversation suddenly echoed in her mind, about the secrecy of the New Charles Xavier School and how they had to protect it at all costs. Was that metal fish spying on them somehow? Did it capture footage of her in Shark Girl form? What if it did?

Panic shot through her.

She did not want to be the one to draw attention to the school. She did not want to fail this test, Wolverine, or the new school.

She had to stop that thing. *Now!*

She shot forth again with a swift kick of her powerful legs, racing after the dented metal creature, wondering where it had disappeared to. She followed Santo's rock wall until it reached the opposite bank where a mass of boulders shot up through the riverbed floor and into the air, forming a ridge wall.

Where did it go?

She swam frantically, peering through the gaps in the rock wall, seeing no sight of it on the other side. Then, suddenly, the senses embedded in the skin across her snout detected the vibrations of it. The vibrations were coming from the vicinity of the ridge wall. She moved closer and noticed a darkened hole, a tunnel, a cave hidden in the wall beneath the waves.

Then she saw it: the dented metal fish, swimming within, staring back at her.

And she saw now that the eyes weren't real. They were artificial lenses, focusing and refocusing on her. Studying her. Maybe filming her. But who was watching?

Iara growled angrily, fueled by the taste of her own blood. She shot forth again toward the creature and was upon it within moments. As she grabbed it in her hands, she felt a strong vibration ripple over her entire body. She heard a loud bang and spun around to see the tunnel opening was sealed behind her.

She was trapped.

She dropped the fish and rammed the sealed door with her muscular torso. It wouldn't budge. She spotted a lever on the wall that she hoped would open the door again. Just as she grabbed it, she heard another sound, felt another vibration. Something mechanical. Then the water around her was draining away fast. She felt pressure at her gills, suddenly starving for oxygen. She forced her human lungs to kick in. As the water drained away, she looked ahead to the dented metal fish that now lay unmoving on the metal floor. Iara listened intently, wondering what would happen next, her hand still on the lever. Squatting like a coiled spring, her gray muscles tensed, her teeth bared, ready for whatever came her way.

The floor moved.

She fell backwards as a conveyor belt propelled her forward toward the opposite wall of the tunnel, which slid open. The conveyor fed her through and she was unceremoniously dumped onto a floor below. She landed with a heavy thud on a square metal plate and heard a clanging sound as bars rose up from the plate, surrounding her. Before she knew what was happening, another plate landed on top of the bars and she found herself trapped inside a cage. A small console on the cage's door beeped, and she knew she'd been locked inside.

Panic and fear shot through her. Where was she? Who was doing this to her? Was this some weird initiation ritual at the school? Had Cyclops and Santo planned this? Where was Sooraya?

"Hey!" she yelled, glancing around frantically into what appeared to be an empty medical science lab. "Let me out of here!" She grabbed onto the bars and pulled, shocked when they gave a little but then bounced rapidly back into place.

"What the...?" She tried again on the other side, pressing her legs against the bars, and pulling with all her might. The same thing happened. The metal moved slightly with her strength but did not break.

"Well, well..." a man's voice came from behind, startling her.

She spun around to see him standing in the doorway. But it wasn't a man she was looking at. Or was it? Instead of a human she saw someone who was once a man but had now transcended that. While human-shaped, she saw patches of exposed skin, but much of him was covered in metallic parts, cables and consoles fused into his body.

This man was half-machine, a cyborg.

Was he working with Cyclops? Or was this something else?

He stepped closer, staring at her with his human right eye and his robotic left eye, which seemed to focus on her raptly as a smile spread across his face. "What a wonderful catch! I have myself an organic," he said, before his voice took on a more sinister tone and the smile vacated his face. "And a mutant one at that."

Coldness swam down Iara's spine. Deep in the pit of her gut, she found the answer she'd been looking for. This wasn't a test.

This was something much worse.

Santo looked up into the sky as the rain began to fall heavily again. In the distance, lightning illuminated the entire sky before the sound of deep rolling thunder rumbled. He even felt it through the soles of his granite feet. He studied the wall of boulders he'd placed across the river, the makeshift levee to hold the rising tide back almost complete. But he was starting to wonder whether it was going to be enough, as the river continued to swell.

He looked over at the choppy water, wondering where Iara had gotten to. The river wasn't that wide that it should take her this long to check things, though he had noted it was much deeper in this area compared to the last two, based on the number of boulders he'd had to lay so far. They were seven or eight deep.

What was Iara doing down there?

A sudden thought struck him.

What if one of those boulders he'd thrown had accidentally pinned Iara beneath the water?

"Oh crap," he muttered, wading into the water as rain spat down. "Way to go, Santo. Accidentally kill the new girl. I'm sure that'll do great things for relations between the two schools… Lucky she can breathe down there."

He peered around as more lightning flashed and the rain fell harder. He wiped his eyes, trying to see through the choppy water, but it was hard, especially with the fading light as dusk neared. As the thunder rumbled louder, he looked up into the sky to see the eye of the storm had well and truly passed and the next front was amassing quickly – a band of dark clouds so thick he worried the levees they'd built wouldn't be enough.

"Yo, Shark Girl!" he called out. "We gotta get moving. Where are you?"

No response came.

"Iara!" he called again. Still no response. "Please don't have killed the new girl…" He glanced back nervously to the riverbank, seeking Sooraya, but she was nowhere to be seen. He looked to the tall ridge sprouting along the opposite bank, then at his levee of boulders. Were these new mutants pulling a prank on him?

"You better not be playing with me, Iara!" he called out. No response came. Concern settled in earnestly now.

"Alright, alright. I'll bite!" he said, then took a deep breath and dove beneath the surface.

Santo pulled himself along the riverbed floor, searching for Iara, but he saw nothing. No living creatures at all. Nothing but rocks, reeds, and the silt floor. He rose to the surface, took a breath, then dropped below the waves again. Where could she have gone? The river was sealed off now. There weren't any gaps large enough for her to fit through.

Lightning cracked overhead and illuminated everything around him. In the ridge wall, he noticed an arched crack of perfect symmetry. Curious, he stared at it, waiting for more lightning to see it better. Bright white light flashed again and confirmed his suspicions. If there was one thing Santo knew, it was rocks, and this line was too perfect to be natural. This was the shape, the outline, of some kind of door. Could Shark Girl be on the other side of it? Trapped even?

He rose to the surface again as thunder rumbled the land and water around him, took another breath, then dove down. He traced his thick fingers along the crack and the surrounding wall, trying to find a way to open it. But he couldn't. There were no obvious handles or levers, and his fingers were too big to fit into the crack to pry it open. His lungs began to burn, craving oxygen, and he growled in anger and punched the rock wall in frustration.

As soon as he did, a bright pink light flashed from somewhere in the rock wall. It pierced his eyes and seemed to travel right back into his brain, stunning him.

He fell limp in the water, semi-conscious, as his heavy body sank, and the last bubbles of air escaped his lungs.

Santo's body hit the riverbed floor and silt wafted up around him. As it did, a metal cylinder suddenly rose from the ground and encapsulated him within.

Then, suddenly, it pulled him underground.

Sooraya, still floating in her dust form, looked up from the riverbed she was inspecting. She turned her eyes upstream, confused by the flash of pink light she had just witnessed out of the corner of her eye. It was too low to be lightning. It seemed to come from the river itself. And that feeling in her head? Like something pressing into her that failed to penetrate her mind. Very little could when she was in her sand-like silicon form.

That light was unnatural.

"Santo?" she called.

There was no answer, but between the rain, the wind, and the bellowing thunder, it didn't surprise her that he couldn't hear.

She flew in her dust form back to where she had left him, but the bank was empty. She studied her surroundings carefully, searching for any trace of him. There was nothing but the angry river smashing against the boulders and the tall ridge wall that lined the opposite bank like a massive, dark shark fin.

Where had Santo and Iara gone?

Perhaps Cyclops had come to collect them? But why would they leave her out here? And that light... the feeling in her head... It wasn't normal. She was sure it had come from within the river itself. Concerned, she quickly floated out over the water, searching for a trace of either of them, but there was nothing. Even in the dim light, surely she would see Santo's granite body beneath the waves?

Buffeted by the wind, she moved over to the tall, arched,

ridge wall for shelter, as she continued to search the banks for them. But the banks were empty. She rested against the ridge wall, her mind turning over.

And then she felt it.

The pull, the suction of air, as it moved from one cavity to another. She turned to face the ridge wall, seeking where it came from. There! A tiny crack in the rock wall, pushing and pulling her sand-like form. Placing her granular hand against the surface she realized it wasn't rock at all. The ridge was artificial and a cavity, a space of some kind, lay within.

Could this be where they were? She glanced around one last time, but there was only herself and the growing storm. She turned back to the crack in the ridge. Maybe they sought shelter? Or maybe they followed that pink light? Perhaps it came from within?

With little choice, she drew in her sand-like silicon form, and began to filter herself inside.

Iara watched the cyborg curiously. For the last few minutes his focus had been drawn to a console against the wall of the room. Originally alerted by an alarm sounding on the small panel in his forearm, he'd been fixed to the larger dashboard ever since, working the keys and tapping the screens, orchestrating something. Now she felt a vibration through the bottom of her cage, a vibration that was getting stronger. A commotion of mechanical sounds grew, and she turned her attention to the wall opposite her, where she sensed it was coming from.

Suddenly a door in the wall rose up, revealing a tunnel, and a wet, unconscious Rockslide fed through and fell to the ground with a thud. Iara's heartbeat kicked up a notch. She watched helplessly as he was sealed within a cage, although given his size, his was much less roomy than hers.

"Rockslide!" she called.

She stared at him, crumpled up into a seated ball, and her mouth turned dry. This was *definitely* not a training exercise; not something Cyclops would've orchestrated.

The cyborg moved toward Rockslide curiously.

"What are you doing? Let us go!" Iara hissed. She surged forward, baring her teeth at the cyborg and pulling the bars that moved with her motion, but failed to yield an escape.

"You're wasting your time," the cyborg told her. "The bars cannot be broken. I created the metal myself. It may not be as strong as Adamantium, but what it lacks in strength it has in pliability. It can bend, yes, but it can never be broken. It's programmable, you see. The metal is embedded with sensors. These sensors will read your body size and adjust parameters to suit. The bars will never bend wider than your frame. You will not escape."

"Who are you?" she growled.

He smiled at her, wide enough this time that she could see his teeth were made of a shiny metal. So shiny she could see her reflection in them. "I am Doctor Yorke Vaile. And you are?"

Rockslide groaned as he began to come to.

"What do you want with us?" Iara asked Vaile.

He smiled again, the silver teeth glinting in the overhead lights. "I'm not sure yet, but I'll think of something."

"Why were you snooping around with that fake fish?" she demanded, as Rockslide finally blinked his eyes open.

"You were trespassing close to my lab," Vaile said. "Just as you mutants don't wish to be discovered in your secret facility, I do not wish to be discovered in mine." His eyes narrowed at her. "But you had to chase that fish, didn't you?"

"Because you were spying on us!"

Rockslide suddenly straightened, saw Iara in her cage, saw Vaile, then grabbed at the bars of his own cage. Eyes burning white hot, he tugged violently at them. Though they bent with his movement, they did not break, nor would they open wide enough to fit his large frame through.

"Let me save you the effort," Vaile said with a bored tone as he turned to Rockslide. "You will not escape that cage. So, please, keep it down."

"You better hope I don't get out of here!" Rockslide threatened, before he looked over at Iara. "You OK?"

She nodded. "He's been spying on the school."

"Who are you?" Santo asked through his clenched jaw. "What do you want?"

Vaile stared at him. "What do I want? Truthfully?" He smiled again. "I want to eradicate mutants from every corner of life as we know it."

Iara and Rockslide stared at Vaile in silence as he moved over to the console against the wall again, turning his back to them.

"I tried to make things work with your kind once. I started my career working on the Weapon X program. I was young and Stryker was a man of vision. So, too, was Colcord at the Facility. But they were wedded to using mutants as weapons. I came to see this was an error in judgment. Boosting a mutant's powers and making them weapons of mass destruction was signing our own death warrant. But they wanted power and believed mutants would help them achieve their goal." Vaile turned around to face them again. "I came to believe we, *humans*, would lose our power if we did that. Mutants are a risk. They cannot be trusted."

"And you think humans can?" Rockslide spat.

"No," Vaile said bluntly. "They, too, cannot." His silver smile shone across the room. "The only beings that can be trusted are synthetics." He worked the console briefly and a screen projected before them, showing all manner of artificial, robotic creatures; variants modeled on species of the animal kingdom. "And so, I created the Weapon S program," Vaile said, eyeing the screen with pride. "Synthetic weapons can be programmed. Their loyalty assured. Few mutants would ever be able to control my machines. They will help restore balance." He looked back at Rockslide and Iara. "My program is close to completion and once it is complete, my synthetics will rise and eliminate all organic threats. Including you and your school."

Rockslide growled with rage as he tugged at the bars of his cage again. Iara felt her teeth sharpen and the fin down her back harden.

Another alarm sounded on Vaile's console, and he quickly turned toward it, muttering, "What now?"

Iara noticed a breeze blowing in from up high. She looked up at the air vent and saw Dust filtering through.

Vaile spun around to see Dust floating before him in her sand-like silicon form. He smiled. "Ah! Another organic for me to destroy."

"Dust is eternal," Sooraya told him venomously, clearly having overheard their conversation, "granite is as old as time, and sharks have survived for millions of years. We will not be destroyed so easily." Iara watched as she raised her arms, whipping her sand-like form into a frenzy, sending it thrashing Vaile's way, ready to flay him alive.

But she wasn't quite fast enough.

Vaile's fingers swiftly tapped over the console in his arm and before Dust's sandstorm could hit him, his entire body was encased in a protective metallic armor. Vaile smiled through his faceplate at Sooraya, then tapped his console again, and before Iara knew what was happening, Dust's silicon form was sucked into the nearest air vent and she disappeared.

"Sooraya!" Iara yelled after her.

"You cannot win, organics," Vaile said, the threat heavy in his voice as he tapped his arm console again and his armor receded. "I have worked with your kind for many years. I have learned how to counter anything you may throw at me. Water, fire, mind tricks, brute strength... *sand*."

"Oh yeah?" Rockslide said. "Then let me out of this cage and let's test if you're ready for *my* brute strength."

Vaile stared at him a moment before a large grin spread across his cyborg face. "What a wonderful idea. Let's do just that."

Iara watched as he tapped at his console again and they heard another mechanical noise sound throughout the lab.

"What are you doing?" Rockslide growled.

Vaile's eyes shone with a dangerous glee. "I've decided what I'm going to do with you."

Iara's and Rockslide's cages jolted backwards as the walls behind each of them opened. Iara suddenly found herself inside a dark tunnel moving along a conveyor belt system at a fast pace. Within moments it passed through another opening and then suddenly it was falling.

Lost in the pitch blackness, Iara let out a scream as her stomach lurched up into her throat. As the cage dropped, another door below her opened, revealing a source of light. Her cage tumbled through the opening, landing with a hard thud on muddy, grassy ground.

Santo spat grass from his mouth and groaned as he rubbed his face where it had smacked into the bars. He heard Iara moan nearby followed by a hissing sound. They both looked back to the wall they'd been ejected from to see Dust being blown out of a vent. Changing in midair from her Dust form, Sooraya landed with a thud between them, a mound of black niqāb. As she came to a stop, she looked up, locking eyes with Santo and Iara in their cages.

Then high-pitched beeps sounded.

The tiny consoles on their cages lit up, and the doors unlocked. Santo didn't stop to wonder why. He kicked the door open wide and crawled through before it closed again. He quickly stood, cracking his granite limbs and clenching his fists as he scanned their surroundings for threats. He saw none, however. There was nothing but trees and a river flowing close to where Iara was now crawling out of her cage.

"Where are we?" Sooraya asked, moving closer to him.

"I don't know," he said, eyeing a rocky outcrop in the near distance and trying to place it. "Are we outside again? Did he let us go?"

"There's no storm," Sooraya said, eyeing the calm daylight skies overhead. "This isn't where we were before."

"So, where are we?" Iara said, back in human form and standing by her cage. "This place gives me the creeps."

"I don't know where we are," Santo said, "but let's get out of here."

A wolf's howl sounded.

"There." Sooraya pointed to the rocky outcrop where a lone wolf stood. It turned its face toward them and they were each taken aback by its red glowing eyes. Then it turned its body slightly to hit a source of light, and they saw it shone silver.

"That's not a wolf," Santo said.

"It's a synthetic," Iara agreed, concerned. "One of his creations."

"Indeed," Vaile's voice sounded from up high. They looked up to see part of the sky opening to reveal the cyborg standing, backlit, in a window. As it did, the sky and surroundings glitched to reveal they stood in some kind of small domed facility. The wolf in the distance had been an illusion projected onto the dome around them.

"It's not real," Sooraya said. "We're not outside. We're still inside."

"Correct," Vaile told her. "Welcome to my simulation arena. This is where I test my synthetics. Thank you for volunteering to be my latest test."

"Volunteering?" Iara growled.

"Test?" Sooraya said, concerned.

"Yes," Vaile said. "You organics believe you are superior to my synthetics, so let's test that theory. May the better creation win."

"You want us to fight your synthetics?" Sooraya asked, appalled.

"This isn't an exhibition match," Vaile said with amusement. "It's a fight, yes, but it is one that will be to the death."

Sooraya and Iara exchanged a worried look with Santo.

Santo heard the smile in Vaile's voice and wanted to rip it from his face. "And if we win this fight to the death?" Santo clenched his fists again, cracking his granite knuckles.

Silence sat for the briefest of moments.

"You won't win," Vaile said coldly.

A sudden splash caught Santo's attention and he turned to see a huge robotic crocodile snatch Iara in its jaws and drag her into the river.

"Iara!" Sooraya screamed, but before they could run to her defense, a deafening roar caught their attention. They turned to see a massive synthetic bear, bigger than Santo, step out from the trees, its eyes glowing red like the wolf's.

And before Santo could process his reaction to *that*, a swarm of wasps appeared, smothering Sooraya and swiping at her with their razor-sharp stingers. She screamed in terror, but Santo could do nothing to help her as the bear charged toward him.

Iara was spinning and shrieking. Bubbles of panicked air escaped her mouth as the crocodile tried to drown her in a death roll, its synthetic teeth puncturing her skin in places, sending wafts of her blood into the water.

But the smell of her blood only made her angry.

Her skin turned gray and hard, her teeth sharpened, her eyes rolled black, and finally her gills started breathing for her. She thrashed violently and snapped her teeth, trying to catch the crocodile's tail. In her struggle, she managed to free an arm from its mouth then thrust an elbow into its head, once, twice, thrice, causing it to loosen its grip on her.

And as soon as it did, her strong legs pushed her body free of its mouth, and she swam away as fast as she could, leaving a trail of blood behind her.

Blood stung Sooraya's eyes, the skin around them the only place visible in her niqāb for the wasps to make direct contact. Her skin burned from the pain and she burst into an angry cloud of sand-like silicon, ready to fight the synthetic beasts on an even playing field – in the air.

They continued to swoop at her granular form, slicing gaps through the dust cloud, but Sooraya twisted this way and that; separating and coming back together, and building up enough fury to whip herself into such a sandstorm frenzy that the creatures struggled to find a way to penetrate her wrath.

It stopped them. But only briefly.

They suddenly pulled back and regrouped, changing their style of attack.

The individual wasps swarmed together as one metallic clump, forming the shape of a single giant wasp – and they mounted their attack.

Santo braced as the bear connected with him like a runaway freight train. He yelled out in pain as the synthetic bear's huge jaws clamped onto his granite neck. The sheer force of the jaws alone sent cracks running down Santo's shoulder and chest. He swung his large fist, smashing it into the bear's head. The bear released its grip and pulled back, showing a slight dent in the side of its face. It roared again and charged, barreling into Santo's chest and knocking him off his feet. He landed flat on his back, winded, as the bear crashed down on top of him. Santo had only seconds to raise his big hands up around the bear's throat before those jaws could finish what they started: tearing his head from his body. Santo channeled all his strength into his arms, squeezing the bear's throat, holding it back. But then a huge paw swiped at him, its metallic claws leaving deep scratches along his cheek and sending small particles of rock flying off in the air.

Santo heard Vaile's laughter bounce around the small arena, punctured only by Sooraya's angry screams.

But what of Iara?

She'd gone silent. What exactly was Vaile laughing at?

Santo roared, pooling his strength as he held the bear's throat with one arm, while his free hand punched the swiping claws away. And then with a quick twist of his body, he flipped the bear over and threw himself on top.

Iara hid on the riverbed floor, among billowing reeds, searching for the crocodile. She knew it was searching for her. She not only saw its radar but *felt* it. The pulse, the red beam of light, arcing out in an attempt to locate her shape. But as she lay floating behind the reeds, her shark senses detected something else.

Its limitations.

The radar beam only covered a certain area. Though it traveled in a three hundred and sixty-degree arc around the creature, that arc was a flat beam, with blind spots overhead and underneath. Blind spots, that if she swam fast enough, she could get underneath and surprise the creature from below. She followed the beam of light and finally saw the crocodile emerge from the darkness. It was massive and metallic, and her puncture wounds hurt just looking at those long teeth. She watched it for a few moments, gauging its speed, its size, and the force she would need to attack it with.

The crocodile swam closer, its metallic parts glinting in the fragments of light piercing the water from above, the red glow of its seeking eyes constant. Iara tensed, readying herself. She watched as the red laser beam shot out again, arcing around the creature, then saw her opening for attack.

With a powerful swoop of her legs, she shot out of the reeds like a torpedo and hit the creature hard and fast from below. The force of her collision pushed it through the water, as her jaws slammed down on its side. She shook her head back and forth, her teeth slicing their way along its metallic hide until they gained enough purchase to hold on.

Upon her impact, the creature's beam cut out and the crocodile almost folded in on itself, her attack swift and brutal enough to stun it with the element of surprise. But the crocodile soon straightened again, despite Iara gnashing her teeth and propelling her body through the water. The creature's large jaws snapped around at her, trying to target the fin on her back. It began to thrash around violently, spinning itself in another death roll until Iara's jaw lost its grip. As soon as it was free, the crocodile whipped its body around and its mighty tail hit Iara, knocking her through the water. Within moments the snapping teeth were threatening again, but Iara darted swiftly out of reach, then sped off, swimming into the safety of the reeds once more.

Sooraya ducked, dove, and pivoted rapidly, avoiding the clump of wasps swiping at her with their now combined razor-sharp stinger, so large it was effectively a sword. Though she assumed the metal stinger would not harm her strong sand-like form, if she tired and became human again, it would surely kill her. Sooraya pooled her strength and sent a sheet of sand its way, in what would ordinarily flay a human alive. But not this synthetic beast. It had no skin to tear. She had to find another way.

She gathered her power again and tried to use sheer wind force to break the creature apart. It worked for a moment, the individual wasps separating as they were buffeted by the gust she sent their way, but they soon recovered. They reformed into their single synthetic beast and shot forward, swiping their tail at her again. Sooraya lurched back in time as the razor-sharp stinger narrowly missed her face. She wasn't sure how long she could keep this up for. She had to think of a solution and fast.

Santo roared as he pounded on the bear's chest but was soon knocked off the creature by the bear's swiping paws again – paws that were larger than his head. He skidded along the muddy grass and turned back to see the beast on its four legs charging at him – a mound of metallic death with glowing red eyes and drill bits for teeth. Santo scrambled up to his feet to face it, then ducked aside at the last minute as the bear charged past him. He watched as it skidded to a stop, and he quickly darted his eyes up to the window where Vaile's silhouette stood watching. Santo snarled and looked back at the bear. He crouched, ready to show Vaile just what he could do to take the towering synthetic down.

The bear charged at him, metal teeth bared, and Santo ducked low, ramming his granite bulk into its gut, lifting it, and throwing it over his shoulder – just like he'd done many times to opponents in his wrestling fantasies. Only, he didn't account for the time it would take to lift and throw the heavy beast. Unfortunately, in the precious seconds it took, the bear had enough time to grab hold of his arm, and as he tossed the creature over his shoulder, his arm tore away with it.

Iara pushed herself backwards as the synthetic crocodile plunged through the reeds, snapping blindly, hoping to catch her in its jaws. She quickly swam past the creature, landing a hard punch in its side as she did. Red laser light shot out as it sought her new whereabouts, and once again Iara deftly avoided it, concentrating on its blind spots: the places where the lack of sensor vibrations registered on her animal senses.

She had no idea how long they'd been fighting, but she felt a desperate urge to get back to the surface in case Sooraya or Rockslide needed help. And there was only one way this could happen. She needed to unleash an assault on the creature that stunned it into submission, a relentless bombardment that destroyed its radar and rendered it defenseless.
She had to pound the crocodile into oblivion.

Iara sped through the reeds, adrenaline numbing any pain as she moved toward the creature, fixated on its vibrations and red laser light. She swooped low, then came up over it, then down low again, circling it swiftly, sending its radar haywire. The crocodile spun, searching for her, as Iara came at it from underneath with all the force she could muster. She slammed into it, hurling it through the water as the stunned creature's legs flailed and tried to fight the momentum. Iara wasted no time, circling around and barreling into the crocodile, leaving a dent in its side. Then again and again, she swam around and came back at it, smashing her muscular body into it, sending its artificial sensors into a spin as it tried to figure out which way was up and which way was down, and where she'd disappeared to again.

As she came back around and under once more, she saw the creature's silhouette against the light overhead, now near the surface of the water. She saw the way the creature twisted and twitched and knew she had it right where she needed it to be. Its senses were confused, overloaded. Now was her chance. She bared her teeth, clenched her fists, and tightened every muscle in her body. Wound like a spring, she let herself go and swam with a speed she'd never experienced before. Twenty yards, ten, five and *boom!* She slammed into the crocodile with such force the momentum shot them both out of the water and into the air.

Iara heard a cracking sound and saw sparks of light shoot out from the creature's belly as the two fell back into the water with a huge splash.

She shook off her own daze from the impact, and quickly swam away from the creature, but soon saw there was little to worry about. The synthetic crocodile had a huge crack running across its belly at the site of her impact, weakened by her previous attacks. Bent and broken, and still shooting sporadic sparks, it slowly sank to the riverbed floor.

Iara watched carefully as the crocodile hit the bottom and sent a cloud of silt wafting into the water around it. As she watched, through the silt, she saw the red light in its eyes dim and fade out.

Gills panting as she caught her breath, relieved, Iara ran her hands across her still bleeding wounds from the crocodile's initial attack. Then more vibrations registered on her senses, and she looked up to the water's surface. As she did, she saw two dark shadows move overhead and wondered what was going on.

Sooraya zoomed over the water with the synthetic singular swarmed wasp in pursuit. Her mind was racing for a way to take this creature down. But how could she when neither the sand nor the force of her wind could not harm its shell? *Think! Think!*

She needed to get out of the open air. She needed cover. She saw the trees and sped toward them, hoping some of them were real, and not all part of the projection. If she could lose the wasp in the trees, then she could buy herself time.

Sooraya flew around the nearest tree trunks, glad they were, in fact, real, but soon enough the projected wall approached, and she had to swerve deftly to avoid a collision – the wasp following her trajectory. As she careened around, she saw there were only a handful of real trees for her to hide in, and too few to lose the wasp with. Still, she had no other choice.

She flew in her sand-like form through each of the trees, spreading herself out among the branches as she did. The singular wasp, still in pursuit, was forced to separate into its many parts in order to follow her through – the loud deep buzzing transforming into a wall of many tiny echoing buzzes.

Sooraya continued to zoom through the trees, ducking and swerving and spreading herself thin, as the reformed singular wasp gave chase. Soon enough she realized it wasn't following her. Not all the way. Instead of chasing her into the leaves, it waited outside, ready to strike in its larger form.

She paused, resting within the branches of a maple tree, her sand-like form scattered throughout the canopy. She watched the creature hovering outside, red eyes fixed on her position, hundreds of tiny silver wings beating with anticipation.

And this made her curious.

The creature preferred to face her as a singular whole and not with its individual parts. Why? It must be weaker that way. Because she, in her sand-like form, was stronger than its individual parts.

Peering through the branches at the creature as it circled the tree's canopy, it dawned on Sooraya that she stood a much greater chance of flaying this tree's branches and leaves than she did its trunk. The smaller parts were weaker. The smaller parts would disintegrate faster than the solid whole.

She had to attack the weaker, smaller parts. But how? Even those smaller parts had their metallic carapaces. She needed to get underneath those carapaces to wreak havoc from the inside. Getting inside the larger creature would be difficult, but if she could separate it, weaken it, then her sand-like silicon form could possibly overpower and destroy the weaker individual parts.

Her face hardened with resolve as she watched the giant wasp pass, then seeped her particles out of the tree to form behind it. Sensing her, it turned.

Sooraya raised her arms and mustered all the force she could to blow the wasp apart into its smaller pieces. She had to dig deeper than before, and she could not stop until the creature was torn apart.

The creature tried to lunge at her, but the force of her sandstorm held it back. As the wind whipped leaves, grass, and mud about, she groaned with the intensity of it all, willing every element of her being to break that beast apart.

Buffeted by the wind, the creature rose and fell in the air, trying to fight through her velocity. But Sooraya held on. Soon enough the giant wasp began to separate into its smaller components, forced apart by the strong wind she produced.

Sooraya's groan was now a full battle scream as her whole sand-like form shook with the power of it all. When she'd pushed the individual wasps apart as far as she could, she focused hard on holding them there as she pooled the last of her reserves for the final attack.

With a swift flick of her hands, the sand shot forward at the smaller wasps, smothering them, the individual granules seeking any way inside their carapaces. She concentrated hard, fighting hundreds of small wars at once as each resisted and swiped at her granules.

But her particles were not like her human form. They were like bonded glass and she pushed into any crack or gap she could find.

The separated giant form of wasp began to disintegrate, too busy with its individual battles to be able to form as one again. Soon, there was no singular wasp to be seen but instead hundreds of smaller wasps buzzing about, trying to stop the granules from penetrating their shells.

But they were failing.

Sooraya felt her particles wreaking havoc on the creatures, thrusting into the smallest of their parts, stuffing into any gap she could find. She felt their minutiae of mechanical parts struggling and failing as her silicon sand wedged itself deep within and began to cause catastrophic failures.

And then the sparks started, like a miniature fireworks display.

One by one they malfunctioned, the silicon interfering with their mechanics, causing them to stall or short circuit and grind to a complete halt.

They began to fall from the sky, landing on the ground as they formed a junkyard of disused parts.

With one final scream and energy burst, Sooraya whipped her sand around in a ferocious whirlwind until every last wasp littered the ground.

And as the last one fell, so, too, did she, to her knees, utterly exhausted.

Santo stared wide-eyed as his arm lay in the bear's claws. The pain he felt in his shoulder was something else. It was one thing to disengage his hands as projectiles himself, but another to have a giant bear rip them off.

"Oh, no you don't!" he snarled in pain. "Give that back!" He disengaged his remaining fist, shooting it like a rocket at the bear's head and landing a vicious punch. "Surprise!"

Stunned, the bear dropped his other arm and Santo ran toward it. He kicked the arm and fist toward a boulder that lay by the river's edge, then leaned into all three as he used the rock and earth matter to reconnect his appendages.

But the bear had overcome its stunned state and rose up.

"Come on!" Santo urged his appendages to reconnect faster, as the bear charged. It rammed him gut-forward into the boulder. The bear reared up and swiped its claws across his back. Santo yelled in pain as granules of granite flew away and the bear slammed down on him again, cracking his back in places.

"Alright, that's it!" Santo groaned, as his appendages finally reconnected. He slammed his fists into the dirt. "I'm done with you!"

The ground began to rumble as shards of rock, like two thick spears, rose from the earth, sending cracks along the dome walls and causing it to glitch. Santo groaned and strained as the bear slammed him into the boulder again, cracking his granite sternum, but he focused his might on pulling the rock spears up from the dirt.

As soon as the spears were free of the ground, he slammed them back into each side of the bear, forcing the creature's bulk off him.

With the bear's weight removed, Rockslide swiftly turned to see the creature scrambling to its feet and running away from him with dented sides. He quickly gave chase, collecting the rock spears as he did and hurling them at the creature. They missed, and the beast soon spun around to roar at him again.

Once more Santo rammed into the bear, knocking it down. As soon as their bodies came to a stop, Santo unleashed a volley of punches at the bear's metallic head, knowing he had to unleash everything he had to stop this creature. Santo yelled in pain as the bear's huge claws scraped down his back. He punched left, he punched right, fast and continuous like a pair of jackhammers, and kept going until the bear's head began to cave in and spark. Finally, its claws loosened their grip and fell away from him, dysfunctional. With a final pop and bright flash, the bear's mangled, crumpled head stilled and its red eyes turned black.

Santo stared down at the creature, breathless, as granules of granite fell off him, but looked around at the sounds of splashing at the river. Iara emerged from the water, bloodied and bruised, but alive. Then they heard a rustle from the trees and Sooraya appeared. She, too, was bloodied and bruised, her niqāb torn.

Santo rubbed his arms where they'd been rejoined with his body, and immediately looked up to the window where Vaile's silhouette stood watching.

"Not so bad for organics, huh?" Santo yelled at him.

Vaile stood motionless for a moment, before he turned and walked calmly away. The light in the window went out.

"Where's he going?" Santo said, granite brow furrowing.

"We have to stop him!" Iara said, teeth bared.

"But how do we get out?" Sooraya asked.

They heard the wolf's howl again, soon echoed by several more.

"We gotta find a way and fast," Santo said, getting to his feet. "Or face more of those things. Hurry!"

Iara, Sooraya and Rockslide raced toward the wall of the small arena where their cages had been ejected from, desperately seeking a way out.

"Here!" Sooraya called, tracing her fingers along a crack in the wall. "I feel a breeze." Iara watched her deftly turn into her sand-like form and vanish inside the crack. Moments later the door opened and Sooraya stood in her human form on the other side.

Beyond, Iara saw a darkened tunnel with stairs at the end.

"Hurry before he gets away!" Rockslide said.

With the flutter of a strong breeze, Sooraya turned to Dust once more and flew down the tunnel. Rockslide quickly followed and Iara came up behind, following his slow bulk as it squeezed through the confined space.

"Hurry up, big guy," she said, "or stand aside!"

Rockslide looked around at her quizzically, and as he did, she squeezed past him, following Dust's wake.

They raced up the stairs to see Sooraya in her human form standing on the other side of another open door. They joined her in what appeared to be a clinical corridor of some kind, reminiscent of the lab they'd been in before.

"Which way?" Sooraya asked, looking down both sides of the corridor.

Iara clenched her muscles as her skin turned gray and rough and the fin emerged from her back. She bent down, wincing in pain from her wounds, and placed her palms against the floor, feeling for vibrations.

She felt them coming from the corridor to the right.

"This way!" she said, racing off.

"Wait!" Rockslide called behind her, but Iara couldn't, the smell of her own blood – and hate – fueling her hunt.

Iara saw a doorway up ahead, and beyond, the laboratory where they'd earlier been kept. She charged through the door but found it empty. She skidded to a stop, confused at first, sure she had felt the vibrations coming from this direction.

Then she felt them again.

She spun around as an armored fist caught her jaw and everything went black.

Sooraya saw Iara's body fly past the lab doorway. She immediately transformed into Dust once more, as Santo charged through her, scattering her form.

"Hey!" she hissed to him as she pulled herself together, then flew into the lab after him. They saw Vaile, dressed head to toe in his armor. He gave a metallic smile through the faceplate, then stepped through a doorway leading off the lab, pressing the console on his arm as he did.

Santo roared, charging him, but the door slid closed, and his granite body connected with it, denting it slightly, before the metal bounced back.

"Come back, you coward!" Santo yelled, ramming the door. "I didn't think you were afraid of us organics!"

Sooraya moved to Iara's unconscious form and hovered over her, seeing her stir.

"She alright?" Santo asked, ramming the door again.

Sooraya nodded, then looked up to the large lab console. Screens were scrolling with all kinds of information, and she floated toward it for a closer look. Thousands of files were speeding across the monitors, and along the top she saw an upload rate.

"He's clearing his files," Sooraya said. She glanced over to another screen registering a security alert for an opening door. "He's preparing to leave!"

"Oh no, he's not!" Santo said, taking a few steps back, then running at the locked door with his shoulder. He crashed into it with a loud bang, but only bounced back from the impact. Iara awoke at the noise. Sooraya transformed to her human form and helped her up, as Santo tried again to knock the door down.

"There must be another way," Sooraya said, moving to the console. "Help me figure out how to open that door," she said to Iara, who stood beside her, rubbing her jaw as she searched the console for an answer.

Sooraya started hitting all manner of buttons, and as she did, one of the monitors switched to security vision outside the lab.

There on the screen was the swollen river. It was about to burst its banks from the driving rain, as lightning flashed incessantly overhead.

Sooraya looked to Santo. "The river. Our levee won't hold it."

Santo turned away from the door and moved to check the monitor.

"We have to stop the river from overflowing," Sooraya said.

"But what about Vaile?" Iara asked. "We can't let him get away!"

"We can't let that river flood the town below, either," Sooraya told her.

They heard a rumbling then, that began to shake the lab.

"What is that?" Iara asked. "Thunder?"

An alarm sounded on the console and all eyes turned to it.

"It's Vaile. I think it's transport," Sooraya said.

"No!" Santo said, punching the console, denting it. "He can't get away!"

"I'm afraid I can." Vaile's bitter voice sounded over hidden speakers somewhere. "But thanks for stopping by. I'm sure we'll see each other again soon."

Suddenly a pink light pulsed out from the corner of the room. Sooraya immediately recognized it and turned to Dust as the wave of light hit Iara and Santo, knocking them off their feet, and semi-unconscious. Sooraya, however, in her dust form, was impervious to it. The light ceased, and Sooraya looked back at the screens, as the rumbling increased to a roar, vibrating the lab.

"Hmm, impervious to the pulse," Vaile mused aloud. "And you're thinking much quicker now, too. How about this?"

Sooraya heard a growl and turned to see a synthetic wolf at

the door. It snarled and lowered its body, ready to attack, as several more gathered behind it.

"Wake up!" she screamed to her companions, as the lead wolf pounced. She quickly flew out of the way, rising up to the roof.

But thanks to her scream and the roar of Vaile's departure, Santo quickly got to his feet, shaking off the daze, and automatically swung a granite fist, which sent the lead wolf flying across the room. He trampled another as Iara, back on her feet in shark form, punched at each leaping wolf that came at her. There were six in all, and in a matter of minutes, Santo and Iara had taken care of the lot of them.

The tempo and vibrations that had been running through the lab suddenly eased off again. Now all Iara heard was the raging storm outside.

"He's gone…" Sooraya said, looking at the screens on the console. "Vaile's gone."

Iara caught her breath, before Rockslide angrily kicked one of the mangled synthetic wolves out of the way.

"The river," Sooraya said, looking at the other monitor again. "We have to do something."

"But what?" Iara asked.

Rockslide glanced at the sealed door Vaile had escaped through, then at the mangled metal wolves, then back to the monitor showing the ferocious storm and bursting river outside.

"We kill two birds with one stone," he said resolutely. "Leave now. Stay clear of this place."

"What are you going to do?" Sooraya asked, concerned.

Rockslide's white eyes were darkly serious. "I'm going to destroy this place and levee the river with it." He walked over to the middle of the room, took a deep breath, and punched his hands into the ground. "Go!" he yelled.

"But what if it floods?" Iara asked.

Rockslide glanced at her. "Then you'll come and get me, right?"

Iara's hard face softened briefly and she nodded.

"Then go! Now!"

Iara ran over to the tunnel door where she'd first been brought in and hit a lever beside it. The tunnel door opened. Water slopped inside onto the floor. "Do you have a way out, Sooraya?"

Sooraya nodded, as the ground began to shake with the strain of Santo's power, the floor tiles cracking and breaking apart. "The air vent," she said, turning back into Dust and swiftly disappearing through it.

Iara climbed into the tunnel, took one last look at Rockslide as his granite muscles strained and he groaned loudly, beginning to pull up rock from deep within the earth. She closed the tunnel door, scrambled along to the external exit, found the other lever and pulled it. A wave of water burst through, knocking her back with the force of the rushing river current. She took a moment, tumbling and being battered into the walls, but she soon had her gills working, and then used her powerful leg muscles to get out of there.

Santo roared as the lab around him began to shake and crumble. Large seams of rock pierced up through the floor. He pulled and pushed and twisted the form, smashing the rock through the walls of the lab, out toward the river. Huge chunks of cement and metal beams fell down upon him, as the sky opened and the rain, and river, poured in. The consoles sparked and debris was strewn everywhere – some from Santo's efforts and some from the wild storm making its way inside.

On the brink of his control, and with his arms aching and exhaustion setting in swiftly, Santo took one last breath, pooled the very limits of his strength and yelled from the pain and effort it took to pull the last of the rock up and whip it around like an Olympic shot putter to flatten the facility around him, sending large sections of rock and lab splashing across the river and cutting off its flow.

Iara and Sooraya stood on the furthermost bank and watched in awe as masses of rock were raised and then used to level everything around them. They cowered behind a large tree as debris flew everywhere, carried by Rockslide's momentum and the raging wind. The earth shook and waves of water rushed over their feet.

But then the shaking stilled and only the storm remained.

As the mass of rock finally settled across the river, halting the tide, they peered back around the tree to see most of the facility had been flattened. Everything except the cages and the bunker, which were made of that strange metal. Not even that mass of rock could destroy it.

"Where's Rockslide?" Iara asked, stepping forward and shading her eyes from the rain. Sooraya joined her and they quickly crossed the river – Iara through it and Sooraya over it. They searched among the ruins until they found him, laying on his back in a pool of water.

"Santo!" Sooraya, back in human form, called. She raced toward him, her niqāb drenched with rain.

The two fell down either side of him, lifting him as best they could out of the water.

"Rockslide!" Iara yelled, over the wind, shaking him. "Santo!"

He blinked his white eyes open and stared at them. "Did it work?" he asked huskily.

They nodded, relieved, and helped him sit up. He looked around at the mostly flattened facility and the newly leveed river. He looked pleased before his smile fell.

"Vaile got away," he said.

"We must tell Cyclops and the others what he was doing here," Sooraya said. "See what information we can dig up from these ruins."

"We should tell Wolverine, too," Iara said. "Vaile's a threat to mutants everywhere."

"What's that?" Sooraya said, looking at something in the distance, in the night sky.

They turned to see a red light soaring toward them at speed. As it neared, they realized it was a drone. It moved so fast, seemingly unhindered by the wind, that they barely had time to understand its purpose before it dropped something onto the bunker.

"Whoa!" Rockslide yelled, grabbing Iara and Sooraya and shielding them with his granite form, just as an explosion shook the earth. Flames burst out before the hard rain dampened its spirit. They stared at the aftermath, panting in astonishment, to see a crater where the bunker and cages had once been, as the drone whizzed away into the night.

"He'll start again somewhere else," Sooraya said, concerned.

"So, we'll find him and stop him," Iara snarled.

"We will," Rockslide said, still catching his breath. He looked around again at all the carnage. "Guess we won this round, though."

Sooraya nodded and smiled. "Today is a day I am proud to be a mutant."

Rockslide smiled back at her, then held his fist out to them both. Iara looked at it, then knocked it with her own, and Sooraya did the same.

"Come on," Rockslide said. "Let's get back to our school."

OF DIRT AND BONES

Pat Shand

Phoebe Cuckoo had found herself alone.

The crunch of her footsteps on the dirt path was the only sound she heard as she walked through the woods. She was certain that if she stayed on the path, she'd remember why she'd come out here to begin with. Whatever forgotten purpose had brought her here seemed important, because she walked with haste, rushing to get...

She came to a stop, looking down at a patch of dirt just off the path. The grass in these woods was patchy during this time of year, so this particular spot looked unremarkable. This, she was sure, was the place.

She knelt in her chosen spot, and heard the light, wishbone-snap of her knees popping. Her breath caught from the sudden sound. Everything – her steps, the snap, the rustle of her jacket sleeves brushing against her sides – seemed so intensely loud without her sisters' thoughts in her mind.

Where are you? Phoebe thought, crouching on the balls of her feet.

There was no reply. Or, there was no reply the way that Phoebe would normally expect. Her sisters shared a mind – they were *Three-in-One*, never alone – so her own thoughts were never without an answer. Being one with her sisters was not at all like three minds in one, but was instead like one mind in three bodies. Here and now, in the woods without her sisters, she felt more than alone. Like a shard of herself.

But something *did* change when she reached out into herself, searching for the presence of Sophie and Esme, and she felt whatever pulled her to this path of dirt strengthen. Before she could question it, she found her hands pressed against the cool earth. Her fingers sank into the soil up to her knuckles, and she pulled.

Handful after handful, Phoebe shoveled dirt out of the spot. Soon, the small hole got deeper by the moment. The more she dug, though, the more she found that the dirt was thick with roots, harder and harder to rip through. She would not be deterred. She shifted her body, watching as her hands, pale in the moonlight and caked in dirt, changed form. Her skin rippled, waving before her eyes like a pavement on a hot summer day. Her flesh hardened, its pigment fading until it became entirely translucent, reflecting the moonlight in a beautiful prism of colors.

In her diamond form, she'd be able to dig as far as she needed.

She ripped through the roots, throwing clumps of dirt aside until finally she saw it. She pressed her diamond fingers into the hole, moving dirt away from the gray thing that glowed underneath. She peered down at it, squinting to see through the darkness.

An eye, milky with cataracts, stared back at her.

"Irma? C- Celeste?"

She didn't know why her mind went to her living sisters rather than Esme and Sophie, the two who had already been lost. The two that made the Five into Three. She was as surprised by her own exclamation as she was by what she saw next.

The eye in the hole rotated and then, to Phoebe's further surprise, rose. She watched as what she'd been certain was a human eye shifted and billowed out of the hole as thick, cold fog. Still in her diamond form, she rose to her feet, watching as the fog spread with terrifying speed. It swirled around her, beginning to take shape. She could do nothing but watch as the mist began to coalesce into a humanoid form… and then another. Then, many, many more.

In every direction Phoebe looked, the mist had taken the shape of people, all of them identical, all of them girls. Hair cut off just below the shoulders, pushed back away from their faces. Glowing blue eyes.

They took a step toward Phoebe, all of their knees popping at once with a sick, thunderous *snap*.

Phoebe Cuckoo's eyes were open before she processed that she'd been sleeping. The first thing she saw was her sister Irma, already dressed, reaching through her sleeve to put on deodorant. Irma looked over at her, raising an eyebrow. "Why are you diamond?"

Disoriented, Phoebe looked down at her arms. Indeed, she was in her flawless organic diamond form, and it felt as if she'd had a reason. She'd forgotten. "How long have I been like this?" Phoebe asked, kicking her sheets off.

Celeste, too, was already up. She had her feet propped up

on her desk, going over some notes. Phoebe realized that, for some reason, she was comforted by the distant hum of Celeste studying in her mind. She felt relieved and she didn't know why.

"As long as I've been up," Celeste said, putting her book aside. She pulled out her phone, flipping it around to show Phoebe.

Phoebe saw a picture of herself, sprawled out on the bed, her mouth wide open and her body set in diamond form.

"You didn't!" Phoebe said.

"Hey, you would've, too! It was too good," Celeste said with a playful smirk. She put her phone back on her desk and cracked open her book again. "Don't worry, I didn't post it. Yet."

Phoebe laughed and transitioned back into her normal appearance. "I wonder if that ever happens to the others. Like, do you think Kitty Pryde ever accidentally *shifts* while she's asleep and falls through the floor?"

"Something tells me probably not," Irma said.

Phoebe sat up and got out of bed, shaking her head at the thought of sleeping in diamond form, wondering why she felt unnerved. She couldn't shake the tension. She had no idea why, but it reminded her of a dream she used to have where she'd be frozen in anxiety, knowing she had something important to do. Those nights, she'd toss and turn, racking her sleeping mind for an answer and coming up with nothing.

Phoebe, wanting to keep her anxiety from her sisters, pushed the feeling down and went about her morning ritual: match an outfit, brush her teeth, wash her face, scroll social. She was drying her face when she heard a gentle knock at their door.

"You don't have to knock," Celeste shouted. "You're thinking *very* loudly, Morph."

The door opened and in stepped a bashful Benjamin Deeds.

He was always dressed like a private school student in a jacket and button-up, with parted brown hair that hung over his brow. He reminded Phoebe of how high schoolers used to look in television from the 1990s and 2000s, which she actually liked about him. She'd never tell him, though, that she appreciated his *Dawson's Creek* vibes. And she hoped her sisters wouldn't either.

"Hey, Headmaster Frost wanted me to come get everyone. We have a combat simulation in half an hour in the courtyard," Morph said.

"You're kidding," Phoebe, Irma, and Celeste said at once.

Morph jumped. It seemed he still wasn't used to that. It made all three of them smirk.

"Uhhh, nope. Not kidding," he said. He went to turn away, but Phoebe spoke, stopping him in his tracks.

"Are we three alone in thinking that we've had *enough* battle simulation?" she asked. "What do you think, Morph?"

"Tell us and we promise we won't look ourselves," Irma said with a smile.

"Promise," Celeste added.

Morph shifted uncomfortably in the doorway. "I mean, I get it. Life for us is dangerous, right? They want us to be prepared." He looked down, pausing as if deciding what to say next. "I don't love it, though. Even the stuff I've seen in these simulations would've traumatized me before I found out I was a mutant. I guess I do worry that we're all getting used to… freaky stuff."

"Like us?" the sisters asked as one. They shared a look, suppressing laughter.

"Nah," Morph said. "You're cool."

"Hey, before you go," Phoebe piped up. "Do you ever change

forms when you're sleeping? *I* think it's pretty normal for people like us, but my sisters think I'm a freak because I turned into a beautiful diamond princess mid-snooze. Instead of machine-gun snoring like Celeste."

"Oh, please," Celeste said, rolling her eyes. "You snore, I snore, we all snore together."

"I … you know, I don't think so," Morph said. "With my powers, I have to be close to someone physically in order to transform."

"And that'd never happen while you were asleep," Irma said, lifting a brow. Phoebe and Celeste looked at her, holding a hand to their mouths to hold back laughter.

Morph chuckled to himself. "Cool, thanks for that. I'll see you three down there. I have to go tell the others to–"

Phoebe, Celeste, and Irma closed their eyes, the three of them forming the same mental message at once, spreading it through the school: *Everyone meet in the courtyard in twenty-five minutes for another traumatizing battle simulation. See you there. Kisses.*

"There," the three said. "Done."

Morph nodded, thoughtful. "You know, I'm realizing now that Headmaster Frost could've easily done that … and yet."

"We have a particularly keen insight into Emma Frost, being, you know, clones of her," Phoebe said. "She's someone who can make her own coffee perfectly well but finds that it tastes *that much better* when she asks someone to go out of their way to fetch her a cup."

"We're trying not to be that way," Irma continued.

"Although, if you wanted to have three cups for us ready in the courtyard when we all meet, we wouldn't protest," Celeste added.

"Kidding," Phoebe said.

Irma shrugged. "Or are we?"

Morph gave an awkward salute as he backed out, leaving the three sisters to laugh together. Phoebe liked Morph – they all did – so it was all in good fun. There was something that felt so good about laughing with her sisters and knowing that everything she said, everything she *thought*, would be perfectly understood. It was beyond that, though. Beyond understanding, beyond even empathy, there was the Stepford Cuckoos. Three-in-One.

Never alone.

When Phoebe, Irma, and Celeste Cuckoo arrived in the courtyard, they realized that they were far less alone in their opinion than they thought. Two of their professors – Emma Frost and Kitty Pryde – were in the middle of a heated debate with a group of students. Others might call it an onslaught.

The students had gathered early to let their thoughts on the recent battle simulations be known. Among them Goldballs, Angel, Tempus, and the tall, dark, and looks-like-Tony-Stark Hijack. Before the sisters even approached, the psychic waves coming off the group of students were palpable.

"The self-control on Tempus," Phoebe whispered to her sisters. "In her mind, she's saying all of this with *way* dirtier language."

"*Way* dirtier," Irma added with a smirk.

Celeste cleared her throat as they approached the student X-Men versus professor X-Men conflict. "We, Three-in-One, agree with those who dissent."

"Oh, come on," Emma Frost said, rolling her eyes. She

stood nearly a foot taller than her younger clones, with blue eyes that spoke to a life of experiences that even the sisters couldn't fathom. Her mind was the one that scared them the most, so they avoided reading it... not that it would be easy these days. Frost had lost some of her powers, which made the Cuckoos previous activity of messing with their least favorite professor's mind not quite as safe as it had been. These days, they knew well enough to leave that particular telepath's mind alone.

Kitty Pryde, who was downright chipper and vibrant compared to Frost's cool demeanor, spoke up. "Listen, we absolutely hear you. Please trust us that we're taking your thoughts into account."

"Key word being thoughts," Frost added sharply, shooting a look at Phoebe and her sisters. "I, too, heard your message to the others."

"And that's OK," Kitty said, forcing a smile at Frost as if to say *I got this one*. "There's so much that we want to teach you, and a lot of it comes from us wishing that *we* learned more when we were younger. There were times when things got scary out there in the real world and I never, in the heat of the moment, thought, *Man, I wish I trained less*. We want to help you avoid making the same mistakes that we did. Taking the same losses that we did."

"And make no mistake," Frost said. "While we *are* listening... you'd be mistaken if you interpret that as us shirking our responsibility to train you in order to spare your feelings. This part of your schooling isn't supposed to be enjoyable."

"Is it supposed to traumatize us?"

Phoebe looked at the source of the voice. Morph approached

them, his hands in his pockets, already looking like he regretted speaking up. She smiled at him.

Frost's stern expression didn't waver. "If it does, that'll be on you to overcome it."

"Well, now–" Kitty said.

"Bad experiences are part of the training at the Institute," Frost said sharply, cutting her colleague off. "You should take those experiences with you. Build on them. Grow from them. If you let a simulation drag you down, I shudder to think what would happen to you when facing off with something…"

The sky began to darken. Phoebe glanced at her sisters, who were already looking her way. She knew what was happening.

"Truly dark," Frost finished. As the words left her lips, the darkness of the sky spread like ink in water. Phoebe and her sisters grimaced. Emma Frost wasn't just responding to their concerns. She was lulling them into a sense of normalcy with the conversation so that she could pull the rug out from under them by starting her psychic simulation.

Phoebe looked around at her fellow students. Irma and Celeste were closest to her, with Morph right behind her. A few yards away were the others, who were reacting to the now pitch-black sky, which began to surge with purple energy. Emma Frost and Kitty Pryde had faded from sight. They weren't players in the psychic theatre that Emma was putting on.

Phoebe knew that something would be coming to attack them soon, so it was just a matter of judging where it would be coming from. To her left was the school, to her right, the large yard stretched on for a long distance before leading to the woods.

I'll keep an eye on the sky. Irma, look left. Celeste, stay right, Phoebe thought.

Silence.

The realization hit Phoebe with a familiar sinking feeling in her gut. She looked at her sisters, knowing from their faces that they'd just made the same discovery.

They were cut off from each other. Emma's psychic simulation had left them *alone*.

Phoebe, suddenly uneasy, scanned her surroundings again. She kept going back to the woods, imagining herself walking through them. Then, for some reason, digging. She shook off the thought, worried that whatever Emma was doing in this simulation was also tinkering with her mind. She needed to focus on the attack that would be coming, so she could be ready.

It came with a sound like a thunderclap. The purple energy coursing through the black sky came down in a concentrated beam, rushing toward where Morph stood. By the time Phoebe turned to see, Morph was engulfed in its light. In a flash of violet, the beam of energy came and went.

Where Morph had been standing was scorched grass, smoke rising from it, the burnt blades slick with red.

Phoebe gaped at the scene, looking back toward her sisters. She knew it couldn't be real, that Emma Frost would never hurt one of them, but *this*...

Turning her eyes to the sky to anticipate the next strike, Phoebe searched for Morph's thoughts in the back of her mind. She reached and reached and... nothing.

Faster than her mind could process, another bolt of purple light came down, narrowly missing Hijack. He had thrown himself to the ground to avoid the blast, landing next to Triage.

He was one of the only ones not to protest the simulation, which Phoebe wondered if he was beginning to regret. As Triage helped Hijack up, using his healing power to get his fellow mutant back to full strength, yet another purple beam came from the sky.

"Look out!" Phoebe called, but it was too late. The beam engulfed them both. More violent than the first, it left a pit where it had hit.

"How are we supposed to fight against this thing?" Angel yelled. "I can't even *see* anything!"

"Well, I'm just gonna start whaling on the sky until something falls out," Goldballs shouted, a ball of pure gold forming from his chest. "Watch my back!"

"Got you," Angel said, flying after Goldballs as the mutant began to shoot golden orbs at the sky one after the other. They came down just as quick, hitting nothing.

"What's our move?" Phoebe asked Irma and Celeste.

"Well, why don't we make like a sleeping Phoebe…" Irma said, her body shifting, her skin beginning to shimmer, "… and go diamond."

Phoebe and Celeste followed suit, the three sisters transforming into their diamond state as two beams came down at once. One of them took out Goldballs and blew Angel back, sending him tumbling across the yard. Another was aimed at Tempus, who used her power to encase the bolt in a temporal bubble. The end of the bolt was suspended before her in a shimmering orb, frozen in time. Tempus looked at the bolt, intrigued.

"Hey, Cuckoos," she called. "Keen on firing back?"

Phoebe, Irma, and Celeste didn't need their hivemind to know what to do next. The three of them activated their telekinesis together, turning the trapped bolt of violent purple energy back toward the sky. They used their power to toss the energy directly at the source that was sending the bolts downward. As the time-trapped bolt sped toward the sky, Tempus deactivated her temporal bubble. The bolt hit the sky, sending veins of red light through the darkness.

The ground shook violently with the reaction of the bolt, knocking Phoebe off her feet. As her diamond back hit the ground, she saw the sky surge with energy, seeming to swell with power before sending a shower of simultaneous bolts of energy directly at them.

Phoebe, covering her head, rolled out of the way. She knew her diamond form could take any blow, but she didn't want to see if it hurt. She sprang to her knees, ready to turn the incoming bolts back toward the sky, when she heard what sounded like the almost musical noise of a crystal glass being shattered.

She looked at the spot where Irma had been standing, which was littered with what looked like a pile of charred glass. Before she could process it, she felt the hard impact of a diamond hitting her in the side. Celeste, her eyes wide with panic, tackled Phoebe.

The violet beam struck the area where Phoebe had been standing a moment before. Where Celeste's lower half had been. Phoebe, horrified, was still holding her sister's hand as the bolt struck. Her vision blinded by the brightness, Phoebe looked at what was left of Celeste, a feeling swelling inside her like she'd never felt.

The reality of the assault being a simulation fell away to pure, blind rage as Phoebe stood and stepped forward. She turned all her telekinetic energy skyward, feeling her muscles tense as she reached inward for the source of the energy. The tension she'd felt since the morning was replaced entirely by fury – hungry to lash out and cause pain equal to hers. Using every bit of power she had, gritting her teeth, and clenching her diamond fists so tightly that she felt her palms begin to crack, she directed all her energy at the sky. Screaming at the top of her lungs, she forced the purple energy up and away, sending rips of red through the dark clouds as if she was making the sky itself bleed. The purple energy was completely overcome with red, which spread throughout the entire field as Phoebe's ripping scream carried on.

She continued reaching, pushing, telekinetically tearing at the sky until–

Snap.

Before Phoebe could process the reality of what had happened, Kitty Pryde was at her side. Her professor was saying something to her, touching her face, but she couldn't hear it over the cacophony roaring in her mind. Voices. Other voices.

Phoebe? Phoebe, are you OK?

Celeste and Irma. Phoebe looked and there they were, right behind Kitty, watching her with concern. As if they hadn't just…

"How do you feel? Can you hear me?" Kitty's voice came into focus as Phoebe gained her bearings. She looked around. Morph was there, already walking back to the school. The sky was bright and cloudless. Emma Frost, her expression blank, stared off toward the woods. The other students were talking amongst each other, some of them laughing and others quiet, but Phoebe could hear their thoughts. She wasn't alone. It had been awful for them all.

"Did you see what I saw?" Phoebe asked, looking at her sisters. "You saw me die, didn't you?"

"No," Irma said. "I didn't."

"I saw Irma die, but then the last thing I did was push you out of the way," Celeste said. "Then it ended for me."

"That's because Phoebe won the battle simulation," Frost said, her tone quiet but her voice carrying. "Not only did she survive, but she was able to use an incorporeal, elemental foe's own power against it. With the help of Tempus, that is. She even managed to physically manifest her power during the simulation, which I was attempting to suppress. Very impressive. And yet… unfortunate for some."

"Come on, Emma," Kitty snapped. She looked at Phoebe, who was confused. "Don't… don't look. You didn't mean to."

"Look at what?" Phoebe asked. She followed Emma's gaze and saw that her professor wasn't looking at the woods, but instead what looked like a small pile of brown and black. Slowly, Phoebe rose to her feet.

"It wasn't your fault," Kitty said. "You don't have to…"

Ignoring her teacher's words, Phoebe walked over to the pile. She could now see that it was a goose. Its long, black neck was twisted at an odd angle, and its wing seemed bent back. Broken. It was dead.

"I did this," Phoebe said.

The goose's eyes stared blankly, and Phoebe's eyes burned with tears. She gritted her teeth and looked away, trying to feign anger rather than the sadness and shame that had replaced it.

"A flock passed by at the wrong time," Emma said. Her tone,

unlike Kitty's, was matter of fact. "You shouldn't have been able to physically manifest your telekinesis, but you had an incredible surge of power that I hadn't accounted for. I–"

Phoebe met Emma's gaze. The action seemed to cut Emma's words off mid-sentence. Rather than look away, Emma held Phoebe's stare.

"I didn't mean for this to happen," Emma finished.

Phoebe had a retort in her head. She wanted to call Emma Frost a psychopath and challenge her for putting them through that horrific simulation as punishment for questioning her teaching methods. She wanted to tell Frost that what she'd just seen was worse than anything she'd even *heard* of a mutant going through. But she'd save that thought for her sisters, who were already hearing it. For now, she wanted to be as far away from Emma Frost as possible.

That night, Phoebe walked through the woods again.

This time, it wasn't a dream.

When you share a mind with two others, even when you love them more than anyone of a single mind could understand, you become skilled at tucking thoughts away. In the days following Emma Frost's battle simulation, Phoebe Cuckoo did just that. She didn't tell the others what she did in the woods and she pretended that, like them, she was fine with what had happened. It wasn't until four days after the simulation that she would return to the woods, and this time she wouldn't be alone.

Phoebe went to Morph, not because she was nursing a crush on him, but because he'd seen the least of the horrors. He was, after all, the first to be struck by the purple energy, which Phoebe later learned had expelled him from the psychic simulation. Like a video game.

When she asked Morph to take a walk, he looked behind her, confused. "Alone?"

"We're not action figures," Phoebe said. "We're sold separately, if we want."

Chuckling bashfully, Morph followed Phoebe as she walked into the woods. She was practicing the art – or what she thought of as an art – of not prying. It was instinct for her to read minds, the same way it was instinct for others to smell, to taste, to listen. To keep the privacy of those around her, on the occasion that she chose to, she had to actively shut part of herself off, constantly pulling back. Why did she do it? She often found that the words people chose to express themselves, true or not, said something more interesting about them than their jumble of thoughts and emotion. She knew how Morph *felt* most days. She wanted to hear him put his thoughts into words.

"You missed out back there," she said.

"Hmm?"

"The simulation. You went first."

He nodded, tightening his lips as if he expected a joke at his expense. Phoebe didn't take offense. She and her sisters had a habit of making an ill-timed joke here and there, and she knew it. When the joke didn't come, Morph looked at her, his expression softening. "Triage and Tempus told me I was lucky."

"Yes."

"What you saw… why do you think she'd do that to us? Do you think she *really* thinks that could help?"

"It can," Phoebe said. She hated to give Frost credit, as she believed that her professor was ill-suited for her role. Frost was everything that Phoebe didn't want to be. She *was* cruel… but Phoebe had come to think that cruelty, in a world that wanted you dead, wasn't the worst thing you could do. Perhaps, if she and her sisters had been crueler, they would still be Five-in-One. For mutants, real life outside the Institute could be closer to what Frost's simulation showed than Phoebe believed the others realized.

"You don't think that," Morph said. "I mean, you three were the ones who said that this stuff was traumatizing. I spoke to Kitty, and she said–"

"It *is* traumatizing," Phoebe interrupted. "Emma Frost is traumatized. It's made her into what she is, and if what happened out there happened in real life… imagine someone like her on our side. She wants us to be like that. Like her."

"Man…" Morph said, looking down. They'd walked along most of the dirt path. Past the spot that Phoebe had visited, where she was struck with intense déjà vu. She'd felt it the night she went to the woods as well. It reminded her of that *what-am-I-supposed-to-be-doing* tension that had haunted her.

Phoebe waited for Morph to continue. She knew he wanted her to reply, but she didn't acquiesce. They stopped and he turned to face her.

"I don't know!" he said. "Don't you think… I mean, this is our *school*. Don't you think it's messed up? That just because we're mutants, that we're, like – we're *drafted* into a war, pretty much. Humans get to choose to fight. Us, it's just a given. Mutants fight to defend themselves, fight to be heroes, and then they die. Is that how it's always going to be? Is that…"

Morph trailed off, his face going slack. Phoebe knew

something was behind her from the way his eyes shifted. The odd thing was, there wasn't a third mind in the forest that she could sense. Slowly, the hairs on her neck standing up, Phoebe looked over her shoulder.

Relief flooded Phoebe's chest when she saw it. A stag, a head taller than her and with antlers that reached for the trees, stood a yard away. Its head was turned away from them, and its fur was covered in what looked like dirt. Had it been rolling around in the mud? Phoebe took a step forward, intrigued by the beautiful animal but still confused that she couldn't feel its mind. That had never happened before. She felt a stillness, similar to what she'd feel from an inanimate object. Or what she'd feel if she tried to work her way into the mind of a more skilled telepath, like Emma. For a moment, her heart sank, and she wondered if Emma had somehow tricked her into another simulation.

Wow, she thought, approaching the stag. *I really am traumatized.*

The stag turned its massive head toward her, and Phoebe got her answer.

"Phoebe, careful! Something's wrong with that thing!" Morph called, but he didn't need to. She already saw.

The stag's fur wasn't covered in mud, but moss and rot. Its face was mostly bone, skeletal at the mouth and around its deep, sunken eyes. It peered at her from those empty sockets, its mind silent. Behind it, the forest began to teem with shapes, moving toward them.

Following the incident with the creature that Morph would refer to as "the zombie deer", Phoebe went to Kitty Pryde. At first, she believed that this was some sort of sick continuation of Emma Frost's lessons, but both Kitty and Cyclops assured her that her accusation was off base. The teachers, Emma Frost included, promised to investigate, but they didn't have to venture into the forest to do so. After seeing the shapes in the forest, Phoebe and Morph had run back to the school and a herd of dead animals followed. Rotting foxes, skeletal deer, headless birds, and all manner of undead creatures emerged from the woods, gathering in the Institute's courtyard.

This, of course, led to panic.

The professors initiated a lockdown, but it was more in an effort to keep the panic to a minimum. The truth was, the dead animals weren't hurting anyone. Efforts were made to study their behavior, but there *was* no behavior to be studied. They weren't even moving after their initial trek. They were, very simply, standing like a gallery of macabre statues. The professors attempted to move them, with Emma using telekinesis and Scott using force, but the animals didn't fight back. They simply returned after being pushed back. Word in the school was that Scott had floated the idea of using his power of optic blasts to incinerate the animals, but the other professors believed it would be better to understand the root of the problem before turning it to ash.

This led to a decision that intrigued Phoebe. Triage, whose sole power was healing, was called forth to join the professors and the undead creatures in the courtyard three days after the animals had arrived. Phoebe, Irma, Celeste, Morph, and Tempus gathered near the exit to watch from the windows. Phoebe and her sisters explained to the others what was going on.

"Triage is scared," Irma said. "One of the very first horror films he saw was an old zombie movie, so this is bringing back memories. He's not saying that out loud, though, so keep it a secret. Shh."

"They think that, as a healer, Triage can potentially expand his powers to help here," Celeste said.

"He can't heal the dead, though," Phoebe continued. "The teachers know that. They're asking him to attempt to feel for the life energy that *was* there, to see if there's a third party manipulating these creatures."

"Cyclops thinks that someone is using them to watch the school," Irma said.

"Yes," Phoebe added. "I think he's wrong."

"Triage is going to do it, but he's uneasy," Celeste said. "He's trying now. I can feel him reaching into them."

As Celeste continued to narrate, the students watched it unfold through the window. Triage stood before the undead animals, his hands spread and his eyes closed, pushing his abilities to their capacity. Phoebe could feel him trying to find some semblance of life in the animals, something to latch onto, but she could tell from his thoughts alone that it was futile. Triage knew well what life felt like. Life was his instrument, the force that he could bring out in people to heal them... and he found none in these animals, neither the life that once inhabited the bodies nor the life of someone using them for a dark purpose.

Triage rolled his shoulders. He spread his feet out, inhaled deeply, and gritted his teeth.

"He's pushing," Phoebe said. "He's–"

Without so much as a sound, Triage was blown off his feet. It was so sudden that it looked as if he'd been picked up by the wind. As he lifted off the ground, Phoebe, who had been pushing deep into his mind, felt a sudden *snap*.

Emma Frost used her telekinesis to stop Triage from hitting the ground. Gently, she lowered him into her arms, where he landed, light as a feather and in her control, but clearly unable to stand on his own.

"Did you see that? He just went flying," Morph said.

"That's so weird. There wasn't any energy or anything. It didn't even look like the grass under him moved. He just got *snatched* up," Tempus said, peering through the window. "What did that?"

Phoebe looked at Irma and Celeste who, too, looked confused… but not the way that she felt. Speaking to their collective hivemind, Phoebe thought, *Did you feel it? The snap?*

Irma and Celeste turned to her. *What?*

When Triage was blown back, I was reading him. I felt…

Phoebe could tell from her sisters' expressions that, no, they had *not* felt the same thing that she had.

That in and of itself was as much of a mystery to Phoebe as the animals.

That night in her dreams, Phoebe returned to the woods. She journeyed down that dirt path, which was now bordered by a parade of decomposing animals. In the dream, they weren't lining up but rather slumped over each other in horrific piles. Phoebe, a buzzing tension building in her, doubled back to run away. However, the path to the school was now blocked by a towering mound of animal corpses. On top of that macabre hill of bones and rot sat four figures – Phoebe's sisters, with Irma and Celeste in matching black dresses in the center, bordered by two skeletal girls in white. Phoebe felt like she would scream, but she opened her mouth and a different sound came out. Five voices, only one of them her own, saying:

"Go back."

Phoebe, nauseated, tore her eyes away from her sisters'. She turned and raced through the darkness until she found the grassless patch of dirt. She dug and dug and dug... and woke up to the feeling of something within her breaking.

The next night, it was the same.

The next, the same.

She'd wake up in her diamond form every time. The third time it happened, Phoebe sat up in bed and looked to her sisters, her sisters that shared the same consciousness, yet who slept soundly, dreamlessly.

Finally, Phoebe knew she wouldn't be able to sleep. Even worse, she was beginning to figure out *why*.

She crept out of her bedroom, careful not to rouse her sisters and walked down the hall. She came to a stop in front of Morph's door. He'd been with her when the animals first came, and she'd want a different sort of company for what she was about to do. However, she couldn't help but feel that he was right about what he said. They *had* been born into an inherited battle, not a battle of choice. Phoebe understood that. The words of her sisters, two of them long gone and still missed, repeated in her mind.

"Go back."

She knew what she had to do. For the first time she could remember, she was facing something entirely alone. This was her battle. She wouldn't force Morph into it.

There was one trip she needed to make, though, before she ventured out.

She knocked softly on Triage's door. She felt his mind stir

from sleep and waited patiently as he got up. He cracked the door, his hair jostled from sleep, looking at Phoebe with his soft, brown eyes. He kept to himself mostly and tried to fence his mind off from abilities like Phoebe's, but the truth was, he felt deeply. He feared deeply and he hoped deeply... he also crushed deeply, with his affections squarely aimed at Phoebe's sister, Irma. Because of all that, Phoebe felt bad about reading his thoughts to the others earlier that day, especially considering how he'd been hurt.

"How are you feeling?" she asked.

"You were watching, too, huh?"

"Yes."

"I'm OK. Felt like I got hit by a truck at the time, but at the infirmary they said there was no damage," he said. "Frost thinks it was a psychic blast, which... you know, hurts at the time but doesn't leave a mark."

Phoebe nodded. That's exactly what she'd come to find out.

"I'm sorry that happened to you," she said.

He looked over her shoulder, his brow furrowed. "Is there, uh... a reason you wanted to talk? It's pretty late."

"No, I... I just wanted to make sure you're OK."

He raised his eyebrows. "Well, I mean... thanks. Thank you. I'm good."

She paused, unsure how to proceed. She wanted to ask Triage something, but she didn't want to show her hand. If all went according to plan, she hoped to bury this without anyone knowing. Without anyone finding out the truth.

"Hey..." Phoebe started, trying to sound casually curious. "What did you feel?"

"Like I busted my butt."

"*Before* that," she said. She forced an eyeroll. He'd expect that. "What did you feel coming from the animals?"

Triage shrugged. "At first, nothing. And then – I mean, I think it was what *I* felt. It all just happened so fast."

"No, what were you going to say? And then what?" She added a sharpness to her tone, trying to sound impatient rather than thirsty for his answer.

"I felt… a *break*," he said. "Like something breaking, over and over again."

Phoebe closed her eyes. There it was. Of course, the healer would be the one to feel it. Frost had been attempting to mine the animals for emotion. Triage found the source of the problem. A final, decisive explosion of pain. A snap.

"That makes no sense," Phoebe said with a scoff and walked away. She heard the door close in the distance and sighed, wondering if he'd bought her performance.

It didn't matter, really. What mattered was that she'd confirmed her fears. She knew what had hurt Triage and if she didn't finish this tonight, so would everyone else.

They'd all know that it had been Phoebe.

Phoebe crept to the door leading out to the courtyard. She knew that she'd have to be quick, as there would certainly be some sort of alert sent to the professors once she opened it. Wisdom cautioned her to wait for the morning, but she wasn't interested in being wise. She wanted to correct her mistake before someone else discovered it. She couldn't be the girl everyone blamed for the herd of zombie forest animals. She reached for the doorknob and, as her fingers touched its cool surface, she was startled by a voice behind her.

"Are you crazy? Where are you going?"

She turned to see Morph wearing a tank-top and sweatpants, looking at her through squinted eyes.

"Don't call me crazy," Phoebe said. "And don't look at me like that."

"You're going to the animals," Morph said. "Do you think you could've picked a creepier time?"

"I think I can end this," she said. "I want to do it before – well, before things escalate. The way that Triage was thrown back today, I just… I think I can get this under control."

"Why you?" Morph asked.

"Excuse me?"

"Why *you*?" he repeated. "Just because you found them first? I was right there with you."

"That has nothing to do with it," Phoebe said. "It's because…"

Her mind raced to find a lie and came up with nothing. Briefly, she considered messing with his mind and sending him back to bed, but she knew she'd have to answer questions from him later if she did that. She wanted to end this quickly and let it go. If *one* person had to know the truth, she could do worse than Morph.

"It's because I think it's my fault," she said. "And if you tell anyone, you'll regret it."

He raised an eyebrow at her. "Fine. Can I at least come?"

Phoebe opened her mouth to decline, but she stopped herself. She'd tried to do this alone, tried to spare Morph whatever this night would lead to… but companionship had just shown up. She knew that she was supposed to push back until he gave in and left her alone. It was the normal thing to do, to resist when someone offers to do something "crazy" just because you're already doing it. Normal, though, was fiction.

"OK."

She opened the door and was instantly greeted by the smell of rot. It carried in the wind, permeated the courtyard, which was now an increasingly dense assembly of death. She and Morph advanced past a staring wolf with its bottom jaw missing, stepped over a squirrel whose skin remained on its face but whose body was a fragile skeleton, maneuvered around a deer with a festering bite mark on its throat. They were all silent, still.

Until, that is, Phoebe stepped onto the dirt path into the forest.

At once, the animals turned toward them in a chorus of cracking bones and rustling fur.

Phoebe's breath caught in her throat as the dark shapes of the animals moved.

Morph sputtered out, "D- Did they just–"

Before he could finish his sentence, the dark wall of rotting flesh took a collective step forward.

"Uh… Phoebe," Morph said, his eyes widening. "We should go back."

Phoebe steeled herself. "You can."

She strode into the woods and an increasingly panicked Morph followed. Behind them, the animals fell into the background… but their dark silhouettes advanced through the woods, following Phoebe and Morph like a macabre shadow. What began as a lumbering, rhythmic sound of paws, hooves, and wings began to increase in speed the further the pair walked into the woods.

"They're getting closer," Morph said. "What are we going to do?"

"Stand close," Phoebe said. "It's going to be OK."

The truth was, she'd had no idea this was going to happen. Ever since the animals took their first step forward, she'd begun to question herself. She knew, though, as the animals began to break into a run behind them, that there was no going back. If she lost faith in her plan, she'd have to call for help. Then, everyone would know.

Phoebe and Morph were halfway down the path when the first animal attacked.

It was so dark that Phoebe didn't even see the bird until it was almost on them. It swooped down, its skeletal wings spread, its claws reaching.

"Watch out!" Morph called as it dove through the air toward them.

Phoebe's eyes burned blue, and the bird hit what looked like an invisible force field before them.

The dead bird collided with the shield. Its brittle bones shattered on impact. It fell to the forest floor as a clump of brown and white. Phoebe looked down at it and thought of the goose, its wing bent and its neck broken. Her eyes welled with tears and, this time, she couldn't stop them from being seen.

Morph looked at her and there was no blame in his eyes. Of course, he still didn't know. Phoebe could feel his mind racing with one emotion: fear.

She didn't have time to think about that, though. She broke into a run, reaching her hand out for Morph to grab. He did, and she widened her telekinetic shield as the animals accelerated to a thunderous pace. Phoebe couldn't help but cast a look back over her shoulder. Behind them, the darkness of the woods seemed as if it was shrinking in on them. The animals could no longer be seen separately in the darkness. Instead, it looked like the mountain of bones and fur and decay from her dream. There was no one sitting on this hill of death, though, and no warning words to be given. It was just coming for them, faster and faster.

Phoebe came to a stop, trying to ignore the sounds of growling wolves, howling coyotes, screeching birds, and gnashing teeth. She knelt before the dirt path. The same one she'd dreamt and then forgotten, only to return to in person the next day. After the incident.

Morph hung close to Phoebe as her telekinetic shield buckled against the animals ramming against it. Panic rose in her chest as she looked down at the dirt, realizing that she wouldn't be able to maintain the shield and do what it was she had to do. Morph had been right. She *should* have waited, but she let shame influence her choice. She looked at Morph with apologetic eyes, about to tell him that they should go back.

But instead, Morph steeled himself. As Phoebe's shield shimmered, getting tighter and tighter, letting the animals dangerously close, Morph turned toward the undead creatures. He breathed in, and then out.

"They're still animals, after all," he said softly. He closed his eyes and began to let out a prominent wave of warmth. Phoebe felt immediately comforted by it before she realized what he was doing.

"Your pheromone power," she said, relieved.

"Their spirits may be gone, but whatever is using them as puppets is still using their bodies," he said. "I can keep them away… but not for long."

Phoebe nodded. She knelt to the ground, shifted into her diamond form, and began digging.

"What are you doing?" Morph asked, his voice wavering. The shield was gone, and the animals were no longer rushing them, but they weren't backing up either. The wolves hadn't stopped growling. "I thought you had an idea how to stop whoever's doing this."

As she dug, Phoebe opened her mouth to tell Morph that she *was* doing exactly that, but another voice cut in, harsh and loud.

"*She* is doing it."

Phoebe looked up to see Emma Frost, glowing with an intense, dazzling blue telekinetic aura, backed up by a horrified Triage who was engulfed in the same aura. They walked through the raging undead animals, unharmed, with the animals even parting to let them through.

"Frost… what are you doing here? Triage? How–"

"Your sisters expressed their concern for you to me earlier tonight," Frost said. "Then, Triage came to me fearful that you came to his bedroom and read his mind."

"I didn't!" Phoebe said.

"I'm sorry," Triage said, looking ashamed. "You were acting weirder than usual."

Emma frowned at Phoebe. "That, paired with you and Morph leaving the school in the middle of the night, left me rather concerned. *What* in the world is all of this?"

"I'm fixing my mistake," Phoebe said, her hands still in the dirt.

Emma turned to Morph. She touched his temple and her glowing blue aura spread to him. "Good work. Clever use of your power. Go back to the school now. With my shield around you, you will be unharmed."

"Can I go back too?" Triage asked.

"Phoebe came to you," Emma said. "She likely had some purpose for that conversation. Am I right?"

"Yes," Phoebe said.

"Triage, stay," Emma said. "Morph, go. Trust me. You will be safe."

Morph shared a look with Phoebe, who was moved that he'd check in with her like that. She nodded. She couldn't imagine how scared he was to go back alone, but she knew that, despite calling her cruel, Emma would be true to her word. He'd be safe.

Without another word, Morph departed. He ran down the dirt path, with the animals parting for him like royalty. Phoebe couldn't help but marvel at Emma's power. What she'd told Morph days before, about how Emma's trauma had made her into an incredible warrior, was true. She'd said that in order to get Morph to talk about his concerns, but it wasn't a lie. The problem was that Phoebe, too, wished that she didn't live a life where she had to aspire to be such an incredible warrior. She didn't want to prepare for a situation in which she could lose another piece of herself. Five-in-One to Four-in-One to Three-in-One to… what next?

Triage stood behind her, watching Morph go, and Phoebe knew that he badly wished to head back as well. Emma stood before Phoebe, expressionless. She'd wait forever for Phoebe to explain herself if it took that long. Phoebe knew it to be true.

Phoebe looked down to the hole. "The goose."

Emma nodded. "The goose you killed. You buried it out here."

"It's not fair that it… That simulation was *insane*," Phoebe said. "It died because of me. And because of *you*."

Emma's expression didn't falter. "You think unearthing it will send these animals back to their resting place?"

"I know that this began when I killed it," Phoebe replied. "And then, when Triage was hurt, I felt… something inside me. My sisters felt *nothing*. I know that all this is because of me."

"What do you mean?" Triage piped up. "*You* sent me flying?"

Phoebe gritted her teeth. "This is exactly what I didn't want to happen. I didn't mean to hurt–"

"You used your powers without thought," Emma said. "You felt severed from your sisters. You tapped into something wholly *you*. You let rage overcome you and you lashed out mindlessly. What would happen if that was something you could control?"

Phoebe glared at Emma. "I would've taken care of this."

"Do it, then. Dig."

Phoebe looked away from Emma, wishing so strongly that Triage wasn't there, that she was scared she'd accidentally invade his mind and make him run away. She breathed in, collected her thoughts, and turned to the ground.

Even with Emma there, the hair on the back of Phoebe's neck stood up as she dug, the growling wolves and incessant cries of the undead birds growing to an almost unbearable cacophony. She ripped the roots with her diamond hands until she felt the cold, damp softness of the goose. Cringing, scared to break its delicate bones, she pulled it from the earth. Clumps of dirt fell from its corpse. She looked at it and gasped.

Its chest glowed a bright red, with veins of crimson glow spiderwebbing through its body. Phoebe looked around and saw the undead animals' eyes all begin to glow red in response to the goose's brightening light. She stepped back in fear. Emma put an arm around her. Phoebe looked up at the woman who she'd grow up to resemble exactly and was, for the first time, comforted. Emma studied her with sharp clarity. Something beyond understanding. Beyond empathy. Something she thought that only her other parts could feel. It made Phoebe's breath catch in her throat and her eyes sting with tears.

"Tell me what happened," Emma said.

"I… I dreamed of this before… before even the simulation," Phoebe said, her mind racing.

"Your power is more than you know," Emma said. "Dreams aren't hitched to time. Not your dreams, anyway. Not ours."

"It felt like they actually died," Phoebe said, and the tears spilled down her cheeks. She wanted to look away from Emma, but she couldn't. "I felt… I felt *severed* from them, alone, and I lashed out. I wanted to break the simulation. I wanted…"

"It's OK," Emma said. "You can say it."

"I wanted to hurt you."

"I'm sorry I made you feel that way. What I want for you, all of you, is to never experience in actuality what you see in the simulation."

Phoebe looked at the goose, its chest glowing red like the sky in the simulation. "I think… I put something *in* it when I killed it. Fear of…"

Phoebe closed her eyes, tears streaming down her cheeks as she remembered her first dream of the woods. The fog forming into many girls who looked just like her. Ghosts. The dream where she alone lived.

"Fear of being one," Phoebe said.

"I think so as well," Emma said. "I felt your connection, but I didn't know what it was. You felt for this creature you killed – that *we* killed – and you buried it, not knowing that you'd left within it a psychic remnant. A remnant that desperately fears death, that wants so badly to cling to life for both yourself and your sisters, and that psychic remnant spread, infecting the woods."

Phoebe knew it was true. She hadn't the words to describe it as Emma did, but she felt it. She looked at Emma who, through the fog of her tears, could've been mistaken for Irma or Celeste.

"What do I do?" Phoebe asked.

"The same thing you did in the simulation," Emma said. "You pushed through even my control, and you tapped into something deeper within yourself. That fear is just a piece of you… *you* are more powerful. Reach into *it* and push through. Push through the terror."

"How?"

"The same feeling you experienced when you saw your sisters die," Emma said. "Use that power. Don't let it be a one-time burst of rage. Make it your own. And Triage?"

Triage's eyes widened. "Y- Yes?"

"The forest needs *healing*," Emma said. "When Phoebe takes care of her business… you will be able to do yours. Be ready."

Triage, nervous, nodded. He put his hands to the ground and closed his eyes. "This isn't anything I'm used to…" he said.

Phoebe looked at him. She wanted to say "sorry" but instead she said, "Same."

She knelt down to the poor goose and closed her eyes. She felt its soft feathers in her hand and winced as she pictured it falling from the sky. She felt the cold energy within its chest push back at her, pulsing in response to her thoughts, resisting her control. She thought of the red lights in the sky as she'd destroyed Emma's simulation. She thought of her sisters, one shattered with her hand still in Phoebe's and the other a pile of rubble. She thought of Emma Frost and how much she blamed her for the past, for the loss of her sisters, and how here she was now, holding her as she pushed. She didn't feel her energy retreating from the forest, though. She felt Triage's mind pushing, trying to use the power he normally reserved for healing people to heal the living forest as well as the bodies that had once been alive in there. It wasn't enough, though. Phoebe's psychic trauma was in them all, festering and rotting.

She had to dig deeper. She had to push not only into herself, but into Triage's mind and accelerate *his* power. She thought about what Emma said.

She'd made a breakthrough when she saw her sisters die in the vision and she acted without them, tapping into a well of psychic power that felt greater than anything she'd experienced before.

There was no way that power could only be hers in the face of tragedy. She wanted to claim it *now*. To make it her own to stave *off* tragedy.

Phoebe took a deep breath and pushed beyond the memory of her sisters' false death. She thought of the pile of bodies and the four who sat on top. She thought of the Five that became Three that she feared would become–

Snap.

Phoebe found herself alone.

She was floating in white nothing, drifting. There was nothing sharing this space with her except a swirling, gray mass, barely distinguishable from the white itself. She looked closer, beginning to think she was looking at a massive eye.

No, she thought. I've been here. It's…

The swirling gray began to form into the shape of girls that looked just like Phoebe. Girls that could've been her sisters, but who were now nothing. Memories. Dead.

Phoebe looked at the lifeless shapes and felt despair creeping through her being. This could be her future.

She could be alone. She could be One.

Then the voice came to her, clear and firm.

"No."

It was her own voice. Not stammering or questioning. Not wavering. Strong and forceful.

She felt it, not coming from her throat but vibrating through her own being. A voice so strong that it was almost impossible to tell that it was three voices speaking at the exact same time.

"We won't *let* that happen."

Phoebe looked at the fog around her and screamed it, not with her voice but with a feeling deep inside beyond sound.

"WE!"

In an instant, the fog was gone and the forest came back into sight. Triage's hands lit up like high beams, sending white light through the forest. Phoebe looked down at Emma and the herd of animals below, watching as they fell to the ground, a pile of bones and fur. The red glow dissipated from the goose, drifting off like fog into the night sky until it was nothing.

Phoebe breathed a sigh of satisfied relief as the darkness was lit by Triage's healing power, now unhindered by her own psychic block. The fear on his face was gone and he let out a whooping cry of joy as he, too, saw that his power was working. She felt so light she could almost laugh.

Then she realized it.

She was floating in the air, her body glowing with a similar blue glow to Emma's telekinetic shield. The power emanating from her was unlike anything she'd ever felt and, from the feeling of oneness in her mind, she could feel Irma and Celeste experiencing it, too, back at the school.

Slowly letting go of the power, Phoebe floated back to the ground. She didn't know if she'd be able to do that again, but she knew that it wasn't just her. It was a shared power that she was part of, not the other way around.

Phoebe's feet touched the dirt and she looked at Emma Frost, who she had blamed for more sorrow in her life than she'd want to say. She hadn't gotten past it all, but tonight, together, they'd taken a step.

As Phoebe, Triage, and Emma walked back to the courtyard, Phoebe entered the hivemind. She knew that Irma and Celeste would be waiting for her outside the school, probably with Morph as well. She'd felt it. Of course, they were.

She didn't want to talk about what had happened. She didn't want understanding, nor empathy. She wanted what only the other two could give.

Phoebe's thought to them was simple, but it was what she needed to express. *I'm sorry I scared you.*

The response came with two voices as one.

Just come back.

KID OMEGA FACES THE MUSIC

Neil Kleid

Look, nobody's perfect.

You know that. Otherwise, how could I be speaking inside your mind, like uploading a podcast about, say, the 1919 Boston Molasses Disaster, directly into your auditory cortex? No, you're not perfect, being both human and susceptible to even the simplest psionic home invasion from a novice telepath.

And I'm definitely not perfect. At least not *yet*.

Well, I *thought* I was. But not anymore. It's confusing.

Wait, I'm ahead of myself. Have a listen to this, sapien.

"What were you *thinking*?"

The indignant voice that you're hearing? It belongs to a man named Scott Summers. You may know him as Cyclops, the clench-jawed, eye-beam-wielding X-Man (or even worse, depending on *how* you know him). Scott is one of the main

headmasters of the Charles Xavier Institute, my current...
well, let's be generous and call the remote, repurposed military
installation a "home". You know what? I'll upload Scott's stats,
powers, and greatest hits directly into your hippocampus,
redhead kissy parts and all.

Anyway, five hours after what we (and by "we", I mean "you
and me") are calling the Incident, Cyclops loomed over my
pink-frilled scalp, screaming his lungs out as I nonchalantly
shrugged behind a metal desk, seated in a filthy little room
located deep beneath the Institute.

"You could have been *seen*, Quentin," Cyclops shouted, "or
worse, you might have put others in danger. Also, let's not forget
that your teammates were expecting you for training today!
Don't you care?"

Honestly, not in the slightest. But I couldn't tell him that.
Cyclops was my teacher, kind of a role-model-meets-headcase.
Not that I was afraid of the guy, but he had leveled up as mutant
messiah over the last few years, sticking his neck out for me
even after all the chaos I'd caused. So, I sat and shrugged again
as his face flushed crimson (an unflattering hue, like the ruby
spectacles covering his deadly eyes). Cyclops had been shouting
for an hour, pacing alongside his co-headmaster, Magneto, the
self-styled mutant master of magnetism.

Ah. OK.

That I felt, sapien. *Him* you recognize.

Good, Magneto's a part of this. Or he was. I mean, he still *is*.

Like I said... confusing.

Anyway, they'd been jointly dressing me down for a while,
and it was Magneto's turn. "You and Glob were seen leaving the
Institute at seven. You were scheduled for Danger Room training

at eight, and four-dimensional strategy at ten. The system has you both on the premises twelve hours later. Where were you?"

A third shrug. Cyclops' face looked like it was going to pop with apoplexy.

Magneto placed his hands on the metal desk. I could feel him unconsciously vibrating its surface as his flinty pupils stared deep into my chestnut browns. "We brought you here to tame your powers, Quentin, but also so you could learn to function in a team dynamic, to be helpful as mutants awaken around the world and require our aid. Wherever you went today, your absence and selfishness distracted from that *and* affected your fellow teammates' training. Don't you care?"

Again, nope. I do now. *Kind* of. But then? Not really.

"Quentin," Magneto's inaudible sigh drowned out the sound of Cyclops' grinding molars. "What will it take for Kid Omega to think about someone other than himself?"

This time I smiled. That was too much for Scott.

"OK, that's it," he grunted, flecks of his spittle sprinkling my spectacles. "We want to know right now, Quire: where were you today?"

So I told them. Sort of. Like I'll tell you.

Sort of.

Oh, but pardon me… where are my manners?

Hello, captive human audience.

My given name is Quintavius Quirinius Quire. Call me Quentin. Unusual? Absolutely, but let's agree that it conveys *gravitas*. I mean, imagine being stuck with the name Jeff your entire life (wait… *you're* not a Jeff, are you? Hang on, I'll check… oh. Oh, dear. That might be even worse than Jeff).

Personally, I prefer my chosen name: Kid Omega. That's my real name, see. My mutant name.

Oh, right; if you haven't guessed by now, I'm a mutant. Surpriiiiise! *Homo superior* here, telepathically unburdening himself inside your precious *Homo sapien* brainpan. As mutants go, I'm a leading man in a cast of thousands, and you might have seen our highlight reel on any news site or social media channel that ever existed, like ever. Or perhaps you've read countless exposés about "the mutant problem"? Oh! Here's a classic: maybe you've tossed trash in our direction, shouting obscenities as we risked life and limb against some universe-ending threat.

Or... maybe not. Are you the type of human that has learned to embrace his mutant neighbor? The rare and few who dream of living alongside *Homo superior*, can stomach us as friends or confidantes, and don't hate-slash-fear our kind? Man, I hope that's the case, Not-Jeff. I'm a powerful telepath, you know; I can root around your mind and ferret out the ugly truth.

Don't worry, I won't. Because this isn't *about* you. It's about *me*.

Tell me... have you ever experienced a moment of true awakening? No? I have. Something like that recently happened to me. It changed my point of view, and even changed... well, hang on for that bit of thrilling fright. But the thing is, I can't tell anyone about it. Not my teammates, not my role models, and definitely not my teachers. Hell, I can't even tell my best friend.

But I had to tell *somebody*.

And there you were, Not-Jeff, sitting across from me in this crowded mall food court.

I simply couldn't resist.

•••

You've probably never heard of me, but Kid Omega is a big deal in the mutant community. I'm one of a select group of omega-level mutants (hence my name) which means I've got mojo to spare. I chose to channel our conversation – sounds, sights, and in some cases, smells included – right into your parietal lobe, but could have easily dragged you into my fabulous mind. And trust me, you would've enjoyed that *far* less than the wonderfully narrated 4D movie playing inside your dome. So, yes: Omega (equals sign) Power. Sure, you might have heard of other omega-level mutants; one of them has a father who's a famous super hero. Several others are attractive gingers. And, of course, there's our pal Magneto.

Anyway, I'm actually several categories better. Yes, Magneto murdered humans and battled the X-Men in a shiny cringe hat, but I touched off a mutant riot, died from partying way too hard, and had guts enough to return for more. Recently, I psionically encouraged several world leaders to reveal their darkest secrets on national TV. Loads of fun, indubitably, but my actions landed me in eternal detention at a *different* lame, fancy, mutant institution labeled the Jean Grey School for Higher Learning (named for one of the aforementioned omega-level gingers). Unfortunately, I and some likeminded pals got into hot water while in attendance, and the exasperated faculty shipped our posteriors to yet a *third* school-shaped gulag, the new Xavier Institute, where Cyclops – remember him? Red-eyed, teeth-grinding, authoritarian mutant influencer? – boasted that he could tame Kid Omega and his unstable pals. The teachers at Xavier's locked the Kid down and encouraged me to play nice. And for a while me and Glob–

–Oh, the best friend I said I couldn't tell? His parents may have chosen Robert Herman, but his real name's Glob. Here, sapien: envision a chubby automaton made of pink, flammable wax inside of which resides a huggable, happy skeleton. See? I'm showing you what he looks like… now. *That's* my adorable life-mate Glob. We've been comrades-in-crime forever. I dunno, maybe we both like pink. Or maybe we just like to manipulate humans. You be the judge.

Anyway, me and Glob played nice at Xavier's, drinking the Kool-Aid and agreeing to use our chaotic neutral abilities for chaotic good. Cyclops kept an eye on us both (ha!), making sure, in particular, that I didn't psionically break into Daddy's metaphorical liquor cabinet. Which I managed to keep myself from doing for a while.

But you know how it is, sunshine. The Kid's gotta be the Kid.

And the Kid *loves* his Simon Williams movies.

Wait, *seriously*? You've never heard of *Simon Williams*?

Not only a notable avenging type, but also famous for appearing in the popular series of *Arkon* films? You know… *Arkon*? Oily, bare-chested barbarian who eviscerates sorcerers, warlords, and movie audiences in multiple thrilling cinematic adventures?

Come *on*, Not-Jeff. Educate thyself.

Simon Williams (whose hero name is – no, I swear – *Wonder Man*) played the titular role in *Arkon III*, a performance that he turned into a string of tour de force roles in other classics such as *Oh, Rebecca*, *Dead Before Arrival* and *Haxan 2*, establishing himself not only in the annals of cinematic history but also my fickle heart – and in turn, Glob's – as an unsung, super-powered talent in an aging, dying industry.

So, yes, I stan Simon Williams. And as it happened, said man of wonder was guest of honor at this year's ArkonCon Calgary, where tickets might be had for an official screening of a trailer for the hotly anticipated, soon-to-be-released *Arkon* remake… along with a meet-and-greet. The tickets were reasonably priced; admittedly even more reasonable for a handsome mutant swain (yes, *me*) who could mentally fool security into believing that he and his waxy buddy actually, y'know, had said tickets.

I had a plan, see. I'd been a Williams aficionado all my life. Sure, I had his films on all types of known media, along with a handful of framed vintage posters. I had the comics, the collectibles, the toys and tchotchkes. All of it. Everything. But I was still hungry for the perfect memento. One that felt so very Quentin Quire. So, I took Glob aside, leveled with my coral compatriot, and said, "Hey, brother, let's hit this Arkon show and *steal Wonder Man's glasses.*"

You know it. *Those* glasses. Strong enough to hold back the ionic power glistening in Wonder Man's crimson cheaters. The glasses that were his trademark. They were custom. They were couture. And they would be mine.

But there was no chance prison warden Cyclops would let Glob and me leave the premises, the two of us being the mutant ne'er-do-wells that we are. Were. Are.

Again, it's complicated.

So, yeah. We skipped school. And, yeah, we got caught.

But what actually happened in between was weirder by far.

"OK, that's it," Cyclops seethed, his face dangerously close to my stylish, pink glasses. "I want to know right now, Quire: where were you today?"

What should I have said, Not-Jeff? Cyclops would never

have believed the truth, not from Quentin Quire, the mutant problem child who'd embarrassed him by televising the verbal pantsing of United Nation leaders during an arms conference (remember that delicious detail? Here's the footage in your hippocampus). And if he had believed me, the Kid Omega-Glob Herman Good Time Roadshow might have been gifted one-way tickets to the X-Men brig; no convention excursions, best friends, or teammates necessary.

So I told him a story. And, honey, it was *good*.

Girls. Single malt scotch from the Blue Area of the Moon. Russian super-apes. More girls. An Atlantean do-it-yourself sushi bar. A madcap plan to steal the Declaration of Independence. Alcohol again. Even *more* girls.

Friend, that story was the rock upon which I built my mutant church.

But it wasn't what actually happened, the tale I couldn't reveal to Cyclops and Magneto. The one I can't even tell my best friend.

But I'll tell you.

Because seriously: who are you gonna tell?

Here's what happened.

"...you've been waiting, Calgary... and now, for the first time – only at ArkonCon! – after months of online teasers, we are proud to present to all you dedicated Arkon-Maniacs... the official trailer for *Arkon: Return to Polemachus!*"

Six thousand grubby fans in stained shirts and passable cosplay leapt to their feet as the MC announced the trailer, waving foam axes and howling with excitement. I could feel their yowls hammering through my psyche as I sat with Glob in the auditorium's fourth row, privately gleeful despite the mass of screeching, sweaty fans. Thanks to a brilliant bit of mental manipulation, I was able to slip us past the guards, get inside the hall, and hide two hundred and sixteen pounds of translucent Glob behind an opaque facade of pink skin, floppy hair, wide-bottom jeans and a custom-made, studded *Arkon* jacket. You know, for effect.

(Before you call me on the hypocrisy, yes, the mutant activist within would shudder in horror at the idea of hiding Glob's beautiful body behind a telepathic illusion. What do I care if he frightens human women and sapien babies? But remember, I had a *plan*. And my boy strutting about in his lustrous glory might have drawn attention and affected our chances to secure my prize. So, for one day, I advocated for discretion. We would swallow our principles, and maybe regurgitate our crow on random humans later that evening, after we had Wonder Man's glasses – and victory cookies – in hand).

"Here we go," I whispered, patting Glob's bulky arm. "Ten minutes from now, and we'll have the ultimate Williams souvenir. Then I'll telekinetically hoist us back to Stockade Xavier before anyone knows that we're gone."

Four rows from the stage, we prepared for the inevitable heist. Once Wonder Man arrived, I planned to telepathically cloak myself as Glob created a loud distraction. During the confusion, I'd telekinetically swipe the shades and abscond stage left before Williams was any the wiser. As far as I knew, Wonder Man's powers were the brawn-versus-brain variety. He had super-hearing and ionic blasts, but I didn't think he was a match for anything I could dish out from beneath my psionic cloak. Truthfully, I wanted to pull this off with as little fuss as possible… like revealing two mutant felons in the middle of an adrenaline-fueled human crowd.

"Are. You. *Ready*?!"

Another howl from the unwashed masses.

"Here to introduce the trailer is the man – no, the *hero* you came to see! You want him… you need him… the smile that saved a thousand galaxies… the West Coast Avenger we love to remember… ArkonCon Calgary, you know him as Wonder Man and the star of *Arkon III*… give it up… for *Simon! Williams!*"

The reaction was deafening. Wonder Man strutted on stage, waving to the audience, a flattering jacket stretched over his midnight-blue costume, a tactful scarlet W cutting across the chest. For a moment, I'll admit to being starstruck… but if I waited too long, Glob and I would miss our chance. As Williams bathed in his well-deserved applause (seriously, stream his filmography one night), I nudged Glob and he headed down front to start a riot. Hunkered low into my seat, I waited for the kerfuffle, preparing to concentrate on the task at hand. But then…

…Hey, so, have you ever had, like, a crippling migraine? The kind where your skull is full of knives, and maybe you have to vomit? Here, I'll show you. It feels like this.

Whoops, sorry. I did warn you.

Anyway, that intense, hammering, bowel-churning throb? That's what I felt after Glob moved down the aisle. Seizing my temples, I psionically tried to protect myself from what I perceived to be a mental attack…

…but then it happened. The Incident.

Yes, of course it was a super villain.

• • •

Kang the Conqueror (I mean, talk about names that conveyed *gravitas*) materialized out of nowhere, shimmering above the main stage in a common villain's ensemble of royal purple and acid green. Kang was (*is?* will be again?) an old-school Avengers baddie; a time-traveling despot with a character arc that'll tie your brain into knots. His unforeseen presence on a Canadian stage definitely had to be the reason my skull was popping like ginger ale microwaved in an aluminum tin.

Kang's glowing eyes, set into an impassive blue face, flicked over the crowd as he hoisted the most technologically advanced weapon I'd ever seen (and I've seen some *weapons*). Smoke gathered about his feet, and despite the frightened con-goers, he clearly only had eyes for the ionic man of the hour.

"Finally!" Kang crowed, triumphantly stabbing a finger at Simon. "My *strategic* calculations have pinpointed the *exact* nexus through which I now draw you to my side... enlisting you, Wonder Man, into a conflict across *space and time*! A battle that destroys the *foundations* of the timeline! The *ultimate* war of destin–"

"Pass." Wonder Man shrugged off his jacket and charged. "Come on, purple-puss, we've done this dance before."

Kang sneered. "Before... and later. Across all of forever."

Their face-off happened so fast, but still I realized that my plans to nab Wonder Man's glasses had been tossed a third millennium monkey-wrench. Thankfully, I seized upon a better plan. I wasn't going to steal the glasses; Williams was going to gift them to me once I helped beat the purple pants off his opponent.

That's right: Kid Omega and Wonder Man team-up! (Cue guitar riff).

Back on stage, Kang evaded Williams' ionic blasts. "You cannot

resist," trumpeted the time-traveling tyrant, "this is your destiny…
and mine!" Kang's technologically improbable blaster started to
glow, and he pointed it in the hero's direction. "Brace yourself,
Avenger, for now I transport you across the continuum… to
key historical flashpoints, in my grand design to–"

Waving away an approaching Glob barreling toward me
through a mob of fans, I launched a focused psionic attack. I can
do this thing, right? Where I drive my mind into another person's.
Like knifing somebody in the brain, but instead of a blade you
hurl your thoughts? Yeah, exactly. I hear the effect is unpleasant,
which made sense because I'd learned it from unpleasant folk. I
knew that I only had seconds before losing my tactical advantage,
planning to follow up my attack with a telekinetic barrage.

Kang shrieked with surprise, which was jarring to hear from
a future despot with extensive knowledge of human history (I
mean, didn't he see that coming?). The long and short of it is,
Purple Pants' hand flinched, forcing his shot to go wide. The
shot from his glowing, ridiculous gun. The shot meant for his
wondrous, avenging target…

…which instead hit me.

Yes, Kid Omega. Your gracious and beloved storyteller.

Everything went backwards from there.

Time travel isn't as comfortable as it appears in the movies.

There are no timey-wimey phone booths or fashionable
DeLoreans. The process is not instantaneous, like snapping
your fingers in one place, then expecting to magically reappear
in another.

Traveling through time is actually, incredibly, horribly
nauseating.

The Kid's body felt... wrong. As if my every molecule had been julienned and then crammed through a blender. Also, I couldn't feel my feet.

Organs raced in multiple directions, as if hooks had been lodged inside my guts and hefty fishermen were reeling them through several dimensions. The sensation was so strong that I needed to close my eyes and stop from losing the minuscule amount of convention food I'd managed to consume.

I knew that I was screaming. But I could hear other shrieks as well: Glob to my left (and to my right... and somehow also behind me?) along with several voices I didn't recognize. Then the lights came on.

At least, I could sense light in the darkness behind my eyes. Reality stopped spinning and all the moving, churning molecules that made up Quintavius Quentin Quire did their best to coalesce, like Humpty Dumpty – that lovable, mutant cautionary tale – back into some semblance of an egg. Suddenly and unexpectedly, my ride came to a complete stop.

The screams continued.

A stifling wind struck my face. I doubled over, and there was sand beneath my knees. Fine grains slipped through shaking fingers, and the Kid's head throbbed like a bongo, pain hammering in reverberating circles. Deciding to risk it, I opened my eyes as wide as they would allow.

Everything. Was. On. Fire.

Squinting, I instinctively summoned a telekinetic shield to protect against the intense, surrounding flames... until I realized that the gusts buffeting my face were stronger than the non-existent heat. Calgary's Convention Center had disappeared, along with the ArkonCon MC, Wonder Man, and

Kang. Thousands of con-goers had vanished as well – all but five: Glob and four very confused, violently ill humans. My fellow *Arkon* enthusiasts, each in a differing stage of regurgitation and fright. Glob's mouth hung open in dumbfounded surprise; the others could see him now, the illusion I'd cast no longer disguising his appearance, and the four sapiens inched as far as they could from Glob's waxy glory while huddling together on the sand. A cursory mental scan revealed a surplus of bewildered terror; Kang's blast must have swept them along for the ride, and the sudden shift in locale had no doubt overwhelmed their tiny human brains.

Hey, not the Kid's problem. My guts were down below my knees.

"Q..." Glob jabbed a single pink digit, pointing at something past my left shoulder. "Where...? What – d- do you see what... *look*!"

Disoriented, I chose to oblige. And what I saw was, needless to say, astonishing.

Cyclops stared down at the two of us.

Not the headmaster we knew, but more radiant. Frightening. Burning.

Hovering several feet above a beach, a bird of prey emblazoned across his chest, Cyclops levitated on a pillar of flame, infernal wings spread as he gazed upon a band of mutant and super powered luminaries, all silhouetted against the blaze. Glancing over my shoulder, I spied landmarks in the distance, many of which seemed strikingly familiar. This was no longer Calgary, but where was it? Had I visited this place before, or seen it as a physical photograph or plucked from someone's mind? If only the searing pain would abate, then I could focus... if I could push aside the pulsing inferno... maybe even use my abilities to penetrate Cyclops' mind and understand what was happening and why. There was fire and, past it, water on every side... as far into the distance as I could see, as if we were on an island...

Oh, right. I *had* been here before, human. Before I *wasn't*.

The fire... Cyclops and the others... it made sense that this was... was...

Freaking hell.

See, I knew it then. I remembered what was happening, why it was happening, and most importantly, *when*. This was recent history to me. Very personal recent history for me and my kind, in fact.

Two things happened next. First, my best friend reached out and grabbed my arm, spinning me away from the flames.

Second, (oh, and far worse) Cyclops noticed me.

Frantic, Glob pulled on my arm. "Quentin! How did we ge–"

Somebody (or *something*) switched off his voice. Glob kept speaking, but the sound didn't reach my ears. A telepathic baffle held me in place; a smothering, invisible hand, preventing the Kid from moving. Glob continued to wave his arms, gesturing to Cyclops and the human con-goers, then back to Cyclops, the flames, and the other mutants. But all I could register was blistering discomfort in my mind, and a seductively greasy voice sizzling at its edges.

Hello, Quentin.

Gritting my teeth, I telepathically replied. *Hello, Scott.*

I swear, sapien, it took everything I had not to call him *Phoenix*.

Give me a moment, Cyclops mentally requested, his voice humming with sibilance in my head thanks to the intergalactic parasite possessing my co-headmaster (soon-to-be-co-headmaster? This *was* our past), whose ancient power dwarfed that of every omega-level mutant on the planet.

I just need to placate our friends, Cyclops/Phoenix said, and then I'll be with you, Quentin. I'm curious to hear why you've come. We both are.

Perspiration ensued, commingling with the mother of all migraines. Cyclops' buzzing drone fell away, and Glob's cries for attention switched on again.

"–know where we are? Look! Xavier is out there, and alive! And Ms Frost!" Glob pointed as another one of our instructors from the Xavier Institute (and a powerful telepath in her own right) joined our flaming co-headmaster on the burning shore, where the Phoenix entity had come to destroy the man for whom our bunker-turned-school was named. Glob grabbed both of my shoulders.

"This is… you know what this is?" Nodding dully, I massaged my temples to relieve the agony, no doubt the result of our proximity to the Phoenix.

"I don't get it?" Glob did a one-eighty, turning around as he tried piecing together what I'd already solved. "One minute we're in the middle of Williams v. Kang, and the next…?" Finally, realization crawled across his translucent face.

"Oh! Oh, Q… what'd you do? We were just gonna swipe the glasses…!"

"I know, Glob. It wasn't… OK, yes, it was me. When Kang threw down, I decided to help Wonder Man. I guess my psionic blast–"

Glob nodded with primitive understanding. "–next thing you know, we're Doc Brown-ing our way through time."

"Got it in one." I nervously glanced down the beach, as the Cyclops/Phoenix entity loomed over its former colleagues and my future, would-be jailers. "But why here? Why now? How did Kang's chronal screwdriver know to send us to Utopia?"

A question I'd like answered, as well.

"Ahhhh!" A psychic storm tore through me as Cyclops/Phoenix eavesdropped back into our conversation. Pushing, I telepathically expelled it from both Glob and my frontal lobes, knowing that I could only buy us a moment. Between the flames and pain, my senses were firing on all cylinders. In fact, it felt like this...

Oh, no. Change your underwear. I'll give you a moment to collect yourself.

All better?

Anyway, I decided that I was sick of being battered on the sidelines and prepared myself for battle with a giant space vulture. But then a second voice murmured through the pain.

Hold your attack, Quentin, Charles Xavier patiently implored. It's taking all my strength to fight Emma and the Phoenix... I can't...

Xavier's transmission ended, as if – like my conversation with Glob – someone had cut his telepathic signal. Apparently, the Phoenix would brook no mental collusion, no psionic plotting, from its most dangerous enemies.

OK. Then it was gonna be war.

"C'mon." I beckoned Glob toward the standoff. "Let's get our hands filthy!" I started forward but Glob hesitated, glancing at the frightened, confused human con-goers, disoriented by the new locale and nearby conflagration.

"What?" I flapped a hand toward the fight. "You know what's going on, Glob. I don't know why we're here, but we can absolutely help!"

"I mean, sure, but should we? What about...?" He nodded to the humans.

"Them? Who cares? They're not part of this. I don't even know why they're here, and I'm not wasting a—"

Cyclops/Phoenix's voice thundered across the beach and tore through our minds – *if you could have stopped me, you would have!* – and the psionic force knocked me down, my head feeling like rotting, splintering wood. Whatever had happened, the Phoenix's mental barrage had shredded my focus. I desperately tried to erect a psionic shield against further psychic outbursts...

...and then I felt a friend's hand on my shoulder.

Glob knelt on the beach, holding out a hand to help me up. "Hey, look." He pointed, and I battled agony to follow his finger. Several bodies lay on the sand. I couldn't make out their identities through the red-gold haze. All efforts to reach them telepathically were being blocked. A field of psionic chaff lay between me and the Phoenix's prey. Grabbing Glob's arm, I struggled to my feet, preparing to telekinetically spike that irritating cosmic bird.

"Come on, Quentin..." Glob dragged me back. "We shouldn't even be here."

"So? Why should that stop me? That's the freaking *Phoenix* over there! D'you know what kind of raw, savage power I could—"

"Yeah! It's the *Phoenix*... and I'm a jello mold! We gotta..."

"Brother, what's with you?" Exhausted, I sighed with impatience as Cyclops/Phoenix lowered itself to the beach, facing off with one more foe. *Last chance, Charles.* The end was near, the moment slipping away. With the Phoenix's focus divided, my head began to clear. Unfortunately, crippling pain had been replaced by collegial annoyance. "You're usually up for any rock and roll type mutant hijinks, no matter the consequences."

"Not like this. This is too big for a guy like me. I just wanna go home."

"This was my home, Glob! Yours, too, or it could've been. And I'm gonna fight for it, even if you want to chicken out and worry about–"

"It's not your home! Your home is years from now! Yours, mine… and theirs," he growled, indicating the frightened humans. "Look, I dunno why we're in Utopia, or for what reason… if there's a reason at all. But I do know the rules of time travel, OK?" Glob counted them off on pink sausage fingers. "Never meet your past self. Don't take your mom to the high school dance. And absolutely do not step on butterflies. The Phoenix is one giant-sized economy-strength butterfly."

He tentatively moved toward the con-goers. "So, let's figure this out, Q. OK?"

I mean, how *dare* he?

Sure, yes, I didn't know why we were in Utopia either, or what made Kang send us to this pivotal moment in mutant history. But I wasn't about to whine about the whys and wherefores or look a gift Phoenix in the beak. Maybe we were here to change history. Maybe I was *supposed* to become the hedonist savior of Utopia, Instagram-chic cosmic buzzard (think of the t-shirts!). Even Scott Freaking Summers, mutant revolutionary, couldn't stop me from wrestling away the power of the Phoenix. I was…

I *am*… Quentin Quire. Kid Omega. One of the most savage omega-level threats on Planet Earth in any time period. Just me, a handful of others… and Magneto.

There he stood, grimacing with anguish as he faced down Cyclops, a former enemy… now one of his staunchest allies. Magneto flexed his hand, and electromagnetic forces crackled to life. I could barely hear his threats against the roaring waves and pulsing energy.

"Listen to me, Scott–"

"–they're here to *kill* us!"

Backed by Emma Frost, Cyclops attacked Magneto. All three would eventually become my instructors at the Xavier Institute, named for an enigmatic mutant dreamer waiting nearby on the burning sands. Less than a decade ago, on the shores of Utopia, Magneto sacrificed his friendship with Scott and Emma – years of earned trust – with no way of knowing what might happen, to save a man with whom he'd quarreled for years, and a resentful human world that hated them both.

Me? I stared at Glob, who'd left me to address our fellow time travelers. The humans shrank from my pal's advance, one of them raising a foam axe to protect the others. But Glob didn't retreat. He… *knelt* next to them, holding out a hand like he did to me.

Honestly, I didn't get him. I mean, these were humans like you, like others we'd tormented under the auspices of mutant revolution. Why should we care what happened to any human, whether or not they called us "mutie" and built Sentinels to stamp us out, even if we'd accidentally displaced them in time?

But then you had Magneto – the original mutant revolutionary – battling his own kind, and for what? I knew what was going to happen today. Hell, I knew what would happen in a year. This was the day Charles Xavier died, who was Magneto's greatest enemy and then his friend. This was the day Cyclops wavered. The day the X-Men splintered...

No, I couldn't stand by and do nothing. "Sorry, Glob." I stepped forward...

...and felt a tug at my guts. I felt wrong again.

That wasn't the Phoenix.

"Quentin...?" Glob stared at his hands; they were more translucent than normal. I knew what was about to happen.

"Hang on," I screamed, stumbling back across the sand to grab my waxy pal. The humans scrambled to their feet and Glob beckoned them close even as I rushed to his side. "It's starting again, hold on, here it–"

Nausea. Screams. Fish hooks in the organs.

And then we were gone.

We reappeared to the sounds of another battle.

Opening my eyes, I saw that Glob and I were still together, as were the other *Arkon* fans. It was daylight. We'd landed on a concrete field at the end of a military airstrip teeming with soldiers, all headed in our direction. Tanks and jeeps rumbled across the tarmac, and a siren blared in the distance, a klaxon no doubt designed to announce the unexpected arrival of six bleary, time-displaced companions.

Swaying for purchase, I tried to lean against Glob's shoulder, but he'd already moved away to check on the humans. One of them – the guy with the foam axe, clocking in at twice Glob's weight – vomited onto the unforgiving pavement and doubled over as he heaved up his guts. One of Foam Axe's companions, an older blonde in barbarian cosplay with a pale, frightened expression, helped Glob check the others, two admittedly beautiful gentlemen with matching sword earrings and *Arkon V* t-shirts (by far the worst of the *Arkon* oeuvre, but I was willing to give the Earring Swordsmen a pass). Though the alarm drilled into my skull, I noticed the blissful absence of any neural chaff or psionic dampeners. No smarmy, sibilant, cosmic vultures snickered inside my soul. The Phoenix was gone, as were Cyclops and Charles Xavier.

Yet, Magneto was still there.

Floating above us, sporting his original uniform and ridiculous helmet, he hovered like a purple and scarlet titan over the cracked concrete. Magneto gestured and half the army vehicles left the ground, levitating on imperceptible magnetic waves to join him high above the installation. He frowned at the scrambling human soldiers, not with disappointment, as he would during my later interrogation, but with anger and mistrust, hate and arrogance. His expression was one I recognized, having adopted a passable imitation in the days before I'd been supposedly tamed by Cyclops. That famous grimace appeared on vintage shirts and strident posters, many of which I've proudly worn or displayed. Younger and slimmer, Magneto radiated an air of earned superiority. This version was no friend to humanity, and had yet to establish a tentative understanding between himself and Charles Xavier or those who believed in Xavier's dream. No, this was the O.G. Master of Magnetism, proud advocate for *Homo superior* rights and leader of the (to me) unfairly named Brotherhood of Evil Mutants.

And there they were now: Toad, manically hopping amid frantic soldiers, indiscriminately striking with his feet and ridiculous, prehensile tongue; Fred J. Dukes, also known as the Blob, planting his immovable bulk before the remaining advancing tanks; Unus the Untouchable, owner of an invisible force-shield that protected him from harm; and Lorelei, whose seductive voice entranced the minds of lesser men. I knew them all. To Quentin Quire, these were poster mutants, not the original Brotherhood but freedom fighters all, and hardly evil to me by any means. When I was younger, I wanted to meet and work with them. Have dinner with them, maybe. Beat up humans together and jointly pants Wolverine. I owned all their trading cards (OK, to be fair, I'd also designed and printed those cards). And here they were, large as life and twice as colorful. Despite the waning nausea, the Kid felt a stupid smile blossom onto his face. And then the Kid remembered that he and Glob were hardly here to join the revolution.

Ignoring the spectacle, I turned to my best friend and his human charges. "Hey, buddy? You OK over there?"

Glob raised a transparent thumb in reply, bleached bone showing beneath the pink as he focused on the gagging axe-wielder. The other sapiens had collected themselves, doing their best to shake off the temporal sickness.

"Hey," I tentatively asked the cosplay blonde, "you, uh… all good?" I could have psionically scanned her mind, accessing Barbarian Lady's fears, hopes, and concerns. But after the telepathic wringer I'd been through on Utopia (not to mention two unexpected time hops) I figured why not use the greatest weapon at Kid Omega's disposal – his mouth – to gauge the group's emotional settings?

Unfortunately, the universe had other plans.

Invisible hands raised me off the ground, dragging the Kid

away from the astonished humans. Psionically grasping the undetectable magnetic waves, I felt along their supposedly imperceptible edges and tore myself free of Magneto's clutches. Telekinetically floating to the ground, I glanced up to see my smirking idol construct a barrier of floating, disassembled jeeps between us – him, me, Glob, the humans – and the rest of the Brotherhood, now engaged in the wanton destruction of the military installation. Satisfied that we wouldn't be disturbed, Magneto lowered himself, stopping short of touching concrete, hovering above us like an amused god.

"Such power," Magneto breathed, his voice purring with pride and delight. "You could have done more than simply break the magnetic hold, my young friend. I sense, in fact, that you could have accomplished far more if you truly desired."

OK, I'll admit it. I blushed like a schoolgirl. I mean, this was Magneto in his prime! He was Che Guevara for mutants like me. Still, I knew that I had to be careful.

"Tell me," he continued, nodding toward Glob and our sapien baggage, "before we discuss who you are or how you've arrived at this godforsaken human excuse for a military refuge... as a powerful mutant, why do you care how *that* one feels?" He pointed now, identifying Barbarian Lady.

Truthfully, Magneto was right (yes, I know it's on the shirt). I could have done more if I'd wanted to. Casting a telepathic cloak, I might have hidden the six of us from his sight. Or if the mood struck, nothing would have prevented me from inducing mental paralysis in the soldiers, the Brotherhood, really anyone in our immediate zip code. So why downplay the Kid's sexy, prodigious powers? Why not tear up the pavement, strip away

Lil' Magneto's mind, and save us a whole lot of grief until we could figure out how to get home? In fact, why didn't I do that to Cyclops/Phoenix back in Utopia?

Hero worship? Yeah, maybe. You wear a guy's face on your chest, it's difficult to mentally eviscerate his younger self. Sheer intimidation? Doubtful. Look, I know that the Kid's a sextuple threat. I know what I can do. So then, why?

Well… maybe it was for the same reason I'd asked Barbarian Lady how she was doing. Hell, I didn't even know her name (I'd taken to calling the humans Foam Axe, Barbarian Lady, Earring Swordsman One and Two). But Glob probably did. I had no idea what was going on with my waxy brother-in-arms, but for some reason he was more preoccupied with the humans than he was with… well, *me*. Definitely more than he was with our unexpected rock and roll joyride through time. Crazy, right? At the time, I couldn't grok it. And frankly, Glob's attitude was starting to hack me off.

So maybe it wasn't that I cared about the sapiens, but I cared about Glob? Was my best friend's crisis of mutant conscience affecting the Kid? Could his same compassionate restraint (*shudder*) be the reason why I didn't instinctively squeegee Cyclops on the beach and psionically humiliate Che Magneto here on the airstrip?

Was… is… *was* Kid Omega going soft?

Rising on electromagnetic currents, Young Magneto turned to face his subversive cronies, gesturing to create a gap so that we could see the Brotherhood beyond the levitating jeeps. "See there," he declared. "The world has persecuted my brothers and sisters for being who they are. Humanity fears what mutants represent, what we may become, and the consequences should we seize what is ours." He smiled from his vantage point, flinty eyes twinkling with determination. "Join our cause, for it is yours. Throw off the shackles of humanity, my friend, and embrace your birthright as one of the true rulers of the world."

He pointed at Glob, standing between us and the conventioneers, attempting to shield them from this younger version of our co-headmaster. "The emotional state of lesser beings is beneath you, pink one, as it is to all *Homo superior*. I see that you are a proud mutant son. Why protect those who fear you? Use your gifts and strike them down for the benefit of mutantkind!"

Yeah, I know. I hear it too.

Hey, a few years ago and the Kid would've spooned it up with both hands. Glob, too. Honestly? Standing on that airfield in nineteen-something-something, I almost did.

Aw, hell. Maybe the Kid is/was going soft.

Shut up, Not-Jeff.

Meanwhile, my buddy Glob rubbed his head and mumbled an answer to the foaming-at-the-mouth Master of Magnetism. "Yeah, I appreciate where you're coming from, sir," he reluctantly replied with a hangdog expression," but, uh… you might want to give it a few years? I think you'll discover a new perspective."

Ha. Good ol' Glob. Worth a few laughs, right?

Magneto wasn't having it, though.

"You dare?" His cape swirled around him as he clenched his hands, clutching Glob and the sapiens in a magnetic vise. "This is no whim, no superficial cause I support! I have been battling humanity's intolerance toward mutants, as well as those they see as different to themselves, since I was a child! No passage of time will deter my aim... and no traitor will stand in my way!"

"You!" Those eyes captured me again. "You are an omega-level mutant. I sense it in you... the raw energy coursing through your veins. We are the inheritors of the Earth, you and I! No god scrapes and caters to," he casually waved a hand, tightening his grip and eliciting groans from Glob and the humans, "the ants at his feet. Join me! Join my Brotherhood and take a step toward mutant dominance by eliminating these *Homo sapiens* and sacrificing your traitorous companion!"

Magneto squeezed his fist again, and I could mentally feel the discomfort he was causing the others. There were fifty ways I might have disarmed my former role model. I had seconds to act, but I'll admit it, man... I hesitated. The words coming out of his mouth, I'd only heard them in recordings and through secondhand anecdotes.

But I didn't think he was exactly wrong.

Thing is, the Magneto I know (*knew?*), the one living in a dirty Canadian hole in the ground, was trying to save the next generation of mutants while making common cause with agreeable, tolerant humans. He still felt strongly about mutant supremacy, by any means necessary, but he'd changed. The passage of time didn't deter his aim, but I guess it introduced nuance? Our Magneto had gotten slightly more tolerant, willing to believe that not all humans were monsters, and as long as they understood mutants deserved to have our rights upheld, left free to chart our own destiny, he was cool with living to let live. And, like the Kid, Magneto's past self probably would have viewed that with sneering disappointment.

Young Magneto's rabid speech, his offer... that was a speech I would have made to others at various times in my life. Heck, I think I *did* make it, or something like it (probably hopped up on Kick, an addictive spray popular with us handsome mutant agitators). Young Quentin – well, *Younger* Quentin; I'm still a youthful Adonis – would have greedily seized Magneto's offer with both mitts. Glob would be a pink smear by now, the humans fresh stains on the concrete. The old Kid Omega would've joined, psionically vivisecting every last soldier on the installation.

So, why *did* I hesitate?

"What will it take for Kid Omega to think about somebody other than himself?" The older, more tolerant Magneto had asked me that question (*will* ask me that question? *Aaaagh*!) hours from now in a dirty interrogation room. This Magneto, however, floating in the air and throttling Glob, only cared about mutant dominance, no matter how evil or twisted the mutants. My Magneto hadn't lost that with age, but he'd improved on it, learning that compromises needed to be made. He understood how to sacrifice rhetoric to form necessary alliances; how to adjust rabid beliefs in order to work with enemies for the betterment of mutantkind, maybe even for the "weak humans" his younger self vowed to eliminate.

And there Glob groaned, writhing in pain because somehow while my back was turned he'd managed to learn the same. He decided to care about someone other than, well, us. Maybe something he'd heard in a speech from Cyclops or a Magneto who had mellowed with age had made a dent in those waxy pink ears, and Glob had learned to... compromise. Did that make him any less of a badass advocate for mutant rights? Did (*does*) it make present-day Magneto? Did (*does*) it mean either of them cared less about *Homo superior*?

"You stall," posed Young Magneto, cutting through my conundrum, "when you should cast aside your friend and eliminate his companions. Sacrifice is necessary for the greater good! Do this and join my Brotherhood." He closed his fist and spit the offer again through clenched teeth. "Take the next step."

Sacrifice is necessary for the greater good.

Weird, right? Thirty minutes ago, I watched a different Magneto sacrifice his friendship with Scott Summers, not to "advance the mutant cause" but to save lives, humans included. Because it was the right thing to do. Because it was for the greater good... though a different version of the "good" in which this Magneto believed.

Glob struggled in the grip of a man who would one day (maybe) teach him what it meant to sacrifice his beliefs – in mutants, in teammates, and friends – because it was the *right thing to do*. And here my boy suffered, because he knew, like mutants, that these four humans had the right to live.

And what did Quentin do? He put them all in harm's way because he had to have a pair of sexy glasses. A chance to meet a bro named Wonder Man.

Oh, I can hear your oozing judgment. You, with a name worse than Jeff.

Well, forget it.

There's only room for one of us to judge me inside my head.

Young Magneto prompted me one last time. "Will you join me?"

My original hero, the mutant who'd defined Kid Omega's earliest incarnation... the radical whose ideals I'd long espoused... whose face I wore on my chest... whose cause I'd supported most of my reckless pink-haired life...

Sigh. Well, you'll be surprised to know that I declined. Heck, I was.

"I know I'll regret this, sir, but I hope you'll understand one day." Telekinetically breaking his grip and shamefacedly shrugging my shoulders, I cast a telepathic cloak over the humans and Glob, who awkwardly fell to the ground. Then I prepared to battle the man I'd long admired.

On his feet, Glob stepped next to me, nodding and slapping me on the back. "We've got this, Q. I mean, I think we do."

I rolled my eyes. "Way to be confident."

Glob smiled. "I'm confident in that I think we've got this."

"Traitors!" Magneto's face turned the same shade as his cape. He raised his hands, gathering the surrounding vehicles. "You side with humans against your own kind? Powerful you may be, but you are no match for the Master of Magnetism, nor the full force of his Brotherhood!"

They thundered down the tarmac, heading our way: Unus with his invisible shield. Toad, in unfashionable motley. Lorelei, beautiful but dangerous. And the Blob, jiggling down the airstrip, every footfall a potential earthquake. Magneto lowered his arms toward us, and a storm of jeeps sped through the air. Waving a hand for effect, I rippled a telekinetic bolt through the approaching vehicles, detonating them from the inside out, creating an impassable barrier of shrapnel between us and the supposedly "evil" mutants. Magneto pressed against my shield, pitting his will against mine, and I strengthened my efforts to separate the Brotherhood from Glob, who whined with frustration.

"Dude! I was gonna go toe to toe with the Blob!"

"Immovable object, buddy. He'd spread you on toast and eat you for breakfast."

This time, Glob rolled his eyes. "Way to be confident, Q."

"I'm confident in that I think he'd eat you for breakfast."

"Enough!" Magneto redoubled his attack, snatching jeep components from the air and crumbling them into fine particles. The Brotherhood surged forward, Glob and I stood our ground...

...and my guts started to vibrate. Glob began to fade. Foam Axe yelped, gathering the other three humans into a tight embrace.

Get on the magic time travel bus, kids.

As nausea kicked in and the six of us disappeared, I locked eyes with Magneto. The anger was there, as was resolve, but also something new: surprise. Although I know it was due to our mysterious magical exit, I hoped that when next we met – either in the present-day or on the next bounce – that he would have learned to embrace that surprise, to understand it could be welcome even if it ultimately contributed to change and compromise. Even if it had to adjust the way he fought for his cause.

Or was that something I hoped for myself?

What do you think, sapien?

Oh, who cares what you think?

Fine. I guess I do.

Right? That's partially why I'm telling you this story.

See, I'm struggling with this – *was* struggling with it, after and I guess *while* we bounced across time. I'd met two versions of Magneto, one who cared nothing for humanity and would sacrifice anyone to uphold his ideals, and another who sacrificed trust and relationships to protect both mutants and humans alike. Oh! And a third, back at the Xavier Institute, fighting for mutant rights alongside a militant Cyclops, but with the understanding that his cause needed a tune-up. *Homo superiors* are GOAT (that's greatest of all time, Not-Jeff), awesome wow, but in a way where we might coexist, as well; a more strident version of the Xavier mantra, I suppose. Three Magnetos but the same, adapting and compromising ideals, friends, and beliefs over time.

Which is (*was*) right? Are (*were*) they all right?

And what's my lesson in it all, human? Like Rocky, if he can change, I can change? That Kid Omega should be chaotic good and understand mutant revolution doesn't have to mean smashing humans? That I can be a selfish, spritely, agent of change and also give a bug's butt about other people?

Yeah, I didn't think you had an answer for me.

But thanks for letting me ramble.

A mass of molecules again, blinking across the space/time continuum, I'll admit those questions were weighing on me. What made Glob focus on humans rather than enjoy our joyride through X-Men history? And why did I care? Truthfully, I didn't have time to dissect it until much later, well after the Incident was in my (ha!) past.

At the moment – my molecules traveling through several of them, in fact – the only thing I wanted to dissect was, "What's next?"

Eventually, we developed the Algorithm.

Here's the gist: establishing a psionic trigger (hang on, I'll dumb it down: "mental alarm clock"), my subconscious made sure that every time we crash-landed in a new time period, it immediately wrapped the six of us inside a comfy telepathic cloak, adjusting for terrain/locale and weather conditions, coupled with a neural baffle to keep out any telepaths it might detect. This provided much-needed breathing room, allowing us to recover from the temporal trots without worrying about being attacked. Once upright, I would always scan our strange new environs for threats while Glob scoped our companions for additional breakage.

We did this at least nine times.

Bouncing more frequently (and, to be frank, less violently after consecutive jaunts), our time on-site shortened significantly as Kang's displacement blast dragged us around the ol' continuum. Events blurred, a potpourri of historical flashpoints, many highlighting Magneto's Greatest Hits. One stop landed us in Paris, where we witnessed his trial for "crimes against humanity". Another bounce shot us into orbit, where we collectively held our breath while hiding behind the bulkhead in a lonely satellite, waiting for the clock to run out as Magneto stared into space, brooding alone for forty minutes.

We did the same in Washington, keeping mum in stunned silence as he plotted vengeance against Earth's heroes alongside a villainous who's who, including the infamous Red Skull – Nazi commandant, intolerant fascist – only to sigh with relief when Magneto sacrificed his involvement to betray the Skull, leaving him for dead in a remote bomb shelter. Finally, on a secret world deep in space, Magneto reluctantly partnered with the X-Men against a multitude of threats and marvels.

Each fleeting moment peeled away another layer of the onion

that was (*is*) Magneto. Charles Xavier's greatest rival, then his staunchest ally; a threat, then partner, and at some point a threat again. Each version offered a point of entry for me to learn why, but instead, I watched and waited… nearly wading in to engage at times despite understanding the potential cost to time, reality, and those sniveling beneath my cloak. Glob, meanwhile, ignored the sights and catered to the snivelers; not quite protecting them, but providing colorful commentary as to what they were seeing and (god, even more frustrating) debating solutions with them for how we might get home.

I mean, what were they gonna do? Did Foam Axe possess super-genius intelligence or think ten million thoughts per second? Was Barbarian Lady an omega-level mutant with the ability to perform instantaneous mental evisceration on a stadium filled with unwashed humans? No. Of course she wasn't. Not on her best *Barbarian Lady day*. So, tell me, sapien, if *you* have all the answers: why the hell wasn't Glob asking *me* how to get home, looking at Kid Omega to save the day?

Fine. To be fair, Kid Omega was busy sightseeing, epically lost in Magneto's redemptive arc, too busy taking ironic mental selfies with his idol's ridiculous helmet. I'll give Glob that, so shut up.

But why wasn't Glob taking those selfies as well? How come he could see the other ArkonCon attendees as anything other than sapien scum and ignore the chronological carnival in order to tend to their boo-boos, making sure their human minds hadn't liquified from one jump to the next? Why was he willing to care about someone other than himself, whether a teammate or a bystander? Did he think he was better than me? Heck, no. He knew that. We all knew that…

...then why couldn't I muster up even half his compassion?

Sure, I'd done the bare minimum and built the Algorithm, but I probably could've done more. Like, learn their names or interface with them the way I'm doing with you (well, not *exactly*, but you get it). Truth bomb? The old Kid didn't care what happened to human collateral damage when he'd waded in at ArkonCon to battle Kang. His focus throughout our journey had been to eavesdrop on Magneto, Cyclops, Phoenix... anything but "other people". But now (*later*), as I sit here (*sat there*) thinking about the Incident, that fact bothers the heck out of me.

I dunno. Maybe I'm no longer the old Kid.

I mean, c'mon, armed with a planet-sized brain and not a single passing thought about how to get us home? Seriously, Not-Jeff, Kid Omega had journeyed across the boulevard of history, cross-referencing the growth of a mutant he loved and respected... and not a bit of self-reflection had dented Quentin's omega-level heart along the way?

(It *must* have... right?)

Finally, we returned to Canada.

The Algorithm kicked in as we arrived. While the others collected themselves, I surveyed the area, immediately spotting a recognizable landmark. Laughing, I tapped Glob on the shoulder, pointing out a gaping stone tunnel leading through a wall, a stone tunnel half-buried in freshly fallen snow. Silence settled upon the tundra. The absence of footprints or scents made it clear that no human had been here for quite some time. But a telepathic scan revealed that the area unsurprisingly played host to a pair of powerful, familiar mutants.

Backs to the wind, Cyclops and Magneto stood shoulder to shoulder before the tunnel, which I knew led into an abandoned military installation. Relief washed through my soul. I sensed the same from Glob, struggling to contain his excitement. No, we hadn't returned to ArkonCon or even back to Calgary, but rather forty steps from a deserted Weapon X facility: the secret, filthy entrance to the Charles Xavier Institute. Home awful home. We'd actually made it back.

Sort of.

Probing to be sure, I let loose an astral projection of myself into the school, sailing on a breeze down inside its musty interior. Damaged, abandoned computers lined the walls. Dust caked their screens and had also settled upon filing cabinets and decaying beds. A cavernous well yawned down the central core, above the school's northern opening. But instead of its hallways ringing with laughter, anger, and unspoken romantic mutant tension, the desolate facility was instead teeming with squealing rodents and a surprising number of mangy goats, snoring blissfully in the darkness.

Of course. We were a year too early, and this pit had yet to become my prison. Fuming in the cold, I returned my astral form to the surface, psionically encouraging my companions to keep their chatter to a minimum. Meanwhile, I floated above the tunnel entrance, hoping to eavesdrop on my pre-destined co-headmasters, both assessing their surroundings.

Cyclops spoke first, of course, never in his life having grace enough to relinquish an opening salvo. "Thank you," he warily offered Magneto, "for... honestly, Erik, I'm not even sure. Freeing me from prison? Helping me? Why am I here, exactly?"

Magneto frowned. "A war is coming, Scott."

Cyclops laughed. "I believe I've heard this one before. Can't you at least set it to music this time, Erik?"

Magneto continued, ignoring the lame jibe. "Mutants, Scott. New mutants are activating all over the world. You know this, and so do the humans, as well as those who serve or avenge their governments' orders."

Scott shrugged. "Yes. I know. What do you want me to do about that? I already tried to stop it, remember?"

Glob breathed in my ear, jarring my physical body as he strained to hear what Magneto had to say. The Earring Swordsmen leaned in close too, distracting me with their admittedly captivating eyes. Annoyed, I blocked everybody out, telepathically fine-tuning my astral focus to mentally capture every sigh, every smirk, every nuance of the conversation below.

Magneto raised an eyebrow. "What do you want to do about it, Scott?"

"Same as before, I guess. Better. Smarter. But…"

Magneto prompted. "But…?"

Scott smiled. "…*but* will they let me? They think I'm a monster."

"And what do you think?"

Cyclops hesitated, frost issuing from his lips as he blew a jagged breath. Before he could answer, Magneto interjected, "It's your powers, yes? You're worried about your powers? Their erratic nature after… well, *after*."

Scott nodded. "I'm broken, Erik, in many ways. The enemies I've… *we've* made… the rights of those I vowed to protect. In the state I'm in, and in the condition of both the world and my 'status', will I end up breaking more than I intend? Will I–"

"Will you break Charles' dream?"

Scott nodded. "The first new mutants in years. Without Xavier, and the state of the X-Men as they are… I worry about breaking the future the way I've destroyed the past." He gingerly touched his eyes, hidden behind a band of ruby quartz. "Our people have a fighting chance. But I don't know if I'm the mutant to help them achieve it."

A spectral vision against the Canadian snow, Magneto raised his hands. Perspiration shone upon his brow as his fingers vibrated. A low rumbling emanated from deep within the facility. After a beat, a billowing landslide of soil tumbled off the hill, and a minuscule avalanche fell before the yawning tunnel. Something burst through the northern opening and tumbled through the air. It shed dirt as it hovered for a moment, and then landed with a slap in Magneto's outstretched hand.

It was a disk drive, virtually obsolete. He gripped it, displaying it to Cyclops like a prize. From my astral self's vantage point, I could see Magneto had doubled over, weakly clutching his chest as he coughed into Alberta's chilly breeze. Slowly, he stood up and handed the drive over to his companion with trembling fingers.

"W… we will help them achieve it… together," Magneto wheezed. "We broken colleagues."

Concerned, Cyclops accepted the drive. "Your powers, too…?"

A tight nod confirmed it. "Together, we must overcome our difficulties and differences to show these miracles the next chapter in mutant revolution."

They turned back to the godforsaken hovel that would soon become an institute. Cyclops crossed his arms and cocked his head to one side, lost in thought.

"And we would live here? Teach them here?"

Magneto smiled. "Absolutely. They require our help, Scott. As does the world."

Scott nodded. "Do they want it? Will they accept it?"

And at that moment, Magneto pointedly looked up, smiling *in the general direction of my astral form.* "We'll discover that together, as well."

Before I could say or do a thing, sapien, I was violently shoved back into my body as the six of us bounced away through time, leaving Magneto and many unspoken questions behind.

All right. Here's where it gets weird. Well, *weirder.*

Here's the bit of the story I really can't tell Magneto, Cyclops, or Glob.

But I'm telling you.

So pay attention.

The Algorithm kicked in. But I was all alone.

Panic set in; I couldn't locate Glob or the other four. As usual, I scanned my surroundings, but was unable to pinpoint their unique psionic signatures. Despite being protected from anyone rooting inside my mind, I sensed that I was far from the only telepath in the vicinity. In fact, I was reading plenty of mutants. Hundreds. Maybe more.

Fresh air assailed my nostrils, seasoned with an exotic aroma I couldn't quite place. The air was dry but cool, refreshing, even. My sculpted posterior lay on a comfortable bed of vegetation, back supported against the trunk of a leafy tree. Sea air wafted from the north, and I turned toward the briny scent, opening my eyes to see tamed jungle surrounding a treacherous cliff, beholding a beautiful sunset in the distance, reflected against a glistening ocean.

"Glob?" Whispering as loud as I dared, I once again tried to locate my companions. But the distracting psyches of a thousand mutants jabbered inside my skull, and instead of the usual stew of mutant desperation, anger, nerves, and fear, I was surprised to find contentment, happiness, belonging... and a peaceful presence binding them together; huge and unknowable... a consciousness that permeated every branch, root, leaf, and blade of grass. The presence had a voice, which blissfully rumbled a warm welcome, whispering its name from every flower and tree.

Standing and perspiring, concerned I had another Phoenix on my hands, I doubled the psionic protection to keep this natural awareness from breaching my mental defenses. Stumbling to the edge of the cliff, I looked down to find mutants dotting a vast island compound, replete with manmade plateaus and clearings accessible via natural walkways and staircases. The mutants – some recognizable, many unknown – strolled amid the greenery.

Curious, I slowly sat down and dangled my legs over the cliff. Placing my hands in my lap, I pondered what to do next.

Where was I? What had happened to Glob, Foam Axe, and the others? Wherever this paradise was in time, why had I bounced here by myself? And most importantly, how the hell was I gonna get home?

You are home, Quentin.

"Yeaaaahhh!!!"

Foolishly believing myself secure in the Algorithm's psionic bubble, I reacted poorly to the second unwelcome intruder inside my head: I jumped up and karate chopped the air, wheeling about and squealing like a pig.

"Who's there? How did you manage to...?"

Idiot, I thought. An island full of mutants and my ego wouldn't allow for the fact that there might be some telepathic hitter powerful enough to pierce the Kid's Algorithm.

Ha ha, chuckled the new, maddeningly familiar voice, *I totally forgot that we used to call ourselves the Kid. C'mon, Quentin. Get up and walk around the corner, OK?*

Cocking an eyebrow, I folded my arms. *No,* I told the annoyingly presumptuous chuckler. *Whoever this is, you come to me.*

Sure, OK. Why did I think the great and powerful Quentin Quire would acquiesce to being ordered about? I felt the mental sensation of rolling eyes coupled with the sarcastic, projected reply. The unseen mutant was beginning to hack me off–

(Yeah, I can imagine that's how you've been feeling all this time. Relax, sapien. We're nearly done).

–and whoever this mutant was, after innumerable hours (days? *months?*) of being bounced across history, panicking in some foreign locale while parted from my best friend, the Kid was hardly in the mood. Standing my ground, summoning all the psionic energy I could muster, I prepared to tangle with whatever might be coming my way. Enough was enough. Despite being dragged around time like a pink-haired yo-yo, Quentin Quire was no man's punchline.

And then – I kid you not – Quentin Quire came strolling around the corner.

Smirking and slightly taller (not by much; maybe a few inches), my mysterious doppelgänger wore a fashionable black blazer over a simple scarlet t-shirt. White slacks and sandals completed this Quentin's ensemble, along with a pair of wraparound spectacles, composed of a harnessed set of pink, sparkly psionic particles.

The fight and wind left my already nauseated gut. I dropped the telepathic cloak, and with a ridiculous "huh" set my butt down again on the fragrant grass. Other Quentin smiled and strolled over, comfortably settling himself next to me on the ground, swinging his legs over the cliff and staring out to sea.

"Weird, huh?" He swept out a hand, indicating the island, water, the mutants, and, well, everything.

Dumbstruck, I scooted away. The rules of time travel! Never meet your past self!

Relax, Quentin, the new arrival assured me inside my mind, that's not something you have to worry about.

Nodding, I crept back and faced the same direction. We sat together, we Quintavius Quentin Quires, listening to rustling leaves and watching the sun descend. Other Quentin kept smiling, clearly waiting for me to start. He could probably tell what I was thinking and had penetrated both the Algorithm and the recesses of my mind. But honestly? I wasn't angry or frightened. I was curious. But mostly, I felt… awed? Relaxed?

Still, my double was waiting, so I got things rolling with an easy one: "Where am I?"

Other Quentin clasped his hands. "A safe place. One you'll come to value. One I've come to value, anyway."

"Value. Not love?"

He grinned. "Value's probably the best word. I don't know that you're ready for love, even now. I mean, I'll admit that we're trying. In fact, the other day… well, she might be listening, so maybe I'd better stop."

"She?" I tried to pluck her out of his mind, perhaps the unknowable presence I'd sensed earlier. But Other Quentin was ably blocking me, and there was too much additional mental noise to solve his cryptic riddle. Despite that, I'd already guessed the obvious answer to one insane mystery.

"So," I decided, "I'm in the future."

"Got it in one, Quentin. Not too far in the future, but far enough."

Eager and excited, I drummed my hands on the grass. "Tell me everything."

"Thing is, I promised certain people that I wouldn't. Just the parts that count."

"Wait… so…" I glanced around, looking for said certain people, "…you *knew* I was coming? You knew I was going to be arriving?"

"Of course. You're my past, Quentin. Your journey was also mine. This is your future, no matter what happens, I believe." Smiling, he ran a hand through his short, pink hair. "It was… is… *was* fairly confusing until I had it explained to me by experts."

Nodding with understanding, I drummed a little faster. "So, what can I know? You said 'the parts that count.'"

He checked a timepiece on his left wrist. Instead of numbers, the hours were marked by runes I didn't recognize, four arms moving slowly across its surface. "How about this? We've got… maybe fifteen minutes before the displacement wave arrives, dragging you to another nexus event–"

"Wait, you learned to measure the jumps? How long does it…"

He held up a palm. "Despite the pun, there's no time for that.

But yes, I have a friend... *you* have a friend who's an expert on all things time related. She and several others helped prepare for this day, this minute. I'm modifying your displacement, but if I don't send you along before the wave hits, it could be bad. So! Before you go, what would you like to know with the fifteen minutes we've got?"

Well, what would *you* ask, human?

Here I sat in some mutant fantasy island, talking to my older, cooler self, and dozens of questions screamed to be posed. Many were trite, and half poorly conceived. Did we have a mutant president? Was I wealthy, loved, and famous? Had the Mets won the World Series? Had anyone yet pantsed Wolverine? Hundreds of questions, some ridiculous but others impossibly sincere: had I found love? Acceptance? Were mutants the dominant species? Part of me figured that Other Quentin was manipulating the choices in my head, shuffling them like cards, helping to steer me toward ones I needed... or those he felt comfortable answering. Doing my best to control the selection process, I grasped at obvious straws. Surprisingly, of all the questions I thought I'd ask about my future, the first was hardly optimal.

"Where are Glob and the others? How come they aren't here?"

That wasn't the question I'd wanted to ask. *Curse you, Other Quentin.*

He grinned despite himself. "Great question," my future self replied, which absolutely confirmed that he'd mentally placed it on my tongue. "Yes, I took steps to divert you from your companions. Glob and the humans are surfing the timeline, sailing back to ArkonCon where I will psionically fuse their displaced molecules together with their past selves, right before Kang sent you hurtling into the time stream."

"Why, though? Why not bring Glob here, too, or send me back as well?"

"I'll do that soon enough. First, I wanted you alone, to make sure you'd learned something from this journey. Quentin, I dragged you here for one last lesson."

Frowning, I flipped him the birdie. "The Kid doesn't need lessons."

"You do. The first is: stop calling us the Kid. It's childish."

I flipped the other bird. "So's this. C'mon, man, you bring me to mutant Hawaii, and won't even–"

Ignoring me, my doppelgänger pressed on. "What have you learned, Quentin, after bouncing across time and space? What lesson will you take home – once I send you back – and affix to your conscience like a moral souvenir?"

"I don't know, all right. What do you want me to say?" But truthfully, I knew even then. I knew what he… I wanted to hear. It lingered on my tongue and psyche, rumbling like the name of the elemental presence upon which we sat.

Other Quentin held up a hand, flexing his fingers until they nearly touched. "You're this close, Quentin. You've already learned the lesson, having eavesdropped on how many instances of Magneto over the years? Listening to his speeches, weighing his actions against your own. Despite your claim to hate humans, you were jealous of the way Glob treated the other con-goers, worried that he'd learned something you hadn't. But you had! You saved them on the airfield, built the Algorithm to protect not only yourself and Glob from harm, but the humans, too. You took your execrable beliefs, inspired by years of imitating Magneto and then Cyclops, balancing your views on mutant rights, Magneto's views, and Glob's against everything you'd seen, and learned how to… what exactly? Come on, you can say it."

"Stop. I don't know!"

Other Quentin grabbed my hands. "Yes, you do. And it freaking sucks, sure. You'd rather give Glob a soapy sponge bath, but you know exactly what it is you need to do. You know why Magneto's…" he grinned and winked, "redemptive arc matters. You know why those four humans matter. Most importantly, you know that what you've learned to do *matters*. But what is it, specifically?"

Squeezing my eyes, I tried to shut him out, getting to my feet and stalking toward the far end of the cliff. But Other Quentin followed in my head, mentally nudging me for an answer along with the cavernous, Entish voice of the island, whispering and *hooming* their shared encouragement, harping on a single word…

You know this, Older Quentin said. It isn't easy, but you've felt it throughout your journey. Acknowledging it will make you a better Quentin Quire – a better Kid Omega – as it did Glob, Cyclops, Magneto, and your older, more handsome self.

My heart burned. I knew what they wanted me to say. I *had* felt something questioning my past and weighing previous actions against my recent few. Why the hell did I want to know Barbarian Lady's name? Since when did the Kid give a Toad's tongue whether or not Foam Axe made it home alive? But I did. I do. I *still* do.

I'd developed a chirpy conscience during my travels through time. The Kid had learned to – *brrrrrr* – care about someone other than the Kid. Not just mutants, but humans. So yes, I knew the word that Other Quentin and the living island of Krakoa wanted me to clutch like a mental lifeboat. The word that wanted to burst from my guts and heart, ride synaptic nerves throughout my body, and, like molecules dancing on the timeline, travel to my brain where every neuron could shout it aloud.

Let's go, Quentin, Future Me psionically encouraged one last time, what did Magneto teach you, even when he felt broken… when his powers failed him? What was Glob willing to do for the humans, even if they hated and feared him? What has Kid Omega learned to do exactly?

Clenching my fists and sweating with nauseous exertion, the answer thundered through every part of my psyche, exploding outward like a firework to illuminate the mind of every telepath on the island.

Sacrifice, OK? I'd finally seen enough examples of sacrifice to understand that maybe I should try it too.

The thunder faded, sapien, and I sank to my knees, crying.

Other Quentin hunkered by my side, gently patting himself on the back.

"It's OK," he assured his younger self. "Yes. Glob learned to sacrifice his beliefs and body for four humans. Heck, more since then. Just as Magneto sacrificed his friendships, his cause, even his mutant birthright, his powers. Not because he didn't believe in them, but because the greater good had changed. He knew that he had to put others before himself – sometimes sacrificing his own desires and wellbeing – in order to save his friends, the mutants he loved… even the humans he'd once hated."

Other Quentin lifted my chin so that he… I could smile into my own eyes.

"And so did I."

"What does that mean?"

He gestured to the island. "This is where it starts, Quentin. Sure, you respect Magneto and are pals with Glob, but the only one who could possibly get Kid Omega to put anyone before himself was… *is*… well, Kid Omega himself."

I smiled, wiping away a tear. "Ha… that… yeah, you're right."

"Quentin, I still believe in mutant supremacy, and that our cause is *the* cause, but over the years I've learned to respect others… yes, even love them. To believe that others – even humans – have something to offer Quentin Quire, I had to learn what it meant to sacrifice… and trust me, I've sacrificed myself thousands of times."

"What do you mean…?"

Old Quentin ignored my unfinished question. "And it starts here," he repeated, "with you. Look, there will always be ways to rebel, to be Kid Omega, but you… *we* can be that and take responsibility for our actions and relationships. We can be rock and roll fashion icon gods, but also know when to help those less fortunate than ourselves. Which, let's be honest, Quentin, is everyone that isn't us." He glanced down at his crazy-runed wristwatch. "And with that…"

"No, wait." Desperate for answers, I grabbed my older self's hand. "I have so much to ask about, well, everything!"

"Patience," he soothed. "You'll get your answers in – dare I say it? Yes, I dare! – *time*. For now, though, it's time to get your ArkonCon on… again."

Future Me placed the watch in my palm. "This will send your molecules on a one-way slide to the present… well, *your* present, my past. Wearing it will keep you from forgetting everything you've learned, psionically retaining your memories of the journey, unlike Glob and the others."

"How...?"

"Don't hurt your head trying to figure it out. It's the madcap result of plying Tempus and Cable with far too many daiquiris and letting them loose in Hank McCoy's lab. Whatever the case may be, it operates like a temporal Algorithm. It'll keep you in your own little bubble, protecting your memories when your molecules fuse with that of your past self. After that, you'll know what to do."

Looking down at the watch, I felt my heart sink. It was clear that time had run out. "So, that's all, folks?"

Other Quentin placed a hand on my shoulder. "Don't fret. It'll all work out. Before you go, I do have a cool parting gift uploading to your brainbox... now."

A flash of pink coated my mind and a smile stretched across my lips. It *was* cool. *Very* cool. And the gift's implications meant more to me than my future self would actually let on.

But we'll get to that later.

Right now... or then... or *soon,* I felt the familiar, nauseating effects of displacement whisk me into the timeline. Fading, I raised a palm to my other self, the cool-as-hell older Quentin who'd given me an illicit glimpse into the future.

"See you soon," he promised, as my molecules winked away.

But I knew that he was wrong.

I'd see him *sooner.*

"–this is *your* destiny, Williams, and mine!"

I rubbed my eyes, blinking away sudden vertigo. A roomful of sweaty humans wailed around me, screaming and rushing for a handful of doors at the rear of ArkonCon's cavernous main hall. I was back.

Well, sort of.

Looking around, I could see that my re-entry into the timeline had barely registered on even Kang's radar. No one was paying attention to Quentin Quire... or to Glob, for that matter, confused and fully revealed, lurking down near the main stage.

The Algorithm had kicked in, see. Both Algorithms.

The first – the one I'd constructed – had gathered Glob, myself, and the four humans into a psionic cloak, telepathically connecting our brains while blocking out any telepaths trying to catalogue our minds... even though we'd yet to (and never *would*) share a jaunt through time. Laughing, I could see Foam Axe, Barbarian Lady, and the Earring Twins try to figure out what was happening and what they were feeling.

Meanwhile, the second Algorithm – designed by future Quentin, implemented by two temporal experts – retained everything I'd experienced, ensuring that though past and present me were having our atoms do the molecular mambo, the Kid still remembered everything that had happened to the six of us. Which also meant...

...if I really wanted, I could stop it from happening in the first place.

"Brace yourself, Avenger!" Kang's blaster began to glow, and he pointed it at Wonder Man. This was it.

Waving away an approaching Glob, I quickly constructed a wide, psionic shield. Opening the shield like an umbrella, I placed it between us and the audience, protecting the remaining, panicking Arkon fans from the battle happening on stage. This time, I launched no mental attack. This time, Kang didn't shriek with surprise, nor did his hand flinch, reorienting his shot. This time, the shot from his glowing, ridiculous gun meant for his wondrous, avenging target...

... actually hit its target.

A portal opened, engulfing Wonder Man. Chortling with maniacal glee, Kang followed him through and disappeared. The portal closed with a whine and all was silent other than the echo of crackling energy and the fading screams of a retreating crowd.

Man, I really hope that was supposed to happen.

Tentatively smiling, I discorporated the psionic umbrella and congratulated myself on a job well done. Glob came up next to me, his illusory disguise having disappeared, and tapped me on the back. "Hey, uh... you OK?"

Offering a satisfied grin, I clasped his translucent shoulder. "No. Not yet. But! I'm gonna be."

Offering a concerned look, Glob glanced at the stage and Kang's portal, now an afterthought of smoke, then down at his transparent pink chest. "Uh, maybe we should go. I dunno what that was about, but I doubt sticking around is a good idea."

"Absolutely correct, my waxy buddy. Just... two minutes, OK?"

I mean, what's two minutes to a couple of dudes who just traveled through time, right? I mean, I couldn't tell *Glob* that, but that's a little joke for the two of us, Not-Jeff.

Glob nodded, and I moved down to where Foam Axe and Barbarian Lady gathered their things, shaking and confused. The two of them shrank away as I approached, but I held out my palms to indicate that all was cool. "Hey, I'm not gonna hurt you. I just wanted to see if you were OK?"

They glanced at the stage and then back at me. Barbarian Lady cautiously asked, "A-Are… are you an Avenger?"

"I am not. I have too much style and self-respect."

"But you did something, right? I mean, we nearly died, and then our heads…"

The Kid grinned and performed a curtsy. "Yes, I did. A simple psionic umbrella, no need for hosannas or viral dance videos in my honor. Happy to help. Just wanted to make sure that you were OK." With that said, I moved back toward Glob.

"You're a mutant."

I turned. Foam Axe was pointing at us both. "I… I mean, the two of you. You're mutants, right? That's how… I mean…"

Cautiously clearing my throat, I placed both hands on my hips. "We are."

Foam Axe grinned. "Cool, I thought so."

"You're… *OK* with mutants?"

He leveled the foam axe at my chest as Barbarian Lady smiled. "Hell, yeah. As long as they're OK with us."

Smiling, I raised my fist to meet his axe. "You know what?" I replied. "Yeah. Today I'm OK with that."

Starting again toward Glob, I hesitated one last time. "Hey, sorry – I'm Quentin, big Simon Williams fan. D'you mind if I ask your names?"

Foam Axe placed a meaty hand over his heart. "I'm Jeff Gooley. My friend is Nancy Sternberg. We both work at Team Comix and Cards in Edmonton."

"Noted. You… look like a Jeff. Very nice to meet you both." With that, I chuckled as we parted ways after decades of shared experience that only I would remember because I'd finally considered others around me before acting. Not a huge sacrifice on my part... but still... maybe a step in the right direction..

Glob met me in the aisle. "What was that? Since when do you give a Toad's tongue about humans?"

"Tell you later. Maybe. Or maybe not."

"Sure, whatever, Q. Can we go?"

"Probably for the best."

As we headed toward the convention doors, Glob nodded at my face. "Shame we never got Wonder Man's glasses, but it looks like you made out all right. Where'd you get the cool specs?"

Smiling, I waved him toward the doors.

"Maybe I'll tell you that, too, when we're back at school."

And that, my captive audience, brings us full circle, seated at a cramped metal desk inside a room deep beneath the Xavier Institute.

Epic cover story told, I waited for Cyclops and Magneto to dole out the inevitable punishment. But Scott just glared at me, teeth grinding, and then jabbed a thick finger in my face. "Fine, Quire. Don't tell us where you went. But you better know that I'm keeping my eyes on you–"

(Don't now. We made an eye joke earlier, and it's just too easy.)

"–and Glob both. You're both going to clean the hangar, without powers. Be on time for training; don't leave the grounds at all. Next time you do, I'll make Glob spit-polish the bathroom with your smirk."

Disgusted, Cyclops stalked out of the room. Magneto lingered behind, sighing to himself as he headed to the door.

"Quentin, I know that this is a joke to you. I know that it

is difficult but, if you can, try to put someone – anyone! – before yourself. For once in your life, I encourage Kid Omega to sacrifice his childish impulses to at least accommodate his teammates." That stated, Magneto followed after Cyclops. That is, until I opened my stupid mouth, stopping Magneto just short of his leaving.

"Sir, I did want to say… this was all my idea. Don't punish Glob for falling prey to my seductive charms."

The master of magnetism turned back with a raised eyebrow, and so I concluded, "I suppose, like you, I've finally learned that sacrifice can have multiple meanings."

Smiling, Magneto slowly clapped his hands. "Well… I was wondering when your past self might finally catch up to your present, Quentin. I will say this: I'm glad to finally have you join my cause."

With that, Magneto left the room.

And with that, my story ends. *Sort of.*

Why didn't I just psionically obscure our absence? Why not mentally rearrange the memories inside Cyclops and Magneto's heads? Why not tell Glob?!

Well, see, the Ki… Quentin Quire had finally learned the meaning of sacrificing his desires – like Wonder Man's glasses, I suppose, which we never did get – in order to help others, maybe even those he hated, in the hope of finding the acceptance and love for which he'd always been searching. He'd… I'd been across time, learning what it meant to care for somebody other than myself, and though I knew I had to change and grow with time and age… well…

…that didn't mean Kid Omega couldn't *also* rebel with confidence and style.

He/I said, wearing the spectacles on which Cyclops, while screaming, had sprinkled flecks of spittle. A pair of wraparound glasses, composed of tightly harnessed, pink psionic particles...

...a pair that young Quentin didn't have prior to his jaunt through time.

So, what does it *mean*, human?

Frankly, I'm curious to discover that myself.

Bringing back the psionic specs – learning to make them from my future self – honestly may have started a whole *new* timeline, one where I have these glasses before I'm meant to have them. Which (equal sign) confidence (plus sign) style. Which (equal sign) rebelling across *two* timelines in my own chaotic neutral way while also acknowledging that my past self could stand to adjust his views on humans' and mutant rights.

(Also, while I *would* love to share this new timeline with Glob... clueing him in would play more havoc with time. I have to sacrifice some desires, right? I dunno, maybe I can still get him Wonder Man's glasses as a consolation prize?)

Maybe not. All I know is, Quintavius Quentin Quire still wants to be a rock and roll fashion icon god, but by sometimes curbing the fun impulse to do whatever I want, I might one day reach the future I saw. A beautiful, island future that seems attainable.

A future where... who knows? I may even fall in love.

What do you think, Not-Jeff?

Like I said, I wish I could tell somebody else.

But for now, I appreciate you listening, allowing me to get it off my chiseled chest and into your very agreeable, receptive mind.

Of course… you do know I'll have to erase it now, right?

Don't worry. I promise, it won't hurt a bit.

Or maybe it will. Beats me. Thankfully, you'll never know.

You've been a great audience, human. Thank you for being you.

Here's to change, my friend.

DEPOWERED

Carrie Harris

ONE

Eva Bell sat uncharacteristically straight in her chair. Her pencil was poised and ready, her feet neatly crossed beneath her at the ankle. In fact, all of the New Charles Xavier School students maintained their best behavior. No one muttered sarcastic comments or tossed balls of paper while the instructor's back was turned. Even Hijack had his eyes glued to the dusty chalkboard hung at the front of the room, and he considered classwork beneath him.

Magneto was teaching, and the students barely dared to blink.

It didn't matter how softly he spoke or how often he praised them. It didn't matter that he would take a bullet for any of them without a second thought. The man oozed intimidation, whether he meant to or not. Eva couldn't look at him without seeing the leader of the Brotherhood of Mutants. The criminal. The killer she'd read about in the papers growing up. Based on the cowed expressions of her classmates, she wasn't the only one.

Age had failed to blunt his effect on her. Just a few days earlier, she'd sat in this same chair, trying desperately not to fidget. Since then, everything had changed. Nothing had changed. She was ten years older and still struggled to meet his penetrating gaze. She could avoid a lot of questions – and had – but if Magneto pushed her, she'd break.

But what could she say? *Sorry, boss; I didn't realize I could time travel, and then I got stuck in the future?* She would have to fess up at some point, but every time she thought about it, her throat tightened and her palms dripped with sweat. At some point, she'd have to figure out what made her so reluctant to talk about what had happened. Grief? Loss? Fury at the unfairness of it all? Was she worried Cyclops would kick her out? That she'd fall to pieces and make a fool of herself? Right now, she couldn't bear to think about it.

But she was visibly older now, and it was only a matter of time before someone pushed the issue. She'd put her money on Christopher Muse. They'd gotten close. She would have confided in him if it had been possible.

"Miss Bell?"

Magneto's stern voice cut through her reverie and brought her back to the present. She met his icy blue eyes and blanched, her gaze dropping. Her heart pounded for reasons she didn't understand. What was she so worried about? He wasn't going to beat the truth from her. They were on the same side. Besides, if he tried something, he'd find that she wasn't the inexperienced teenager she used to be. She'd faced down alien invaders and held the hands of dying men. She'd fought to the death to protect her child. But she didn't want to think about her daughter ever again. It hurt too much. Even facing the likes of Magneto was preferable.

She met his eyes again, ignoring her racing heart. Stuffed the memories of her loss deep down inside and locked them away tight. She hadn't used her mutant ability to control time ever since she'd come back, and that made her a liability here at this rundown school for mutants. As Cyclops always said, they were at war, and without her mutant abilities, she was a fighter without a weapon. She would have to get back on the horse and accept the risk that came with it or leave. Of all the instructors, Magneto was best suited to help her with that. He never coddled. If she was truly broken, he'd tell her so and not lose a wink of sleep over it.

They locked gazes for what felt like an eternity. The corner of his mouth twitched, and he nodded at her, a slow gesture of approval that should have made her veins run cold. But it reassured her instead. Magneto had his faults, but he did not suffer fools or failures. He was just what she needed.

"Are you with us, Miss Bell?" he asked.

"Yes," she said, willing it to be true.

"Good, because you have some experience with our discussion topic for today, and I expect your full participation."

He turned away without waiting for an answer, sweeping the room with his stern glance. Objectively, he wasn't any more intimidating than the rest of the instructors. He wasn't particularly big. He didn't carry a giant sword. His short hair had gone gray, and age lines had begun their inevitable creep over his square-jawed face. But he held himself with the unshakeable confidence of a man who knew exactly how much he would sacrifice to reach his goals. He would act without hesitation or regret, and that made him dangerous.

Maybe she could learn something from that. Or maybe

trying to follow in Magneto's footsteps would make her into a psychotic criminal. Probably best not to find out.

"Today, we will be discussing Sentinels," he continued, marching toward the front of the room. "We will review each generation and its attributes, and then we will study a few battles and review appropriate survival and attack strategies."

At the desk next to her, Fabio Medina shuddered, his face going pale. Magneto turned on him, arching a brow.

"Does this discussion topic bother you, Mr Medina?" he asked.

"Those killer robots scare the bejeezus out of me, Mr… uh… Magneto, sir," replied Fabio.

"By all means, respect them. Learn about them. Practice in the Battle Room until your dreams are full of the screams of tortured metal. But do not for a moment fear them." The quiet intensity of Magneto's voice held them rapt. No one moved as his gaze swept them once again. "Mark my words: any Sentinel that comes to this school will not leave again. *They* should fear *us.*"

"Sure," said Fabio. "You and the rest of the instructors would crush them. But that doesn't do me much good if they come to the dorms first."

Now Magneto smiled outright, and if his glares were frightening, his smile chilled the blood. Even the psychic Stepford triplets shifted in discomfort, and Christopher blanched visibly.

"I wasn't talking about the instructors. I was referring to you, my mutants." He looked them over, his gaze pausing almost imperceptibly on Eva before it continued on. "You are more than you appear to be. I pity any adversary – Sentinel or otherwise –

that stands against you once you fully accept your powers." His eyes danced. "Or I would, if they deserved my pity."

No one had any answer to that. Eva glanced at Christopher, who turned wide eyes to her. Perhaps she should have been scared, too, but all she felt was a surprising wave of determination. Magneto wanted to push them to excel? Well, she was ready to be pushed.

She put her hand up.

"Yes, Miss Bell?"

"Christopher and I faced some Sentinels when our X-Copter flight was diverted," she said. "They had different weapons systems than the ones we've seen with Cyclops. Are there markings that would help us know which generation of Sentinels we're facing and what their capabilities are?"

"Excellent question. Let's look at some images and see if we can identify your adversaries. Benjamin, if you'd get the lights, please."

Benjamin turned off the overheads while Magneto flicked the switch to turn on an ancient projector. The machine rattled incessantly, its yellowed bulb dim at first but growing in strength as it warmed up. It projected a fuzzy-outlined, silvery-blue robot onto the tattered screen at the front of the class, and Eva turned her full attention to it. If she'd learned one thing from her unintended time travel, it was this: she had to squeeze the most out of every moment. The next time things went sideways, she'd be prepared.

TWO

Although the discussion topic was of particular interest to him, Christopher Muse couldn't concentrate. His eyes remained locked on the black and white hair of the young woman sitting in the front row, right under Magneto's watchful eye.

Eva.

She was inexplicably older now. He'd suspected it for a while, and when they'd brushed shoulders on their way into the classroom, he'd used his healing ability to run a quick diagnostic on her. He didn't do so lightly – it wasn't right to go rummaging around people's bodies for fun – but he had to know. One touch, and he could feel her body as if it was his own. The strain in her shoulders. The ache of brows constantly furrowed with stress. The tense muscles of her jaw. The body, straining against the aches and pains that came with the passage of years. He could no longer deny what his eyes told him. Somehow, in the past week, she'd aged ten years.

But she'd said nothing, not even to him.

After class was over, he would corner her. This time, he'd push a little harder. Refuse to take no for an answer. Even if he couldn't help, at least he could listen.

But the opportunity never came. As Magneto wound up his lecture on the Sentinels, the ancient loudspeaker mounted over the door came to life with a static crackle. Magneto froze mid-word, alert and ready for anything.

"Magneto. You're needed in the hangar bay immediately. There's a situation," said Cyclops, his voice even more tense than usual.

The connection cut off before Magneto could reply. Christopher pursed his lips, wondering what the Crisis of the Day would be this time. Over the past few weeks, he'd grown used to the constant trouble that mutants seemed to attract, but that didn't mean he had to like it.

But Magneto didn't even bat an eyelid. He flicked off the projector, bathing the classroom in darkness. Before he even spoke, the Stepford triplets stood up and began to collect their things, picking up on some unsaid order. Confused, Christopher half-stood, wondering what he was supposed to do.

"Come," Magneto ordered, making a beeline for the door.

The Stepfords fell into place behind him while everyone else scrambled to catch up. Christopher jogged up to walk with Eva, whose brow creased in concern. He gave her what he hoped was a reassuring nod, and after a moment, she broke out in an answering smile. That more than anything convinced him that everything would be OK. He could face anything so long as he had his team – and his closest friend in particular – by his side.

They rushed through the musty-smelling hallways and past blocked-off corridors, winding through the old military installation-turned-school with confidence. When they'd first come here, Christopher had been firmly convinced that he would never become comfortable in this terrible place. The food was awful, prepackaged junk. None of them could cook. Fantomex had taken over cooking duties with relish while he was here, but after he'd left with Weapon XIII in tow, they'd run out of food that didn't come in packages. Now, it was back to soggy sandwiches and microwaveable meats. The smell of damp and age had sunk into the walls and refused to budge despite constant cleaning. Once, this had been a place of violence. There was a bullet hole over his bed. At the end of their brief stint as roommates, David had drawn a smiley face over it. The bullet hole was the nose.

Despite all of this, Christopher had gotten used to the place. Maybe it still didn't feel like home, but he navigated its hallways with ease. They all did. They followed Magneto to the hangar bay where the rehabilitated X-Jet and an ancient X-Copter waited, their exteriors sparkling.

Cyclops, Emma Frost, and Magik all waited next to the jet. The women were in black pleather, while Cyclops had exchanged his standard brightly colored uniform for a similar suit all in black. They looked like super heroes in mourning, and maybe they were. After all, the events of M-Day still loomed over them all. Christopher hadn't manifested his mutant abilities until afterwards, so he hadn't known many of the depowered mutants, but all of their teachers knew people who'd died. You didn't recover from that overnight.

Magneto joined them, his sober black and gray jumpsuit blending in nicely. Even if they were monotone, they still looked impressive as heck. Christopher spared a moment to wonder where they got those outfits – at the super hero Walmart? – and if he'd ever qualify for one.

The instructors had a quick conversation, too hushed for

Christopher to pick up on. It didn't last long anyway. Cyclops broke from the group and marched over, sweeping the students with his visored gaze. He cut an imposing figure, the kind of man you'd follow into war. But he wore his regret like an invisible cloak. This was a man who had lost things and couldn't let go.

"I'm sorry to say that we're going to have to cut your classes short for today. There's an emergency that requires our immediate intervention," he said. "Stay here. Stay safe. We'll be back ASAP."

"Wait," Christopher blurted. The details of the mission didn't matter. It wasn't his job to stay safe anymore. Cyclops paused, staring him down. "We could help."

The headmaster's mouth twitched. "I appreciate the offer, Christopher, but I don't think you can–"

"He's proven himself, and you know it," said Eva, stepping up next to Christopher. "All of the students have. At least let us fly backup." Her voice, which was strong and assured at first, seemed to lose steam toward the end, as if she wasn't entirely sure she believed what she was saying. He frowned, overcome by a pang of uncertainty.

David didn't share his misgivings. On the contrary, he jumped in with unshakeable confidence. "You know I can handle the chopper," he said. "We'll stay out of sight."

Christopher nearly snorted. Subtle wasn't usually in David's playbook. He could control vehicles, and more often than not, he made them crash and found it amusing. But after a rocky start, he'd proven that he could be counted on in a pinch, and this sure felt like one.

Still, Cyclops remained unconvinced. He shook his head, and Christopher readied himself for the inevitable disappointment, but it didn't come. Instead, support came from an unexpected corner.

"They must bloody themselves some time, Scott," said Magneto.

But Cyclops shook his head.

"I trust their combat skills," he said. "That's not the problem here." He sighed. "But Magneto's right about one thing. You deserve an explanation. We've got an emergency meeting about the time-displaced mutants, and most of the people at that meeting want to knock my block off."

"Not without reason," murmured Emma.

Cyclops waved a hand. "Neither here nor there. The point is you students need to stay out of this disagreement. Not because you're incapable, but because I won't let our past differences become your future problems. I'm sorry, but the decision is no, and it's final."

Christopher couldn't come up with any arguments against that, although he had a ton of questions. Now wasn't the time, but he'd table them for later.

"I suppose you have a point," said Magneto. "I concede."

Without further comment, he turned and climbed aboard the X-Jet. Emma and Illyana followed him, and after one last regretful look in their direction, Scott Summers joined them. The jet engines roared to life, driving them back toward the entrance. Wind whipped them as the enormous aircraft took to the skies and soared out of sight. In its wake, the doors trundled shut, squeaking in protest.

"I hate being left behind," Christopher muttered. "Makes me feel like an X-Men Lite. Same mutant powers, but only half the calories."

Eva snorted. David edged up next to him, slinging an arm over his shoulder with a casualness that put him instantly on high alert.

"The chopper's still here," David offered. "We could follow."

"What good will that do? I'm willing to break the rules if necessary, but we gain nothing by sneaking into that meeting," replied Eva.

"But I'm bored," said David. He fell into a pensive silence and then raised a finger as inspiration struck. "I know. We've got this place to ourselves. We've gotta take advantage of it."

Christopher fixed him with a look of dawning worry. "Oh, no. Whatever you're planning, it's a no."

But David just grinned wider, slinging his other arm over Eva's neck and trying to pull her in, too.

"Come on, Muse. Lighten up a little," he said. Eva peeled his arm off her and smacked it. "See? Tempus is ready to throw down. How about you, Chris?"

"Don't call me that," Christopher said, with the fatigue of someone who has made the request a million times before and anticipates doing it again sometime soon.

"Fine. You come to my party, and I promise not to call you Chris ever again."

"Party?"

David nodded. "The Danger Room. Half an hour. I've got an idea."

Eva and Christopher both groaned, and David pretended to be offended, but his grin gave him away.

THREE

Eva Bell wasn't in a party mood, but she needed the distraction. So she twisted her hair up into a pair of pigtails and tried to remember what it felt like to be excited about mundane things like parties. Back in her university days, she would have gotten ready with music blasting, bursting with excitement over what the evening might hold. She couldn't scrape up even a fraction of that excitement, no matter how hard she tried to psych herself up.

The environment didn't help. Any party that the New Xavier School could offer would be underwhelming by default. After all, the facility was located in the middle of the Canadian wilderness. No one could make bologna sandwiches festive, and here, it was cheap lunch meat or nothing. But at least they could play a little music and pretend for a minute that they were home, and everything was normal, and most of the world's population didn't want to kill them.

As she neared the Danger Room, flashing colored lights spilled out into the hallway, and the deep thump of bass shook the walls. Had David unearthed a still-functional stereo or found a way to patch into some Wi-Fi? Excited despite herself, she hurried to the door and looked inside. An honest-to-goodness party greeted her. Streamers hung from the ceiling, and a loud punk band played on a dais off to one side, thrashing and gyrating to the music. Flashing lights and disco balls hung from the ceiling. The students stood clustered beside a laden drinks table dominated by a giant punch bowl.

For one heart-stopping moment, she wondered how he'd managed it. But, of course, none of it was real. The spiky-haired singer and his bandmates were nothing but holographic simulations courtesy of the Danger Room's programming. The refreshments didn't exist either. The cups would feel solid enough if she picked one up, but the liquid inside didn't taste like anything. Consuming Danger Room food gave her nothing but a headache as her brain tried to reconcile the smell and sight of food with the absence of taste. After a week's worth of crappy sandwiches, they'd tried it.

Most of the students clustered around the table anyway, clutching red plastic cups and swaying awkwardly. David sat in a corner, staring up at the band with slumped shoulders, all of his gung-ho excitement faded away. The drastic transformation concerned Eva. She bypassed everyone else and pulled up a chair next to him. But as soon as she settled into the uncomfortable seat, he brushed her off.

"I already told everyone else. I'm not in the mood to talk," he said.

"OK." They sat in silence for a short while. She stared up at the band, who danced as if playing before thousands of screaming fans. "Who's that?"

"One of my favorite indie acts. You wouldn't know them," David sighed. "I saw them in concert once, but this isn't the same."

"It's not." Eva looked around the room. "But it's still impressive. Does the Danger Room respond to your mutant abilities, or did you figure this out on your own?"

"I can only *really* control vehicles. Which is weird when you think about it, right? How does my mutation know the difference between a car and a toaster? All I know is that the car will listen to me, and the toaster just burns my bread."

"Mmmm. Toast. I miss toast."

"Yeah. I programmed a big buffet table, too, but it was too depressing. I took it out."

"Good call, mate."

"I'm not sure it helped." He sighed, running a hand through his spiky hair. Somehow, he'd dug up some styling gel despite the fact that there was nothing but snow, rocks, and wild animals for miles. "This is the most depressing party I've ever been to."

Eva glanced at the small cluster of students half-heartedly bobbing to the music, a small island of humanity in the middle of the empty floor. A few feet away, the Stepfords watched their classmates, so motionless that they could have been statues.

"It's not your fault. I think we're all just too tense to really let loose," she said.

"I'm not sure some of our classmates were ever the party type to begin with," he chuckled. "What about you, Bell? You got any good party stories?"

She shook a finger at him, unable to keep her lips from twitching.

"None that I'm going to tell you. If you want blackmail material, you're going to have to work harder than that," she said.

He snickered. "I'd call that a big yes."

"Not that it matters. I'm not that girl anymore."

That was one of the most honest things she'd ever said. Time travel had changed her. Now that she was back to her original timeline, she would never see her husband again. Never hold her daughter. Even if she did learn to control her ability, she'd watched enough sci-fi shows to know that she would probably never behold them again. She'd tried, but she couldn't seem to get to the right future. There were too many variables. For all she knew, the timeline in which she had her family might not even exist anymore.

In short, she was screwed.

A single tear spilled down her cheek. She brushed it away with the back of her hand as soon as it fell, but David was no dummy. He saw it. But one look at her forbidding expression convinced him to keep his trap shut.

"I think I'll turn off the simulation," he said, instead. "That music is giving me a headache."

"Good idea."

He went to the soundboard that sat in the middle of the room, punched a single button, and the simulation vanished in a blink. It took a moment for Eva's eyes to adjust to the sudden dimness. Her ears rang.

"Why'd you turn it off?" asked Christopher.

He was resplendent in a black suit and crisp white shirt, his locs springing out from behind the goggles he always wore on his head. His deep brown skin glowed in the dim light.

"What're you complaining about? You hate my music," said David, teasing.

"It was a good party," Christopher replied. "Not your fault that we suck at whooping it up."

"Hey, I like a good party," Fabio broke in. "Just not today."

"You OK, man?" asked Christopher, with a keen once-over.

"Yeah. Just not in a party mood. I can't chill, you know? Got too much on my mind."

"God, me too," said Eva.

As they chatted, the rest of the students drifted progressively closer, drawn into the conversation despite themselves. Even the Stepford triplets, who didn't speak to outsiders unless they had no other choice, were sucked in. Phoebe, Celeste, and Irma "Mindee" were identical, or they had been until Mindee dyed her hair black. Eva appreciated that, because without that visual cue, she never had any idea which one of them she was talking to, and they never bothered cluing people in.

"It's been a difficult transition," admitted one of the blondes.

"Even for us," added the other.

"But we did the right thing by coming here," said the first.

"How do you know?" asked Benjamin Deeds. He hung at the edges of the group as usual, an unassuming figure that no one would look twice at. His Adam's apple bobbed as he gulped, uncomfortable under the weight of their stares. "How do you know this is the right thing?"

"Well, for me, it was the only option," said Christopher, trying to make a joke out of it. But the humor fell flat. They all knew what was at stake for mutants that manifested their abilities at the wrong place and the wrong time.

"We just know," said Mindee. The other two shot disapproving looks in her direction, but she ignored them. "We're psychics, after all."

Eva stiffened. The Stepfords might be terrific people, but the possibility that they could rummage through her mind really bothered her. It would have even if she wasn't trying desperately to avoid thinking about the past. Or the future. Whatever. Time travel made things so complicated.

As soon as she thought that, Mindee turned and stared straight at her. Eva blanched, the color draining from her face.

I don't want to talk about it, she thought as hard as she could. *I won't.*

Mindee said nothing, but the damage had been done. Christopher glanced between the two of them with a stubborn expression that was all too familiar to Eva. He wasn't going to let this go. Eva would have to tell him to stuff it or confess everything.

Neither option was a good one, but luckily, the alarm saved her from having to choose right then and there.

FOUR

WAH! WAH! WAH!

The ear-splitting bleat of the perimeter alarm made Christopher nearly jump out of his skin. He recognized it immediately. Cyclops had spent one painful afternoon running all the students through the various alarm tones until their heads threatened to crack under the pressure. At the time, Christopher had resented it, but now he conceded that it was handy to know what this specific tone meant.

An unauthorized vehicle approached the school.

For a moment, everyone froze. Benjamin and Fabio wore identical wide-eyed expressions of panic. The Stepfords couldn't have been more blasé. Then David clapped his hands together with evident relish, his bad mood washed away in a new wave of enthusiasm.

"Finally!" he exclaimed. "It's about time something happened to shake things up around here."

Christopher rolled his eyes, but there was no sense in urging caution. David wasn't a take-advice kind of guy.

Eva sidled up next to him. Her neutral expression suggested that she was ready for anything, but her eyes flickered with excitement. Just a few weeks earlier, he would have thought her certifiably insane. He would have urged caution. But not anymore. He understood what they were capable of now, even if he didn't savor it like some people.

"What do we do?" asked Benjamin, his shaky voice barely audible under the continued blare of the alarm.

Christopher went to the control panel, his eyes roving over the array of buttons and switches before him. He knew the big red emergency stop button – Cyclops had drilled them on that, too – but otherwise he had no idea how to use the thing.

"David, can you silence that thing? And get any info on what's setting off the sensors?" he asked. "Kinda tough to make decisions without knowing what we're dealing with. Maybe one of our instructors got separated from the rest of the group and decided to come back. We could all be worried about nothing."

"Of course. Piece of cake."

But it wasn't a piece of cake. It took a lot of button-punching and quite a bit of annoyed muttering before David figured it out. Meanwhile, the alarm blared on.

"By the time he figures it out, they'll be here," muttered Fabio, looking over his shoulder in obvious paranoia.

"Stuff it, Goldballs. Think you could do better?" David snapped. The alarm cut off mid-*wah*, and he pumped a fist before returning to his button-mashing.

"We'll monitor the perimeter," said Mindee. "If anyone enters the building, we'll warn you."

"Any idea who it could be?" asked Eva, perking up.

"We could try to find out," said one of the blondes, "but there's a risk. We don't want to show all of our cards too early if we're under attack."

"Subtlety? Who are you, and what have you done with Phoebe?" murmured Mindee.

Phoebe rolled her eyes but otherwise ignored her.

"I think I've got it," said David.

He punched one final button, and a grainy image flickered up on the screen before him: a small plane against the backdrop of a pale blue sky.

"Can you zoom in?" asked Christopher. "So we can figure out what kind of plane it is?"

"How far away is it?" added Eva.

"Can you tell how many people are on board?" asked Fabio.

"Jeez. One question at a time." David held up a hand for quiet. "I can try to zoom, but these are long-distance images filmed by cameras that are out in the snow and wet. The picture isn't going to be great no matter what magic I do." As he began punching buttons again, he added, "And no, I can't tell how many passengers are on board. You think I'm psychic, too?"

"How far is it?" Eva repeated.

"Lucky for us, the sensors have a pretty wide range. But they could be here in a minute if they wanted to. Right now, they're just circling." His eyes lit up. "I could bring them down. That would answer all those questions."

"No!" exclaimed Christopher. "We're not inviting strangers to our secret mutant school."

"If it was a friendly, wouldn't they radio in or something? Would we be able to hear that?" asked Benjamin.

"I'm sure the computer would notify us of an incoming transmission." David threw his hands up. "But I wouldn't know how to answer it. I'm doing my best here, but this isn't easy."

"Course you are, man." Christopher put his hand on David's shoulder. "And we appreciate it."

David nodded, his burst of annoyance fading away as a readout on the screen caught his eye.

"They're coming in for a landing," he said. "It looks like…" He squinted at the screen, leaning forward until his nose nearly bumped into it. "Is that an X-Jet?"

Fabio threw back his head, laughing out loud. "It's our instructors. They're back, and we've been flipping out over nothing. Come on! Let's go meet them!"

"They wouldn't set off the alarm," explained Christopher, but they didn't hear him. Fabio rushed through the door with Benjamin in tow. The Stepfords followed arm in arm, murmuring to each other.

David stood up, still frowning at the video image. "I'd better go, too. I'll turn that jet around and send it back where it came from if it comes to that."

"Yeah, we should stick together," said Christopher, sighing. "What do you think, Eva?"

She shrugged. "I don't see how we have much choice. When will they touch down?" she asked.

David punched a button or two and winced.

"We'd better run," he said. "Unless you want Fabio to pelt the newcomers with gold balls before we can get there in time. You know how he gets when he's nervous."

Christopher needed no further encouragement. He sprinted for the door, Eva and David hot on his heels.

FIVE

Eva ran as fast as she could, but her height, or lack thereof, put her at a disadvantage. Christopher and David quickly outpaced her, leaving her the last one to enter the hangar bay. Most of the students clustered near the empty stall, watching as the sleek form of the jet lowered itself, bringing the elements with it as it descended. A cold wind whipped through the bay, tossing Eva's hair into corkscrews. Snowflakes pelted her cheeks. Her favorite short-sleeved dress was quite comfortable indoors, but it wasn't remotely suitable for the Canadian cold. She shivered, hugging her arms to her chest, and joined David and Christopher off to one side.

David said something, but the roar of the engines swallowed his words.

"What?" she shrieked.

He grabbed her by the shoulder and shouted directly into her ear.

"This isn't our X-Jet!" he said.

"How do you know?"

He fixed her with an exasperated look.

"I'm Hijack, and that's a vehicle," he said, jerking his thumb in the direction of the plane.

She nodded, thinking fast. It could be an X-Jet from the other campus, or maybe some enterprising villain had painted their plane to look like an X-Jet. Without any way to know if the aircraft contained a friend or foe, they ought to be cautious. None of the senior X-Men would take it personally if they turned out to be aboard.

If they were under attack, she couldn't sit on the sidelines. If she did, and one of the other students got hurt, she'd never forgive herself. Christopher could heal them, but it wouldn't matter. She would still have let them down. Besides, she had the most experience out of all of them, even if she was the only one who knew it.

So she swallowed her nerves and got to it.

"If this goes badly, I've got the best chance of stopping whoever is on that plane in their tracks. Hijack, can you take control of the plane and keep them on the ground until we know what we're dealing with? I wouldn't want any of our enemies to get away with information on where we are," she said.

"Yeah, I'd kinda like to know how they found us," David replied, cracking his knuckles. "I'm on it."

"I'll stick with you," said Christopher, his jaw set in that stubborn way he had. "If something goes wrong, I want to be close enough to put you back together."

It wasn't worth arguing, and they didn't have time for it anyway. The plane's engines wound down as the bay doors slid shut overhead. The rest of the students surged forward, eager to greet their visitors. She pressed her lips shut against the fearful – and angry – tirade that wanted to escape. At their age, she'd thought herself untouchable, too. The poor lambs would learn soon enough.

"Get behind cover," she ordered, her voice lancing through the sudden quiet. "That's not our X-Jet, and we don't know who's on it."

The Stepfords did as requested, as poised as ever. She considered asking them what they picked up from the plane, but if they had something to report, they'd say so. Benjamin hesitated, looking toward the silent aircraft.

"I could help," he said, obviously frightened. "I could morph."

She was happy to see him begin to trust in his powers. Benjamin was a transmorph; he could alter his appearance and emit psychochemicals to make people accept and trust him. But this wasn't the time to test their limits. They had the Danger Room for that. Better to stick to the tried and true, at least until they knew what they were dealing with.

"Not now," she said. "If it goes poorly, I'll bubble them. If that doesn't work, David'll run them over with the plane. We've got it covered."

"Oh," said Benjamin, crestfallen. "OK."

Shoulders slumped, he joined Fabio behind a pile of crates. Eva regretted turning him down – the kid only wanted to help – but she had no time for pep talks now. She linked arms with Christopher. He might not be any older than Benjamin, but they'd been through the wringer together, and she knew he'd have her back.

If someone attacked the school, she would freeze them, but every use of her mutant ability came with a risk. At any moment, it could flare out of control again, hurling her through time. Lord only knew where it would dump her. With her luck, she'd end up as a dinosaur's midday snack or enslaved to some unknown future's alien overlords. She would only use her time bubbles if she had no other choice.

The X-Jet hatch cracked open, and the stairs began to descend. Beside her, Christopher tensed, his hand clamping down on hers with an almost convulsive strength. By all rights, she ought to be terrified, too. After all, they were facing a potential threat with a group of largely untested heroes who hadn't yet figured out how to be a team. Magneto hadn't been wrong; in time, they'd be formidable. But that time hadn't come yet. Still, Eva's initial burst of nerves had faded to numbness. She'd lost enough to grow jaded. It wasn't a positive, but that didn't make it any less true.

She and Christopher both took a step forward at the same time. With an exasperated look, he tugged at her hand, urging her backwards. With everything that had happened, she'd nearly forgotten about his insistence that he go into any dangerous situation first. Initially, she'd taken it as an insult, a commentary on her ability to handle herself. But to Christopher, it had been cold logic. His mutation made him difficult to kill. Sometimes, she wondered how far that ability would stretch, but it wasn't the kind of thing you asked a friend. No need to make him worried about immortality if he hadn't already considered it.

Time and time again, he'd put himself in harm's way despite his fright, earning her trust and respect in the process. So she released his hand and allowed him to take the lead without argument. If she hadn't known him well, she would have thought him fearless. His head was held high and proud, his narrow shoulders thrust back. He betrayed no hesitation as he approached the plane. But his hands clenched at his sides, tense with anticipation.

She couldn't hold back, not after he'd shown his willingness to risk himself to protect her. She owed him nothing less.

As the stairway unfolded from the side of the plane, she peered out from behind Christopher, waiting for any sign of movement. A pair of feet appeared inside the plane, waiting for the steps to lock into place. Movement suggested at least one more person behind them.

She couldn't chance waiting any longer. She focused, holding the moment in her mind. A glistening blue bubble popped into existence around them, freezing them in time and space. A sudden panic gripped her limbs as she waited for her powers to spiral out of control, pulling her through the time stream. But it didn't happen. Not this time.

Slowly, she relaxed. Holding time bubbles was much easier now than when she'd first started. Back then, it had taken a great deal of concentration, like juggling chainsaws. But now, the bubbles came with a sickening ease and a feeling of completed purpose. She'd never been a runner, but she imagined the endorphine rush felt very similar. If it wasn't for the constant chance of backlash, she would have made bubbles all the time.

Christopher relaxed, his breath escaping him with a low "hah!" of relief. He glanced back at her, shaking his head.

"Should have known you'd pull a stunt like that. How am I supposed to be a hero and pick up chicks if you keep stepping in like that?" he asked, teasing.

She arched a brow. "The only 'chicks' here are me and the Stepfords, and you're like my brother."

"Yeah, that would be awkward. But the Stepfords are cute..."

"At least pick the brunette so you can be sure the girl you're dating is the one you're supposed to be dating," she said.

He grinned.

"What made you such a Romeo all of a sudden?"

"Distraction technique. It's either this, or I run screaming through the streets," he said. "And there aren't any streets here. We should check on our visitors before your bubble pops."

Moving in tandem, they edged toward the plane and peered inside. The bubble glinted as the light hit it, its iridescent surface making it difficult to see details. Eva tilted her head this way and that, unable to believe what she was seeing. The young woman's long black braid had frozen mid-flip over her shoulder. She wore simple clothing – a black leather jacket over a bright yellow t-shirt, jeans, and a pair of sturdy boots. A beaded choker encircled her neck, and the top of a longbow poked out over one shoulder. She looked different without her X-Men uniform on – younger somehow – but still recognizable through the blue-tinted globe that held her frozen in place.

Dani Moonstar, aka Mirage. Telepath. Illusionist. Former team leader.

The figure behind her was more difficult to make out, shrouded in the shadowy jet interior. The fit young woman wore a turquoise or green bodysuit; the time bubble made it difficult to tell. She had turned back to look at something inside the plane at the precise moment that Eva had bubbled her, obscuring her face with a sheaf of hair that matched her suit. Eva had a few vague guesses, but it was near impossible to make a firm ID under these conditions. Still, she relaxed. Dani wouldn't put them in danger. Eva had never met her, but she'd studied enough of her Danger Room fights to know that Dani would give anything to protect the students of the various mutant schools.

Still, it didn't hurt to be thorough.

"Anybody else in there?" she asked.

After a moment, Christopher shook his head.

"No one alive that I can sense," he said. "Stepfords? Can we get a hand here?"

After a moment, the psychic triplets joined them at the bottom of the steps. Their emotionless expressions gave away nothing of their thoughts, but Eva thought that Mindee's gaze flickered toward her for just a moment. She concentrated on the jet.

Nothing else to see here, she thought.

"I've scanned the jet, and I'm fairly confident that there are only two people on the plane. Before we release them, can you make sure they aren't under any kind of compulsion or psychic influence?" asked Christopher.

Phoebe arched a brow, seeming amused by the request, but she turned her pale blue eyes toward the aircraft. The other two Stepfords followed suit.

After a moment, Phoebe said, "The woman in front is Dani Moonstar. She is free of any psychic influence, although she's under significant mental strain. Behind her is Lorna Dane."

"Polaris?" Eva arched a brow, impressed. Maybe that explained their sudden appearance. Even Magneto's daughter had to come visit her dad every once in a while, although this was her first appearance. Eva wouldn't have recognized her at all if not for the class Cyclops taught on mutant profiles. Maybe they weren't close? Eva didn't pry into her instructors' lives, so she wasn't sure. They hadn't exactly had a lot of leisure time for family visits since the school had opened.

"She is similarly agitated," added Mindee.

"I sense no other mental signatures in the plane," said Celeste.

"Thanks," said Eva. "Are we ready for me to release them?"

Christopher nodded, edging in front of her again. In response to her exasperated look, he explained, "I know they're friendly, but the Stepfords said they're agitated. There's no harm in being cautious."

"We can assist in diamond form if things turn ugly," offered Phoebe.

"That'll work, but back off just a bit for now, will you? They might get edgy if we shove psychics in their face right off the bat," Eva suggested.

Maybe that could have been construed as an insult, but the Stepfords didn't seem to mind. Perhaps because they knew it was true. They backed off, hand in hand, ready for anything. Eva met Christopher's eyes, and he nodded.

It was go time.

SIX

The time bubble popped, releasing pressure in Christopher's head. Normally, Eva's bubbles didn't bother him, but trying to use his powers through them made it feel like his head was stuck in a vise.

He kept a careful eye on the two mutants as they returned to the normal flow of time. Confusion flitted over Dani's face as they seemingly appeared in front of her out of nowhere, but she recovered quickly. After all, she'd led enough mutants to be used to this kind of thing. She held up a hand in greeting as she descended halfway down the stairs and then stopped.

"I'm Dani Moonstar," she said, looking from Christopher to Eva and then on to the Stepfords, who had retreated a few paces back. "Who's in charge here?"

"You can talk to us," Christopher replied. "How can we help you?"

Lorna Dane stepped out onto the stairway behind her, the overhead lights glinting off her emerald-green hair. After the past few weeks, Christopher had begun to get used to the sight of Magneto in the hallways. The former villain's appearance still unsettled him, but it was tough to get too worked up over the man who gave you peanut butter and jelly sandwiches and swore at the overhead projector. The mundane reality of life at the school had begun to counteract the man's enormous reputation.

Still, the sight of Magneto's daughter made his heart skip a beat, and it wasn't just the skintight jumpsuit that did it. Polaris somehow seemed more approachable than her father, and maybe that made her more dangerous. No matter how accustomed he got to Magneto's presence, they'd never be friends. But Lorna was a blank slate.

She scowled.

"What just happened?" she demanded. "How did you all appear like that?"

"Let it rest, Lorna," Dani said softly. "It's fine."

"No, it isn't. We don't use our abilities on other mutants. Don't they teach anything in this dump? Coming here was a mistake."

"Didn't anyone teach you to call first?" Eva broke in. "For all we knew, you were coming here to kill us. You're lucky all we did was freeze you."

"Yeah?" Lorna demanded.

"Yeah."

The two women went nose to nose, glaring at each other. Christopher was simultaneously dismayed at the argument and impressed by Eva's guts. She never hesitated to stand up for herself. He'd been trying to follow in those footsteps, but a lifetime of trying to be smaller wasn't easily unlearned.

"That's enough, you two. We need help," said Dani, drawing their attention back to her.

"What's wrong? Is someone hurt?" Christopher asked, tensing.

Lorna unhinged her jaw enough to say, "No one's hurt. No thanks to you."

"Are you looking for your dad?" asked Christopher. "He's not here."

"No, we wanted to talk to you in private. You're Triage, right? And Tempus?" said Dani.

Mirage and Polaris knew their names. The resulting shock made Christopher's throat close up. Eva forgot about her anger. She stepped back, her eyes wide.

"That's us," said Eva. "How do you know who we are? Don't you want the instructors?"

"Definitely not," said Dani. "I'll explain if you're willing to listen. I think we could stand to start over."

"Yeah, I'm sorry about the reception," Christopher said, pouring on as much charm as he could in the hopes of defusing the situation. "We didn't know who you were, and we're a little on edge. Something about people trying to kill us really sets us off, you know?"

Dani smiled slightly, and even Lorna thawed a little.

Eva sighed. "Yeah, me too. I forget how scary it can be to lose time and not know what happened." She took a deep breath, summoning up the words with obvious effort. "I'm sorry."

"Apology accepted." Dani looked around. "Maybe we could sit down somewhere to talk?"

"Somewhere less freezing?" Lorna added, hugging her arms to her body.

"Absolutely," Christopher responded, leading the way to the door and gesturing with a flourish. "We could head to the cafeteria. The food's not great, but there's instant hot chocolate."

"I'll take it," said Dani, following him.

"It's safe to come out now," said Eva.

Neither Dani nor Lorna batted an eye as the rest of the students came out of hiding. They'd been young mutants, too. They knew the dangers.

In the small, utilitarian cafeteria, the students and their two visitors clustered around one of the larger tables, pulling up chairs and hunching over steaming Styrofoam cups. Once everyone had settled in, Christopher opened the conversation.

"So, what brings you here?" he asked. "How can we help?"

Dani and Lorna exchanged glances. Lorna's jaw remained tense despite Christopher's attempt at hot-chocolate-assisted reconciliation. She no longer snapped at them, but she'd picked a spot as far away from Eva as possible. He hoped that wouldn't be a problem.

"I'm not entirely sure you can," she said. "We've been here for fifteen minutes, and it's obvious that you have no idea what you're doing. And no wonder. This place is trashed. How do you learn anything under these conditions?"

"Did you really come here to judge us?" asked Eva, fatigue saturating her voice. "Because if so, get in line."

Lorna stared at her in silence, clearly trying to decide whether or not to take her up on the challenge or maybe march straight back to her aircraft. Christopher met Dani's eyes and saw his frustration mirrored in them. If only they'd stop bickering for two seconds, maybe they could have a conversation.

"Look," he said, "we need to table this for now. Maybe you have a legitimate beef, but it doesn't matter. The world's out to get us, and we need to have each other's backs. No one else will. Maybe we're newbies, but we all know that whether we like it or not."

He paused, taking in the nods of his fellow students. Even Eva subsided, the corners of her mouth turning down as some painful memory washed over her.

"Maybe the bubble was a misstep, but you've got to understand that we're still trying to figure this out, Lorna. We can't learn if no one will give us a chance. You came all this way. Give us a chance," he continued.

Lorna's expression didn't soften, but she nodded.

"Fine," she said. "At least it'll give me some time for my toes to thaw. Is it always this cold here?"

"You think this is bad? You should see the showers," muttered David.

Fabio snorted.

Dani sat back, arms folded, watching it all play out. When it became evident that the conflict had truly resolved itself for the moment, she leaned forward over the table, her gaze intent.

"I've never been one to beat around the bush, and I won't start now," said Dani. "M-Day kicked our butts."

Christopher winced. His abilities had manifested after that awful day, but that didn't make him immune to its effects. He'd thought he understood them up until one day last week when Magneto had taught a class about it. Magneto had cried as he listed off the names of lost mutants, which made Christopher tear up, too. Besides, the anti-mutant sentiments that drove M-Day still lingered on. He felt them every time he returned to civilization.

Dani's eyes fell, her face spasming with some remembered pain.

"My powers are all but gone," she said. "When I was younger, I wasted a lot of time wishing that I didn't have them. But they're a part of me whether I like it or not. It's like missing an arm."

Polaris rubbed Dani's shoulder, offering what little comfort she could. With a grateful smile, Dani broke from her mournful reverie and sipped her hot chocolate. The students sat spellbound and silent. After all, what could any of them say that would make this better? No words could fix this loss.

"What about you?" Christopher asked Lorna.

"I still have mine, but I can't use them," she replied. "At first, I thought they were gone, but I was wrong. I have the strength of a mutant in her prime and the control of a two year-old. No amount of practice has helped. I had to stop or risk killing someone."

"I'm sorry," Eva blurted, her eyes locked on Polaris. "I know how–" She broke off, shaking her head. "I'm just so sorry. How can we help?"

Dani perked up. "I still have coffee with Illyana every once in a while. Even if I'm not an X-Man anymore, we were teammates for a long time, and those connections don't just go away. Last time we met, she was telling me all about the school. She hypothesized that combining your abilities could restore mutant abilities to depowered mutants."

Christopher and Eva exchanged glances. Her eyes were wide with shock, and his felt like they might fall out of his head. It sounded like crazy talk, but M-Day itself was crazy. It had taken power to steal the mutant abilities in the first place. Why shouldn't the right combination of powers be able to put them back?

"How?" asked Eva.

"That's the real question, isn't it?" asked Dani. "At a minimum, you'd need healing and time, since the injury happened in the past. We're essentially trying to rewind the clock on our DNA. Putting it back to how it's supposed to be."

Christopher stroked his chin, thinking through the theory. He'd never even considered the possibility of healing the damage done by M-Day, but it intrigued him. He and Eva would have to learn how to combine their powers, but how hard could that be? They already worked well together.

"Wait a minute. If it's Magik's idea, why isn't she part of this conversation?" asked Eva.

"She likes the idea in theory, but when I suggested trying it, she balked," Dani admitted. "Said it was too dangerous."

"Dangerous how?" asked Christopher.

"As I understand it, most of the danger would be borne by us," said Dani. "Manipulating someone through time can have unforeseen effects. We could end up as toddlers or senior citizens, with no idea how to reverse it. But it's our choice. Our risk. Unfortunately, 'Yana doesn't agree, and she threatened to pour coffee on my head if I didn't drop the subject."

Eva snorted. "That's on brand."

"No kidding. So I went home and called Lorna. A bunch of us depowered mutants are in an informal support group. She and I talked it over, and we agreed that it's worth the risk."

"Is there any risk to us?" Eva pressed.

Dani clamped her mouth shut, and for a long moment, it looked like she might refuse to answer. Then she said, "If word gets out that you can fix broken mutants, you're going to get popular. This school won't stay secret any longer. And there are a lot of people who don't want mutants to return in numbers."

Eva nodded quietly. "Yeah, I can see that. Thanks for being honest."

"But if you can fix us, we could help keep you safe. My father lost his powers, too. And now they're back," said Lorna. "But he won't tell me how he did it. In fact, he's been avoiding me. We had to track him just to find this place. It took forever."

"That stinks," said Fabio.

"Magneto has his reasons for acting the way he does." Lorna lifted her chin proudly. "I don't always agree with them, but I know he doesn't play games."

"It might not matter," said Christopher with regret. "We didn't restore his powers. We don't know any more than you do."

"Emma's are nearly back to full strength, too," added Mindee. "Maybe yours will come back with time."

"Or maybe it's the environment," Lorna countered. "Because the mutants here are the only ones who have shown this kind of improvement. We've talked to a lot of other people who lost most of their abilities. None of them have regained half of what your instructors have."

"We think maybe it's you. After all, you're training together in the Danger Room with them. You're freezing them in time bubbles. You're healing them. Right? Maybe you've been helping without even realizing it," Dani suggested.

"So join the staff here," said Eva. "See if it works for you, too."

"I'm afraid I've got other things on my plate, or I would," Dani replied.

"And I'm not interested," Polaris added.

"Why not?" Eva persisted. "I'm honestly not trying to be a jerk here. I swear."

Lorna considered this, her lips pursed, before answering reluctantly.

"If I join this school, it'll be on my own terms and at full strength. I've spent my life living in my father's shadow, whether I knew it or not. But I make my own way, and my own decisions. I can't risk it any other way," she said. "I don't expect you to understand, but just imagine it for a moment. Imagine having Magneto – *the* Magneto – as your father."

Christopher had had a complicated relationship with his parents, but even he had to concede that it would be nothing compared to what Lorna must have gone through. Magneto wasn't the purebred villain the media painted him as, but he operated from an unshakeable belief in his version of the truth. That bone-deep certainty made him powerful. He was a born leader, and Christopher could admit to having fallen under his sway a few times.

It would be quite a shadow to live under. But maybe not enough to justify a more direct approach. He wasn't sure.

"Eva, what do you think?" he asked.

She hesitated.

"I don't know yet. Maybe we should see what we're working with first. Would you two mind demonstrating your powers?" she asked. "Or lack thereof?"

"Sure thing," replied Dani. "What do you want us to do?"

SEVEN

The more she heard about the situation, and about Polaris's problems in particular, the less Eva liked it. But she couldn't force out the words. She couldn't make herself say, "This is a bad idea. Fooling around with the timeline ruined my life. It marooned me in the past, stuck me in the future, and made me lose my husband and daughter at the same time. You want to talk about uncontrolled powers? I should be the poster child."

But she couldn't bring herself to say so. For starters, she still couldn't bear the thought of talking about her family. Saying it aloud would make the loss final in a way she just couldn't handle yet. It would be like twisting the knife in deeper, and it had already cut deep enough. But there was more than that. After all, her lack of control wasn't anybody's fault. She had instructors who would teach her how to leash her abilities, how to deepen them. Even if she couldn't get her family back, at least she had hope that her entire existence wouldn't be defined by this flaw. Someday, things would be different.

On the surface, their situations were very similar except for one important thing: Polaris lacked that hope. Her control problems had been forced on her through no fault of her own, and from the sounds of it, she'd tried everything Eva would have. Training wouldn't fix it. Waiting might get the job done, but that was no guarantee. But how ironic was it that Polaris would have to rely on her – who suffered from exactly the same problem – for help? What if Eva somehow made things worse? But how could she refuse to try when she could empathize with what Lorna was going through?

She waffled back and forth as the group headed towards the Danger Room. But as they entered the room, Polaris hesitated.

"Maybe we should head outside for the demonstration," she said.

"Weren't you complaining about the cold just a minute ago?" asked David from his spot right on Christopher and Eva's heels.

"Yeah, but there's lots of metal in here, and when I said I don't have control, I wasn't exaggerating," she explained. "The last thing we want is for your instructors to come back and learn that we tore a giant hole in the wall. I'm not sure that even the safeguards in here could contain me."

"OK. Outside it is," Christopher declared. "We've got some heavy coats in that locker in the foyer."

He opened the creaky door and distributed the coats. They smelled just as musty as everything else in the place, but Eva snuggled in anyway. She didn't hate the cold as much as she used to – a few years in the hot and humid future had cured her of that – but she still didn't relish the thought of spending a lot of time outside.

As she emerged out the front door and into the dazzling light of midday, she tented her hand over her face to shield her eyes. The bright sun bounced off the glittering snow, illuminating the sloping hill that led down from the school into the wilderness beyond. Her eyes slowly adjusted, and she looked around even though there was nothing to see but rocky slopes covered with snow, punctuated by the occasional evergreen. The school couldn't have been more remote. The instructors occasionally took them on lengthy hikes, but they had never encountered another person, nor any signs of their passage. No hikers. No road winding through the hilly tundra, punctuated by a single solitary gas station. Once she saw a deer, and it had been an event.

There were no deer today. Only a single bird carving circles in the sky off in the distance. The movement attracted her attention in the vast stillness.

"Let's move away from the building to be safe," Polaris suggested.

"There's a flat bit down here that should work," Christopher suggested. "We sometimes train hand to hand out there."

"Perfect. But before we go…" Polaris held up a finger, urging them to wait, and then returned to the building. A scattered handful of crates were clustered against the exterior wall, a remnant of the prior occupants. Either they hadn't been great with tidiness, or they'd pulled up shop and left in a hurry, because the place was full of half-packed equipment, like some alien invaders had beamed them all up before they could completely move out.

She scanned the crates before reaching into one of them and pulling out a long length of rebar. The heavy metal thunked against her palm as she tested its weight. Satisfied, she slung it over one puffy-coated shoulder and rejoined them.

"I need some demonstration material," she explained. "Carry on."

Christopher led the way through the crust-covered snow,

tamping it down with his heavy boots. After a few paces, Fabio joined him, and together they forged a path that kept most of the snow out of Eva's shoes. Her socks would thank them later.

After about five minutes of hiking, they reached the clearing. The students clustered beneath the trees at the edge, drawn together by cold or nerves. Maybe both. Christopher turned to Polaris and arched a brow.

"Is this far enough away from the school, do you think?" he asked.

"It should work," said Polaris. "Dani, you go first."

Dani pulled down her hood, her face drawn in resignation.

"There's not much for me to demonstrate. You know what I do? Or what I… did?" she asked.

"I don't," said Benjamin hesitantly.

"I cast empathic illusions. I can read your mind and project an image of your greatest fear or your happiest moment," she explained. "But of course, now it doesn't work. Sometimes when I practice, I see a shimmer in the air, and it feels like I'm close, but nothing ever manifests. And sometimes I get glimpses of emotion or thought, but they're like a radio station in the mountains. The reception is never good enough to hear anything clearly."

"So nothing happens when you try?" Eva prompted.

"Nothing really. But I'll give it a go so you can see."

"I'm watching," Christopher said. "Stepfords?"

"If there's a mental block, we'll pick up on it," Phoebe assured him.

"OK, Eva, I'm going to try for something that will make you happy."

Dani stared deep into her eyes, jaw clenched in concentration.

At first, Eva was flattered to be the guinea pig, but that emotion quickly gave way to a torrent of other feelings. What would make her happy would be to see her daughter again, but the illusion would only serve to remind her of what she'd lost. But she wanted it more than anything. She wanted it so bad that her hands shook with need.

She stood there, waiting, unsure of what to wish for, torn apart by her conflicting emotions. Her stomach heaved. She tried to control it, but there was no use.

"I think I might throw up," she said, clutching her belly.

Dani blinked. "I'm sorry. That's never happened before."

In a flash, Christopher was by her side. His cold hands pressed against her cheek, and slowly the nausea eased.

"Better?" he asked.

"Yeah. Thanks."

But she couldn't meet his eyes. Shame flooded her. How was she supposed to help people – and Dani and Lorna in particular – if she couldn't hold it together? Her loss was real, and she deserved a chance to grieve. But she still had a job to do, and she'd better get a grip or someone was going to get hurt because she was too busy feeling sorry for herself.

She straightened, forcing herself upright. "I'm better now," she said.

"So did you feel something?" Dani prompted, her eyes alight.

"I'm not sure if it was you or my breakfast. Ever since Fantomex left, we've been back to prepackaged crap," Eva explained regretfully.

Christopher rubbed her back, turning back to Dani. "I can't pick up on anything physically wrong with you. Either of you," he added.

"And it's not a mental block," added Mindee.

"Well, there you go." Dani sounded disappointed. "That's all I can do."

"You can still shoot a bullseye from all the way across this clearing with one hand tied behind your back," Lorna corrected her. "So that's not all you can do. Remember what they used to say in group. Don't sell yourself short."

"I know. But it still feels like I'm missing my arm," Dani sighed. "Your turn."

Lorna nodded. "I'll head out to the middle of the clearing. You should be able to see fine."

"What's going to happen?" asked David, his eyes alight with interest.

"Who knows? I'm going to try to bend this rebar. It might work. Or maybe nothing will happen. Or maybe it'll explode. It's like the world's worst guessing game."

With that, Lorna began to slog across the snowy clearing. Eva watched her go, fists clenched. For some reason, this felt personal. Important. If Lorna could get a handle on her powers, Eva could, too. And right now, she needed that hope.

Lorna stopped and turned to face them, holding up the bar.

"Can you see OK?" she shouted.

"Yeah, it's good," Christopher yelled. "You ready, Stepfords?"

"We're always ready," said Phoebe, sounding affronted.

"Go ahead!" he yelled.

Polaris held up the length of rebar, the metal silhouetted against the bright white of the snow. Nothing happened. The bar remained intact and straight, without a bend in sight. Eva stared at it, clenching her fists as if that might help somehow. Still nothing.

"Come on!" Lorna cried, staring at the metal bar.

"You can do it," Dani murmured, clenching her fists just as tightly as Eva's.

From somewhere in the distance, a loud boom shook the trees. The ground quaked beneath Eva's feet, and she looked around wildly, trying to find the source of the noise. A flock of birds leapt into the air, cawing in alarm. She couldn't see anything over the trees. But if she moved out from underneath them just a bit…

A shadow crept over the clearing. As Eva sprinted out from beneath the tree cover, she saw an extraordinary sight. A giant electrical tower, hundreds of feet in length, soared down the slope toward them, dragging long lengths of broken wires behind it. As she watched, one of the wires snagged on a full-grown tree and pulled it out of the ground with the protesting groan of wood.

It was headed straight for the students, leaving a trail of destruction in its wake.

Eva could barely believe what she was seeing. Was Lorna doing this somehow, by accident? It was the only explanation that made sense, and when Eva concentrated, she thought she could see a faint shimmer in the air running from Lorna's outstretched hand to the levitating tower.

"Lorna!" yelled Eva. "Make it stop!"

But the magnetic mutant didn't answer. It was like she didn't even hear. The rest of the students had frozen, too, staring at the astonishing sight in shock and fear, their feet seemingly rooted to the ground. They wouldn't move unless someone herded them.

"Get them to safety, Christopher!" she yelled.

She sprinted towards Polaris, not looking back to see if he followed her instructions. She trusted him. He wouldn't let her down. Now all she had to do was get Lorna to stop the tower before tragedy struck. She'd never forgive herself, and even though the two of them hadn't started off on the right foot, Eva refused to allow that to happen.

But Lorna's eyes remained locked on the bar. She was concentrating so hard that she'd blocked out all other input.

"Lorna!" she shouted.

Still no answer. So, Eva did the only thing she could think of. She tackled Lorna to the ground, running at full speed. Lorna wasn't a short woman, but Eva had grown up with a brother. She knew how to take someone down if she had to. She hit the taller woman hard, wrapped her arms around her waist, and took her down into the snow.

Lorna yelped.

"What the heck?" she shouted.

Instead of answering, Eva grabbed her chin and pointed her face towards the levitating tower. Sparks hopped along the snowy ground as it continued its slow approach, hovering like an alien ship moments before it fired a laser blast at the ground below. The enormous structure creaked, metal straining to breaking point.

"No!" Lorna moaned, pushing her hands toward it. "No no no no no!"

She strained, tears gathering at the corners of her eyes. Her teeth gritted together. At first, Eva could see nothing, no indication that Lorna had any power at all, no slowing of the giant structure that bore down on the copse that sheltered the students of the New Charles Xavier School.

If she didn't manage to turn the tower, they might not survive.

"I'll freeze it," she said, although she was less than confident about her ability to do so. The tower was bigger than anything she'd ever bubbled before, and with her luck, her powers would pick this moment to act up again, too.

Then the necklace that hung around her neck levitated in front of her face. The pendant, a silver-plated heart, had been a gift from her mother. Now it floated, held aloft by a power she couldn't feel, although maybe she wasn't imagining the shiver that ran down her spine.

"I've got it," Lorna said through gritted teeth.

The tower slowed, metal groaning as momentum struggled against the opposing force of Lorna's magnetic powers. She pushed harder, groaning with effort. Blood trickled from one nostril. When Eva concentrated, she thought she could see the power travel through the air, a heat-like shimmer stretching from Lorna's outstretched hands to envelop the electrical tower. But maybe that, too, was her imagination.

With a shout of effort, Lorna wrenched her hands downward. The tower jerked out of the sky as if she'd tugged on its leash. A loud crash shook the ground, and trees snapped as the tower dropped down mere yards from the fleeing students. Christopher had herded them away, just far enough to escape harm. But it had been close. If they'd been a few seconds slower, someone would have been badly hurt.

Lorna's bottle-green eyes turned to hers. She looked like she'd just awoken from a nap only to find that her nightmare was real.

"I'm so sorry!" she exclaimed. "I told you…"

She leapt to her feet, surveying the damage. As she took in the tower, all the blood drained from her face.

"You see?" she asked. "If I don't do something, if I don't fix this, someone will die. I know it's a lot to ask, and I know we don't get along, but please. Please at least try to help me."

Eva struggled to stand, brushing the snow off her knees. "I'm willing to try, but I should tell you something first. My powers aren't much better controlled than yours. I could make things worse without meaning to. *Much* worse."

"Eva? Lorna? You guys OK over there?" Christopher yelled.

"Yeah!" Eva responded. "We're good! Just a minute, and we'll join you."

"What's going on?" Polaris stared her down. "Is it something we ought to know?"

"Most of it's personal, and I'm not ready to share. But… I've lost control, too. I know how awful it feels."

"You're still young," Lorna said gently. "It'll come with time."

Eva snorted. "Time. That's ironic. You say that now, but what if I fling you through time and you can't get back? You'd be cursing my name then, I bet."

"Ah. So that's the problem." Lorna fell silent for a long moment. "I don't talk about this much, but I think you need to hear it. When I was small, I was on a trip with my parents – or the people I thought were my parents, anyway. They were arguing, and I didn't like the yelling. I didn't even know I was a mutant back then. I brought the plane down without even knowing I'd done it."

"Oh no," said Eva. "What happened to them?"

"They all died," Lorna said simply. "But here's the thing: that's not a reason to deny my abilities. I could have refused to use them ever again. But that would just make it happen again. I need control. I need to use my abilities to make up for that day. To choose to be something different."

"Easier said than done."

"Tell me about it. But we've got to try. Moping around and feeling sorry for yourself isn't going to help anyone."

Eva snorted. For some reason, the lecture stung a little less coming from Polaris. Maybe because they were facing some of the same problems. Maybe because Eva had already come to the same conclusion herself. She might not like it, and she might struggle against it with all her might, but deep down she knew that Lorna was right.

She took a deep breath, trying to steel herself.

"OK," she said. "I'll try. But Dani needs to fully understand the risks first. If you could find a private time to tell her about my problems, I'd appreciate that. My friends will fuss once they know what happened, and I'm just not up for that yet."

"But you will tell them, yes?" Lorna demanded.

"Eventually, yeah."

"Good." Lorna paused. "Dang it. Dani was right."

"About what?"

"I am a good teacher." Lorna sighed. "She's always right. It's aggravating."

"I'll keep your secret if you keep mine," Eva offered, chuckling.

"That's a deal," said Lorna, and they shook.

EIGHT

As the electrical tower plummeted to the ground, Christopher kept up a steady stream of reassurances. "It'll be fine," he kept saying. "Don't worry. Stay together. It'll be fine," despite his panicked visions of students crushed by the sliding tower of metal, or buried under a mound of snow and suffocating alone. His voice didn't even shake. No one would have known how close he came to going fetal unless he told them, and he'd take that secret to his grave.

The tower touched down and began to slide through the snow, pushing great mounds of it toward the treeline that sheltered the students. Christopher urged the group on, but they needed no prompting. They helped each other over the uneven ground, moving as quickly as possible through the knee-deep snow. Christopher followed, his heart thumping so fast that he thought he might keel over. Logically, he knew that he'd survive being buried alive in the snow or crushed by a giant hunk of metal, but that didn't stop the wave of adrenaline from overwhelming him.

Thankfully, the tower didn't slide long, but it felt like an eternity anyway. Every moment was packed with enough terror for an entire year. Once it finally creaked to a stop, he leaned down to put his hands on his knees, struggling to catch his breath. The snow mound blocked his view, and the greenery right at the edge of the clearing had been scrambled, but enough landmarks remained to orient him. They'd run maybe a hundred yards, but if he'd had to guess, he would have said a mile.

It didn't matter. They'd escaped unharmed, and that was what counted. The students clustered into a big group, exchanging hugs and exclamations of relief. Fabio sat right down in the snow, unable to support himself on legs shaky with adrenaline. David dropped next to him, talking to him in low and soothing tones. A few steps away, Dani Moonstar watched all of this with the wistful expression of a teammate without a team.

"Everyone OK?" Christopher asked. "Anybody need healing?"

"I think we're good. We lucked out," said Mindee.

He looked back towards the clearing, but the giant mound of snow continued to block his view. Eva and Lorna had been well out of range of the toppling tower, but he still needed to be sure.

"Eva? Lorna? You guys OK over there?" he yelled.

"Yeah!" Eva shouted back. "We're good. Just a minute, and we'll join you."

When he turned his attention back to the group, Dani was rubbing her ankle, her brows drawn in pain. He hurried over, eager to do something – anything – substantial to help.

"Let me heal that for you," he said.

"It's just twisted. I've dealt with much worse," she explained.

"I'm sure you have, but there's no sense in limping when you've got a healer right here."

"Fair enough."

She allowed him to take the injured ankle into his hands. The injury practically leapt out at him, a minor disturbance in the overall harmony of her body. One tendon pulled slightly beyond its limit. Muscles tensed in an effort to spare the joint from further harm. Repairing it was nothing, but it still felt like a million bucks to have her wilt with relief.

"Thanks," she said.

He looked back toward the tower. A clump of snow fell off one of the girders as the structure continued to settle. It was huge, defying his efforts to mentally calculate its height.

"How tall do you think that thing is? Five hundred feet? A thousand?" he asked, awe saturating his voice.

"No idea. I bet it weighs a ton, though. You see why we need help now? It's not safe for anyone to walk around with that kind of power and no control."

"Yeah." He rubbed his chin. "I'm trying to think of where it came from. We've walked around the area a lot, and I know I've seen those towers, but it's hard to make a mental map without many landmarks. It's not close, though."

The rest of the students joined them one by one, prompting a new round of check-ins and exclamations of relief. Christopher surveyed them with pride. As new as they were, they'd held it together during a dangerous situation, without the aid of their instructors. Whether they realized it or not, they were getting the hang of this X-Men thing. When he pointed it out, Dani immediately stepped in to confirm it.

"He's right," she said. "I've seen experienced teams do much worse."

"Yeah? I nearly peed when that thing came flying down at us," Fabio joked.

A wave of relieved laughter ran over the group.

"Can we climb over, do you think?" asked Benjamin, his thin face pinched with worry. "Those wires aren't live anymore, right?"

"I don't think so, but I'm not sure how sturdy it is," Christopher replied. "We should probably go around."

"Speaking of wires," said David, "that thing transmitted a lot of power. Someone's going to come looking for it. I'm not sure we want the attention."

"No, we definitely do not." Christopher frowned. "I'm not sure we want to chance asking Lorna to move it. You think you could tow it? Drop it into a lake or something?"

"The X-Copter can't carry that kind of weight. To be honest, I'm not sure that the X-Jet would do much better. It'll spin when we pick it up, and that's a recipe for potential disaster," David responded. "It might be better to wait for Magneto to get back. They can't be gone that long."

"If it takes too long, you could use the chopper to dump a bunch of snow on it so it's not visible from above," Dani suggested. "Buy yourself a little time."

"That sounds like a plan," David nodded. "Although that brings up another question. Did that thing power the school?"

Christopher's stomach sank. They'd been worried about breaking the Danger Room, but now they might have broken the entire school. Peachy.

"Oh no," he said. "We'd better go find out."

He led the way around the fallen structure, only losing his footing once. He took a step forward, expecting to meet solid ground, and plummeted into the snow to his waist. Fabio and David pulled him out without any harm done, but it shook him.

Luckily, they made it the rest of the way to the clearing without further incident. Eva and Lorna finished talking just as they approached, and it only took a few moments to bring them up to speed on the new power-related concerns.

"I'm so sorry," said Lorna. "But you see why we're here."

"I do. And I'm in. But we've got to check on the school first. I don't relish the idea of freezing to death out here without power," Christopher replied. "I'd feel much better if we could go back and check before we do anything else."

"Of course," said Dani. "This predicament is our fault. We'll help fix it if necessary."

The group hurried back to the school. As they climbed up the slope toward the front entrance, Christopher scanned the sky. A silent, still expanse stretched out before him. He saw no helicopters full of curious humans, desperate to know what natural – or unnatural – disaster had befallen their power grid. Maybe they'd lucked out. Maybe the tower hadn't been in use. Maybe no one would notice.

It didn't hurt to dream.

When he pushed open the door, warm air blasted his frozen cheeks. The small foyer was cloaked in darkness, but the lights had been malfunctioning for some time, and they kept the hallway doors closed for security reasons. If anyone ever broke into the school, they'd have to blow their way through every door, giving the students precious time to get to safety.

"So is the power on or not?" Fabio asked, too impatient to wait.

Everyone clustered in behind Christopher, eager for answers, and he held up a hand for quiet. To his surprise, this time they listened. In the sudden stillness, he could hear the rush of air through the vents. The heating system wouldn't work without power, would it?

"I think so," he said, crossing the floor to the first door. The palm reader didn't work, but the keypad next to it lit up when he flipped up the cover. He grinned, overcome with a wave of relief. "The power's on."

"Thank god," said Benjamin, clapping his hands. "They would have killed us."

There was no need to ask who "they" were. All of the students had shared the same worries in one form or another. No one wanted to be the person to tell Cyclops that their school no longer had electricity because they'd accidentally torn the power wires down.

"We should check the computer just in case," David suggested. "We could be on emergency power only."

"Is that possible?" asked Christopher, his relief ebbing.

"If I built this place, I'd divert emergency power to the doors and the heat. Otherwise, you're one power failure away from turning this entire school into a tomb. Better to check just in case."

"You know a lot about this stuff," Eva said.

David shrugged. "My old man was an engineer. This is all he'd talk about at the dinner table for years. So I know the basics, but that's about it. Cyclops and I have been trying to figure the system out in our spare time."

"We'll take it," Christopher replied, punching in the code. "Let's go check."

He led the way down the hall, glancing at lights and keypads and trying not to overreact when they remained dark. Flipping every switch between here and the Danger Room would prove nothing except that he was unhinged. But his worries weren't unreasonable. Cyclops was already overprotective. If they damaged the school, they'd be in training wheels forever.

He said a silent prayer as they entered the Danger Room. The computer bay cast a reassuring electric glow on the countertop below, but as David had pointed out, that didn't guarantee that all was well. Christopher would wait for verification before he got too excited. David slid into the cracked leather seat, scanned the array of screens, and began pushing buttons, his hands moving with surety over the complex control board. As he worked, the rest of the students clustered around him, waiting with bated breath for his analysis.

Christopher glanced around, taking a head count to reassure himself that they hadn't lost anyone in all the chaos. Even in a small group, such things were possible, and right now he was feeling extra paranoid. But they were all present and accounted for. Even Dani and Lorna, although the latter hovered near the doorway, her face twisted with worry and guilt.

Christopher sidled up to Dani, catching her attention with a tug on her sleeve. A quick flick of his head toward Lorna directed Dani's attention.

"You think she's OK?" he murmured.

Dani arched a brow and shook her head. "Would you be, under the same circumstances?"

He opened his mouth, thought better of it, and shut it with a click.

"That's what I thought," Dani continued.

"Should somebody talk to her?"

"I'll check on her, but words are useless. We need our powers back. Otherwise, this is just going to keep happening," said

Dani. "I'm sorry if that's harsh, but it's the truth. I hope you can see that now."

She excused herself then, and he thought it through as he watched her join Lorna, exchanging a few quiet words. Of course, Dani was right. Once they knew that the power was operational, he'd try to help. He'd do his best to talk Eva into it if she wasn't on board. He didn't exactly know where to start, but for the longest time, he hadn't really understood how he healed people either. He'd just done it, completely by instinct, when he was needed. It didn't really matter, anyway. If it was possible, he had to at least make the effort.

"How's it looking?" he asked David, unable to wait any longer.

"Yeah," added Fabio. "It's taking a while. You ordering takeout or something? If so, I want some."

He snickered, elbowing Benjamin.

"Don't I wish," replied David. "I'm going through all of the electrical systems to verify that they're operational. Just a couple more to go, but so far, we're golden. I think we're completely off the grid, but I'd have to get a look at the generator room to know for sure, and they keep it locked for a reason."

"Why's that?" asked Eva curiously.

"Because if some idiot kills the generators by accident, we all freeze to death," David replied.

"Oh. I feel stupid now."

"Don't worry about–" A familiar klaxon broke the silence. The perimeter alarm again. "Uh oh."

"It's probably just the instructors coming back," said Benjamin. "Right?"

"The instructors wouldn't set off the alarm, remember?"

Christopher explained. "Unless they ditched the X-Jet and came back in something else."

"After all the work Summers and I put in to fix it? No way," said David, punching at the control panel with increased urgency. "Come on, you piece of crap. Let me out of this submenu."

"So who is it then?" asked Eva.

"That's what I'm trying to find out," said David. "If you all would just shut up and let me concentrate. This thing isn't easy to navigate, you know."

"Sorry," she said. "I just thought after what you did for the party…"

"What's going on?" Dani asked, rejoining the group with Lorna in tow. "What's that alarm?"

"It's not the electrical system. That's fine. But it's…" David pushed one final button and then stared at the readout with wide and disbelieving eyes. Then he burst into a long string of swear words.

Christopher didn't want to ask, but he needed to know.

"What is it?" he asked.

"It's a Sentinel," David answered.

NINE

At first, Eva wondered if David was playing a prank on them. When he'd arrived at the school, he'd made it clear that he considered the entire situation beneath him. He was older. Wiser. A man of the world. That David would have yanked all of their chains and found it hilarious. But after he'd been expelled, he'd come back a different person. One who wanted to be here. He still teased his fellow students, and sometimes they disagreed, but at the end of the day, she knew he had their backs. He wouldn't joke about something like this.

"How?" she demanded. "How did it find us?"

"The computer can do a lot of things, Bell, but reading the minds of hostile robots isn't one of them. How would I know?" he shot back.

"Sorry!" she exclaimed, holding up her hands in a placating gesture.

He rubbed at his face, worry creasing his brow. "I shouldn't have snapped. You were probably being rhetorical."

"How long do we have before it gets here?" asked Dani, frowning. "Do we have enough time to run? Everyone can pile onto our jet, and we can take you somewhere safe until it's gone."

"Hard to say," David replied, tapping on the keyboard to his left. "But I don't think so. It's closing in on the tower pretty fast, and as soon as we take off, it'll follow."

"Besides, once it finds the school, it'll tell all its robot buddies," said Eva. "The whole point of this location is that it's secret."

"The tower attracted it," Lorna said, scowling. "Darn it. I'm so sorry. I wish I could..."

She trailed off, her meaning obvious. If she'd only been at full strength, she could have torn the Sentinel out of the sky without even breaking a sweat. But it wasn't worth the risk. She slammed her hand against the nearest wall, snarling. Dani patted her shoulder, but there wasn't much else she could do. Still, Lorna got herself back under control as quickly as she'd lost it.

Excitement and fear swelled in Eva's belly. They'd faced Sentinels before and won; heck, she and Christopher had taken on a few of them alone on their trip to Chicago. As a result, she didn't underestimate them, but she knew they could be beaten. It would just require them to work together on a level they hadn't managed before.

"OK," she said. "David, can you take it over, or is it too far?"

"I think so..." he said, hesitating.

"Do it. Fly it as far away as you can and run it into a wall."

"But what if more of them come to investigate?" asked Christopher.

"If it finds us, we'll have an entire squadron of them on our heads," said Eva. "At least this way, we buy ourselves a chance. And we get time. We need that time. Do it, David. If we waste too much time arguing, we won't have a choice any longer."

"On it," said David.

No one argued as he turned back to the control panel and cracked his knuckles. He pushed a few buttons, and a grainy video image flared to life above his head. Then he stared at it.

It was very anticlimactic.

Christopher edged over to Eva and whispered in her ear.

"You sure this is a good idea?" he asked.

"It's the least bad one," she replied. "Someone has to step in and make the call."

He frowned. "I hate to say this, but we need to radio for help."

"You've got to be kidding me." Eva threw up her hands. "I thought we'd gotten past this."

"We have! Honest. But hear me out: if we don't at least try to contact Cyclops, and he comes back to see signs of a struggle, he's going to trust us even less. The protocol says that we send out an alert if we can. We follow the protocol, just like any other X-Man."

Eva sighed. "I suppose. David can do so after he crashes that Sentinel. We can't distract him."

They watched the tiny figure on the screen soar over snowy hills. Eva squinted, trying to figure out where it was, but the low-quality image didn't help with an already difficult landscape. As she watched, the ground disappeared as the Sentinel climbed up into the cloudless sky.

"That's a great idea," Dani murmured over her shoulder.

"I don't get it," Eva replied.

"He's taking it up into the atmosphere. That'll suggest an airborne threat and concentrate any searches in that direction. The school could escape detection after all," she explained. "It's very smart."

The image began to flicker, dissolving into staticky bars.

Moments before it disintegrated entirely, the Sentinel exploded in a somewhat underwhelming burst. David slumped in his seat, wiping at his sweaty brow.

"That's done," he said.

"Nice work!" Christopher clapped him on the shoulder. "That was some quick thinking."

"Thanks." David gave them a thin-lipped smile. "Did I hear correctly that we wanted to radio the instructors as well?"

"It's the right thing to do," Christopher replied.

"I'm honestly not sure they'll answer," said David. "We haven't gotten all of the wrist communicators to work properly yet. I can leave a message on the X-Jet, though. As soon as they board, they'll hear it."

"It'll have to do," said Christopher, ignoring Eva's satisfied smile.

David punched a few buttons.

"Home Base to One-Eye. Home Base to One-Eye. We have a perimeter breach. Return to base immediately," said David. "Home Base out." He toggled the radio off and stretched elaborately. "That's done."

"Did he pick that call sign?" asked Dani, her brows arched.

"Nope," David grinned.

"He's probably gonna kill you."

He shrugged. "So what now?"

All the students began talking at once, eager to share their plans. Some thought they should go into hiding. Others thought they should take the X-Jet and run. David loudly proclaimed that they should arm themselves like Rambo and lie in wait for the next wave of Sentinels, but maybe he was kidding. It was always difficult to tell with him.

Eventually, Lorna held a hand up, pinching the bridge of her nose.

"Please stop," she begged. "I haven't had my caffeine today, and all this shouting is going to make my head explode."

"This team needs a leader," Dani added. "I can't believe you don't have one yet."

"Well, it can't be either of you. We don't know you," said David. "No offense. I know you've got experience coming out your ears, and I'd listen to advice from you any time. But I'm not going to blindly follow someone I barely know. That sounds like a recipe for disaster."

"Me either," said Christopher.

Eva's heart skipped a beat. This was their chance. After everything they'd been through, she and Christopher were the ideal choice for this job. They'd faced down Sentinels completely on their own. They'd handled Sabretooth. They worked well together. She didn't know how to classify their bond – best friends? Siblings by choice? Partners? But the semantics didn't matter. She could count on him, and that was enough. They were the ideal choice to lead this team.

"It should be us," she declared. "Me and Christopher."

"Shouldn't Cyclops pick our leaders?" Fabio asked nervously. "It seems like he should at least have input."

"He's thought about it," said Mindee. "But no final decision yet."

"But he's not a part of this group," Christopher argued, warming to the topic. "Eventually, we're going to have to work on our own. He won't have to deal with the fallout. We do. So we ought to pick."

"I can get behind that," said David. "But if we're gonna do this, we better speed things up."

"Do we have any more Sentinels on the radar yet?" asked Eva.

"Nothing yet, but it's probably just a matter of time."

"OK. Does anyone else want to do this?" asked Eva.

"I think I'd be a good leader," said David. "I'll throw my hat in."

They all stared at each other. No one spoke. Meanwhile, the seconds ticked by, bringing the Sentinels closer to their door. Eva wanted to break the silence, but she worried how that would look. She wanted to lead. Casting the first vote for herself seemed tactless.

Luckily, Dani waded into the breach. She stepped into the middle of the group, dusting her hands off briskly as if preparing for heavy work.

"As a neutral party, I'd like to volunteer to take the votes," she said. "Any objections?"

No one objected.

"Good," she continued, turning to her right. "I'll start here and move around clockwise. Phoebe Stepford?"

The Stepford triplets exchanged glances. Eva wondered what conversation they were having, in the depths of their minds where no one else could eavesdrop. Did they argue? Tease? Discuss everyone's deepest secrets in great depth? Whatever they discussed, it displeased Phoebe. She turned to Dani with a faint frown creasing her brow.

"We vote for Eva and Christopher," she said.

Dani blinked. She wasn't used to the three-in-one and their habit of presenting a unified front regardless of the circumstances. Her gaze flickered over Mindee and Celeste, unsure of how to handle the situation.

"You both agree?" she asked. "That's three votes, right?"

They nodded in eerie concert. Dani shivered a little, but

pulled out a sheet of paper and marked off three ticks before moving on.

"OK," she said. "Benjamin?"

"I vote for David," he said with an apologetic glance at Eva and Christopher.

"Fabio?"

"I vote for David, Christopher, and Eva," he said.

"You can't vote for all the candidates, Fabio," Dani protested.

"No one said I can't." He folded his arms. "They're the ones who want to lead. Everybody knows it."

"Eva?"

Eva took a minute to think it over, trying to set her personal feelings aside and consider the group as a whole. Yes, she wanted to lead this team. Taking the position would distract her from her personal woes. But it would also take advantage of her years of experience, and her natural partnership with Christopher. They would make good leaders. Not that David wouldn't, but he'd burnt a few bridges with his early behavior. Those bridges could be mended, but they didn't have the time for it. She honestly felt that voting for herself wasn't just a selfish choice, but the right one.

"Fabio isn't wrong. But I think Dani's right, too. Three leaders would just complicate things, and I have experience teaming up with Christopher. So I'm going to vote for us. But I think David would be a great leader, and he deserves a team of his own someday," she said.

"Thanks," said David. She shot him a look, and he threw up his hands. "No, I really mean that. I know I can be a smart aleck sometimes, but I think regardless of how this vote goes, we'll be in good hands."

"Thanks," she said, genuinely touched.

"I agree with Eva," said Christopher. "David would be a great choice, but when that tower came sailing over the trees, Eva went sprinting across that clearing, and I led the students out of the way. I vote for us."

Dani turned to David. He nodded.

"I mean, with a few notable exceptions, I've been looking to you two for leadership, too, if we're being honest," he said. "But we gotta choose these things for ourselves. And if we trust you to lead us, you have to trust in our skills and our input. Can you do that?"

"You've more than proven your smarts," said Eva. "We'd be crazy not to."

He nodded, and the two of them shook hands.

"Then you've got my vote, which means you're in," he said. He didn't seem remotely bothered by the fact that he'd lost, and Eva admired him for it. He just shook it off and turned on to the next thing. "So what next? We've..." He paused, glancing down at the control panel. Then he cut off entirely. "Oh boy."

"What?" Eva demanded. She already had a sinking feeling that she knew what he was going to say next.

He nodded.

"Yeah, they're coming," he said. "It's a whole squad of Sentinels by the looks of things."

He spun around in his chair and began typing madly, pulling up screens and data readouts. Within moments, they could see the familiar grainy video monitors, but this time, instead of a single Sentinel, there were too many to count.

"How soon will they be here?" asked Eva.

David pursed his lips in thought. "Five minutes tops," he said.

Christopher and Eva exchanged looks. When it was just the two of them, decision making had been easy, but now the dynamics had changed, and neither one of them wanted to go first. But there was no time to waste. They'd done enough waffling around already.

"OK. Where will they come in?" asked Christopher. "The front door and the hangar bay, right?"

"Unless they find the emergency exits, and those are tough to locate if you don't know what you're looking for," answered Eva. "Two teams?"

"Makes sense to me. I'll take Dani, David, and Fabio. We can stay here."

"Then I've got the Stepfords, Morph, and Polaris at the front door." Eva nodded. "That works."

"That's a great idea. Let's roll," said Christopher.

TEN

As Eva's team hurried toward the front door, Christopher turned to look over his mutants. His X-Men. This felt like the kind of momentous occasion that deserved a speech, but he would have felt like an idiot giving one. Besides, the Sentinels would arrive before too long, so he had an excuse for skipping it.

"OK," he said. "We need a plan."

There was just one problem. He didn't have one. Dani might have suggestions, but she didn't know the new mutants the way he did. Besides, he'd been given the opportunity to lead. If he turned around and passed the buck on to someone else within the first five minutes, that wouldn't exactly inspire his fellows to follow him. That kind of thing could tear a team up in a heartbeat.

He would just have to apply some logic. The Sentinels were dangerous adversaries, but their greatest strength lay in their numbers and their ability to call up reinforcements as soon as they discovered a potential target. In order to win this battle, the mutants needed to keep that from happening. If they could shut down the Sentinels' long-distance communications, then they'd only have to face the squad nearby. If not, they'd be overrun.

He turned to David, nearly bouncing with excitement. For the first time, being a mutant was fun. He'd proven himself, and now all he had to do was put his brain to work. It felt like one of his favorite strategy games.

"Do we know if they've radioed in our position to their… home base, or whatever they call it?" he asked.

David smirked, but he turned to the keyboard. After a moment of typing, he said, "I don't think so. We probably would have picked up on that."

"Can you jam their outgoing communications?"

"I'm not good enough with the computer, but I might be able to turn off their long-range transmitters with my mutant powers. I haven't had the chance to try something like that before. You want me to give it a go? I won't be able to monitor the computer. There's so many of them that I'll pretty much be dead weight."

"I can take over on the computer," Dani offered. "I've used a similar system before. It would just take me a minute to orient myself."

"Perfect."

The two mutants switched places. Dani began to type, her fingers skimming over the keyboard with an assurance that reassured Christopher. She wouldn't have volunteered if she didn't know what she was doing – at this point, Dani Moonstar had nothing to prove to anyone – but still. He wanted this to go well. Not because he was desperate to prove himself as a leader, and not because he was worried about their safety. He could heal just about anything short of death, and he'd trained until he could wield that skill with confidence. That confidence made all the difference, and many of his teammates didn't have it yet. Or if they had self-confidence, they didn't have trust. If the instructors always had to haul them out of the fire, they would never make a difference.

David stood in the middle of the hangar, looking up toward the closed bay doors. His face went blank as he reached out toward the Sentinels with his mutant powers. Christopher didn't know exactly how those powers worked – how did his DNA recognize a vehicle compared to other mechanical contraptions? But it worked somehow, and that was all he needed to know. He'd leave all of the theorizing to the experts in the field of mutant studies.

"Looks like they found us," said Dani. "They're closing in fast."

"You got them, Hijack?" asked Christopher, trying not to sound as anxious as he felt.

"Don't distract me," said David, clenching his fists. "I'm busy here."

"Oh. Sure." Christopher turned his attention back to the doors. The Sentinels would come through, and then ... what? He tried to think back to the conflicts they'd been in when the school was young. Cyclops had taken the students along on recruiting missions, where they'd been attacked by mutant-fearing police, Sentinels, and even the Avengers. They'd gotten sent to Limbo once, fighting off hordes of grotesque demons against a hellish landscape that still haunted his dreams sometimes. The students had been entirely green during those fights, and Cyclops had gotten them through. How had he done it?

Christopher thought back, racking his brain for some leadership strategy he could use. But even in retrospect, those fights had been nothing but organized chaos. Cyclops hadn't really told the students what to do beyond the basics like, "Get out of the way!" or "Watch out!" But he and the other instructors had worked together like clockwork. They seemed to have eyes in the backs of their heads, or some sixth sense that told them when a fellow mutant needed help. Christopher hoped that someday their team would have that kind of connection, but they definitely weren't there yet. As a result, those memories of Cyclops gave him nothing he could use. That wasn't a ding against Scott Summers; just a recognition of the fact that their team wasn't ready for that kind of hands-off leadership in a combat situation. Christopher would have to come up with something else.

Quickly, if possible. He looked around wildly, only to realize that Fabio was nowhere to be seen. Had he decided to go with Eva's group after all? Did he get beamed up by Sentinels? Could they even beam people up? He had no clue. Some kind of leader he'd turned out to be. In the first minute or two, he'd already lost a mutant.

"Fabio?" he called, hoping that he'd say, "I'm right here, you idiot. What are you, blind?" But he didn't respond.

Well, hopefully he'd just gone to make sure the doors were all closed and he'd be back in a second. Christopher needed to have a plan by then. If he didn't, his team members would just wander off on their own again. He dropped down to a crouch next to Dani, looking over her shoulder and trying to make sense of the readouts that scrolled past at a breakneck pace. How could anyone even read that?

"Dani?" he asked. "Can I ask you for advice?"

"Hmm?" she asked, distracted. "Advice about what?"

"How do you make people listen to you?"

For a moment, she looked from his worried expression to the screen and back again, as if trying to decide which of these potential crises deserved the more immediate attention. But then she removed her hands from the keyboard and turned to face him. A small smile creased her lips as she took in his expression.

"This isn't funny," said Christopher, wounded.

As he spoke, a series of thumps overhead announced the arrival of the Sentinels. The control panel lit up with red flashing lights. Christopher frowned, gesturing toward it, but Dani kept her attention on him.

"That can wait a second. This is important," she said.

"No, it can't!"

"They're going to get in no matter what we do," Dani replied patiently. "But we'll survive it if we work as a cohesive team, which means that talking you through this is more important than buying us an extra two minutes by manually controlling a security system that I don't fully understand. This system is similar to the one at the mansion, but it's not exactly the same. It's better if I let it run its automated processes. Besides, you asked for my advice. Do you want it or not?"

Christopher closed his eyes. She was right. He was letting his nerves get the best of him. He needed to quit obsessing and solve the problem.

"Yes, please," he said.

"Just stop trying to force something that isn't there yet," she said. "I remember when I got my first team. I went in confident, because if Professor Xavier and the rest of the team chose me as the leader, that meant I was worthy. I thought that the title alone would make my team listen to me."

"Did it?"

She shook her head, sending her braid flying.

"Heck, no," she said. "It was a disaster. Because the title doesn't make you a leader. Being a leader does."

Overhead, metal screeched and sparks rained down as the Sentinels began to cut their way through the doors. Dani didn't bat an eye. She stared at Christopher as if willing him to understand. He got the idea, but putting it into action would be another thing entirely. Taking action had been so easy when it was just him and Eva, and they'd had Sabretooth's backup then, for better and for worse. But at the end of the day, this wasn't much different. There were just more pieces on the board, and he excelled at complex strategies.

"So I lead, and then they'll follow," he said. "But what if they don't?"

"That's their choice." She offered a tight smile. "Although if they try that while I'm here, I'll happily smack them upside the head until they see the light."

He laughed. "OK."

Fabio came running back in, his eyes wild. "They're cutting in through the doors!" he exclaimed.

It took Christopher a moment to catch up with the abrupt conversational change. Then he nodded. "I know," he said.

"What do we do?" Fabio demanded.

Christopher looked around, still second-guessing himself. If this was a game, he'd play it conservatively, since he had fewer pieces than his opponent. So he needed to protect his pieces and create a situation where he could pick them off from a safe position. He could do that.

"David's distracted. We need to get him out of the way," he said.

They all looked to the middle of the floor where David stood, his gaze abstract and his hands held out. His fingers curled, straining toward some unseen goal. Sparks showered the ground around him, but he didn't so much as flinch.

"OK," said Fabio. "I can do that."

With a loud, metallic screech, a piece of the hangar bay tore free, missing Dani's X-Jet. The large hunk of metal plummeted toward David's unseeing face. Christopher didn't have the time to think over the wisdom of his actions. The only thing he could do was react. He threw himself at David's legs as the door closed in, knocking his friend out of the way. His calf stung as a piece of sharp metal ripped through his skin, and David whuffed as they fell onto the hard floor, knocking all the wind out of him. The door impacted on the ground with a crunch, flying high into the air and nearly hitting Christopher in the face before it finally came to a stop on the floor.

"I think I've got their communications locked down," David murmured. "And that really hurt."

"Sorry, man," said Christopher, but there was no time for further explanations. A purple and gray metallic head stuck itself through the opening in the ceiling and swiveled, its glowing eyes sweeping the space.

A Sentinel.

<<MUTANT ACTIVITY DETECTED,>> it said in a voice that echoed off the hangar bay walls. <<INITIATE APPREHENSION PROTOCOLS.>>

ELEVEN

Eva led the way toward the front door, thinking as quickly as possible. Under different circumstances, she would have been the perfect mutant to lead a defense of the foyer. After all, she could freeze the small area in a bubble, and then they could pick off the Sentinels at their leisure. But she had horrific visions of making her first bubble only to have her powers flare out of control and whisk her away to the Paleolithic Age, leaving the rest of her team to wonder what had happened to her while any Sentinels that she missed hunted them down like deer.

She couldn't let that happen, which meant that she needed another plan. Lorna couldn't help without risking tearing holes in the school. And the Stepfords couldn't use their psychic powers on a bunch of robots.

The answer eluded her, and there was no time to waste. The foyer sat around the corner and through that door, and she still had no idea what to do once they got there. If they entered the room to find that the Sentinels had already gotten into the building, someone could die.

She skidded to a stop, watching in horror as Benjamin reached out toward the keypad that opened the door.

"Stop!" she yelled. "Wait."

Benjamin snatched his hand back like the keypad had burned him, and she immediately wanted to kick herself. Panicking her team would accomplish nothing. Cyclops and Captain America were born leaders because they built their people up rather than tearing them down. She would have to do that. It would be no more difficult than getting her daughter to brush her teeth at night. Kids could be so stubborn.

"Sorry," she said, trying to explain away her shout. "I'm a little hyper here. There could be Sentinels in there. We need to be prepared."

"Oh. That's easy," said Benjamin, his narrow face eager. "You bubble them all, right?"

Eva hesitated. "Maybe. But I might not catch them all."

"We'll go through first," Mindee Stepford suggested. "In diamond form. We should be able to absorb anything they throw at us, at least for a few seconds."

Phoebe shot her a look but sighed. "Yeah, I guess we could do that."

"Great. Thanks," said Eva.

Mindee met her eyes, and although Eva had suspected they'd picked up on her secret, now she knew it for sure. The psychic practically dripped sympathy. That annoyed Eva, but at least Mindee hadn't said anything. It could have been much worse.

"Please transform, then," Eva urged. "Every moment we waste is another minute they could get into the building."

Phoebe nodded, closing her eyes, and the other two

Stepfords followed suit. Their skin began to shimmer from within, as if caught by great lighting. Then it hardened, supple human skin changing into hard living diamond, the transformation creeping out from their torsos to the tips of their fingers and the tops of their heads. Soft slopes of human flesh sank into flat planes and rounded corners. When it was over, the three young women glittered as the light struck them, their figures impossibly translucent. What happened to their internal organs? Eva wondered. Did the transformation hurt?

The Stepfords opened the door to the foyer, shielding the rest of the students from view. Nothing happened. Eva peered over their shoulders and let out a sigh of relief. Not a single killer robot in sight.

Before she could comment on their luck, a metallic *rat-a-tat-tat* echoed through the small chamber. Eva reassessed the situation: the Sentinels were here, and they had good manners. Under different circumstances, she would have laughed.

"We gonna answer that?" asked Benjamin querulously.

"Definitely not," answered Eva.

They didn't wait for an answer anyway. Instead, the edges of the door began to glow faintly as the killer robots applied some heat-based tool to it. They'd melt their way in. The bright, glinting forms of the Stepfords stepped toward the door, hand in hand. Their expressions betrayed no fear. They couldn't have been more blasé if they'd been walking to the corner store for a gallon of milk.

The red ring around the edge of the door grew with steady implacability. The entryway would be breached within a minute or two.

"Got any weapons around here?" asked Lorna.

"I'm afraid not. The previous occupants left a few boxes of guns, but no ammunition," said Eva.

"I'm not a great shot anyway. Never learned," Lorna frowned, looking around the entryway. "What's that?" she asked, indicating a closet in the corner opposite the door.

"Cleaning supplies."

Lorna pinched the bridge of her nose, closing her eyes. Eva wished she could manifest weapons out of thin air, but it hadn't been a priority in a facility where people could shoot gold balls from their pores and turn into living diamond.

"I'm sorry," she said.

"What?" Lorna blinked. "Oh, it's not that. Caffeine headache. I really should have brought some coffee, but I thought you'd have some here. What kind of place doesn't have coffee?"

"How can you think of lattes at a time like this?" Benjamin squeaked.

"This isn't my first rodeo," said Lorna. Then, in an unexpected display of humor, she grinned, making a lasso motion over her head. Eva snickered. Lorna nodded appreciatively before turning her attention back to the door.

"Cleaning supplies, huh? Maybe there's something I can use," she said.

She opened the closet. A broom toppled out, clattering on the floor. The overstuffed space burgeoned with half-empty bottles of ancient cleaner, stiff rags coated with unidentifiable substances, crunchy mops, and other useless paraphernalia. Most of it hadn't been touched in years. Lorna picked up the broom, tested its weight, and then tossed it to the side. Then she plunged into the musty space, knocking a plastic bottle containing a sliver of bright green fluid across the floor.

The door shuddered, emitting a hiss of protest as the airtight seal disintegrated.

"Oh, god," said Benjamin. "Is it too late to ask to go home?"

"Just stay behind us," said Phoebe. "And be quiet."

"What's this?" Lorna asked.

She emerged from the closet with a long metal pole clutched in her hand. It must have been six or seven feet in length, topped with a sturdy-looking hook. The green-haired mutant swung it experimentally, testing its strength. It smacked against her hand with a satisfying clunk.

"I have no idea," said Eva, "but you're welcome to it."

"I think it opens the protective shutters in the hangar bay," said Benjamin. "Cyclops has been looking for it for ages."

"Yeah?" said Lorna. "Well, he might have to do without it for a little while longer." She took a spot a few paces behind the Stepfords, brandishing the pole in a confident, relaxed grip. "There's a second one in there," she said. "If anyone needs it."

"Should I get it?" Benjamin asked Eva. The thin young man's hands shook as he brushed his hair out of his eyes, but he met her gaze with determination. "What do you want me to do?"

His voice cracked on the last word, and his cheeks went scarlet, but he still didn't cave. The mulish expression on his face reminded Eva of her daughter Doll. She'd been stubborn like that, too, always dashing into dangerous situations in her desperation to prove that she was "really grown up". Eva and her husband had had their hands full keeping the little girl out of trouble. One time, Doll had wandered into a fight with a Sentinel and barely escaped with her life. Eva had screamed at her, her terror at almost losing her child transforming on the spot into mindless fury. She would have given anything to take the words back, but now it was too late. Or too early, to be precise.

Benjamin was much older than Dolly had been, but he was still out of his league. His transmorphative powers made him an ideal candidate for spy work, and if she'd needed someone to sneak into a secret facility and steal some papers, he would have been at the top of the list. But he wasn't particularly good in a fight. No one could doubt his bravery, but in the Danger Room, he tended to hang back. He could sneak up on an enemy by disguising himself, but there wasn't much he could do once he got there. Sometimes, he could buy the team a moment to regroup, confusing the enemy with his sudden appearance and strangely comforting presence. But that skill had limited usefulness in a fight.

He was a part of the team, and Eva knew that he deserved a task, but she couldn't come up with one that didn't strike her as a needless risk. She could ask him to morph, but wouldn't the Sentinels see through that with all their sensors and scans? Fooling a robot was a very different thing than a person. One blast from a Sentinel laser cannon, and he'd die. She could bubble them. Lorna could tear them apart with her pole or her powers. The Stepfords could absorb the blasts with their diamond form.

But as much as she hated to say it, Benjamin was a liability here. She should have sent him with Christopher. He could have used the computer.

She hesitated, torn between her duty and her fear. Benjamin's keen gaze picked up on her reluctance, and his face fell. He took a step backwards, stuffing his hands in his pockets and trying to look casual.

"I'll stay out of the way," he said. "I get it."

"Benjamin," she said, searching for the right words to say.

"There's no need to explain. Really."

He took another step back, obviously trying not to allow his disappointment and embarrassment show. But his face had gone scarlet to the tips of his ears, and his mouth trembled despite his best efforts.

With a bang, the door collapsed, and the Sentinels streamed in.

TWELVE

Christopher climbed to his feet and went to meet the Sentinels, a lone mutant in a rumpled suit against all that firepower. A strange wave of calm overtook him as he looked them over. He didn't underestimate them for a moment. Although he'd defeated them multiple times, he knew what they were capable of. During class, Magneto had provided various examples of overconfident mutants that had lost their lives to the deadly automatons. Despite their skill, things could still go horribly wrong, and while Christopher had the utmost faith in his ability to heal anything, he couldn't heal death the way he'd healed his injured calf – barely even registering the effort. At some point, he would be too late.

So, by rights, he should have been afraid. After all, only a few months earlier, he'd been a normal college student. The most excitement he'd had was when a girl showed up at board game night. Now, if he searched for it, he could still feel the fear, but it had been buried beneath a layer of determination. He had faced these things and triumphed, and he would do so again, regardless of what they threw at him.

The first Sentinel pushed through the hole in the ceiling, intent on the small cluster of mutants that awaited below. Two more heads popped up in the gap behind it, and a quick series of thumps on the roof suggested that they weren't alone. The students would have to take them out quickly or risk being overrun.

<<HALT, CITIZENS, AND PRESENT IDENTIFICATION,>> ordered the Sentinel, its metallic voice implacable and emotionless.

"Fabio," Christopher began, but he didn't get a chance to finish his sentence. The Sentinel dropped like a stone, its heavy metal body plummeting toward the ground. Right toward David.

At first, Christopher expected Hijack to roll out of the way, or maybe divert the Sentinel's trajectory by taking over its propulsion system. He'd done it once before, ramming the robots into buildings and walls, or pulling them off to the side as they fired at one of their fellow students. That expectation cost him precious milliseconds. Then he realized that David wasn't budging. Again. Although his head was turned up toward the ceiling, his eyes remained closed. Sweat ran down his temple as he strained.

"There's too many..." he gasped, completely unaware of the fact that he'd be smashed in at any moment.

Christopher launched himself at David a second time, nearly losing his footing in his desperation to get there. He knocked his fellow student out of the way at the last possible second.

"Oof!" said David. "You trying out for football, Muse?"

The Sentinel landed in the spot they'd been just moments before. It turned to face them, its robotic head swiveling until it pointed the wrong way. Christopher met its eyes, wondering what they thought of him. Was it all just ones and zeroes in there, like your average computer, or did the Sentinels reason for themselves? Magneto hadn't said so for sure, and Christopher didn't think this was the time to engage the killer robots in a philosophical debate.

So, instead, he said the first thing that came to his mind, which was, "Go away."

Brilliant.

Behind him, Fabio barked out a hysterical laugh and choked on his own spit. Dani shifted in her seat but otherwise said nothing. A second pair of Sentinels dropped down next to the first one, and for a moment, Christopher debated taking the initiative, but he decided to hold off. The Sentinels were talking. In his experience, they shot first and asked questions later. Maybe they wanted something.

<<SENTINEL UNIT B45C7-ALPHA DETECTED AN ELECTRONIC ANOMALY ON PATROL. UNIT B45C7-ALPHA IS OFF GRID,>> The Sentinel's eyes bore into his with an intensity that made Christopher wonder if it truly was worried about its compatriot. If so, it wouldn't be happy to find out that they'd blown it to smithereens. <<WHERE IS UNIT B45C7-ALPHA?>>

"I don't know," replied Christopher. "We've done nothing wrong."

<<REMOTE DATABASE ACCESS UNAVAILABLE. SCANNERS OFFLINE. IDENTIFY THIS FACILITY.>>

Both their database and scanners were offline? David had really managed to shut them down. Impressive. He'd bought them time; now Christopher had to figure out what to do with it.

"It's a school," he said. "And I don't know what you're talking about or why you put a hole in our ceiling. Are you gonna pay for that?"

"That's not going to work," murmured Dani.

His cheeks went hot with embarrassment, but there was nothing to be done about it. Of course it wouldn't work. David couldn't block their scanners forever, and the students couldn't allow the Sentinels to return to their base to report on the presence of a school out here. He didn't know what else to do other than fight them, though. But how? They would have to be creative. With Hijack completely engrossed in blocking the Sentinels' transmissions, they'd lost their strongest weapon against the killer machines.

<<ACCORDING TO STATUTE 14B OF THE MUTANT REGISTRATION ACT, HARBORING A MUTANT IS A CRIME PUNISHABLE BY LAW. SURRENDER ALL MUTANTS ON THE PREMISES.>>

Christopher sighed, edging backwards. As much as he hated to admit it, this battle was inevitable. He caught Dani's eye and nodded. She put her hands to the keyboard and typed a few things before nodding back. He didn't know what she had planned, but something told him the Sentinels wouldn't like it. He had no choice but to trust her.

"Fabio?" said Christopher. Adrenaline flooded his veins, making his fingers twitch. He curled them in, willing it to stop.

"Yeah?"

"Go," said Christopher.

Fabio blinked, not understanding the order. Christopher gestured with his hands, trying to simulate the process of shooting hundreds of gold balls out of his skin. It wasn't very easy, and he'd never been great at charades.

"Oh. Yeah. OK." Fabio took a deep breath, then flung his hands toward the Sentinels with a dramatic flourish. Golden globes about the size and consistency of volleyballs poinked into existence around him, rocketing toward the Sentinels. "Goldballs!" he shouted, making the nonsensical word sound like a threat.

Christopher had been on the receiving end of a Goldballs deluge once before, and he'd be happy not to ever do that again. The balls had a little give to them, and they weren't particularly weighty. But they'd hit hard enough to knock him off his feet, and there were so many of them. They'd overwhelmed his senses until one hit at just the right angle to knock him unconscious.

The Sentinels were a little sturdier than he was, to say the least, but Fabio showed no signs of slowing. Balls streamed from his body in an unceasing deluge. The rain of goldballs was so thick that Christopher could barely see the robots on the other side. But he could hear them.

<<Hostile mutants detected,>> said one, which seemed like stating the obvious to Christopher.

Then they began to fire.

THIRTEEN

Smoke and snowflakes came streaming into the foyer as the front door exploded. Pieces of molten metal flew into the room, pelting the diamond bodies of the Stepfords. They didn't so much as flinch when the red-hot shards of what had once been the front door burnt holes in their clothes, but Eva thought they might sing a different tune later. Clothing and other necessities weren't easy to come by out in the Canadian mountains, and none of the students had arrived at the school with much of anything at all. Every shirt was precious, and now theirs had extra aeration.

Although the Stepfords soaked up most of the damage with their impervious bodies, Eva still flinched. She would have felt stupid if not for the fact that Lorna did the same thing.

Debris and smoke quickly filled the room, coating everything in a difficult-to-penetrate haze. Eva didn't like that at all. The Sentinels would be able to pierce the fog easily with their sensors and scanners, putting the mutants at a distinct disadvantage. Every second they wasted was another moment that they could possibly be overrun. They couldn't afford to delay.

"Advance," she urged. "Create a bottleneck."

"Good idea," Lorna murmured. "Limits the numbers we're facing."

The praise warmed her. In unison, the Stepfords advanced, blocking the space where the door once stood with their crystalline bodies. As they moved into position, a single metallic head came swimming out of the haze, lunging toward them with surprising speed.

Lorna reacted the quickest. She drove her pole forward like a spear over Celeste's shoulder, the wicked hook passing centimeters from her ear. The hook hit the Sentinel right in the crease where the robot's head met its body, punching through the armored exterior and lodging in the delicate electronics inside. Sparks flew.

The Sentinel brought its arm up, the armored compartment opening to reveal a giant laser cannon. But Lorna's strike must have disrupted the Sentinel's delicate power supply, because the weapon crackled and sparked. While the robot struggled with its weaponry, the Stepfords lunged forward once again, their every movement coordinated with eerie perfection, and slammed their diamond fists into its head in perfect unison. Metal crunched under the impact as their fists drove so deep, they nearly touched in the middle.

The Sentinel wavered and fell to the ground with a crash. Eva had barely a second to celebrate. Then, metal screeched as another pair of Sentinels began to tear at the hole in the wall, widening it. The Stepfords attacked with everything they had, battering the robots to a pulp. But the damage had been done. By the time the second Sentinel went down, the hole was nearly big enough to drive a car through. Their small group would be overrun by the Sentinels' superior numbers. They needed to change tactics, and fast.

Eva remembered a similar combat situation. Before she settled down with her family, she'd run with a mercenary group for a little while, trying to get access to a machine that could supposedly send her back to the present day. Of course, it had turned out to be a hoax, but that wasn't what mattered now. The mercs had been bottled up and outnumbered just like this, so all she had to do was call the same shots.

"There are too many of them. Pull back and draw them in," she ordered. "I'll have to bubble them, and then we'll take them down and use their corpses as cover."

She looked around. Benjamin was nowhere in sight, and for a moment, she worried about him. But he'd probably fled into another room, and honestly, that would be the best place for him right now.

The Stepfords gave ground gradually, engaging another wave of Sentinels in hand to hand combat as they edged back into the room. Phoebe took a brutal punch to the face without even blinking. Celeste grabbed a laser cannon in one shimmering hand and squeezed, crushing the delicate electronics within. At first, it looked like they were winning.

But the tide turned quickly. The Sentinels poured in under the cover of the smoke, and by the time Eva realized how many there were, it was too late. An angry red beam hissed past Eva's ear, burning a hole in her dress. The air lit up as if at the deadliest rock concert ever.

Lorna took shelter behind a large piece of the door, pulling the heated metal up to provide cover. It was just in time. A red blast of laser fire struck the door moments after Lorna pulled it into place, making her yelp in surprise. Eva looked around wildly for cover, but in this small and unfurnished room, there was nothing else that would hold up against the advanced weaponry of the Sentinels.

A red light skittered over her eyeballs as one of the robots took aim.

There was no time to second-guess herself. No time to worry about unintended after effects. She threw herself through time as the red and buzzing beam came hurtling through the space she'd occupied only milliseconds earlier.

Sickening vertigo gripped her stomach in a vise. Her senses told her that she was rushing forward at inhuman speeds, but her body knew that she hadn't moved, and the conflicting input made her stomach churn. Then she emerged back into the time loop with one last twist of her insides. She looked around, her heart in her throat, terror making her palms sweat. Had she ended up in the right time? She half-expected to see an abandoned husk or an empty cave where this building would one day exist, but instead, Lorna gestured to her from beneath the door.

"Come on!" she yelled. "Before they fire again!"

Eva threw herself out of the way just in time. Another laser blast carved a chunk in the floor where her feet had been. The two of them clung to each other, trying to fit behind the insufficient armor. She could still hear the tinny smash of the Stepfords' fists against Sentinel bodies, but Eva had lost her chance to bubble them. Now they were all spread out, and she would freeze her friends as well as her enemies. It would only delay the inevitable.

Lorna stared at her intently. "You held back," she said. "If there was ever a time to let loose, girl, that time is now."

"I lost my family," Eva blurted. "I can't control my powers any better than you can."

"So you'd rather die?" Lorna demanded. "Is that what you think your family would want?"

Eva stared at her, unable to form an answer. The door flared red, caught by another laser blast. She had no time to consider the consequences. She knew what she had to do.

But she was just so scared.

FOURTEEN

At first, Christopher stood frozen while the Sentinels fired on them. He'd had visions of the whole squadron of robots buried in a sea of gold balls without a single shot fired. Of course, that would never happen, but he indulged in the daydream anyway. A bit too long, as it turned out.

The laser blast caught him on the arm, spinning him around and knocking him into David, who let out a startled yelp. Christopher grabbed him around the waist, pulling him out of the line of fire, and the two of them tumbled onto the floor as the air above them filled with hostile fire.

David glanced down at him, his gaze still abstracted. "You... are you OK, man?" he asked in a faraway tone.

"Just a scratch," said Christopher, already healing it. "Come on."

He led the way across the floor, and David followed with agonizing slowness. Fabio yelped as another stray blast grazed his ear.

"Dani!" Christopher yelled. "Do something!"

"Already on it," she said, her voice calm and collected. She still sat at the control panel, slumped down in her chair to present as small a target as possible. As he watched, she typed again, and the giant hydraulic arm that lifted the X-Jet into and out of its storage bay reached down and plucked one of the Sentinels from the pack. It struggled briefly, bringing its weapons to bear on its captor, but it was too slow. With a crunch of metal and a spray of hydraulic fluid, the robot hand crushed the Sentinel into mush, throwing the pieces onto a growing pile in the corner.

Christopher grinned, giving her a thumbs up.

"Take cover!" he ordered Fabio. "Don't stand out there and wait to get hit and expect me to heal your lazy butt."

Fabio grinned, too, picking up on Christopher's sense of elation. They were doing it. They were standing up to an entire squad of Sentinels. And it was *easy*.

A loud whining sound cut through the air like a hot knife through butter. Christopher craned his neck, trying to find the source, but Dani didn't pause a moment. She launched herself out of the chair, ignoring the laser fire that continued to patter the wall behind them, and hurried toward the door.

"Run!" she yelled, her eyes wide. "Missile!"

Christopher needed no further encouragement. He tore toward the exit, pulling a still-distracted David along behind him. The vehicle-controlling mutant stumbled over his own feet, muttering a stream of broken apologies.

"Sorry," he said. "Sorry. I'm…"

"Don't worry about it!" Christopher yelled.

He shoved David through the door as the missile exploded, throwing Fabio into them. The three of them flew through the exit, hitting the opposite wall with a bone-crunching impact. Blood filled his mouth, and his head swam, but he pushed himself up. Nothing broken, and he could deal with the minor injuries later.

Fabio hadn't been so lucky. He lay on the ground, his eyes wide as he clutched at his leg. Dark red blood stained his pant leg, and a jagged piece of bone jutted out just beneath his desperately clutching hands.

"Help!" he gasped, his face pale and clammy.

"Hurry!" Dani demanded.

Christopher needed no further urging. He put his hands to Fabio's injured leg, willing the bone to heal, ignoring the flare of pain in his own leg as his body aligned with his patient's. Within moments, it was over, and Fabio pushed himself up to his knees, dry heaving with remembered pain.

"I'm good. I'm good," he said, trying to reassure himself as much as them.

"It's too bad David can't control the chopper, too," said Christopher. "He could shoot them all down. They wouldn't even know what hit them."

David's brown eyes focused on his for a moment. "My hands are full," he said. "But…"

There was a pause, and then the sound of laser fire. But the blasts didn't pelt the door frame or streak across the hallway. They were firing at something else.

David smiled, a thin-lipped expression of utter satisfaction. "There," he said.

"What did you do?" asked Christopher, but David just waved a hand at him, closing his eyes.

"Need to concentrate," he said. "Too many of them."

Christopher needed to know. How else could he decide what to do next? He peeked back into the hangar and grinned at the sight that awaited him. When he pulled back, he shook his head with delight.

"What?" asked Dani.

"They're all shooting each other. David must have hijacked one of them. We could pick the rest of them off if we had access to the computer," he said.

"There's another terminal in the Danger Room," Dani suggested.

"That's where we'll go then."

He led the way down the hall toward the Danger Room without looking back, confident in the knowledge that they would follow. He wondered how Eva's team had fared, but of course they would be fine. He'd seen her in action. She'd made mincemeat out of Sentinels before, and there was no reason to believe that this time was any different. He'd take his team straight to the Danger Room and use the computer to help track down and pick off any stray intruders. While they were at it, they could peek in on Eva's team and offer assistance if necessary.

With a shocking level of confidence, Christopher opened the door to the Danger Room. On the other side stood a Sentinel, hand raised as if to knock. But that made no sense. Why would an invading robot knock on a door in a facility they were trying to take over? The robot's laser cannon hummed loudly, suggesting it had been cranked up to full power. That would make one heck of a knock …

The blast took him in the chest, slamming into him with the force of a bullet train. Pain flared; every cell in his body screaming out in unison. But it dissipated as quickly as it had come, shut down by shock or maybe his body's natural healing power. His head floated, his body numb. When he hit the wall and slid down to the floor, he didn't feel a thing.

He lay there, his eyes half-open, letting his mutant ability take over. By this point, he'd been fatally injured enough times to not panic. Instead, a strange peace came over him, broken only by his worry for his team. How had the Sentinel gotten in? Were there more of them, roaming the halls at this very moment, looking for students to capture? Maybe they'd found the emergency exits. Maybe it didn't matter. Maybe the only thing that mattered right now was keeping his team intact.

Fabio let out another barrage of balls, driving the Sentinel back into the Danger Room. Dani knocked him out of the way just in time to avoid the answering laser blast, which took out the hallway light fixture instead. The lights crackled and died, plunging the area into a deep blanket of darkness only punctuated by the dim lights from the Danger Room control panel. Christopher had never seen a darkness so complete as in this underground facility. When the lights went down, nothing could penetrate the gloom. Unless you were a Sentinel. It would be able to see just fine regardless of the lack of illumination. Christopher's heart sank. He needed to get up, but his legs still refused to do more than twitch. He was lucky he hadn't died.

Heck, maybe he had. That thought both reassured and terrified him. He wouldn't need to worry if it was true, but then he'd have to deal with the fact that he couldn't die.

<<SCANNING,>> said the Sentinel. Then, after a long pause, it said, <<SCANNERS INOPERABLE. RUNNING DIAGNOSTICS.>>

"Yeah, not gonna happen." David's voice came out of the darkness, and then a red glow lit the room for a moment as the

Sentinel shot itself in the head. The clatter of its body hitting the floor echoed down the hallway, giving Christopher a bit of a headache. Or maybe the lingering pain was just a side effect of healing a laser blast to the torso. It didn't really matter, and he wasn't about to complain.

He pushed himself up to a sitting position just as David turned on the Danger Room lights. The sudden brightness stabbed at his head, but he was so relieved that he didn't care. They'd survived. David had saved them.

Maybe David deserved to lead the team after all. Christopher had protected the team, and that wasn't inconsequential, but David had led them to victory. Christopher tried to think it over with impartiality, but his emotions got in the way. He wanted this. He wanted to feel like he mattered, but David had taken action. All he'd done was gotten himself shot.

Dani crouched down next to him, looking at the burnt circle in his shirt and the bare skin beneath. Worry furrowed her brow as she scanned his body, unable to believe what she was seeing.

"You OK?" she asked.

"Yeah." He tested his legs again and found that this time they worked. Stretching them was blissful. His spine popped as it realigned, and he let out a sigh of relief. "I'm fine."

"When they said you were a healer, they weren't kidding," she said, obviously relieved.

"Yeah, but what kind of leader spends the fight trying not to bleed out on the floor?"

He tried not to sound bitter, but it crept in there. After all the time he'd spent working up the nerve to put himself out there, it stung to do so and find out he didn't have what it took to be exceptional after all.

Dani sighed. "If I knew you better, I'd smack you upside the head. But since I don't, I'll tell you this: good team leaders don't micromanage. You gave your people direction when they needed it, and you stood out of the way and let them do their jobs when they didn't. Maybe you'd feel more impressive if you were shooting lasers out your eyeballs, but that's not what makes Summers a good leader. Your powers are irrelevant as long as your team will follow your lead when it counts."

"By that logic, you could lead an X-Men team right now," he countered.

She blinked, taken aback by the sudden twist in the conversation. Her mouth opened and shut a few times as she struggled with potential responses, but finally, she just nodded.

"I'll take that under consideration," she said.

"I'm not saying I won't help if you still want to try and get your powers back. But if you really mean what you said, is it worth the risk?"

"Yeah, I get what you're saying," she responded in a tone of voice that made it obvious that she considered the subject tabled for the moment. She straightened, offering him a hand up. "We should check the computer and take care of the last few Sentinels."

"I'm already five steps ahead of you," said David. He sat at the control panel, his mouth stretched in a satisfied grin as his fingers danced over the keyboard. "Now that there aren't so many Sentinels to block, I can multitask. There were so many of them before that it was like trying to juggle cats. Killer cats with laser cannons."

"That's... graphic," said Christopher.

"I used to be an illustrator. It's what I do," said David, smirking.

"Now, if you'll shut up for five seconds, I'm going to steer this Sentinel around and have it shoot its friends."

Christopher met Dani's eyes. She had a point about his leadership worries. He couldn't do everything himself. After all, he didn't need to be the star of this team. He just needed to step out in front and take the blow when the time came.

He could do that.

FIFTEEN

Eva's heart beat so hard that she could feel it in her jaw. Her fingers trembled as she reached up to brush her hair out of her eyes. A few inches over her head, the broken piece of the door grew redder, emitting so much heat that she thought she'd be sunburned later. Lorna gritted her teeth and maintained her grip on the improvised shield, but it had to hurt.

"Stepfords!" Eva yelled. "A little help here?"

"Negative. We're–"

Phoebe's response was cut off by another laser blast and the sound of falling rubble. Eva wanted to scream, but she forced herself to call out calmly.

"Phoebe? Mindee, Celeste?"

There was no answer. Eva met Lorna's eyes and saw the same resignation she felt. If they were going down, they'd go down fighting. Together.

"We're going to do this," Lorna said. "You and me. If we don't, we all die."

Eva gulped against the lump in her throat and nodded. "You fling the door at them, and I'll freeze anybody you miss. It'll be fine," she said, trying to believe it. It probably wouldn't be, but anything was better than being roasted to a crisp beneath a broken door.

"On three," said Lorna, holding up her fingers.

Eva fought for confidence as Lorna counted down swiftly. They could leash their uncontrolled powers, just this once. If Polaris could believe in them, she could, too.

One. Two. Three.

Lorna tensed. From this close, Eva could feel Lorna's powers activate. The hair on her arms stood on end, and she knew that if she touched something, a spark of electricity would dance from her fingertips. The sensation reminded her of the good old days when her brother used to drag his feet across the carpet and chase her around the living room, trying to shock her.

The door shook, threatening to buck free of Lorna's grip. Then the ceiling on the far side of the room exploded into pieces. The entire building shuddered, its metal framework caught in the grip of Lorna's formidable magnetic powers.

<<UNSTABLE STRUCTURE. RETREAT,>> said an emotionless Sentinel voice.

Somewhere deep in the bowels of the building, unseen metal screeched. Eva's hair crackled with electricity, standing straight out in all directions. Eva put her hand to it, stomach clenching in fear. Lorna hadn't stopped. Maybe she couldn't. She could bring the entire building down on them all. Even if her team managed to make it outside, the Sentinels would cut them down. She could hear them tromping out of what remained of the front door.

Unless Eva stopped it. She could freeze the Sentinels, but then they might all die in the twisted wreckage of the torn-apart school. Or… she could freeze Lorna. All she had to do was focus with every ounce of her being. She couldn't afford to be distracted by her emotions, or her worries, or her past. If she did, Lorna would pay the price, and Eva saw too much of herself in the older mutant. She didn't want to hurt anyone, but if she lost Polaris in time and space, she would take it hard.

But she couldn't afford to dwell on those fears now. She'd done that long enough.

With the precision of a brain surgeon, Eva deployed her bubble. In the past, she'd flung them around like Fabio's goldballs, mistaking quantity and size for quality. Maybe that was what had gotten her into trouble before. If so, she couldn't blame herself. She hadn't known better. But now, she would focus on making a single, perfect time bubble. One that did no more nor less than she wanted it to.

The blue, glistening bubble popped into existence, encasing Lorna in shimmering stasis. The electric shiver in the air immediately cut off. The building shuddered and then fell quiescent, but Eva knew that silence could be deceptive. Who knew what damage had been done? Lorna might, once she was unfrozen, but Eva couldn't risk unbubbling her long enough to ask.

A red pulse of energy hit the door, taking Eva by surprise. The Sentinels had regrouped and were shooting at them from the relative safety of the expanded doorway. She yelped as a second laser blast skimmed her thigh, trying to squeeze more fully under the makeshift shield. But despite her best efforts, the bubble took up space in an already cramped shelter. Some part of her would remain exposed.

"Eva!"

Benjamin hissed her name from the hallway, sticking his head out just far enough to gesture for her to join him. The angry buzz of another laser strike cut through the air, and he ducked out of the way just in time.

<<SURRENDER, MUTANTS,>> ordered one of the Sentinels.

Eva eyed the distance to the hallway and shook her head. The Sentinels would pick her off before she made it even halfway there, and she couldn't bubble them all. She couldn't even see them. Also, she couldn't leave Lorna. The bubble would pop eventually, and then she'd be vulnerable.

So Eva shook her head with regret and gestured for Benjamin to flee. He hovered there for a moment, uncertainty and despair written all over his face. For a moment, she thought he'd run. Then his mouth firmed and his shoulders straightened.

Eva clenched her hands into worried fists. What was he going to do?

"Don't!" she blurted, not even sure what she was cautioning him against.

Benjamin Deeds stepped out into the lobby without a single weapon to protect himself from the Sentinels. He held his empty hands out from his body in a demonstration of his vulnerability. Not that anyone would have ever looked at him as a threat. He was a reedy boy with flyaway hair and a terminally haunted expression. Eva could have taken him in a fist fight with one hand tied behind her back.

"I'm surrendering!" he yelled in a quaking voice, taking a step forward. "Don't shoot."

<<IDENTIFY YOURSELF.>>

"My name is Ben. What's yours?"

He spoke in a soothing voice that struck Eva as ridiculous.

Hadn't he listened to anything Magneto had taught them? The Sentinels couldn't be charmed or reasoned with. Not even by Benjamin. His psychochemicals might lull people into complacency, but the Sentinels didn't have any emotions to manipulate.

<<IDENTIFY YOURSELF. WHAT IS YOUR FULL NAME, MUTANT?>>

Benjamin took another step forward, gulping. Eva's heart leaped. Was he *trying* to get himself killed? Maybe he sought to buy her time, but she didn't know what to do with it. She refused to run, and there was nothing else she could think of. Maybe they would luck out and Christopher's team would come to the rescue. She would have called for help, but the entryway had no computer terminal, and she wouldn't have known how to use the thing anyway.

"Oh, sorry. My name's Benjamin. I still didn't catch your name. Do Sentinels have names?" he replied, edging forward again.

<<HALT. ANY FURTHER MOVEMENT WILL BE TAKEN AS AN ACT OF AGGRESSION.>>

"Sure, man. Whatever you say."

Benjamin took another step forward, his brow furrowed in concentration.

<<HALT, OR YOU WILL BE TERMINATED. THIS IS YOUR LAST WARNING.>>

"Benjamin!" Eva cried, unable to stop herself. "Don't!"

He took another step. Eva thrust her fist in her mouth to choke off a cry of despair. She'd made him feel useless, and now he was sacrificing himself to save her, because he thought that was the only thing he was good for. His despair – his death –

would be on her hands. She peeked out from behind the door, hoping that the motion would go unnoticed. She might not be able to freeze all the Sentinels, but she had to try. If he died, she'd never forgive herself.

The overhead lights flickered and died in a dramatic rain of sparks, thrusting them into a darkness broken only by the white glare off the snow outside. Luckily, it outlined the pair of Sentinels standing in the ruins of the front door. Eva tensed, trying to focus, but her emotions whipsawed out of control, and the necessary concentration failed to come.

<<IDENTIFY... MUTANT... SCANNING MALFUNCTION.>>

The Sentinel's suddenly halting speech, combined with what sounded almost like confusion, caught Eva's attention. She risked another peek out from behind the door, watching as Benjamin took another step forward, his expression full of determination.

"Everything's fine," he said.

<<RUNNING DIAGNOS... MUTANT REGISTRATION... ELECTRICAUUUU...>>

The machine's words trailed off in a mechanical whine. Benjamin took another step forward, glancing back at Eva with wide eyes. "Help!" he mouthed. "I can't keep this up forever."

The tromp of metallic feet approaching from the hallway made Eva's throat constrict. They couldn't catch a darned break. Whatever Benjamin was doing to scramble those Sentinels, she didn't know how many he could handle at once. She would have to bubble this one and hope the disruption didn't mess with whatever he was doing.

<<STAND DOWN,>> said the Sentinel. <<WE ARE GOING TO PARTY.>>

Eva paused. Maybe Benjamin had things under control after all, because that hadn't sounded like the usual Sentinel monotone at all. She looked at Lorna to gauge her reaction to this strange statement, but of course Lorna did nothing.

<<MAYBE WHEN WE'RE DONE, I CAN MAKE IT BREAKDANCE. OUT OF THE WAY, DEEDS. YOU'RE MESSING WITH MY VIBE.>>

Eva poked her head out from behind the door to see the Sentinel doing a very poor rendition of the robot as it continued to the front door.

"David?" she asked hesitantly. "Is that you?"

The Sentinel paused, looking over its shoulder at her.

<<GOOD GUESS. BE BACK IN A SEC. GOT SOME SENTINELS TO OBLITERATE.>>

The Sentinel blew up the two confused robots in the doorway, stepped outside, aimed its laser cannon, and squeezed off five more quick shots. It was over with obscene speed, and then it returned back to the lobby and looked around.

<<NICE REDECORATING,>> it said, and then it shot itself in the head.

SIXTEEN

Once David gave them the all-clear, Christopher led his team toward the entrance at double speed. The Stepfords had been buried in rubble, and while their diamond forms made them nigh invincible, he wanted to evaluate them for himself. When he arrived at the entrance, he stopped in shock, surveying the damage. They weren't going to be able to clean this up and pretend it hadn't happened. The foyer had been obliterated. The Sentinels hadn't just taken out the door; they'd blown out the entire exterior wall and a sizeable chunk of ceiling, too.

"Holy crap," he said. "You sure you guys are OK?"

Lorna levered a huge metal pillar out of the way with apparent ease. Either she was cheating with her powers, or she'd been working out.

"Everyone's OK," she said. "I've almost got the Stepfords out. Dani, you want to give me a hand with this last bit?"

"Sure thing."

As the two elder mutants got to work, Eva edged up to Christopher, her cheeks smudged with dust from the destroyed building. But her eyes were alight with triumph.

"How'd it go?" she asked.

"We had our moments," he replied. "You?"

"Same." She glanced over her shoulder and grinned, gesturing. "Benjamin, get over here. What the heck did you do to that Sentinel?"

The scrawny young man shrugged, stuffing his hands in his pockets. But despite his awkwardness, Christopher could feel the waves of pride coming off him. He clapped the transmorph on the back. Out of all of them, Christopher could best understand what it was like to question your usefulness in a fight and to finally realize that you'd been selling yourself short all along. But now he was dying to find out what had happened.

"Not sure, really. I tried to soothe it like I do people, but instead I think I scrambled its brain," Benjamin replied. "I'll have to practice more and figure it out."

"Definitely," she replied. "Whatever that was, we need more of it. I was wrong when I told you to run. I'm glad you didn't listen."

He nodded. "I mean, I don't blame you, but me, too."

Christopher arched a brow. In response, Eva shrugged.

"I'm a little overprotective sometimes," she said. "I'll tell you all about it later."

"Deal."

They shook hands, and a wave of relief came over Christopher. Whatever weirdness had gripped Eva over the past couple of weeks seemed to have passed over now. Things were back to the way they were supposed to be. They had the makings of a really great team, and for the first time, he knew without a doubt that they belonged at the forefront of it.

"Listen, Eva," he said, but before he could finish, a loud and desperate voice came booming from the hallway.

"What in the heck is going on here?" demanded Cyclops.

Christopher whirled around to see him standing in the hallway, arms folded and lips pursed as he surveyed the wreckage that used to be the entrance to the New Xavier School. Magik and Magneto stood to either side. Illyana's mouth twitched uncontrollably, but she said nothing. Magneto's gaze went to his daughter and stayed there, but his expression remained neutral. It would have taken a mind reader to pry out his thoughts, and the Stepfords were otherwise occupied.

"Well?" Cyclops barked. "I'm waiting."

Christopher stepped forward, clearing his throat. Eva kept pace without being asked, because of course she did. They were on the same wavelength again, as if he'd needed proof.

"Triage and Tempus, team leaders, ready to report," he said.

He could barely believe that he'd said those words in that order. He definitely couldn't believe the fact that they fit. He'd never been the most confident of guys, but for the first time, he knew he'd earned his place. Maybe he still had a lot to learn, but he couldn't deny that he belonged here, in this time and place, at the head of this team.

"Team leaders?" asked Cyclops, tilting his head. His mask obscured most of his face, but there was no mistaking the warning in his voice. Scott Summers didn't like surprises. Today, he'd just have to deal. "Says who?"

"We do," David interjected. "We took a vote."

"They did a good job, too," added Dani, as she helped one

of the Stepfords out from beneath a large sheet of metal. The triplet's diamond skin glittered in the bright sunlight that streamed in through the broken wall.

"Is anybody hurt?" Cyclops persisted.

"I've already healed everyone, sir," said Christopher. "I'll double check the Stepfords once they transform, but they've reported that they feel fine."

Cyclops sighed, running a hand over his face. He suddenly looked weary, and more than a little resigned to dealing with this new development. Christopher should have felt guilty over this, but he couldn't manage to scrape any up.

"So what happened?" Cyclops asked.

"It sounds like the Sentinels picked up on us during a routine patrol," Eva explained. "We had Hijack cut off their communications, so they couldn't report the presence of the school once they found us. That appears to have been successful. If they'd been able to call for reinforcements, they should have gotten here by now."

"Then we fought," added Christopher. "As you can see. We've run a full scan with the computer system, and David has also gone through the entire building. All of the Sentinels have been neutralized. I know we did a lot of damage to the school, but the students are safe, and that's what's important."

"I know, Christopher," said Cyclops, sighing again. "I just wish…"

"We called for help," said Eva. "We followed protocol."

"We teleported in as soon as we could," said Magik. "Emma is following with the X-Jet. But I can see that we aren't needed." With a wink and a surreptitious thumbs up, she turned and left the room. "I'm going to go check on the Danger Room computer. Run a full diagnostic," she said. "Although I don't expect to find anything."

She hurried off with the speed of someone who thinks the stuff is about to hit the fan and wants to get out of the blast radius.

"And what are Dani and Lorna doing here? Did you throw a party while I was gone?" demanded Cyclops, rallying himself for another round of irate questioning.

"We came for a visit," said Dani, evasively.

"You weren't here," added Lorna.

Christopher had hoped that they'd come clean about the reasons for their visit, but their evasiveness spoke for itself. Maybe they thought Scott would be upset that they deliberately approached his students in his absence. Maybe they'd changed their mind about asking for help. Maybe they just felt bad about bringing the Sentinels here to destroy half the building. It didn't matter, really. He had no desire to throw them under the bus. He'd cover for them as long as necessary.

"We told them they could wait," he added. "Good thing, too, because they helped with the Sentinels."

Cyclops frowned, scanning the array of innocent faces. "Why do I get the feeling that you're all trying to put one over on me?" he asked.

Christopher had no idea what to say. Vehement protests would only make Cyclops suspect that something fishy was going on. He probably wouldn't take it out on the students, but Dani and Lorna would likely get into a lot of trouble, and given the status of their powers, he didn't want to risk it. They were on thin ice as X-Men already.

Help came from an unexpected quarter.

"I invited my daughter to view the school," said Magneto. "If our student body continues to grow, we will need more instructors."

"And I brought Dani," added Lorna. "She's an excellent teacher."

Cyclops nodded slowly. "I still don't buy it, but if you don't trust me with the truth, there's nothing I can do about it." He paused as if waiting for someone to speak up and spill it all. No one said a word. He sighed, looking around. "Well, I'm glad no one's hurt, at least. I'll run a full diagnostic, and we'll have to get to work on the repairs immediately. We're losing too much heat for the generators to keep up."

"Lorna and I should be able to handle the bulk of the repairs," offered Magneto. "The structure is mostly metal."

"Good. Once the Stepfords are checked out, get to work on cleanup. I'll leave it to your team leaders to make specific assignments." A ghost of a smile flitted over Cyclops's face. "I suppose I should also congratulate you on a job well done. Taking out a full squadron of Sentinels is no small feat."

"Thanks," said Christopher. "Everyone did their part."

Cyclops acknowledged this with a nod before marching off. It took only a few seconds for the Stepfords to return to their human forms and for Christopher to certify them as ready for duty. There wasn't a scratch on them, despite the large slab of ceiling that had pinned them in place. Then he and Eva split them into teams, sending them to collect cleaning supplies from the cafeteria and get to work.

Finally, everyone else cleared out, leaving only Christopher and Eva, Dani and Lorna, and Magneto. Christopher and Eva began to lug some of the larger pieces of debris out of the way.

After a moment, Dani and Lorna joined them. All the while, Magneto watched them with a curious glitter in his dark eyes.

Finally, he said, "I covered for you. I deserve the truth."

Protestations of innocence rose to Christopher's mouth, but he swallowed them. Magneto was right, and out of all of the instructors, he would be the most understanding. After all, Lorna was his daughter. But it was her choice whether or not to tell, and he couldn't rob her of it.

She lifted her chin proudly, but her eyes were still drawn with pain.

"M-Day has made my powers uncontrollable. I accidentally caught the attention of the Sentinels while they were on patrol. Pulled out an electrical tower and dumped it on a clearing not too far away. It'll need to be returned to its home," she said.

"I'll handle it," Magneto replied.

"Your powers recovered. If you're not at full strength already, you're close. So Dani and I theorized that you must have discovered some kind of treatment. And then Magik told us about the students' powers here."

"And you assumed that it was a combination thereof that restored me." Magneto's icy gaze swept over Christopher and Eva. "Healing and time. It's not a bad theory. Did you try and fail?"

"We didn't try," Eva blurted. "Because my abilities aren't under control either. I time traveled. By mistake."

Christopher had known it, deep down. She'd aged so quickly; time travel was really the only explanation that made sense. Still, hearing it said aloud wasn't easy. How long had she been adrift, wondering if she'd ever get back home? Even imagining it made him queasy.

"How far did you go?" Magneto demanded. "What did you see?"

"It doesn't matter. As soon as I returned to present day, any future that I saw ceased to exist. And my family with it," said Eva, in obvious misery.

"You are a powerful mutant indeed," said Magneto.

"Please don't tell anyone. I don't really want to talk about it," said Eva.

"That's why you've been hesitating to use your bubbles," said Christopher, the lightbulb going on. "You're afraid it'll happen again."

Eva nodded.

"I will help you with this. We will practice until you gain full and complete control of your powers," said Magneto. "With time, you will master this new talent of yours."

"Thank you," said Eva, tears in her eyes. "I can't risk it happening again. I don't think I could take it."

"The offer extends to you as well, daughter," said Magneto. "I don't know whether your difficulty is due to the tragic events of M-Day or because you have manifested too much power too quickly, but it, too, can be mastered, if you will agree to train here."

Lorna began to shake her head, opening her mouth to deliver the inevitable refusal, but then her eyes fell on Eva. She paused, considering, her gaze shifting to the imposing figure of her father, waiting with implacable patience. She let out a heavy sigh.

"OK," she said. "But only on my terms. I have a few other obligations, so I can't stay full time, but I'll come train with Eva whenever I can. We have a lot in common."

Eva nodded. "That's an understatement."

"What about me?" asked Dani. "I have no powers left at all. Nothing to train with."

Magneto frowned. "If Tempus and Triage wish to try and restore you to yourself, I won't interfere. But it is not my choice to make. You are still our mutant sister, and I will fight for your right to be welcome here."

"I'm willing to try once I get my powers under control," offered Eva. "But it would probably be wise to wait until then, unless you fancy living in the Renaissance era."

Dani wrinkled her nose. "I'd smack the first person who tried to put me in a corset. Probably not a good idea."

"So you'll wait?" asked Christopher.

"Yeah." She smiled at him. "Some wise young mutant I met reminded me that we're more than just our mutations. I've got some other things I can work on in the meantime. I trained as a Valkyrie once, you know. I've always been meaning to brush up on my sword skills. Maybe I'll check in with them and see if they'll let me do a little training."

"I'd pay good money to see you on a flying horse," Christopher declared.

Dani smiled at him. "You're sweet."

"So we have a plan," said Eva. "Yeah?"

Christopher nodded. "Sounds like it. We'd better get to work, though, or Cyclops will throw a fit."

Eva snorted, picking up another piece of metal and chucking it out into the snow. The four of them got to work under Magneto's watchful eye. The scrutiny wasn't exactly comfortable, but it didn't make Christopher as nervous as it once had.

"I'll leave you to it, then," said Magneto. His gaze took them all in, lingering on Lorna. "I am proud of you, my X-Men. Over the past few years, I have sometimes despaired for our future. But seeing you take the reins to your own destinies gives me hope."

With that, he swept from the room, leaving them to set things right.

CONTRIBUTORS

JALEIGH JOHNSON is a *New York Times*-bestselling fantasy novelist living and writing in the wilds of the Midwest. She has also written several novels and short stories for the *Dungeons & Dragons Forgotten Realms* fiction lines. Johnson is an avid gamer and lifelong geek.

jaleighjohnson.com
twitter.com/jaleighjohnson

ROBBIE MACNIVEN is a Highlands-native History graduate from the University of Edinburgh. He is the author of several novels and many short stories for the *New York Times*-bestselling *Warhammer 40,000 Age of Sigmar* universe, and the narrative for HiRez Studio's *Smite Blitz RPG*. Outside of writing his hobbies include historical re-enacting and making eight-hour round trips every second weekend to watch Rangers FC.

robbiemacniven.wordpress.com
twitter.com/robbiemacniven

CATH LAURIA is a Colorado girl who loves snow and sunshine. She is a prolific author of science fiction, fantasy, suspense and romance fiction, and has a vast collection of beautiful edged weapons.

twitter.com/author_cariz

AMANDA BRIDGEMAN is a Tin Duck Award winner, an Aurealis and a Ditmar Awards finalist. She is the author of eight volumes of the award-nominated Aurora series of near-future space thrillers, the SF police procedural *The Subjugate*, which has been optioned for TV by an Oscar and Golden Globe nominated production company, and a Stephen King-esque mystery *The Time of the Stripes*. She's also worked as a TV and film actress.

amandabridgeman.com.au
twitter.com/bridgeman_books

PAT SHAND is the creator/co-creator of numerous comic books including *Destiny NY*, *Snap Flash Hustle*, *Breathless*, and *Afterglow*, as well as writing extensively for properties such as *Charmed*, *Adventure Time*, *Disney Villains*, and *Angel*. He has also written and produced off-off Broadway theatre and original stories for Marvel, including *Guardians of the Galaxy: Space Riot* and *Iron Man: Mutually Assured Destruction*. He runs the independent publisher Space Between Entertainment in New York, where he lives with his wife Amy and their army of cats.

twitter.com/patshand

Xeric Award-winning graphic novelist NEIL KLEID authored *Ninety Candles*, and the acclaimed graphic novels *Brownsville* and *The Big Kahn*. He has written other several comic books and graphic novels, as well as adapting Jack London's novel *Call of the Wild* into sequentials, and the reverse for Marvel Comics' *Spider-Man: Kraven's Last Hunt*; and co-authored *Powers: The Secret History of Deena Pilgrim*. *Savor*, his culinary adventure graphic novel with John Broglia and Frank Reynoso, was released by Dark Horse Comics. He lives with wife, kids and dog in New Jersey by way of Detroit.

twitter.com/neilkleid

CARRIE HARRIS is a geek of all trades and proud of it. She's an experienced author of tie-in fiction, former tabletop game executive and published game designer who lives in Utah.

carrieharrisbooks.com
twitter.com/carrharr

A book dragon from the beginning, GWENDOLYN NIX has amassed a hoard of science fiction and fantasy stories and is always hungry for the next tale to devour. Once upon a time, she'd been a marine biologist, but through a series of events, has ended up as an editor. Like Sasquatch, she can be found somewhere in the Rocky Mountains writing her next novel, researching things that go bump in the night, and taking the road less traveled.

twitter.com/gwendolynnix

WORLD EXPANDING FICTION

Do you have them all?

MARVEL CRISIS PROTOCOL
- ☐ *Target: Kree* by Stuart Moore

MARVEL HEROINES
- ☐ *Domino: Strays* by Tristan Palmgren
- ☐ *Rogue: Untouched* by Alisa Kwitney
- ☐ *Elsa Bloodstone: Bequest* by Cath Lauria
- ☐ *Outlaw: Relentless* by Tristan Palmgren
- ☐ *Black Cat: Discord* by Cath Lauria
  (coming soon)

LEGENDS OF ASGARD
- ☐ *The Head of Mimir* by Richard Lee Byers
- ☐ *The Sword of Surtur* by C L Werner
- ☐ *The Serpent and the Dead* by Anna Stephens
- ☐ *The Rebels of Vanaheim* by Richard Lee Byers
- ☐ *Three Swords* by C L Werner *(coming soon)*

MARVEL UNTOLD
- ☐ *The Harrowing of Doom* by David Annandale
- ☐ *Dark Avengers: The Patriot List* by David Guymer
- ☐ *Witches Unleashed* by Carrie Harris
- ☐ *Reign of the Devourer* by David Annandale
  (coming soon)

XAVIER'S INSTITUTE
- ☐ *Liberty & Justice for All* by Carrie Harris
- ☐ *First Team* by Robbie MacNiven
- ☐ *Triptych* by Jaleigh Johnson
- ☑ *School of X* edited by Gwendolyn Nix
- ☐ *The Siege of X-41* by Tristan Palmgren
  (coming soon)